Dale Brown

Former US Air Force captain Dale Brown was born in Buffalo, New York, and now lives in Nevada. *Act of War* is his seventeenth novel. He graduated from Penn State University with a degree in Western European History and received a US Air Force commission in 1978. He was still serving in the Air Force when he wrote his highly acclaimed first novel, *Flight of the Old Dog*. Since then he has written a string of *New York Times* bestsellers, including, most recently, *Air Battle Force* and *Plan of Attack*.

'When a former pilot with years of experience in America's Strategic Air Command turns his hand to writing thrillers you can take their authenticity for granted. His writing is exceptional and the dialogue, plots and characters are first-class . . . far too good to be missed.'

Sunday Mirror

'A master at creating a sweeping epic and making it seem real.'

CLIVE CUSSLER

'Dale Brown is a master at mixing technology and action. He puts readers right into the middle of the inferno.'

LARRY BOND

DALE BROWN

ACT OF WAR

HarperCollins*Publishers*

HarperCollins*Publishers*
77–85 Fulham Palace Road,
Hammersmith, London W6 8JB

www.harpercollins.co.uk

This paperback edition 2006

First published in Great Britain/USA by
HarperCollins*Publishers* 2005

ISBN 978-0-00-784247-6
ISBN 978-0-00-721479-2

Set in Meridien by Palimpsest Book Production Limited,
Polmont, Stirlingshire

Printed and bound in Great Britain by
Clays Ltd, St Ives plc

This book is dedicated to my close friend U.S. Army Reserve Command Sergeant Major Raymond Jefferson. Two tours in Vietnam, two decades repairing avionics for the Air Force, and a lifetime training infantry soldiers for combat in the Army Reserve, Ray was one of the most professional, dedicated, generous, and trustworthy men I have ever known.

He didn't want a gravesite or even a marker – instead, he wanted an American flag raised above his fellow veterans' resting places. Ray's flagpole is there, in front of the new Veteran's Court of Honor. He's still leading his troops, just as he had been most of his life in the Army he loved.

Job well done, Command Sergeant Major. Rest easy.

ACRONYMS

APC – armored personnel carrier
ARG – Accident Response Group (Department of
   Energy)
ARL – Army Research Laboratory
CID – Cybernetic Infantry Device
DOE – Department of Energy
GAMMA – originally *Grupo do Abaete de la Movimento
   Meio Ambiente,* the Environmental Movement Group
   of Abaete; changed to *Guerra Alliance de la Movimento
   Meio Ambiente,* or the Environmental Movement
   Combat Alliance
GSF – General Security Forces (Egyptian interior para-
   military forces)
GUOS – Grenade-launched Unmanned Observation
   System ('Goose')
HEAT – High Explosive Antitank
HMMWV – High-Mobility Multipurpose Wheeled
   Vehicle (Humvee)
ITB – Infantry Transformational BattleLab
LAWS – Light Antitank Weapon System
MILES – Multiple Integrated Laser Engagement System
NBC – Nuclear/Biological/Chemical
NEST – Nuclear Emergency Search Team
NSC – National Security Council
ONC – octanitrocubane
PME – *Policia Militar do Estado,* Brazilian State Military
   Police
PPD – Presidential Protection Detail

SA – Special Agent
SAC – Special Agent in Charge
TGE – TransGlobal Energy
THREATCON – Threat Condition
TO&E – Table of Organization and Equipment
TOW – Tube-Launched Optically Tracked Wire-Guided
  Missile
UAV – Unmanned Aerial Vehicle
UCMJ – Uniform Code of Military Justice

REAL WORLD NEWS EXCERPTS

DEFENSE ADVANCED RESEARCH PROJECTS AGENCY (DARPA), http://www.darpa.mil, August 2000 – The Defense Advanced Research Projects Agency (DARPA) is soliciting innovative research proposals on Exoskeletons for Human Performance Augmentation (EHPA). The overall goal of this program is to develop devices and machines that will increase the speed, strength, and endurance of soldiers in combat environments. Projects will lead to self-powered, controllable, wearable exoskeletal devices and/or machines.

The technological challenges that must be addressed are energy sources, power by generation, haptic interfaces, control algorithm development, as well as integration of actuation systems and all previously mentioned subsystems into a machine with an anthropomorphic architecture. Highly efficient actuators must be developed that can utilize a high-density, man-wearable energy source in both a safe and quiet manner. The power provided to the EPHA system must support the exoskeleton for a duration of military significance, initially estimated to be four to twenty-four hours. Control approaches must be devised that enable direct and seamless interaction between human and machine. Finally, these devices and machines will be demonstrated in order to evaluate their utility to various military operations.

EHPA will enable new capabilities for ground forces. Inclusion of exoskeleton technology into land-based operations will extend the mission payload and/or mission range of the soldier. Exoskeletons will also increase the lethality and survivability of ground troops for short-range and special operations. The enhanced mobility and load-carrying capability provided by the exoskeleton will allow soldiers to carry more ballistic protection and heavy weaponry.

To meet the challenges set forth, DARPA is soliciting devices and machines that accomplish one or more of the following: (1) assist pack-loaded locomotion; (2) prolong locomotive endurance; (3) increase locomotive speed; (4) augment human strength; and (5) leap extraordinary heights and/or distances. These machines should be anthropomorphic and capable of bearing distributed loads, such as that generated by extensive armor protection, as well as typical pack loads.

UC BERKELEY RESEARCHERS DEVELOPING ROBOTIC EXOSKELETON THAT CAN ENHANCE HUMAN STRENGTH AND ENDURANCE – University of California-Berkeley, http://www.berkeley.edu, March 2004 – The mere thought of hauling a seventy-pound pack across miles of rugged terrain or up fifty flights of stairs is enough to evoke a grimace in even the burliest individuals. But breakthrough robotics research at the University of California, Berkeley, could soon bring welcome relief – a self-powered exoskeleton to effectively take the load off people's backs.

'We set out to create an exoskeleton that combines a human control system with robotic muscle,' said Homayoon Kazerooni, professor of mechanical engineering and director of UC Berkeley's Robotics and Human Engineering Laboratory. 'We've designed this system to be ergonomic, highly maneuverable, and technically robust so the wearer can walk, squat, bend, and swing from side to side without noticeable reductions in agility. The human pilot can also step over and under obstructions while carrying equipment and supplies.'

The Berkeley Lower Extremity Exoskeleton (BLEEX), as it's officially called, consists of mechanical metal leg braces that are connected rigidly to the user at the feet, and, in order to prevent abrasion, more compliantly elsewhere. The device includes a power unit and a back-pack-like frame used to carry a large load.

Such a machine could become an invaluable tool for anyone who needs to travel long distances by foot with a heavy load. The exoskeleton could eventually be used by army medics to carry injured soldiers off a battlefield, firefighters to haul their gear up dozens of flights of stairs to put out a high-rise blaze, or rescue workers to bring in food and first-aid supplies to areas where vehicles cannot enter . . .

STRATEGIC FORECASTING INC., www.stratfor.com, 21 May 2004, © 2004 Stratfor, Inc. – Although Stratfor believes that [terrorist] strikes could be carried out against multiple targets of opportunity, certain factors – including time and al Qaeda's targeting criteria – lead us to conclude that Houston, Texas, is near the top of the list. Not only is it home to much of the nation's oil infrastructure, which carries significant economic implications, but it also is a city of 5 million people – and the home of former President George H. W. Bush. A strike here would lend a personal nature to the attack that would send a clear message across the desk of President George W. Bush. . . .

In this case, we believe a truck bomb is the most likely delivery mechanism – perhaps a stolen delivery van, helping to mask the driver's intentions. This scenario was discussed by a sleeper cell in New York City before the first World Trade Center attack in 1993, and al Qaeda has shown a tendency to return to previous attack plans. The assailants might use a ramming car to break through perimeter fences while either shooting or running over security guards. However, it also is feasible that they could use legitimate company identification cards in order to slip past the guards. Once near the target, the explosive would be detonated, killing the attack team . . .

'WHO'S GUARDING U.S. MILITARY EQUIPMENT?' by Michelle Malkin, posted October 29, 2003, on WorldNetDaily.com, © 2003 Creators Syndicate Inc. '. . . A possible terrorism nexus here is clear. . . . There are at any given time several hundred military vehicles on [the Maine National Guard Facility, Limestone, Maine] site, and security is nonexistent. The fact that undocumented foreign nationals are illegally transporting this equipment throughout the U.S. with access to the Limestone facility and other military facilities also would seem to pose a threat . . .'

. . . This is not the first time suspicious foreign nationals have been caught around the Maine National Guard site. In June, according to the Border Patrol, a Humvee was stolen from the Limestone facility. While searching for the missing vehicle, agents apprehended a Russian illegal alien nearby. He had a valid New York State commercial driver's license allowing him to haul hazardous materials and a pass that granted him access to seaports along the East Coast – including high-level security bonded customs areas. Also this summer, two other Russian nationals, dressed in military battle dress uniforms, were stopped by Canadian authorities as they attempted to enter the U.S. at an unguarded crossing approximately 20 miles south of Limestone . . .

Act of War

Prologue

Kingman City, Texas
Present time

Just twenty precious minutes more – and the global war for freedom from death and tyranny would enter the next level. The closer the driver came to his target, the more his blood boiled and his adrenaline level kicked up to even higher levels.

I am a man of peace, the driver told himself for the umpteenth time as he made his journey, but if any man on Earth deserved to die, it was Harold Chester Kingman, president and CEO of TransGlobal Energy Corporation. The man's destructiveness and greed were exceeded only by his immense ego. The highways and roads leading to his target were so audaciously named, the driver noted with disgust, that one could practically make the trip without once referring to a map of any sort: from Interstate 45, take the Harold Chester Kingman Parkway off-ramp, head west on Kingman Parkway to TransGlobal Avenue, then south on Dominion Street to the front gate. Kingman had even changed the name of the town itself: known as Texas City since 1893, the oil, gas, and nuclear energy mogul changed the name when he purchased the entire area just a few years ago. Why, thought the driver, didn't Kingman just put his name on every street sign in the city, perhaps with the title 'King,' 'Lord,' or 'Slave Master' added for good measure?

The driver followed the signs to the truck entrance a

bit farther south, noting the security cameras arrayed along every portion of the road. As he got closer, he noticed more and more roving patrols in sport-utility vehicles, with supervisors in sedans, enforcing the enforcers. Yes, paranoid: Kingman trusted no one. From many previous trips here, the driver knew that those SUVs were heavily armored and could probably withstand a rocket-propelled grenade round, then return fire with their own heavy weapons, including assault rifles, machine guns, and grenade launchers. But as tight as security was, the driver remarked to himself that it got tighter and more sophisticated every time he came here. Was it merely the nature of post–9/11 American industrial society, or was it Harold Chester Kingman's supreme ego and paranoia at work? Whatever it was, TransGlobal Energy was surely expending an even greater percentage of their enormous profits on security these days.

Not that Kingman was paying for it, of course – it simply meant that his workers worked harder for even less pay, and he jacked up prices across the board for his products and services, perhaps double the cost of the added expenses. Kingman obviously wasn't suffering because of all these outlays for an elaborate and even outlandish show of security – in fact, he was profiting handsomely from it, telling the world that it was these security measures responsible for the steep price increases, layoffs, and pay cuts.

The front gate to the immense TransGlobal Energy Transshipment and Refinery Complex, about twenty miles south of Houston, resembled some kind of futuristic sci-fi fortress – or prison, depending on how you looked at it. The incoming gate was an entrapment area, with two gates enclosing an arriving vehicle so that there was no direct opening to the outside at any time. In addition, the moving gates were massive barriers made with twenty-centimeter-square steel posts, topped with coils of razor wire. Those gates looked strong enough to stop a main battle tank.

The driver approached the outside guard shack and parked just outside the steel gates, despite a large sign that read 'DO NOT APPROACH GATE UNTIL CLEARED.' The guard shack was no longer a 'shack' – this was now a brand-new concrete bunker, with gun ports and thick one-way mirrored bulletproof glass instead of the old simple wooden building, screen door, and smiling, mildly bored guards. He had been here only a couple weeks and this bunker wasn't here the first time he'd arrived. He stepped over to the large glass window, idly flipping through a metal form holder.

'Move your vehicle away from the gate, Officer,' an electronic voice ordered through a hidden speaker.

The man on the outside looked up, squinting through the spotlights shining on him from around the window. 'Is that you, Tom?' the man asked. 'What's with the lights?' He knew what the lights were for, of course – they darkened and obscured his view of the inside of the guard bunker, and also allowed them to take more detailed digital photos of him.

'You need to move your car away from the gate until you're cleared in, Patrolman Kelly,' the voice said again. 'Back behind the yellow line.'

Texas Department of Public Safety (DPS) Sergeant Frank Kelly squinted in mild irritation and looked back down at his forms. 'Well, clear me in then, and I'll be on my way, Tom,' he said. He looked at his watch impatiently, hoping they'd get the hint. Usually the sight of

someone in a DPS uniform made folks nervous, from
young motorists right up to CEOs of Fortune 500 companies, even if they were totally innocent. The DPS enforced
not only highway traffic laws but safety and security laws
for important public transportation facilities such as ports,
harbors, and truck terminals. They had the authority to
shut down any facility that didn't strictly comply with
Texas law, so every trooper was usually treated with a
high degree of respect.

'Procedures have changed, Frank,' a different voice
said. 'You obviously didn't get the memo.'

'You're going to make me back the damned car up
twenty lousy feet before you'll let me in, Tom?' the officer
asked, the exasperation more evident in his voice. 'All I
want are the tanker inspection logs and I'll be out of
your hair.'

'Frank, the entry procedures have changed,' the invisible guard inside the bunker said apologetically. 'We notified DPS headquarters and all the area substations last
week. I'm sorry, but you know, procedures are . . .'

The officer held up his hands in mock surrender.
'Okay, okay, I know: procedures are procedures,' he said.
'I'll back up behind your big bad yellow line.' He slapped
the metal form holder shut with a loud *bang*! and walked
back to his marked Crown Victoria cruiser.

So much for the rock-solid intelligence they had so
far been receiving, Kelly thought, fighting to act inconvenienced and put off. All this added security was unexpected. And the new guardhouse – where in hell have
the lookouts been all this time? It should have been plain
enough to even untrained observers to notice that these
damned blockhouses were being built at the entrances!
He glanced in his rearview mirror, noting that the street

behind him was still clear – no trucks or other security vehicles were boxing him in.

A moment later, the guard he knew as Tom stepped out of a revolving steel security turnstile and approached the cruiser, an M-16 rifle slung on one shoulder. Kelly noted that he also wore an automatic pistol instead of the cheap standard-issue revolvers most security guards here wore. Another serious breakdown in intelligence. At that moment, one of TransGlobal's royal blue armored Suburban security vehicles appeared on the street behind him and stopped about fifty yards away, a gun port on the right rear door open. Now Kelly was starting to sweat.

A knock on his driver's-side window startled him, but he quickly regained his composure and hit the switch to roll the window down. It was Tom. 'You okay, Frank?' he asked.

'You guys expecting a war or something, Tom?' Kelly asked, ignoring the question. 'Now you're toting M-16s? I'm not even issued one anymore.' Tom made a quick glance around inside the cruiser but quickly returned his eyes to Kelly's. 'Is there a fucking problem here, Tom?' He reached over and snatched the cruiser's microphone off its clip with an angry pull. 'Okay, I didn't read the memo, or if I did, I forgot about it. You want to bust my balls over it so you look good in front of all your new security cameras, fine. Should I call my supervisor, or did you already do it?'

'Relax, you big Mick chump, relax,' Tom said with a smile. He held up a piece of paper. 'I just came out to give you a copy of the memo. We haven't implemented most of the procedures on there, but the new guys are pretty gung-ho and they feel pretty tough with their assault rifles and Berettas.'

Kelly took the memo and glanced over it, trying like hell not to look too relieved. 'New guardhouse, new weapons, cameras out the wazoo – what else you got in there?'

'Half the cameras aren't hooked up, and I swear to God these kids haven't a fucking clue – if I got a dime for every time I've told these jerkoffs to keep their damned fingers off the triggers of those M-16s, I'd be as rich as you troopers.'

'Har har.'

'I'm serious, dude – as soon as my application is accepted, I'm out of here and going to the Highway Patrol Academy,' Tom said. 'Working for Kingman is like what it must have been like working for Napoleon, Hitler, or Clinton.'

'Bill or Hillary?'

'I thought they were one and the same – they both liked their power and their women,' Tom said. Kelly was pleased to note that his laugh sounded normal. Tom's face turned serious as he went on: 'Starting next week, we'll be instituting an electronic identity verification program for both individuals and vehicles. We'll be asking everyone to have biometric prints taken, and your cars will have to have coded transponders on them, like on airliners. Give everyone at the station a heads-up.'

'More fun and games, huh?'

'This antiterrorist shit is no fun and games, especially with Mr Kingman,' Tom said. 'We'll soon have security in this place that'll make Fort Knox look like a day at Disneyland.'

'I can't wait.' Kelly noted with relief that the big outer steel gate was starting to open. 'Why don't you just have Kingman's transportation guys transmit the vehicle logs over to headquarters rather than have us pick them up all the time?'

'I guess Mr Kingman likes seeing troopers around.'

'Well, recommend that he make us feel a bit more welcome next time, or we'll make *him* bring the logs to *us* rather than the other way around, the way it's supposed to be.'

'With all the political muscle Kingman has, I'm surprised he doesn't have the governor build a DPS substation here at the terminal – or better yet, have the President build an entire army base here,' Tom said. He slapped the door sill. 'You take care, Frank. Sorry for the inconvenience. I'm afraid it's only going to get worse, though.'

'No problem, buddy. Thanks for the heads-up. Later.' As Tom assumed a port-arms stance to guard the open gate area, Kelly pulled his cruiser inside the entrapment area when the green direction light came on. After he was inside, he waited until the outer gate closed, shut off the engine, popped open the hood and trunk, and then exited his vehicle to allow the security guards to search. They shined flashlights in the engine compartment, opened glove boxes and storage compartments, looked under the seats, flipped down sun visors, inspected under the spare tire, and rolled a mirror underneath the cruiser to inspect under the chassis.

Kelly then handed a guard a logbook marked FIELD KIT SECURITY LOG, and the guard compared the last number on the log to the number stamped onto a steel truck seal that secured a large metal case in the trunk. The trunk contained a shotgun, ammunition, a Taser gun to subdue unruly citizens, road flares, flashlights, strobes, ropes, and other safety and security devices carried by all DPS sergeants, but they were prohibited in TransGlobal's complex unless they were sealed by TransGlobal security personnel. The numbers matched, and the security guard closed up the trunk, handed the logbook back to Kelly, and nodded at the guardhouse to allow him to pass.

Kelly got into his cruiser and started it up. Just when he was expecting the inner gate to open, he saw Tom enter the entrapment area. He rolled the window down again as he approached. 'What's up now, Tom?'

'Just a glitch.' He noted Tom had his M-16 rifle hanging in front of him this time with his hand on the grip, not over his shoulder like before.

'Need me to step out?'

Tom shook his head. 'Shouldn't take a minute.' Kelly could see Tom touch an earpiece in his left ear as he listened to radioed instructions. 'Pop the trunk again for me, buddy. They want me to check something.'

Kelly hit the trunk release button. 'Sure. Need the logbook?'

'Why don't you let me see it? These new guys are starting to blabber. They're driving me nuts. Let me straighten this out.' Kelly handed Tom the truck seal log, and Tom went around to the trunk, opened it, and started to work inside.

Kelly got out a moment later and casually strolled around to the back of the cruiser. He noticed three more guards outside the bunker, their M-16s also slung in front of their bodies but not upraised, watching him. Tom had his flashlight out and was inspecting the truck seal on the field kit box, the logbook open. 'Problem, dude?'

By way of reply, Tom ran a gloved finger under the truck seal, feeling all around the underside of the steel strap. After probing the entire seal, he gave a light pull . . . and the seal came apart and clattered to the carpeted floor of the trunk.

'Why did you do that, Tom?' Kelly asked.

The security guard stood up and faced the DPS sergeant, a dark, blank expression on his face. 'It shouldn't have come off that easily, Frank,' he said. 'And it looks like the band itself was cut right at the clasp to make it hard to detect the cut.'

'Probably just a bad seal,' Kelly said. 'No big deal. I'll pull out, and you can reinspect the field kit, reseal it, and sign the log again.'

'There's another problem, Frank,' Tom said. 'There's a radiation alarm going off.'

'A what?'

'Radiation alarm. We installed radiation detectors here at the facility.'

'Yeah? That's pretty cool. Well, the shotgun and my sidearm have tritium sights – your guns probably do too. That'll set off a radiation alarm.'

'This alarm is going off the scale, Frank,' Tom said. He raised his M-16 and clicked off the safety. 'Turn around, walk forward to the fence, then place your hands on the fence, lean forward, and spread your legs.'

Kelly did as he was told. 'Jesus, Tom, put that thing down. It's me, man, remember?'

'I've known you for a grand total of two weeks, Kelly – stop making like we're brothers or something. Cover!' he shouted. Two of the security guards started to enter the entrapment area. Tom took Kelly's pistol and Mace canister out of his holster and tossed it aside, then held his rifle aimed at Kelly until the other guards could cover him. 'Okay, asshole, what's in the case?'

'It's my field kit, Tom. What do you think it is?'

'You can't get away, so whatever that thing is will kill you along with everyone else if it goes off,' the security guard said. 'Give it up. What's in the fucking box?' No reply. '*Answer me*!'

Kelly hesitated for a moment, and then replied in a low voice, 'If I were you, Tom, I'd get out of here, now, as fast as you can. Head for the train tunnel on the other side of the deep water canal – you'll be safe there.'

'What did you fucking say?'

'I said you'd better get away from here. Leave me with the two Rambos. A kilometer should be far enough as long as you're underground. Two would be better.'

'Better for what?'

'I like you, Tom,' Kelly said. 'You're a good guy. You always have been.'

'What are you fucking talking about, mister?'

'You've treated me with respect even though you've had your doubts about me – I like that. You should have followed your instincts, though. That just makes you a bad security officer, not a bad guy.' Kelly started to turn around.

'*Don't you move*!'

'Don't shoot me. Let me explain.' He continued to turn until they were looking into each other's eyes. Kelly's eyes motioned up to his left hand, and it was only then that Tom noticed he had a small device resembling a remote car door opener attached to a clump of keys in his hand. 'You should order me to turn around again, Tom,' Kelly said in a low voice. 'You tell the Rambos to cover me while you report this to security headquarters in person, and then you should get into that armored Suburban back there and start driving toward the tunnel on the other side of the canal. Even if you don't make it all the way, inside that Suburban, you should be okay.' Tom started to reach for the device. 'Don't do that, Tom. I've already activated it. It's a dead-man's switch. If it leaves my hand, it'll trigger it.'

'Trigger what?'

'You know what it is, Tom,' Kelly said. 'My mission has failed, and it's time to give it up. But I can save at least one nice guy here. TransGlobal is filled with nasty, sleazy, uncaring persons. You're the only good guy I've known that works for TransGlobal. You deserve a second chance. Get as far away from here as you can. I'll hold them off, don't worry.' Tom raised the M-16 and aimed it at Kelly's head. 'Don't be stupid, Tom. If you shoot, I'll let go of it, and you'll die. That's foolish. Do as I say. Get away from here. You don't owe Kingman a damned thing.'

'He's not here. You won't be doing a thing to him.'

'Maybe not to him, but to his company – *this* facility, this abomination to nature that pollutes Galveston Bay, pollutes the air, pollutes the drinking water, and enslaves workers all over the world.'

Tom lowered the rifle slightly. '*What*?'

'Kingman is a bloodsucker, Tom. He'll do anything for profit. The only way to hurt him is to kill his profits.'

'Are you some kind of environmentalist wacko?'

'I am a soldier of GAMMA – the Environmental Movement Combat Alliance.' Tom's face fell and he looked at Kelly over the sights of the M-16 with shock and surprise. 'I see you've heard of us.'

'You blew up that dam in Paraguay recently . . .'

'Uruguay.'

'You killed hundreds of people . . .'

'TransGlobal paid almost five million dollars in bribes to government officials to get approval to build that dam,' Kelly said. 'The government uprooted thousands of persons who had lived in that river valley for centuries. Hundreds of peasants, who were working for pennies a week, died during the construction – and *then* when they flooded the river valley, they wiped out hundreds of thousands of acres of rain forest, priceless Indian artifacts, and the graves of thousands more.'

'Where in hell did you get a nuclear weapon?'

'There are governments all over the world anxious to sell nuclear weapon components,' Kelly said casually, 'and there are many socially and environmentally conscious persons willing to pay to obtain them, and even more dedicated, selfless soldiers willing to plant them in the places where they'll do the most good – not against mindless soldiers or isolated military targets, but against the real killers of planet Earth, men like Harold Chester Kingman.'

'Is it a real bomb? Full-yield – not a dirty bomb?'

'So-called "dirty bombs" are the joke of the century – they would do nothing but scare a few people, certainly not someone as devoid of conscience and morality as Kingman,' Kelly said. 'No, this is a real weapon. GAMMA has sent a tape with all of the data on it, including its yield and components, in order to validate its authenticity. I notice that since the tape also warned TransGlobal Energy to evacuate the area that either no one listened to it, or Kingman *did* listen to it and ordered his security staff not to do anything about it. I tend to believe the latter.'

'I thought GAMMA was an environmental protection group. You'll contaminate this entire region and kill thousands when that thing goes off.'

'Kingman dumps enough pollution in the air worldwide every *day* to equal a full megaton nuclear blast,' the terrorist said. 'Besides, I like the irony of that . . . using weapons of mass destruction to punish those like TransGlobal Energy and Kingman, men who build weapons of mass eco-destruction.'

'You're crazy. Do you know how many people you'll kill in this area with that? Thousands . . . no, maybe *hundreds of thousands.* You'd do that just to try to hurt Kingman?'

'He's killing thousands of people every day around the world with his harmful deep-water drilling, leaky unsafe single-hulled tankers, outdated wells and storage facilities, wanton pollution just to make more profits, and miserable working conditions that enslave entire generations of workers,' Kelly said. 'I truly believe that Kingman is capable of killing the entire *planet* if his practices aren't revealed to the world and shut down *now*. If I can shut this one plant down, it'll really hurt him right where he lives – in the wallet. Maybe he'll give up after that, after what I'll do wakes up the world to his lies, corruption, and criminal activities.'

'You . . . you can't do this. It's *insane* . . .'

'Get away from here, Tom,' Kelly repeated. 'It's your last chance. Get far away from here before your cowboys get their hands on me. Tell them to stay away. I'll give you ten minutes. That should be enough time.'

The two guards started to enter the entrapment area, but Tom raised a hand. 'Stay back!' he shouted. Kelly smiled, nodded, and started to turn back toward the fence. But Tom ordered, 'I'm going to take that detonator away from you, Kelly. I can see what button you're pressing. I'll put my finger on it, and you let it go. Don't try to stop me.'

'Don't try it, Tom. I'm giving you a chance. You have a wife and kids. Don't let this chance slip away.'

'My house is less than a mile from here, man. If it goes, they'll go too. They're innocent. You'd be killing them and thousands of other innocent people.'

'I'm sorry to have to do that. You can call them – tell them to get belowground. Or you can go there, be with them – maybe even get them into that Suburban. At that distance, the armoring might protect them . . .'

'*You sick bastard*!'

'This is a war, Tom, and in war, innocent people are killed,' Kelly said quietly. 'It's what makes war so horrible – it's the reason why we need to end it. This is my blow for freedom. Maybe it'll be the beginning of the end of Harold Kingman.'

'I'm going to take it from you, Kelly,' Tom said, his voice shaking. He had to concentrate to keep from thinking about his family. Where were they? In school? No, it was Sunday . . . they might be safe if they went to the grocery store or . . . but if they went to the park, they'd be out in the open . . . oh shit, oh shit, oh *shit* . . . 'Listen, man, you don't have to kill thousands of people to make your point,' he went on. 'Once the world finds out what you've done here, they'll all want to know about your beef with Kingman and TransGlobal. That's the best way to get your message out. If you kill thousands of people here today, you'll be nothing but a terrorist. No one will ever listen to you.'

'I don't care about that, Tom – I only care about hurting Kingman. He's the target. Now get out of here.'

'I'm reaching up to your hand, and I'm taking that detonator.' His hand touched Kelly's. They looked into each other's eyes. Tom must've seen something akin to surrender in the other's eyes, and he thought it meant that he would give him the detonator.

'You're a good guy,' Kelly said. 'You didn't run. Maybe you would have made a good trooper. But we'll never know.' And Tom watched Kelly's eyes go blank, and then close . . .

. . . just as his own thumb closed over the button to the detonator. Kelly did not struggle. Tom was able to take it out of Kelly's hand, his finger firmly on the button, keeping it safe. He did it.

Just then, Kelly's eyes snapped open. He grinned at Tom, winked, then yelled, 'Open fire!'

'*No*!' Tom yelled, but it was too late. The two young security guards drawing down on Kelly opened fire, their M-16s on full automatic. Slugs ripped mercilessly into both men. Tom remembered through the pain and dizziness to keep his thumb on the button, keep his thumb on the button, keep his . . .

. . . and then as a slug entered his brain, and he died, the world disappeared in a blinding flash of white-hot light . . .

Multipurpose Range Complex, Joint Readiness Training Center, Fort Polk, Louisiana
That same time

With a tremendous 'CRAAACK!' as if from the world's largest and meanest bullwhip, the lightweight thirty-millimeter projectile disappeared from view as soon as it was launched. The radar trackers on the instrument range followed its flight path flawlessly. 'Good shot, J,' Dr Ariadna Vega, a civilian research engineer assigned to

Fort Polk, reported, checking the range telemetry data. Ariadna was in her early twenties, dark-haired, slender, and beautiful, and seemingly very much out of place on this muddy tract of land in central Louisiana. 'Launch velocity . . . seventeen hundred meters per second. Awesome. Range two point three-five kilometers . . . two point four . . . two point four-seven kilometers at impact. Not bad.'

'I can do better than that, Ari,' her partner, Major Jason Richter, responded confidently. 'Reset the sensors and throw me another ball.' The two were very much alike and could have been mistaken for brother and sister. Not much older than Vega, tall, lean, and dark-haired, Jason Richter too was an engineer, assigned as the special project office director of the U.S. Army Infantry Transformational BattleLab, a division of the Army Research Laboratory, tasked with developing new ways for infantry to fight on modern battlefields.

'You got it, J,' Ariadna said with a proud smile. She reactivated the radar scanners briefly to scan for any vehicles or unwanted observers in the area, then reset them to track another projectile. 'Range is clear, sensors reset and ready.' She reached into a padded metal case beside her, withdrew an orange object, ran it under a bar code scanner to log its size, mass, and composition, and tossed it to Jason. 'Keep your head down.'

'I got this nailed,' Jason said. He put the orange projectile on a golf tee, leveled his 'Big Dog' composite driver – slightly modified for these experiments and definitely not PGA tour–certified – addressed the projectile, brought the head of the driver back, paused just for a moment on the back side, then swung. They heard another loud whip-crack sound, but this time with a much less solid, tinny tone. Just a few hundred meters away, an immense cloud of mud and standing water geysered into the air, and the projectile could be seen skipping across the ground, soon lost from sight.

'Told you, J,' Ari said, resetting the range telemetry sensors again. 'You're bringing your head up and topping the ball. Head *down*.'

'All right, all right,' Jason murmured dejectedly. 'Toss me another one.'

'This is the last one,' Ari said, tossing him the last orange projectile from the case. 'Make it good.'

Jason reached up and snatched the ball from mid-air – but it was not *his* fingers that grasped it. The fingers belonged to a three-meter-tall robotic figure. Its arms and legs were thin, covered in composite nonmetallic skin. Its shape was like a human, with arms, legs, a head, and torso; its bullet-shaped head was an armored sensor ball that swiveled and moved in all directions; its joints were fluid and massive, matching strength with dexterity. But for its size, the machine was incredibly agile – its movements precisely mimicked a human's movements in amazing detail, even to subtle movements of its shoulders and hips as it precisely, casually placed the orange projectile on another golf tee and stepped back, ready to hit it downrange. The robot parted its feet and centered up on the ball – it was almost comical to watch, like some weird child's caricature doing a completely human thing.

'No using fire control sensors now,' Ariadna reminded Jason. 'You said you wanted this completely manual.'

'I'm not using fire control,' Jason said. The robot was fitted with a variety of sensors – millimeter-wave radar, imaging infrared, and laser – that fed a computer that could steer weapons with zero-zero precision, or the data could be uplinked to other aircraft or forces in the area via satellite. Jason smoothly brought the club back, paused, relaxed his 'body,' and began his swing . . .

. . . just as a cellular phone rang. The robot's head jerked up just as the club head made contact. The projectile veered sharply right, ricocheted off a steel revetment with a sound like a heavy-caliber gunshot, then blasted through a concrete range officer's building a hundred meters away just in front of the vehicle assembly area. '*Dang*!' Jason shouted. 'No fair! I want a mulligan!'

'The range officer's going to be pissed – again,' Ari said as she reached for her cell phone. 'Hop out and help me get packed up – that was the last projectile.'

The robot tossed the golf club toward Ari, then assumed a stance with one leg extended back, the other knee bent, leaning forward, and arms extended back along its torso. An access hatch on the robot's back popped open, and Jason Richter climbed out from inside the machine. He was a little sweaty and his face was lined with ridges from where the oxygen mask and sensor helmet plates sealed on him, but he was still grinning from ear to ear like a schoolkid who had just hit a home run in a Little League game.

Ari opened the flip on her phone. 'Vega here.'

'Put Major Richter on, Ari.' She recognized the agitated voice of the staff NCO, Army Master Sergeant Ted Gaines.

Ari held out the phone to Jason. 'It's the Top, and he sounds weird,' she said.

Jason barely finished saying hello when Gaines asked breathlessly, 'Are you listening to the news, sir?'

'You just ruined my last test shot, Top. I was . . .'

'Turn on the radio, sir! *Houston has been bombed*!'

'*Bombed*? Bombed by whom?' Jason motioned to the Humvee parked a few meters behind them, and Ariadna flipped on the satellite radio receiver and turned it to SATCOM One, the all-satellite news broadcasting station . . . and in moments, they were both stunned into absolute speechlessness. 'I . . . I can't believe this,' he finally stammered. 'Someone set off a *nuke* near Houston . . . ?'

'Major! Are you still there?' No response. Richter's mind was racing. This was unbelievable . . . too horrible for words . . . '*Major . . . ?*'

'Sergeant, get the Chinook ready to fly,' Jason said breathlessly. 'I'm taking the Humvee and CID One to the flight line right now. We're going to Kingman City.'

'*Kingman City*? You can't go there now! It's a radioactive hole in the ground!'

'CID will be the only system that can operate in that environment,' Jason said. 'Just get it moving. I'll call the boss and get clearances. *Move*!'

Chapter One

The White House, Washington, D.C.
That same time

The President's National Security Adviser, Robert Hall Chamberlain, strode into the White House Situation Room ahead of a wall of military officers, civilian advisers and analysts, and Secret Service agents. They had to scramble to stay out of Chamberlain's way as he quickly entered the room and took his seat, not at the center of the oblong table but just to the right of the seat apparently reserved for the President of the United States. A former oil executive with TransGlobal Energy, an expert and adviser in foreign affairs and commerce, a wealthy political supporter and friend of the President and many other world leaders, Chamberlain had been described as having the geopolitical savvy of Henry Kissinger, the military affairs expertise of Condoleezza Rice, the wealth of Bill Gates, the charisma of Colin Powell . . . and the ruthlessness of Saddam Hussein.

'All right, let's get started,' Chamberlain said brusquely. He was of average height and size, but he made up for his lack of physical stature by his high degree of energy – it always seemed as if he had someplace else he had to be; and in this current emergency situation, he was moving twice as fast. 'Just to bring you all up to speed: the President, Vice President, most of the Cabinet, and the congressional leadership have been evacuated. The President, his chief of staff, SECDEF, SECSTATE, CJCS, and the congressional leadership went aboard *Air Force One;* the VP, Attorney General, the Chief Justice of the Supreme Court, and a few other senior Cabinet officials went aboard a C-37B, the Vice President's transport; the congressional leadership are in alternate secure locations throughout the East Coast. All are safely away and secure, and it is our opinion that the continuity of government has been assured to the best of our ability. As you all know, the President has already made one radio broadcast from *Air Force One* and plans on making another in a few hours. Except in southern Texas, the nation seems to be as calm as can be expected after a horrifying attack like this.'

Chamberlain then turned to the woman beside him to his right, putting a hand on her shoulder. 'Before we begin, I want to extend my personal condolences to Secretary of Homeland Security Calhoun, whom I understand lost some family members in Kingman City. It is truly a devastating loss, and I for one intend to see it avenged and the guilty persons destroyed. I thank her for staying here in Washington to oversee the defense and security of the United States. I'll postpone her briefing for a few . . .'

'No . . . no, I'm ready, Mr Chamberlain,' Calhoun said, wiping her eyes. She took a deep breath but kept her eyes on the table. Donna Calhoun was tall and statuesque but fragile-looking in her current emotional state. 'Let me begin with a short synopsis: the attack occurred approximately three hours and twenty minutes ago, at three-thirty P.M. Central Time. We have no details of the incident itself yet, only the aftermath. The destruction, the death toll, is . . . is immense. Approximately three square miles has been destroyed or dam . . . damaged.' She had to choke back a whimper, trying like hell to replace her sorrow with anger. 'Estimated casualties are in the . . . thous . . .' This time she couldn't hold back the tears no matter how hard she tried.

'That's okay for now, Donna,' Chamberlain said. He waited a few moments until her weeping subsided, then turned with a stony expression to the three-star general across from him. 'General Hanratty?'

Lieutenant General Colin Hanratty was deputy commander of U.S. Northern Command, or NORTHCOM, the unified military command responsible for the defense of the fifty states; the commander of NORTHCOM was also triple-hatted as the commander of NORAD, the North American Aerospace Defense Command, the joint U.S.–Canada military alliance defending the entire North American continent; and also commander of U.S. Space Command, in charge of all of America's satellites and space boosters. 'The commander of NORTHCOM, General Joelson, is at the Cheyenne Mountain Complex and is on duty with the senior duty controller monitoring the global military status and assessing North America's defense readiness. Although we are in constant communications with the Mountain, at the present time it is sealed up and ready to cut itself off from all outside communications and utilities at a moment's notice.'

One of the wide-screen monitors on the wall showed a map of the world, with several annotations across mostly green shading. 'The map shows the global defense status as of the latest observations, none of which are more than two hours' old,' Hanratty said. 'Our strategic adversaries are at normal defense configurations and we have observed no unusual strategic weapon movements. All of our detection, warning, intelligence, navigation, communications, and surveillance spacecraft are operating normally. Consequently, at this time Northern

Command believes that this incident was a singular act of terrorism and not a coordinated attack or prelude to any sort of military action against the United States.

'As the lead military organization in the defense of the homeland, NORTHCOM was asked by the FBI to do some initial analysis of the explosion itself,' Hanratty went on. 'We estimate it was a point seven-five kiloton thermonuclear blast – a so-called "backpack nuke," actually about the size of a very large suitcase, with approximately ten kilos of fissile material, comparable to a Soviet-era one-hundred-and-thirty-millimeter tactical nuclear artillery shell. The double-pulse characteristic of a small but potent thermonuclear blast was detected from space by our thermal and nuclear detectors.'

'Are you saying the weapon was Russian, General?' Chamberlain asked pointedly.

'I have no information on its origin, Mr Chamberlain. I was just making a comparison. But I've read lots of reports of former Soviet military weapons on the black market, including weapons of mass destruction, and since I've never heard of a Western WMD up for sale I can only assume it was Russian.'

'Let's not leap too far ahead here yet, folks,' Chamberlain said. 'Before we know it, this will leak out and the Russians will be screaming denials at us, and that will only ratchet up the pressure for military action. I don't need to remind you all that everything discussed in this room stays in this room. The press will be clamoring for an explanation and what we're going to do about this, and we need to give the President the time he needs to make some hard decisions. Move on, General. What about fallout?'

'As far as we know, sir, serious, but not catastrophic,'

Hanratty said. 'Prevailing winds are from the southwest – New Orleans, Little Rock, Shreveport could all be affected, perhaps even as far north as Memphis or St Louis. I haven't seen the reports yet from environmental analysis and atmospheric testing, but my guess would be that the explosion was not large enough to cause a very large volume of radioactive material to be dispersed into the atmosphere.'

'Compared to Hiroshima, how big was this blast?'

'Quite a bit smaller, sir – in fact, about ninety percent smaller,' Hanratty said. 'The effects are similar but on a proportionally smaller scale. Also, this explosion was in a mostly industrial area of Houston, quite a distance from populated areas. Kingman City is mostly oil refineries, petroleum and natural gas storage, docks, and inland waterways. The destruction might be horrible, but the loss of life will be relatively small. Hiroshima and Nagasaki were major population areas.' He nodded to the assistant secretary of Homeland Security. 'With all due respect for your loss, Madam Secretary, the loss of life is probably a lot less than 9/11.'

'That may be some small comfort to the nation as a whole, but it is not any comfort to me at all,' Robert Chamberlain said angrily. 'I will accept for now that this is not a prelude to a *traditional* military attack, but my recommendation to the President will clearly state that this is most assuredly an attack on the nation, and that we should respond accordingly.'

The 'hotline' phone rang just then, and Chamberlain answered it on the first ring. 'Chamberlain . . . yes, go ahead, Signal . . . I'm here, Mr President. I've assembled representatives of the National Security Council here in the Situation Room.'

'Thank you, Robert,' the President of the United States, Samuel Conrad, began on the secure line. 'I've got the secretaries of State, Defense, and Transportation with me, along with the chairman of the joint chiefs, the Speaker of the House, and the majority and minority leaders of the Senate. The Vice President, Attorney General, and some of the other Cabinet members are also patched in.'

'Yes, Mr President,' Chamberlain said. 'We've just been briefed by General Hanratty of Northern Command, and he tells us that there appear to be no indications of any nation mobilizing its armed forces. It looks like we were the victim of another terrorist action – but this time with more dire implications.'

'Christ . . .' the President breathed.

'I strongly recommend you return to Washington immediately, sir,' Chamberlain said forcefully, glancing at the drawn, shocked faces of the men and women around him in the Situation Room. 'There's no imminent danger, and you have already made it clear to the world that you and the government are safe. You need to get back to the White House and take charge, in person, right *now*.'

'Are you sure it's safe, Robert?'

'Safety is not the issue, sir – leadership is,' Chamberlain replied. 'You need to get back here so the American people can see you not just alive and safe, but in charge and leading the defense. Now I advise you to tell the chief of staff to turn the plane around and get back to the White House as soon as possible. I'll advise the press you'll be on the ground at Andrews and back at the White House shortly.'

'I . . . all right, Robert,' the President said hesitantly. 'I plan to address the American people immediately as soon as I arrive back at the White House, Robert,' he went on a moment later, 'and I want a full situation briefing and intel dump as soon as I get off the plane.'

'Yes, Mr President.'

'Is there any information on who did this? Anyone claim responsibility yet?'

'No, Mr President,' Chamberlain said. 'We hope to have more by the time you return. We'll transmit a complete casualty and damage report, defense status report, and up-to-the-moment world situation report to the chief of staff so he can have Communications draft an address for you.'

There was silence for a few moments; then: 'I want to hunt them down and slaughter them, Robert,' he said angrily. 'I want every resource of the United States of America mobilized to find those responsible and eliminate them. I'm not interested in bringing them to justice. I want them *gone*.'

'Everything will be done that can be done, sir . . .'

'That's not good enough, Robert,' the President said acidly. 'I'm tired of America being the target, the hunted – I want America to be the *hunter*.' He paused, then went on, his shaking voice evident even over the secure telephone connection: 'Robert, I want to declare war on terrorism. And I don't mean a "war" like our "war on drugs" or our current "war on terrorism" . . .' He paused again, and Chamberlain could hear a slow uptake of breath before he said, 'I propose to go before Congress and ask for a declaration of war against terrorism.'

'A . . . say again, sir?' Chamberlain responded in shock and confusion. 'Mr President, I . . . I don't know . . .'

'Robert, I intend to ask Congress for a declaration of war against terrorism,' the President said firmly. 'The attack on Kingman City may or may not be state-sponsored; it may be radical fundamentalist Islam or some other fanatical group – it doesn't matter. I want the full and unfettered resources of the nation to find who did this unspeakable act, hunt them down like the sick cowardly dogs they are, *and destroy them*. I want a congressional declaration of war. I don't care how we get it, I just want it *done*.'

There was silence on the line for several long moments; then: 'Mr President, I am behind you all the way on that idea,' Robert Chamberlain said. 'We should discuss this as soon as you land. It will take an enormous amount of courage and tenacity to pull it off; undoubtedly your political opponents will call it a grandstanding gesture that will throw the world into chaos. But I believe the American people will be behind you one hundred and ten percent.'

'I'm not going to sit around and wait for Congress or the Supreme Court to wring their hands and debate this,' the President retorted. 'Robert, I'm tasking you with implementing this idea. Get together with Justice, Defense, and the congressional leadership and draft me a proposal that I can present to a joint session of Congress within thirty days. I want a plan of action set into motion immediately. Military, Central Intelligence, FBI, Homeland Security, every branch of the government – everyone's going to work together on this to find the bastards who attacked us.'

Chamberlain swallowed, nervously looking around the Situation Room at the faces looking worriedly at him. 'Yes, Mr President. I'll get right on it,' he said finally. 'I'll have some suggestions for you as soon as you return.'

'Thank you, Robert,' the President said. 'You're my go-to guy, Robert. I'm relying on you to push this, hard.

The entire world watched me run in fear from my own capital, and I'm not going to let that happen ever again on my watch. I want to take the fight to the enemy. Whatever it takes, whatever we've got – I want the terrorists who did this to suffer. I'm going to stake my entire political career on this. I need a strong hand on the wheel. I'm counting on you, Robert.'

'I understand, Mr President,' Chamberlain said. 'I'll see you when you get back. Thank you, Mr President.' The connection went dead, and Chamberlain returned the phone to its cradle with a stunned expression on his face.

'What's going on, Robert?' Donna Calhoun asked.

'The President will be back in Washington within the hour,' he said, quickly composing himself. 'He wants to address the nation as soon as he returns. I want a complete report on Kingman City, our defense status, and the world situation in twenty minutes. I'll transmit it to Air Force One so the President's communications staff can draft a speech.' He paused, his mind racing furiously; then he added: 'He wants it to be a tough, no-nonsense, decisive speech. He wants blood. He doesn't want to reassure the nation, or offer his condolences – he wants action, and he wants heads to roll.' He paused again, thinking hard, until he realized that the National Security Council staff members present were looking rather concerned. 'On my desk in twenty minutes.'

'Is there something else, Robert . . . ?'

At that instant the phone rang again, and Chamberlain snatched it up as if it had electrocuted him. He listened for a moment; then his eyes widened in surprise, and he motioned excitedly to a staffer. 'Turn on the damned news,' he shouted, '*now*!'

Another computer screen came to life, and all heads

turned to watch. It showed a person in a silver radiation protection suit inside a helicopter, talking into a handheld video camera. The captions read KRISTEN SKYY, SATCOM ONE SENIOR CORRESPONDENT and LIVE OVER KINGMAN CITY, TEXAS.

'Holy shit,' someone murmured. 'It looks like Kristen Skyy is going to fly over ground zero!' No one had to ask who Kristen Skyy was: she was by far the most well-known, popular, and trusted foreign affairs journalist on television since Barbara Walters. Her beauty, on-camera ease, and charm would have been enough to get her international attention, but it was without a doubt her drive, ambition, determination, and sheer courage that made her a media superstar.

No one, therefore, was *that* surprised to see her in the middle of a nuclear death zone.

'I thought the airspace over the entire nation was closed down!' Chamberlain thundered. 'What in hell is she doing up there?'

'She's on the ground in five minutes, sir,' Hanratty said, picking up a telephone in front of him.

The sound was gradually turned up, and they heard, '. . . *assured repeatedly that it was safe at this point to fly near the blast site, the danger from radioactive fallout has subsided, my cameraman Paul Delgado has a radiation counter with him and as you can see the needle is hardly moving so I think we're all right . . .*'

'The radiation will be the *least* of her problems once I get done with her,' Hanratty murmured angrily. Into the mouthpiece, he shouted, 'I told you, Sergeant Major, I'm watching her *right now*. She's broadcasting live from a helicopter right over the damned blast area. I want an Apache up there to force her away and back down on the ground in five minutes, and if she doesn't comply I want a broadcast warning her that she'll be shot down. And when they land, arrest all of them. And I want the persons producing her news program to be arrested as well *right now.*'

'*. . . been told that the FAA is ordering us to land,*' the correspondent went on. '*It's an order apparently from the Departments of Defense and Homeland Security, but we think this story is just too important to simply fly away. We've been told that there are injured people at a park on Swan Lake, about a mile and a half from ground zero. Emergency responders are ordering everyone away from the blast area, so no help has arrived from Galveston or League City.*'

'Are there any rescue units heading toward that area?' Chamberlain asked.

'All traffic for five miles around ground zero is being stopped, and that includes traffic on Galveston Bay,' Calhoun responded. 'Radiation levels hit the danger mark at two miles out. No one can get close enough to the area to attempt any kind of rescue.'

'So what in hell is that reporter doing out there?' Chamberlain asked. 'And why isn't her radiation meter picking up anything?'

'Either she doesn't have it on or she's got it set up incorrectly,' Hanratty said. 'Our detectors definitely picked up danger levels of radiation out to three kilometers. Kristen Skyy is going to get hurt if she stays out there – I don't care what kind of suit she's got on. And if that pilot and cameraman don't have suits on, or if they're not fitted or sealed-up properly, they're dead – they just don't know it yet.'

'Get them out of there, General!' Chamberlain shouted. But they could do nothing else but watch in horrified fascination as the report continued:

'*We can see the blast area, ground zero,*' the reporter in the radiation suit went on. '*It looks like a forest after a huge fire, with nothing but blackened sticks sticking out of lumpy rocky black soil. The fires look like they've gone out, but we see what used to be the refinery and petroleum storage tanks still smoking. Here and there we see immense piles of metal glowing reddish-orange, like a pool of lava. I see what the term "vaporized" means, because everything looks as fragile and decimated as ash on a cigarette. I apologize to the families of the victims of Kingman City for my harsh graphic descriptions, I'm not being insensitive, it is hard to put this nightmarish scene into words.*

'*Okay . . . okay, I understand . . . ladies and gentlemen, my pilot is telling me that he is getting some high-temperature readings from our helicopter's engine, so it may be time to turn around; apparently the incredible heat still emanating from ground zero is superheating the air and causing some damage. The military is now warning us that they will shoot us out of the sky if we don't leave. I don't care what the military says, but if our helicopter can't stand this heat then maybe it's time to leave. We can't help any survivors if we can't safely evacuate them. The air is bumpy, obviously from the turbulence created by the heat, and it's getting harder and harder to breathe in these suits, so I think we . . . hey, Paul, swing around over that way – my God, I see them! There appears to be an overturned school bus about a kilometer east of us, right at the edge of Swan Lake!*'

'Oh, Christ,' Chamberlain breathed. And a few moments later, the camera focused on an overturned bus, which appeared to have either been blown over by the blast or the driver had steered or been pushed off the road and the bus flipped onto its side. They could count at least two dozen men, women, and children lying on the ground, motionless or writhing, obviously in pain. Several adults and children were in the lake, trying to stay away from the intense heat, but it was obvious that the water itself was getting uncomfortably hot as well – adults were carrying several children on their shoulders, trying to keep screaming children out of the water. There was a playground nearby; watercraft of all kinds were scattered around the edge of the lake, along with more bodies. The earth was scorched a pale gray, with 'shadows' of natural color where larger objects had blocked the roiling wave of heat energy from the nuclear blast.

'Paul, tell him to go over there . . . yes, set it down over there!' Skyy was saying. *'We've got to help those children out of there. Maybe if we can get them on the boats we can save them!'*

'We're watching it,' Hanratty said on the telephone. 'Get some choppers out there to rescue those civilians in the lake. I want all other aircraft kept away from that entire area – yes, you are authorized to fire warning shots if necessary.' Chamberlain nodded when Hanratty looked to him for confirmation of his order.

'What are their chances, General?' Chamberlain asked.

As if to respond to his question, suddenly the image being broadcast from the SATCOM One news chopper swerved and veered. They heard a man cry out, but at the same time they heard Kristen Skyy say, 'Oh, shit, it looks like the engine has seized up, and we're going down. Paul, drop the camera and hold on, for Christ's sake!' Chamberlain had to admire her courage – the cameraman was screaming like a child, but Skyy was as calm as ever. She even sounded embarrassed that she let an expletive sneak past her lips.

The image showed the view out a side window as the

helicopter headed earthward. They saw the deck heel sharply upward moments before impact, and then the camera bounced free and went dark. 'Shit – more civilians in the hot zone. How soon can we get some rescuers out there, General?' Chamberlain asked.

'Several have already tried, sir,' Hanratty replied. 'We've got more on the way, but they're running into the same problems. The heat is just too great out there.'

'*I'm okay, I'm okay*,' they heard Kristen Skyy say. '*Paul, are you all right? What? Your back . . . oh, Jesus . . . Paul, we've got to get out of the chopper, it might catch on fire . . . if you can move, get out and get away from the chopper . . . no, screw the camera, just get out . . . I know you signed for it, Paul, jeez, okay, okay, take it if you can, but just get the hell out and head toward the lake. We've got to get out of this chopper, Paul – the heat is getting worse and it might set off the fuel. I'm going to check on the pilot.*' They heard rustling and opening and closing helicopter doors. '*The pilot is unconscious but alive. Can you help me, Paul? I don't think I can carry him by myself. We've got to get him out of here.*' They could see the image jostling about as Kristen and her photographer pulled the injured pilot, wearing no protective gear but a Nomex fireproof flight suit and rubber oxygen mask, out of the cockpit.

The camera was picked up a few minutes later, focusing unsteadily on Kristen Skyy, running toward the playground in her radiation suit. '*I'm okay, and I hope you can hear me*,' she said via a wireless microphone. The radio connection was scratchy but still audible. '*Paul will stay with the pilot in Swan Lake. I'm going to check to see if there are any survivors.*' She checked the first body. '*Oh God, it's a teenage girl. She didn't make it.*' She rolled her over onto her face, exposing severe burns on her back. She went quickly to the next. '*This one, thank God, is alive.*'

Maybe her boyfriend or brother.' She dragged him to the edge of the lake, where others taking refuge there helped him into the relatively cooler water. Then she went back to check on another.

'She's got guts, I'll say that,' someone said.

'*The ground feels very hot, like I'm walking on very hot sand,*' Skyy said. '*The air is very uncomfortable, like a sauna, but not moist – very dry, like a desert, like the Mojave Desert. I'll go over to the bus and see if . . . hey, it looks like a rescue helicopter has arrived. Paul, can you see the helicopter coming? It looks like an army helicopter.*'

'That was quick,' Chamberlain said. 'Who is it, General?'

'I don't know, sir,' Hanratty said. 'I'll try to get a confirmation.'

The photographer swung his camera up, and they could see a twin-rotor Chinook helicopter quickly approaching. It had a small device slung underneath the fuselage. '*It's carrying something underneath,*' Skyy said, '*like a raft or maybe a net of some kind of . . . well, I can't make it out, but it's coming toward us fast so we'll find out in a moment. I wonder if he can land and take all of us out of here in that thing, it certainly looks big enough. We should . . .*' And then she paused, and then exclaimed, '*What the heck is that?*'

The officials in the Situation Room stared in amazement as the cameraman zoomed in. The object the helicopter had slung underneath looked like a man . . . no, it had the figure of a man, but it looked like a *robot*. 'What the hell is that?' Chamberlain exclaimed.

'I have no idea, sir,' Hanratty responded. 'It looks like someone in a protective suit, but I've never seen anything like it before. It's like some kind of high-tech deep-sea diving suit.'

Robert Chamberlain turned to a soldier in battle dress uniform standing behind him, calmly standing at parade rest while the action swirled around the room. He was of average height and build, and his pixilated camo BDUs were adorned with only a few badges – most notable were helicopter pilot's wings, master parachutist's wings, a Combat Infantry Badge, and a Ranger tab – but the man exuded an indefinable aura of power that prevented anyone in the room from locking eyes with him or even coming near him, even the three- and four-star generals. 'Sergeant Major, get someone from the Pentagon to identify that . . . thing, whatever it is.'

'No need, sir – I know exactly what it is,' Army Command Sergeant Major Ray Jefferson responded. The blue-eyed, wiry Ranger looked at the monitor carefully, then nodded. 'I didn't know it was ready for the field, but if it is, sir, it might be the only thing that can save those people now.'

'We're going to redline in about two minutes,' the Chinook pilot said. 'Sorry, sir, but we've got to leave ASAP.'

'You copy that, Jason?' Ariadna Vega asked on their tactical communications frequency. 'The chopper is going to melt in a few minutes. How are you doing down there?'

Jason Richter saw the temperature and radiation readouts in his electronic visor, and he couldn't believe it. The outside temperature was over sixty degrees Centigrade, even suspended twenty meters under the Chinook by a cable, but inside the Cybernetic Infantry Device's composite shell it was still a comfortable twenty degrees Celsius. 'I feel okay,' he responded. 'Everything seems to be working fine so far. Let me down and I'll get to work.' The helicopter slowed and quickly descended. As soon as Jason's feet touched the ground, he disengaged the cable. 'You're clear. Get out of here before your engine goes.'

'We're outta here, Jason,' Vega said. 'Good luck, dude – you're gonna need it.'

God, Jason thought, am I nuts? I'm wearing a contraption that has hardly been tested, let alone ready for exposure in a nuclear environment. Oddly, Jason felt as if he was standing naked, although he was surrounded by forty kilos of composite material and electronics. He experimentally moved his arms and legs and found the limbs remarkably easy to move and control. Jogging was effortless. He saw the survivors down by the lake, about two kilometers away, and started to pick up the pace . . .

. . . before realizing he had hit *fifty kilometers an hour*, and was standing at the edge of Swan Lake in seconds. Kristen Skyy and her photographer stood before him, motionless – but the photographer was not stunned enough to stop filming. Jason scanned the radio bands from his suit's communications system and found her wireless microphone's FM frequency. 'Can you hear me, Miss Skyy?'

'Who in hell is this?' Skyy asked. 'How can you be on this channel?'

'My name is Major Jason Richter, U.S. Army.'

'Where did your helicopter go? Can't it come back and take any people away?'

'The heat is damaging its engine, like your helicopter. I'm here to get you out.'

'How do you think you'll do that – carry us out two by two? Most of these people can't make it. If they leave the water, they'll die – and if we stay here much longer, we'll die.' Jason looked around, saw the school bus lying on its side, and went over to it. 'Get your helicopter to come back,' she was saying, 'and put a cable on . . .'

Jason simply reached down, grasped the edge of the roof of the bus, picked it up, and pushed with his legs. The bus flipped over onto its wheels, its springs bouncing wildly.

'*Oh . . . my . . . God . . .*' Skyy watched in pure amazement as the man . . . robot . . . whatever it was . . . as he walked to the front of the bus, picked it up with one arm, and walked it around until the back of the bus was facing the lake. Then he began to push . . . and in less than a minute had pushed the rear end of the bus into the lake.

'Let's go, Kristen!' Jason shouted. 'Get them on board now!' In moments, the survivors had waded through the water and were helped aboard. The inside of the bus was almost unbearably hot, but it was their last hope. Kristen sat down at the wheel and, after a few frantic moments, got the engine started. With Richter pulling from the front, the bus moved out of the lake. Kristen managed to drive it over the sand and grass until they reached the park road before the engine died, but by then Jason was able to push the bus with ease along the road. With Kristen steering, they reached the highway leading to the town of Bayou Vista a few minutes later, and five minutes after that reached the police roadblock outside the blast area.

Kristen Skyy's photographer captured it all, live, to astonished television viewers around the world.

The men and women in the Situation Room were on their feet, stunned into complete silence, motionless, almost unable to breathe. Finally, Robert Chamberlain put his hands on the conference table as if unable to support himself otherwise. 'What . . . did . . . we . . . just . . . see, Sergeant Major?' he asked, his head lowered in absolute disbelief. 'What in hell *is* that thing?'

'It's called CID, sir – Cybernetic Infantry Device,' Jefferson responded. 'An experimental program run by the Army Research Lab's Infantry Transformation BattleLab in Fort Polk, Louisiana. It's an Army research program trying to find ways to modernize the combat infantryman.'

'I'd say they'd found it, wouldn't you, Sergeant Major?' Chamberlain asked incredulously. 'What is it? Is there a man in there?'

'Yes, sir. CID is a hydraulically powered exoskeleton surrounding a fully enclosed composite protective shell. The system is fully self-contained. A soldier doesn't wear it like a suit of armor, but rides in it – a computer inter-face translates his body movements into electronic signals that operate the robotic limbs. As you saw, sir, it gives the wearer incredible strength and speed and protects him from hazardous environments.'

Chamberlain's eyes were darting around the room as his mind raced again. Finally, he looked at Jefferson as an idea formed in his head, and he pointed at his aide, his voice shaking with excitement. 'I want a briefing on this CID thing before close of business today,' he said, swallowing hard, 'and I want that . . . that suit of armor, whatever it is, its wearer, and the men and women leading that research program here to meet with me as soon as possible for a demonstration. That thing is going to be our new weapon against terrorists.'

'Yes, sir,' Jefferson said. He picked up a phone and

gave instructions. When he hung up, he said, 'I believe the program is still experimental, sir – I don't think it's ready for full operational deployment.'

'It doesn't have to be,' Chamberlain said. 'Heck, just one or two of those things can do everything a damned truck loaded with troops can do! I want to know everything about it, Sergeant Major – and I want to know how fast we can build more of them.'

The crowd of onlookers and police applauded wildly as Kristen pulled off her radiation suit's helmet – but the applause and cheering was deafening when the robot assumed a weird stance, a hatch popped open on its back, and Jason Richter climbed out of the machine. Paramedics started to reach for Kristen to help her into a waiting ambulance, but she pushed them away, stepped quickly over to Jason, threw her arms around his neck, and kissed him, long and deeply. Jason could do nothing else but enjoy the moment – after all, he thought, these things didn't normally happen every day at the Army Research Lab. The crowd cheered even louder.

'Thank you, Major Jason Richter, United States Army,' she said between kisses. 'You saved my life.' She kissed him again, then took his face in her hands. 'And you're cute, even. I will never forget you, Major Jason Richter. Call me. Please.' Finally, she allowed herself to be pulled away by the paramedics and taken to the ambulance.

'Man oh man, you got the prize of a lifetime – a lip-lock from Kristen Skyy herself!' Ariadna Vega shouted after she pushed her way through the crowd. She was wearing a nuclear-biological-chemical protective suit of her own and was sweating profusely, but she was close enough to ground zero that she decided not to completely take the suit off, even though no one else nearby had one on. 'Jason, my man, you were *awesome*! CID worked great!'

Moments later, their celebration was cut short by two columns of troops, each with infantry rifles, who stepped quickly up and surrounded them. Jason issued a command, and the robot folded itself up into an irregular rectangular box large enough to be carried by him and Ari. They were led to the back of a troop-carrying truck, which was covered with a tarp once they and the folded robot were on board.

Ari's cell phone was beeping with numerous messages waiting, and while she was listening to them, another call came in. She hardly had a chance to say 'Hello' before she handed the phone to Jason. 'The boss sounds pissed.'

'Duh.' Jason put the phone up to his lips but not to his ear, expecting the tirade to come. 'Major Richter here, sir.'

'*What in hell was all that*?' screamed Lieutenant Colonel Wayne Farrwood, loud enough to be heard by Ari without the speakerphone. Farrwood was the director of the U.S. Army Research Laboratory Infantry Transformation BattleLab, or ITB, at Fort Polk, Louisiana, near Alexandria. Part of the Joint Readiness Training Center, the ITB was tasked with developing next-generation technology for army ground combat forces. 'Who gave you permission to take a classified weapon system all the way to Houston *in the middle of a nuclear terrorist attack*?'

'Sir, I . . .'

'Never mind, never mind,' Farrwood interrupted. 'If you didn't get us both shit-canned or thrown into prison, you'll probably become a national hero. The truck you're in will take you to the airport and put you and Vega on a military flight. The National Security Adviser wants to talk to us in Washington. Bring the CID unit with you. We're sending one of the support crew Humvees out on a separate flight.'

'What's this about, sir?'

'I don't know, Richter,' Farrwood admitted. 'I just hope we're ready for whatever the hell they have in mind for us.'

Chapter Two

**The Pacific Ocean, thirty kilometers west of the
Golden Gate Bridge, San Francisco, California
The next morning**

The Gibraltar-flagged cargo ship *King Zoser* rode at five knots, barely enough to maintain steerageway, in choppy three- to four-meter seas, with waves and wind combining to keep the decks perpetually damp and the men angry. Most of them were manning the starboard rail, either puking or trying to, when the Coast Guard *Barracuda*-class patrol boat *Stingray* finally approached.

The *King Zoser* was a six-thousand-ton cargo ship, heavily laden and lying very low in the heaving water. It had two thirty-meter-tall cranes that could each sling as much as a hundred tons out to fifty meters over the side, making it one of the few older ships on the high seas able to load and offload itself without extensive shore equipment. Its twin nine thousand horsepower diesels propelled it as fast as twenty knots, although it rarely did more than fifteen. It had a ship's complement of about fifty men and could stay at sea for as long as three weeks.

The *Stingray* launched a large fast intercept craft from its stern ramp, with three two-person inspection teams, four security officers, the detail commander, and a records officer, plus three K-9s that would accompany the inspection teams. The intercept boat had a .50 caliber machine gun mounted in front, and another Coast Guardsman with an M-16 rifle beside the helmsman.

Once alongside the steel-runged ladder on the starboard side of the cargo ship, the boarding party tied off and began climbing the ladder up the vessel's gray slab hull. The K-9s hopped into large canvas backpacks and were carried up the ladder to the deck.

A Coast Guard lieutenant was the first up the ladder. He nodded formally to the man who approached. The captain of the *King Zoser* saluted brusquely with two fingers of his right hand. 'You are either very brave or very foolhardy,' the man said loudly to make himself heard over the swirling winds, 'to board a vessel like this in such rough seas. You would have been better advised to wait until we reached the harbor.'

'Lieutenant Matthew Wilson, executive officer of the Coast Guard patrol vessel *Stingray*,' the officer responded, returning the captain's salute. 'Operating in such sea conditions is routine for us, sir.'

'Is that so?' The captain sniffed. 'I am Yusuf Gemici, master of this vessel. I trust this will not take long. I have a schedule to keep, and I have been at sea for over two weeks.'

'I have checked your manifest filed with the U.S. government,' Wilson said. 'All is in order, so this is just a routine prescreening. My headquarters has notified the harbormaster at Richmond that you will be delayed for a routine inspection. Your berth will be waiting for you whenever you arrive. We'll try not to detain you too long, sir.'

Gemici sniffed again, obviously his signal that he didn't believe what he was being told. 'Very well. You may proceed.'

'I have eleven crew members and three dogs to perform our inspection,' Wilson went on. 'We require access to all spaces, berths, and holds. I request one crew member accompany my search teams in order to expedite movement through your vessel. Any crew members we find belowdecks who are not at required duty stations will be detained by my search teams and may be placed under arrest. Do you understand, sir?'

'More delays,' Gemici growled. Wilson looked as if he expected an argument; the master thought it better to change his tone. 'Yes, I understand.'

'This is Chief Petty Officer Ralph Steadman, my noncommissioned officer in charge of this detail,' Wilson said, motioning behind him without taking his eyes off the captain, his voice a bit more authoritative now. 'If you have any specific questions about this search, you may ask him at any time.'

Gemici looked the CPO over and decided he did not want to get on this man's bad side. Steadman said nothing and did not offer any greeting, obviously not in a diplomatic mood. He carried an M-16 on a shoulder sling and a sidearm and wore a bulletproof vest under his orange life jacket – obviously Wilson was the good guy, Steadman the bad. The rest of the search teams were likewise heavily armed and outfitted, with stern, determined, no-nonsense expressions. The recent attack in Houston had obviously altered many attitudes about securing the homeland.

'I have no questions,' the skipper said. 'My crew will cooperate in any way possible.'

'Very good,' Wilson said. 'If you can lead me to the bridge, sir, I would like to inspect your logbooks, then meet with the crew to check their documents and address any immigration issues.'

'I understand. *Buyurunuz*.' Gemici used a walkie-talkie and assigned some men to take the search teams where they wanted to go. As they spread out, Gemici noticed the Coast Guardsmen activating small black boxes attached to their life jackets. 'What are those devices, Lieutenant?'

'Radiation detectors, sir,' Wilson replied.

'Ah. The attack on your port city of Houston, Texas. Terrible. Terrible.' He spat overboard, being careful to do so with the wind. 'Such crazed terrorists hurt all without regard. I curse them all.' Wilson said nothing, but activated his own detection device. 'I have been at sea for many days,' he reminded Wilson.

'We're not singling you out for any particular reason, sir,' Wilson said. 'All vessels entering major U.S. ports will be inspected several times before they are allowed to offload their cargo; any vessels already in port will be inspected as well.'

'*Evet, anliyorum,*' Gemici said, sniffing. 'I understand.'

Chief Petty Officer Steadman had gone down to the main deck to check in with the above-deck search team, which was inspecting hundreds of tons of steel pipe and massive house-sized oil field transfer pumps chained to the deck. After asking about their progress, Steadman checked a few of the articles on deck himself. The straight pieces were open and easy to inspect, but the angled pipes and pump flanges were closed with steel security caps, bolted in place and the bolts and nuts sealed by local customs officials with numbered steel wires and lead seals that passed through the bolts, which prevented the nuts from being removed without detection. On an oil pipe with over fifty bolts on it, Steadman checked every third or fourth bolt to save time, examining the seal for the proper registration number and gently tugging on the wire to make sure it was not broken.

After reporting that the above-deck inspection was

almost completed, Steadman went belowdecks to check his other inspection teams. These inspections were drier and warmer but not any easier. The usual procedure was to walk slowly up and down the passageways, picking every third or fourth cabin, storage space, or berth to enter and inspect, plus any other suspicious-looking areas such as freezers, flammable-liquid storage areas, and overhead drop ceilings. Each Coast Guard inspection team was briefed daily on the latest intelligence and results of recent searches, which usually provided clues to areas on which to concentrate a search: sometimes patterns emerged, such as using broken-down equipment, 'malfunctioning' engines, or spaces with lots of corrosive chemicals in it to throw off a dog's scent. Searchers were trained to look up as well as look down; they also learned that items were hidden in plain sight as often as they were hidden in the most obnoxious, darkest, smelliest, untouchable places.

As the chief petty officer and senior enlisted man in the inspection team, Steadman tried to show his support for his men by picking the noisiest, smelliest, nastiest places to do his own inspection, which usually meant the propulsion and steering mechanical spaces. But after twenty minutes of careful searching, nothing else showed up. Steadman examined some firefighting equipment that he thought looked odd – finger-to-shoulder heat-resistant gloves, hooded respirator, heat-protective coat, and thick heat-resistant boots, all in a new locker located outside the engine rooms. It was all fairly new and rather high-tech for this ship; only one man, the engineer's mate, had the key – unusual again, since it might be important for every watch stander to have that key in case of emergency. Steadman made a mental note and moved on.

'Got another weather report from the ship – winds

gusting above fifty knots,' Wilson radioed to Steadman after he reported his search of the engine rooms was completed. 'Unless you have something special, let's wrap this up before we're stuck on this bad boy.'

'Copy.' It was almost time to wrap this search up – but not before he tried one last time to stir up some shit.

Each engine room was supposed to have just one watch stander and one oiler during this inspection, but upon entering the port side engine room, Steadman found a third crewman who was listening to a Walkman and smoking a foul-smelling hand-rolled cigarette, taking some readings from an electrical panel. Without any warning, Steadman pressed the man face-first up against the panel. 'Don't move!' he ordered, placing him in plastic handcuffs. The man was about to struggle, but quickly thought better of it and offered no resistance.

Steadman brought the suspect up to the bridge, still in handcuffs, and his papers were handed to Wilson. 'Do you speak English?' Wilson asked.

'Yes.'

He looked carefully at the man's eyes, then asked him, 'Name?'

'Boroshev. Gennadyi Vladomirivich.'

Wilson examined the man's documents, then turned to the skipper. 'Most of your crew is Turkish and Egyptian, but this man is Russian.'

'We have crew members from all over.'

'We asked that only two crewmen remain in each space during the inspection. Why did this man disobey the order?'

'I do not know. Perhaps he thought he was the one who should stay.'

Wilson's face remained stony, and his eyes locked first

on Boroshev's, then Gemici's. Both men remained impassive. Wilson radioed in a request for a records check on Boroshev. Like most of the other crew members, his passport and seaman's license were in horrendous condition, difficult to read and badly weathered. 'Skipper, you know that the United States has regulations on the condition of official documents,' he said. 'These papers are virtually unreadable. Any documents in this bad a condition will have to be replaced before shore leave for those individuals can be approved.'

'My men are professionals, sir,' Gemici said. 'They know the rules, and if they fail to follow them, they must suffer the consequences.' He shook a finger at Boroshev. 'Shore leave for you is not approved until suitable replacement documents arrive – which will probably not be on this trip.' Boroshev said nothing, but bowed his head, ashamed of being scolded in front of the American.

'We'll request a replacement set through the San Francisco consulate – they might have temporary documents waiting for you at your port stop in Victoria,' Wilson offered.

'Bremerton,' Gemici corrected him.

Wilson made a show of checking the manifest, but Gemici was sure he knew his schedule by heart. 'Yes, sir. Bremerton,' Wilson said. He stayed very close to Boroshev, putting his radiation detector right in the guy's face as he scanned as much of his body as possible. The guy was too confused to look nervous. Wilson made a show of staring at the man's eyes carefully. 'This man's pupils look dilated – pretty unusual for someone who was belowdecks and then outside. You do drugs, Gennadyi?' He made a tokeing motion with two fingers up to pursed lips. 'You like the weed, Gennadyi?'

'No, sir.' A hint of perspiration appeared on his forehead. 'I . . . seasick. Very seasick.'

'Seasick, huh?' He stared at the sweat popping out of his forehead, then glared at Gemici. 'You approve of your crewmen using marijuana for seasickness, skipper?'

'My men are professionals, Lieutenant,' Gemici repeated. 'While on this ship, their responsibilities are to their captain, their fellow crew members, their ship, their cargo, and themselves, in that order. As long as they do the job, I do not ask questions.'

'What you do on your ship is your business, Captain,' Wilson said, 'but if any drugs leave the ship while you're in an American port, you could be in danger of having your ship and its cargo confiscated.' After a negative watch list message came back from the *Stingray*, Wilson cut off Boroshev's plastic handcuffs with a folding knife. 'A word to the wise.'

'Yes, sir. I will take care of it.'

A short time later, Steadman radioed to Wilson that they had finished inspecting the ship, checked and verified the crew, and the inspection team assembled on deck awaiting orders. Wilson ordered them to start boarding their intercept boat to return to the *Stingray*, then held out his hand to the skipper. 'Thank you very much for your cooperation, sir,' he said to Gemici. 'I hope the rest of your trip is safe and successful.'

The skipper sniffed but shook hands anyway. 'You be careful riding that little boat of yours back to your patrol vessel, Lieutenant,' he said with a toothy smile. '*Gunaydin*. Have a nice day.' Wilson nodded, saluted, and was the last man down the ladder. With not some small amount of difficulty, the fast intercept craft detached from the cargo ship and finally rendezvoused with the patrol boat; in very short time the Coast Guard vessel was headed back to shore.

The bottom line, Gemici thought, as he made his way back down to the main deck with Boroshev silently behind him, is that there was simply no way any government agency could search every square centimeter of a ship that was over three hundred meters long and weighed more than six thousand tons. The major items on any inspection – the manifest, the logs, the crew, the cargo, and a visual inspection – could be anticipated and handled easily. Everything else that happened was by pure chance. But the odds favored the smugglers, not the inspectors. Unless they dry-docked this ship and cut it apart with torches, plus emptied out every container and cut open every piece of cargo larger than a suitcase, any skilled smuggler could hide thousands of kilos of anything – or hundreds of men – in it.

Case in point: The chain locker in the bow of the *King Zoser*. In most ships, the chain locker and anchor mechanical spaces were in the very forward part of the bow; during an inspection, it was a simple matter to open the door, see the tons of chain and the huge electric winches, and move on. They had even put in false walls to make it appear that the hull was sloping in as expected. But there was yet another compartment forward of the chain locker, accessible only through the false walls, that was even bigger than the chain locker.

Gemici looked mad enough to chew nails as they arrived at the chain locker. Boroshev was nursing the abrasions on his wrists from the handcuffs, and he looked as wobbly and dazed as ever. 'You stupid ass!' the captain shouted at him in Russian. 'Didn't you hear the announcement that the American Coast Guard was approaching and preparing to board us? You could have . . .'

In a flash of movement, Boroshev's left hand whipped out and slapped Gemici full in the face, hard enough to make the captain stagger backward. 'Don't you *dare* talk to me like that, you old donkey-fucker!' he roared. 'You may be the captain of this tub, but you are not my commanding officer!'

The captain wiped blood from his mouth. 'Do you think that smoking dope right before entering American waters was a good idea, Boroshev?' The Russian didn't answer. Instead he pounded on the steel bulkhead at the rear of the chain locker with a code tap, and moments later the wall started to move.

'About fucking time!' a soldier inside said in Russian, lowering his shotgun. 'It's freezing cold in there!'

'Shut up and go check the pumps and the uppermost pressure relief U-pipe on deck – they opened both of them up for an inspection,' Boroshev said. 'Scan for listening devices.' The man nodded and hurried off. Boroshev issued more orders, and one by one another nineteen men hidden in the false room inside the chain locker filed out.

'They had radiation detectors, every one of them,' Gemici said. 'What in hell are we carrying? What is in those pumps?'

'Your job is to get us and our equipment to Richmond, not to ask questions,' Boroshev said. 'We have all used the highest level of security. Believe me, the less you know, the better.'

Gemici looked skeptical. 'Tell me, Boroshev. I won't tell another soul. Drugs? Weapons? Money? If the Americans come back, I should . . .'

'I said no questions. Don't worry about the damned Americans. They left, didn't they?'

'You think they'd try to arrest us all if they found something? They'd get off the ship, alert the entire U.S. Navy, and surround us.'

Boroshev hesitated, licking his lips apprehensively, but finally shrugged. 'Well, it would be the shits to come all this way and get caught within sight of our objective,' he said, 'but that's the way it goes. But I'm telling you, we're fine. As long as we find any bugs they may have planted, and we stay on the lookout for aerial surveillance anytime we're on deck, everything will be fine.'

'They found your private locker too. They made the engineer's mate open it.'

'They didn't take anything, did they?' Boroshev shook his head. 'You see? If they found anything critical, they would have seized this ship, I'm sure of it. You worry too much, you old hen. The Americans are not stupid: after the Houston bombing, they are on full alert. We can expect their security to get tighter as we get closer to port, but if we stay cool everything will be fine. When do we get out of this rough water?'

'We'll be in U.S. waters in about two hours,' Gemici replied. 'We'll take on a pilot entering the bay, probably have to undergo another inspection – we should be in San Pablo Bay in three to four hours. They'll make us anchor in the bay overnight, and then we should be allowed to dock sometime the next day. We should clear customs a couple hours afterward, and then start offloading the shipment.'

'Good,' Boroshev said. 'We'll check for bugs, but I tell you, we're fine. Good job.'

Gemici was worried, but in the end he didn't really care.

His job was to get the package onto the wharf in Richmond, California; Boroshev's job was to get it to its destination, wherever that was. When the pumps and whatever they contained hit the trailer beds and the men stepped foot on the wharf, the money would hit Gemici's Cayman Islands bank account. Then, Boroshev was on his own.

'Let's get out of here, dammit, I'm freezing,' Boroshev said, patting Gemici on the shoulder. 'Another few days, and you'll be finished. Then we'll be on our way back to Alexandria or Damascus or anyplace warm.'

Gemici nodded and left the chain locker. Boroshev was right behind him, but stopped and grasped the arm of one of his men who was waiting nearby. 'Those radiation shields were all in place, weren't they?' he asked in Russian.

'Yes, sir,' the soldier responded. 'We checked the readings carefully for leakage. They're secure.'

Boroshev nodded, silently hoping that was true. 'Very well. Carry on.'

The Americans were making it tougher and tougher to infiltrate their borders, Boroshev thought as he made his way topside to join the captain, but they had anticipated this and were ready. They'd passed their first test that day – or so it seemed. They had a few more tests to go, but they were that much closer to their ultimate objective.

The White House, Washington, D.C.
The next morning

Robert Chamberlain strode through the door to the Oval Office with a single folder in his hand. The President was at his desk, with his chief of staff, Victoria Collins, looking over his shoulder. 'What's up, Robert?' the President asked. He saw the folder Chamberlain had in his hand. 'Comments on the speech?'

'Mr President, do you really mean to say this?' Chamberlain asked incredulously. 'This part about asking folks to go on with their lives?'

Victoria Collins blinked in surprise. Collins was a former college track and field star, Fortune 500 CEO, and two-term Illinois senator. As the first female ever to hold the office of chief of staff, she was very comfortable in the rough-and-tumble world of politics and had been in plenty of high-stress situations in her ground-breaking career; her presidential aspirations were well known to the entire nation. 'Exactly what do you recommend we say to the American people, Robert – run and hide in your homes because we can't handle the situation?'

'Exactly the opposite – I think we should be telling the American people to *offer* their services and help in this time of crisis,' Chamberlain responded. 'I think we should tell them that they should step forward and do everything they can to help their nation and their neighbors get through this crisis.'

'*What*?' Collins cried. 'What do you expect them to do – pick up a rifle and go hunt terrorists in their backyards?'

'I would like all retired civil servants to go back to their old jobs and volunteer to help,' Chamberlain suggested. 'We will need thousands of new background security checks, baggage screeners, record checkers, instructors, and countless more jobs done in the coming months, and we simply don't have the manpower or the money to hire and train new personnel. The budget is already blown through the roof, and our existing employees are already overworked. We need help, and the best solution is to ask for volunteers.'

'This is crazy, Robert!' Collins retorted. 'They'll think we're out of control. And who will retrain the retired guys?'

'The current trainers will, of course,' Chamberlain replied. 'It'll be more of a recertification rather than a full-blown initial training program, since they already know their business. They will . . .'

'And you expect these people to *volunteer* to do this?' Collins asked. 'Why should they? They put in twenty or thirty years in their job, they have a good pension, a comfortable retirement . . . you think they'll respond to a call to leave their comfortable lives and return to those jobs for no pay?'

'I think they will, enthusiastically and in large numbers – if we ask them,' Chamberlain said. 'Mr President, that's why this speech is so important. After 9/11, the message was "Don't panic, be aware, be vigilant, but go about your normal lives because otherwise the terrorists win." It was a good sentiment, but it was the wrong message. The *last* thing we want is for Americans to go about their lives as if nothing has happened.'

'You're inviting panic, confusion, chaos, and a tremendous backlash against this administration, Chamberlain . . .'

'Nothing like the panic and confusion there would be, Miss Collins, if we didn't do anything and there was another nuclear terrorist attack in the States,' Chamberlain said. 'Look, it's simple: We need the help, but we can't afford to hire *half a million* new civil servants. We inspect ten percent of containerized cargo coming into our ports right now. What if Congress orders us to inspect even fifty percent? It'll take at least *five times* the manpower we have now! Who's going to do the background checks for all those people? Who's going to train them? Who's going to train the trainers or check the checkers?'

'But you're suggesting that *volunteers* do it?'

'Exactly,' Chamberlain said. 'These retired and former civil servants, military personnel, teachers, and experts know their business. We can rescreen then, recertify them, and let them work their old jobs when they want. We gain a new pool of help for very little additional cost.

'But more important, we communicate to the American people that we *are* at war,' he went on. 'Telling the people to go about their lives as if nothing has happened doesn't convey the sense of danger or urgency we need if we want to go forward eventually with a declaration of war . . .'

'You obviously didn't get my memo,' Collins said. 'The staff attorneys for the White House, State, Justice, and Defense all are recommending that the President *not* go to Congress to ask for a declaration of war against terrorism. There's no legal or historical precedent for it, and it would be too unpopular and politically dangerous . . .'

'I read the memo, Vicki, and it *stinks*,' Chamberlain snapped. 'It's incomplete and based on opinion only, not on hard evidence or factual research. The political damage has already been done here when the terrorists attacked Kingman City and we were completely unprepared and unaware of the plot – now is the time for the President to step forward and pursue an offensive, forward-leaning, aggressive program to stop future attacks. I realize it may take time and some convincing to get the congressional leadership on board . . .'

' "Some convincing"? The leadership thinks we'd be *nuts* to try it, and there's no way anyone will endorse it,' Collins interjected. 'I've spoken informally and off the record about it, and there's no way it will ever fly . . .'

'Can you possibly be any more negative and wishy-washy here, Collins?' Chamberlain asked angrily. 'The President directed the staff to lay the groundwork for a declaration of war against terrorism. You're not supposed to ask "pretty please" and float trial balloons – you're supposed to implement the President's directives. This speech does nothing to advance the President's agenda.'

Collins stepped forward and was about to take on Chamberlain face-to-face, but the President touched her arm to stop her. 'So what are you suggesting, Robert?' he asked.

Chamberlain handed him the folder. 'I've redrafted your speech to include my recommendations,' he said. 'This speech should be a *call to action*, not a "Don't worry about a thing" lullaby. The speech directs the departments of Justice, Defense, Homeland Security, and State to put out a call to all former employees and contractors to volunteer to assist in helping to ramp up operations, and directs all agencies to make retraining and recertifying these volunteers a top priority. We need at least a thirty percent across-the-board increase in manpower in the next six months to help in border security, security screening, background checks, record checks, surveillance, inspections, support services, and administration . . .'

'That's five percent a month!' Collins exclaimed. 'It can't be done!'

'It can and it *must*, for the sake of our nation,' Chamberlain said. 'If we don't get volunteers, we should consider drafting citizens to do it – not drafting citizens to go in the military, but drafting them to serve their country to help in the war on terror. High school graduates and everyone between the ages of eighteen and thirty will be required to do at least one year of paid government work in a field of their choice, and will then be required to work at least four weeks per year until age sixty . . .'

'Where in the world is this idea coming from, Chamberlain?' Collins retorted.

'Israel has been doing a similar program for decades, and it is highly successful,' Chamberlain said. 'The United States could be under siege like Israel if we don't act.

'I'm proposing a straight volunteer program right now, but I also propose we ramp up the volunteer program so we can increase our manpower by one hundred percent within the next fifteen to twenty-four months,' Chamberlain went on. 'I suggest we offer Americorps or G.I. Bill–like incentives for volunteers: credits for home loan programs, tuition rebates, discount Medicare cards, job training opportunities, tax deductions for volunteer expenses, even tax cuts if necessary.

'I also propose bringing home each and every Reserve Force soldier from overseas duty and putting them to work on domestic security tasks,' Chamberlain said. 'The National Guard and Reserves were always meant to be there to help protect the American people on American soil, not helping the active-duty troops fight overseas. We should increase pay for the Reserve Forces and strengthen the laws that protect their civilian jobs while they're away on Reserve duties, even if it means the government pays their salaries for the jobs that were lost.'

'This is *insane*, Mr President!' Collins said as she read

her copy of the draft. 'None of this has been staffed. We won't be able to address the most basic questions – how much this will cost, who will be accepted, who will be rejected, who will oversee the program, and a million other questions! Legal hasn't even been alerted that you were going to recommend any of this. We're not going to get the media and the American people all hot and bothered with this idea and then find it's not legal or constitutional. You can't expect the President to make a speech about this *tonight* without doing the staff work first!'

'Mr President, I've already got my staff doing the basic legal research,' Chamberlain said. 'They'll have their results to me this afternoon in plenty of time to brief you before your speech to the American people at nine P.M. So far there's nothing we can't address. The union or civil service status of the volunteers and draftees is a prime concern, but that's not a barricade. Vicki is over-reacting, and as usual she's erring on the side of extreme caution, which is precisely what we *don't* need at this time. What we need is bold, decisive, determined *action*.'

The President looked over at Collins, who was silently reading the edited speech, shaking her head, a grim expression on her face. 'Victoria?'

'I can't even begin to list the holes in this proposal, Mr President,' she responded. 'Who will assume legal responsibility for the volunteers? How do we work this program into the departments' budgets? How do we handle information and operational security issues . . . ?'

'That's all flak, Mr President,' Chamberlain said. 'It's details. My staff hasn't uncovered any major glitches in the idea so far. Once the department and congressional staffs jump on this I'm sure they'll uncover problems, but I'm also sure there won't be anything that can't be solved. More important, sir, it shows you doing something positive and proactive. Extreme times call for extreme measures.'

The President finished reading the speech, thought about it for a few moments, then nodded. 'Victoria, give this to Communications and have them polish it up and put it out to the staff. I want comments and changes forwarded by four P.M. this afternoon.'

'Do you want the press and Congress to get a whiff?'

'Yes,' the President replied immediately. 'The more eyes looking at this proposal, the better. Might as well have as many folks as possible vet this idea – might save our staffs a lot of legwork.'

'Do you want this idea to come from the White House or the office of the national security adviser?' Collins asked. 'Since you haven't had time to think about it, it might be better to give credit for the proposal to Mr Chamberlain at first.'

'His office and mine are the same,' the President said. 'I'll give credit but take responsibility for the proposal. It's a good idea, Robert. Thank you.'

'Thank you, Mr President,' Chamberlain said.

'Try to give us more of a heads-up next time, but with this Kingman City crisis, everyone is on the run.'

'Yes, Mr President.'

Collins shot Chamberlain an evil glare as she departed the Oval Office. The President read the edited speech over once more, then commented, 'I see you scheduled yourself to view some kind of demonstration over at Andrews Air Force Base. What else are you working on, Robert?'

'A demonstration of that manned robotic exoskeleton technology that did that rescue out at Kingman City at

Andrews Air Force Base this morning,' Chamberlain replied. 'I'm going to propose that we build a unit of those things and put them to work hunting down terrorists.'

'Sounds good.'

'I'm also going to propose that we build a joint task force – the military and the FBI, working together, to hunt down terrorists,' Chamberlain went on. 'I want this task force to have the mobility and lethality of a special-ops unit, the striking power of a Marine expeditionary unit, and the legal and investigative capability of the FBI; it should be able to operate worldwide.'

'You don't believe in thinking small or forming a consensus with your fellow advisers, do you, Robert?' the President commented with a chuckle. 'All right, you're authorized to put together such a task force under the National Security Council's authority and discretionary budget. Don't have them do a thing without my express written authorization – they can form, organize, and train together, but they can't do anything in the field yet. You're in for an uphill battle on this volunteer program idea, and even more of a turf war over this joint civil-military task force idea. But if anyone can get these programs approved, it's you.'

'Thank you, Mr President.'

'Who are you going to propose to lead this joint task force?'

'My aide, Army Command Sergeant Major Raymond Jefferson.'

'Not an officer?'

'Jefferson is the best of the best in special-operations fieldwork, Mr President,' Chamberlain said. 'He's led both Ranger and Delta Force teams in missions all around the world for almost twenty years. He's tough, he's got lots of special-ops experience, and he's itching to get out of Washington and back into the real world.'

'Who will command?'

'I picked an intelligence agent from the FBI, and I thought of using the officer that developed that manned robot contraption as a cocommander. I'll meet with both of them this morning at the demonstration.'

'Putting the FBI and the military together like this will be like mixing gasoline and air: Do it right and it produces horsepower; do it wrong, and it . . .'

'Creates a big explosion. I know, sir,' Chamberlain said. 'I'll make it work.'

'Keep me advised, Robert. And thanks for the hard work.'

'Thank you, Mr President.'

Just before he reached the door, the President called out, 'Robert?'

'Yes, Mr President?'

'What is it with you and Victoria?' he asked. 'You know she doesn't like being called "Vicki" but you do it anyway, and it just creates tension. You two seem to be butting heads constantly, and I'm starting to feel more like a referee than the chief executive. What's up with that?'

'I don't like it when folks slam ideas before they've had a chance to study them, that's all, sir – especially *my* ideas,' Chamberlain replied. 'Victoria Collins is a political animal. She's not interested in real solutions, just political expediency.'

'Maybe she's just giving advice. That's what she gets paid for.'

'She gets paid to run the White House staff,' Chamberlain said. 'She acts as an adviser, yes, but her primary job is to get things done. When I get a directive from the President of the United States, it's an order, not a suggestion. You directed the White House staff to lay the groundwork for you to ask for a congressional declaration of war on terrorism. It didn't mean list all the ways it *can't* or *shouldn't* be done, but to *do it*.'

'Is that the way you did things at TransGlobal Energy, Robert?'

'Actually, sir, that's what I *learned* at TGE – unfortunately, I learned it too late,' Chamberlain admitted. 'I learned there are those who lead, those who follow, and those who don't know their ass from a hole in the ground. I thought Harold Chester Kingman was a leader, and I was happy and proud to be his lieutenant. I found out soon enough that he is a morally bankrupt, totally corrupt, completely uncaring, and utterly emotionless bag of shit. I became his fall guy and was disgraced simply because I made the mistake of following him when I should have been voicing my opinions and standing up for what I believed to be right.'

'You're referring to the Russian oil deal?'

'Yes, sir. Kingman had an opportunity to unite TGE with one of the world's largest oil producers and build an alliance that would span half the globe. I believe he could have been instrumental in uniting Russia and the U.S. politically and economically too, similar to the alliance between the U.S. and Japan, for which we would have been recognized for decades. Instead, he turned the deal upside down. He fired the entire Russian board and top officers of the company, then dared to threaten the Russian government by withholding *their own oil and natural gas* if they didn't cooperate with the takeover. When I stepped out of line and argued against the move, I was fired as well.'

'That was years ago. You still sound upset.'

'It was a harsh lesson, sir,' Chamberlain said stonily. 'Harold Kingman just doesn't fire someone – he destroys them, just to make sure they don't rise up against him some time in the future. I lost millions in stock options. I paid hundreds of thousands of dollars to fight off corruption, embezzlement, fraud, and conspiracy charges that were all frivolous and unproven, and now I'm having to pay thousands more to keep my countersuits alive against TGE's constant delays, countersuits, and slanderous attacks in the media. In the meantime, my wife left me – amid allegations of adultery, all of which were not true and completely baseless – my kids disowned me, and I became a pariah in the eyes of every corporation in the world.'

'I know the story, Robert – but what does it have to do with Victoria Collins?'

Chamberlain paused, then averted his eyes before replying: 'Maybe . . . maybe I see some of the "play it safe" attitude that I had at TGE in her sometimes, the attitude that ruined my corporate career. Maybe I'm still angry at myself for my indecisiveness and lack of courage, and I take it out on others that I perceive as being the same.'

'You have nothing to prove here, Robert,' the President said, getting to his feet, walking around the desk, and putting a hand on his National Security Adviser's shoulder. 'You have been a tough, courageous, no-nonsense, and dedicated adviser and confidant to me and this administration since the first day you set foot in the White House. TransGlobal Energy's and the corporate world's loss is my gain.'

'Thank you, Mr President. That means a lot.'

The President stepped back and seated himself at his desk again, signaling the end of the brotherly role and the resumption of the chief executive role. 'You have nothing to prove, Robert – which means take the damned chip off your shoulder and start being a member of the team rather than the ideological taskmaster,' he said sternly. 'You are an important man in my personal and professional life, but you are just one of *many* important persons around here. Start thinking of ways to build bridges instead of walls; stop torpedoing the other staff members in this office. I expect you to share your ideas with the others before you present them to me and get as much of the conflicts ironed out so we don't waste a lot of time in bickering and confusion when you walk in here looking for a decision. Are we clear on this?'

'Yes, sir,' Chamberlain responded. The President looked down at the edited speech, signaling an end to their conversation. 'Thank you, Mr President,' Chamberlain muttered, and walked out.

I serve at the pleasure of the President, Chamberlain reminded himself as he headed back to his office to get ready for the visit to Andrews Air Force Base – and right now, the President wasn't too pleased with him.

Facility H-18, Andrews Air Force Base, Maryland
A short time later

'With all due respect to the Brazilians, I think they should get their heads out of their asses and try a little harder,' Special Agent Kelsey D. DeLaine said into her secure cell phone. She kept an eye on the partially open warehouse door for any sign of activity, but so far nothing was happening. Inside the empty building there were only a few Air Force Security Forces guards and one lone guy in camouflage battle dress uniform standing near a high-tech-looking Humvee. His hair was a little long, he was skinny and white-skinned, and he had horn-rimmed glasses strapped to his head with a black elastic band. If he was a military guy, he was definitely the geekiest-looking one she had ever seen. 'There's an attack on a TransGlobal facility in Brazil on the same day, almost the same *hour*, as the attack in Houston, and no one sees a connection?'

'Kel, there have been a total of nineteen attacks against TransGlobal or affiliated companies in South America in the past year,' her associate, Special Agent Ramiro 'Rudy' Cortez, Federal Bureau of Investigation, said on the other end of the connection. 'All of them involved small dams and power-generating plants, and all used only home-made explosives. Strictly small-time. I'm not sure there's a connection.'

'Rudy, we can't start to piece it together until we get more information from our "friends" in the Policia Militar do Estado, but they seem to be dragging their feet on our requests,' DeLaine said impatiently. She had long brown hair, but it was put up now off her collar, which irritated and aggravated her to no end – she hated the feel of cold air on the back of her neck. Her black Reebok power-walking shoes were in her bureau car outside, and after standing in heels for the past twenty minutes she wished she'd brought them along. She shifted the Glock 29 pistol on her right hip for the umpteenth time, trying to find a comfortable position for the compact weapon, and wished that the bureau would reinstate the option for agents to carry their weapon in a purse in non-hostile environments.

'They're doing the best they can, Kel,' Cortez said.

'Their country is as big as ours but nowhere near as connected. We only made the request yesterday. My, we're cranky this morning, aren't we?'

'The eight A.M. meeting hasn't happened yet, the place is empty, no one but some grungy-looking army gopher is here, and my feet are killing me. What do we know about this Brazilian group, GAMMA?'

'Brazilian environmental and human rights activist organization. Targets multinational petroleum and energy-producing corporations in general but appears to be going after TransGlobal Energy Corporation assets more and more in particular.'

'I want to know every detail possible about GAMMA,' Kelsey said. 'If the PME won't give the information to the FBI office in Rio de Janeiro, we should send a request to the CIA Americas desk for support. And we should start pulling data on Brazilian nuclear material and weapons research programs. Brazil could be a source for bomb-making materials, if not the actual weapons themselves.'

'As long as you're asking for the impossible, why don't you get me a sleepover with Jennifer Lopez?' Cortez quipped. 'Kel, we've got every agent in our office pulling sixteen-hour days since the Houston attack. Everyone is concentrating on how a backpack nuke got into the U.S. undetected. No one is looking at Brazilian ecoterrorist groups yet – we're looking at the more credible perps, like al Qaeda, missing Russian tactical nuclear weapons, the Chinese . . .'

'Then get a clerk or records officer to check – it's all computer work,' Kelsey said. 'They can pass the info to you and I'll brief the chief and get the extra manpower if we need it. But we're just doing surveillance – it's not fieldwork, not yet.'

'Kelsey, you've already pressed every clerk, records person, secretary, janitor, and doorman into doing research for us,' her partner said. 'You've even gotten clerks in other agencies doing work for us, which I'm sure is a breach of security. At the very least you're going to owe a lot of lunches.'

'Ramiro . . .'

'Uh oh, the ethnic first name – discussion must be over,' Rudy said. 'Okay, I'll get on it. Any idea what your meeting is about, and why they scheduled it for an empty building at Andrews?'

'This is not just a "building," Rudy – the Redskins could play here if they laid down some artificial turf and put up goalposts,' Kelsey said. 'I have no idea. I'm hoping they're going to fly in a witness that'll break the Houston bombing wide open for us, but I'm not that lucky.'

'Probably has to do with that memo you sent to the director a few months back,' Cortez surmised. 'Didn't you mention something about nuclear weapons then?'

'I talked about a memo I wrote based on reports from our London and Warsaw offices about Russian tactical battlefield nuclear warheads being converted to "back-pack" weapons,' Kelsey said. 'It was a collection of reports from our bureaus and from European sources spanning three years and three continents, and I had no concrete conclusions – I thought my office should start an analysis and try to come up with some definite links. I thought the report got circular-filed.'

'Obviously after Houston, folks noticed.'

Just then she noticed the warehouse door opening, and several security officers taking positions inside and out. 'I should find out soon – someone's arriving. Talk to you later.'

'Break a leg.'

Kelsey closed her phone, then straightened her shoulders as three dark stretch limousines approached. The warehouse doors closed, with guards both inside and out. The limos pulled over to Kelsey . . . and she was at first surprised, then shocked, at the figures that stepped out of those cars: the director of the FBI, Jeffrey F. Lemke, from the first; Secretary of Homeland Security, Donna Calhoun, from the second; and the President's National Security Adviser, Robert Chamberlain, from the third.

'Kelsey, good to see you again,' Director Lemke said, holding out his hand. She shook hands. Although she worked at FBI headquarters in Washington, she'd attended just a few meetings with the director and maybe said six words to him in two and a half years. Jeffrey Lemke was a former FBI agent turned federal prosecutor and politician, first as a state attorney general and then as a two-term congressman from Oklahoma before being appointed FBI director. Kelsey liked him and thought he was an effective director, although he looked and spoke more like a politician than an FBI agent – which was probably a good thing.

Lemke turned and motioned beside him. 'Secretary Calhoun, I'd like to introduce Special Agent Kelsey DeLaine, deputy director of our intelligence office in Washington and one of our best analysts. Agent DeLaine, Secretary of Homeland Security Calhoun.'

'Nice to see you again, Madam Secretary,' Kelsey said. 'We met about two months ago when I briefed you and your staff on my report on backpack nuclear devices.' The pain on Donna Calhoun's face, which Kelsey remembered seeing in a press conference on TV just last night and was obviously still with her, deepened to a look of stony agony. Kelsey meant her remark to make the secretary feel more comfortable with her, but she saw that it only made her sadder. Calhoun nodded in greeting but said nothing and stepped away to speak with Chamberlain.

'Sorry about that, sir. I wasn't thinking. I remember she lost some family in Houston.'

'Don't try to make polite chitchat here, DeLaine,' Lemke said pointedly. 'This is not a damned cocktail party.'

'Yes, sir.' She was not accustomed to being admonished like that, even by the director, especially after recognizing her gaff and apologizing for it, but she tried not to let her indignation show. 'Can you tell me what *is* going on?'

'We'll all find out together,' the FBI director responded woodenly. The military officers remained apart from the civilians, talking between themselves at first and then with Chamberlain as he approached.

Kelsey found it odd that the lone guy by the Humvee had stayed by himself as all this brass arrived, so when curiosity finally overcame her, she excused herself from Lemke and stepped over to him. The guy didn't look like a GI at all: his hair was rumpled and a bit longer than the other military guys in the hangar wore theirs; his boots looked as if they hadn't been polished in eons; and he had a slight stubble as if he hadn't shaved in a couple days. He was wearing crisp, new-looking military fatigues but there was no rank or insignia on them – they were obviously borrowed or just recently purchased. A very attractive dark-haired woman in a green olive drab T-shirt and black fatigue trousers was sitting behind the wheel with a headset on – she looked more military than the guy did, but she didn't *seem* military. Neither of them displayed any ID. 'Excuse me,' she said. 'I saw you over here all by yourself and thought I'd introduce myself. I'm Kelsey . . .'

'Special Agent Kelsey DeLaine, deputy director of intelligence, FBI, Washington,' the officer said. 'I'm Major Jason Richter, ITB, Army Research Lab, Fort Polk, Louisiana.'

'*You're* in the army?' Kelsey asked, glancing up at his unkempt hair.

'We've had a long couple of days,' Richter said a little sheepishly. 'This is Dr Ariadna Vega, assistant director.'

'ITB?'

'Infantry Transformation BattleLab. We try to think of ways to make infantry soldiers more lethal.'

'Sounds interesting – and a little scary.' She extended a hand, and he shook it. He seemed a little nervous – his hand was cold and clammy, and there was a slight sheen of perspiration on his upper lip. His handshake matched his appearance – he seemed more like a computer nerd than an army officer. But in the intelligence field she learned that very often appearances were deceiving. He would look a lot cuter, she decided, if he weren't wearing those geeky glasses. She shook hands with Vega as well. 'Nice to meet you. How do you know who I am?'

'Because we're monitoring all conversations taking place inside this building and all movement within a mile,' he replied.

'You are? How are you doing that?'

'Surveillance units, both inside and outside.'

Kelsey motioned to the Air Force guards. 'You mean those guys?'

'No. Unmanned probes.' He pointed toward the roof.

'I don't think you can see it, but there's a device on the roof right about there that looks like a giant cockroach, about the size of a serving tray. It can pick up, record, jam, analyze, and transmit voice, video, electromagnetic signals, and data for two square kilometers. It can crawl around walls and ceilings, and deactivates itself if it thinks it's being scanned.'

This guy was a little too cocky and calm for her liking. He was not wearing a sidearm, but his hands were behind his back where she couldn't see them. She fished out an ID badge that she had been given after checking in at base security. 'Do you have one of these, Major, Doctor?' she asked, her voice a little sterner. 'Can I see it?'

Richter smiled. 'No, I don't,' the guy said. His smile sent a warning chill up and down her spine. 'I didn't arrive via the front gate.'

'Then let me see some ID, both of you,' she ordered in a loud voice.

'Agent DeLaine . . . ?' Director Lemke said behind her.

'I don't have any ID to show you, Kelsey,' Richter said. 'We're here to dazzle the brass over there.'

Now she was thankful that she didn't have her gun in her purse. Kelsey quickly drew her Glock from her holster and held it at her side where it was clearly visible but not pointed at him. 'Then let me see your hands, above your head, both of you, *now*!' she ordered.

Richter's eyes lit up in surprise. 'Oh, goody,' the army officer said with a quirky smile as he slowly raised his hands. They were empty. 'We get to start the demonstration early.'

'What did you say?' She watched as the army officer reached over and touched some buttons on his wrist-watch, which she could now see was a very large device, more like a small computer keypad. *'Don't touch that! Keep your hands up!'*

'What's going on here?' the National Security Adviser was demanding. 'Put that pistol down . . . !'

At that moment Kelsey noticed a blur of motion. Someone, a woman – Secretary Calhoun, Kelsey realized – screamed. Kelsey glanced to her right . . . just in time to see a large robot-looking thing running at her as fast as a track and field sprinter. She dropped to her left knee and just had time to aim her pistol at the running machine.

'CID One, stop,' Richter spoke in a quiet voice – not as a warning but as a gentle command. The machine stopped instantly – Kelsey couldn't believe a thing that big moving so fast could stop so quickly. 'Please don't shoot it, Agent DeLaine,' he added. 'It won't like it very much.'

Kelsey froze but kept her pistol aimed in the center of the machine's torso. The machine had both its arms upraised, mechanical fingers extended like claws – and mounted on its right shoulder, Kelsey was staring into the muzzle of the biggest machine gun she had ever seen, not ten feet away from her face. 'I believe I have the drop on you,' Richter added with a smile.

'I see you've decided to start the demonstration on your own, Major Richter,' Robert Chamberlain said. 'Agent DeLaine, you can put your weapon away. Major Richter's machine is part of the reason we're here this morning.'

'Sorry, sir,' Kelsey said a little sheepishly, rising to her feet and holstering her pistol. 'I asked for this man's ID, and he said he didn't have any.'

'Obviously you don't watch much television, Agent

DeLaine – you're probably the only person in the world who's never heard of Major Jason Richter and his robot here and what they did at Kingman City yesterday,' Chamberlain said. He nodded toward Jason and Kelsey. 'Major Jason Richter is deputy director of the Army Research Lab's Infantry Transformation BattleLab, the creator of the Cybernetic Infantry Device, or CID, unit you see before you. Major Richter, this is FBI Special Agent Kelsey DeLaine, deputy chief of intelligence in Washington.' To Calhoun and Lemke, Chamberlain said, 'I propose that these two individuals together with this hardware, among other innovations, form the backbone of America's war on terror.'

Jason's eyes bugged out in surprise, and he looked at DeLaine, who immediately looked at him with the same expression. Neither of them knew what to expect after that announcement, but what they got . . . was bedlam.

'You mean, you propose to use *that thing* to hunt down terrorists?' Secretary of Homeland Security Calhoun retorted. 'You're joking, aren't you, Chamberlain?'

'I've never been more serious – and neither has the President,' Chamberlain said. 'It will be the first federal law-enforcement task force created to specifically detect, identify, pursue, and destroy terrorists around the world. I intend it to be an ultra-rapid response force that will be primarily investigative in nature but equipped to handle a wide array of threats, including military adversaries.'

'You can't do that, Mr Chamberlain – it's prohibited by the Posse Comitatus Act,' Homeland Security Secretary Calhoun pointed out. 'We've stretched the boundaries of that law for years, but having a military unit actively and purposefully involved in law-enforcement actions is against the law.'

'First of all, Madam Secretary, CID doesn't belong to a military unit – it's just an experimental design,' Chamberlain pointed out. 'Second, CID will be used in a support role, which is permitted under the law. I've verified this with the White House counsel. The President will issue a classified executive order secretly implementing this new FBI task force, code-named TALON, reporting directly to the White House and funded by National Security Council discretionary funds . . .'

'Meaning, run by *you*,' Jeffrey Lemke interjected skeptically.

'The President will be responsible for all of TALON's activities and will be briefed on a daily basis of its operations and status.'

'But *you* will be managing it for the President, right?'

'I will propose that the operational unit be supervised by Command Sergeant Major Ray Jefferson, a veteran special-ops leader and the noncommissioned officer in charge of operations for the National Security Council,' Chamberlain went on, motioning toward the soldier standing behind him at parade rest. Like Richter, Jefferson was wearing a green camouflage battle dress uniform, but with a very large sidearm. 'They will set up operations at a secret location and begin organizing, planning, and training together.

'But we will go farther than this, Director Lemke, Secretary Calhoun,' Chamberlain went on. 'The President proposes to use the current Threat Level Red condition to ask Congress to repeal the Posse Comitatus Act of 1878. He will then reveal the existence of Task Force TALON and request full funding, provided by Department of Defense, Homeland Security, and Justice Department allocations.'

'But . . . but what about *this* thing?' Calhoun asked. 'Where does this thing come in?'

'Madam Secretary, technology like CID represent the evolution of the U.S. infantry and possibly law enforcement. This is the perfect opportunity to put this new weapon system into action.' He turned to Richter. 'Mount up, Major, and let's give them a demonstration. Tell us what we're seeing.'

'Yes, sir.' Jason stepped forward and stood before the machine. 'Ladies and gentlemen, CID is more than a robot and more than an exoskeleton – it is designed to be a fighting unit all by itself. It can replace an entire four-man infantry or special-operations squad, except it has capabilities that are far superior to a normal rifle, machine gun, or rocket squad. It has the firepower of an infantry squad but is as fast and as self-protective as a Humvee, has the communications- and intelligence-gathering capability of a Stryker light armored reconnaissance unit, and the rapid deployment capability of a Marine Corps special-operations platoon.

'The Cybernetic Infantry Device is composed of a light-weight composite framework, many times stronger than steel but only a fraction of the weight, covered in impact-resistant composite armor,' Jason went on. 'It is powered by several different sources: a rechargeable hydrogen fuel cell, lithium-ion batteries, and solar power. Locomotion is provided by very small hydraulic systems that support the structure, coupled with a computer-based haptic interface that precisely translates human muscle and limb movement into exoskeleton movement, even against forces that would make a human muscle fail. This CID unit has the strength of ten men, and that strength can be enhanced even more with improvements we're making in its microhydraulic systems. Other CID systems provide global communications, satellite datalink, multi-spectral sensors, and precision-weapon fire control.

'As you can see, this CID has one weapon already installed, a twenty-millimeter cannon. CID One, about-face.' The machine smoothly and quietly turned around. 'The weapons are modular, contained in quick-don, reloadable backpacks that allows weapons to be employed without having to lift or point them with the arms and hands or aim them with the eyes. We have developed other modules including grenade, rocket, unmanned aerial vehicle, missile launchers, and even long-range reconnaissance and communications relay.'

Jason motioned to the side of the warehouse, and a Humvee drove up. 'CID One, stow the backpack,' Jason spoke. The machine stepped over to the left side of the Humvee, turned around, and backed into a cutout on the side of the vehicle. Seconds later, the cannon folded itself inside the backpack, and the backpack detached itself from the machine and disappeared inside the vehicle. 'Inside the special Humvee, the module is automatically tested, serviced, and reloaded in about five minutes, while the CID can attach another module. The Humvee is designed to support two CID units and can carry four modules with one reload apiece along with the two CID troopers, a driver, and a support technician.

'Here's the best part: CID One, retire.' At that command, the machine started to fold itself. Seconds later, it had compressed into a box-shaped object that resembled a large old-fashioned steamer trunk, complete with handles. Jason and Ari Vega squatted down and picked the object up. 'Weighs about eighty to ninety pounds – easily transportable by two persons.'

'So, this thing does . . . what?' Lemke asked. 'Follows a couple special-ops guys around? Runs beside the soldiers? Sounds pretty ridiculous to me.'

'You called it an "exoskeleton," ' DeLaine asked. 'Is there someone inside?'

'I'm sorry – I got a little ahead of myself,' Jason said. 'CID One, activate.' The machine unfolded itself in less time than it took to fold. 'CID doesn't follow you around, sir – the pilot *wears* it. CID, pilot up.' At that command, an access door opened up in back of the machine. Using the backs of the legs, Jason climbed up and slid inside the machine, and the door closed behind him. A few seconds later, the machine came alive.

It was almost comical to watch: unlike before, when the machine moved in a characteristic robotlike gait, the machine now moved exactly like a human – smoothly, fluidly, almost randomly. Its arms, fingers, head, neck, shoulders, hips, and legs articulated as if they was real. Every unconscious gesture, quirk, reflex, and adjustment that a normal human made could be seen, except it was being accomplished not by a human being but by a three-meter-tall machine. They could not see his face – his head was completely covered in armor, his eyes with an electro-optical visor; the machine's ears were dielectric sensor panels – but it almost seemed as if they could feel him looking at their stunned reactions just by observing his body language – yes, they could all notice *body language* in this amazing machine.

'As you can see, CID's haptic interface, powered by fast computers, fly-by-wire controls, and even faster microhydraulic actuators, gives the pilot a very easy, free range of movement,' he said, his voice amplified via a hidden speaker. Its right foot lifted up, and the machine did a perfect spin on its 'toes.' He then started to hop, skip, and jump around the warehouse, resembling some sort of hulking child. The jumps got longer and higher, eventually reaching several meters, but he landed with virtually no noise. After the jumps, Jason started running around the hangar – and within moments, his speed was breathtaking, circling the entire football-field-size building in about twenty seconds.

Jason then jumped back over to the Humvee. Ari threw him three tennis balls, and Jason began to juggle them. 'That concludes my demonstration,' he said as he juggled. 'Any questions?'

There was no reaction to the amazing showing for several long moments. Finally, Kelsey asked, 'How . . . how long can your power last, Major?'

'Depends on the activity,' Jason replied. Ari retrieved a bowling ball from the Humvee and threw it at Jason, and he started juggling it along with the tennis balls. 'Full combat operations with a couple backpacks and reloads, covering an AOR of twenty square miles: five to six hours. A reconnaissance mission or light armed patrol: perhaps two days. The fuel cells can be changed in a few seconds; the battery lasts between fifteen and sixty minutes for emergency power; and the solar panels can charge the batteries in about two hours.'

'Can you please stop that, Major?' Donna Calhoun asked perturbedly. Jason caught the three tennis balls in one hand and the bowling ball in another. Calhoun shook her head. It was very hard to take this machine seriously – or maybe it wasn't the machine, but the *man* inside it, that she couldn't stand. 'Mr Chamberlain, it's very impressive, but if you expect Homeland Security support for this project, you have to give us more time to evaluate this system and design performance and operational guide-lines for it. You can't just take something like this out of the lab and put it in the field without tests, evaluations, measurements, and some planning about how it can be used. We have no idea what it's capable of.'

Jason handed the tennis balls to Ari, as casually as a grade school kid passing a note to a buddy – and then he took the bowling ball between his two hands and, with a loud 'POP!' crushed it into black powder, right before their eyes.

All of the observers jumped in complete surprise. 'Goddamn it, Major, *as you were*!' Sergeant Major Jefferson snapped in a voice that made even the civil-ians jump. Jason immediately dropped the powderized bowling ball and assumed parade rest – Kelsey practi-cally had to bite her tongue to keep from laughing at the sight of this horrific yet impressive machine standing before them like a Marine guard at the White House. 'Take that thing off . . . I mean, shut that thing off . . . I mean, get out of that damned thing, Major!' The machine assumed its special stance, with its left leg extended backward and both knees bent; the access hatch flipped open, and Jason climbed out. His hair and uniform were slightly rumpled, but he looked as he did when he first climbed inside. He stood at parade rest beside the machine.

'This is all very impressive, Mr Chamberlain, but I'm not going to sign off on this thing without some study,' Lemke went on, impatiently looking at his watch, obvi-ously ready to depart.

'I'm afraid I agree with Jeffrey,' Donna Calhoun said. 'The Department of Homeland Security can't even begin to start designing doctrine and training with the CID units until we can study how it works, how it's maintained, what its flaws and limitations are . . .'

'You don't understand, Madam Secretary,' Chamberlain said with a tone of firm exasperation in his voice. 'This project is going forward. Sergeant Major Jefferson prepared an operations plan, including the initial TO&E, and the President signed it.' He withdrew envelopes from his jacket pocket and handed one to each of them. 'Full authorization from the President for a pilot program, ninety days. We are requesting a written report within the next three days on the budgetary, equipment, and personnel support you can provide TALON, and all of the listed support items delivered to the base within fifteen days.'

'*What*?' Lemke exclaimed. He snatched an envelope from Chamberlain's hand, opened it, and quickly read. 'You want a hundred personnel, an *airbase*, computers, satellite Earth stations, aircraft . . . *all in fifteen days*? Mr Chamberlain, I can't even guarantee I can staff this request within fifteen days, let alone deliver all this stuff . . .'

'Then you'll personally explain to the President why you can't comply,' Chamberlain said. 'Director, I know you've done a lot more in a lot less time. I'm sorry you weren't given more time to provide your input . . .'

'I wasn't given *any* time!'

'. . . but Kingman City has changed everything. We want to do everything we can to prevent another incident like this, and the way we're going to do it is form a task force that can deploy at a moment's notice and hit the enemy hard.'

'We have that already, Robert – it's called U.S. Special Operations,' Calhoun said. 'It's called the U.S. Marines. You don't need to start all over again.'

'I agree,' Lemke said. 'It sounds to me as if you need to bring the FBI in on this.'

'It's been considered and rejected because of our legal limitations,' Chamberlain said. 'I suggested, and the President concurred, that to carry out these operations with the current legal and political limitations would not be efficient or effective. When I was made aware of the CID weapon system and the other innovations being developed by the Army Research Lab, immediately after the Houston attack, I decided that making TALON a separate unit instead of part of the FBI was a better way to proceed. Again, the President concurred.'

'Mr Chamberlain, it's a little unusual for the President's National Security Adviser to be setting up any kind of direct action military unit,' Donna Calhoun said, 'let alone one that combines direct action military hardware like this with a federal law-enforcement agency like the FBI. We already have such paramilitary organizations in place, like the Coast Guard, Customs Service, and Alcohol, Tobacco, and Firearms, which frankly work very well with the FBI. It seems like you're duplicating your efforts.'

FBI Director Jeffrey Lemke nodded in agreement. 'After Kingman City, Robert, we're stretched to the breaking point,' he added. 'We can't afford any manpower to hand over to this task force of yours, especially not my deputy for intelligence.' Lemke motioned to Kelsey DeLaine. 'Kelsey is one of my best and most trusted analysts.'

Lemke nodded to Richter, then let his eyes roam over his unkempt hair and unshaven face with a disapproving expression. 'The major here . . . well, he *seems* like a fine young man, but how well do you *really* know him? How long have you known him? Have you checked out his background? Is that his real name? Who are his parents, his relatives?' He glanced at Special Agent DeLaine and saw her looking at him suspiciously. 'Did he really graduate from Georgia Tech? Is he really twenty-nine years old? Did you even *know* how old he was? Do you . . . ?'

'Stop, stop – I get the picture,' Chamberlain said, holding up his hand. He stood silent for a few moments, collecting his thoughts; then: 'No . . . no, I'm determined to see this through. I don't care if this is not the way it's usually done; I don't care if the military doesn't like the way I'm doing it. It's got to be done. It's been years since 9/11, and I don't think enough has been accomplished – and the attack on Kingman City proves it. It's time to get tough on terrorists before they attack and destroy Washington, not just an isolated oil terminal outside Houston or a couple skyscrapers in New York City.'

It was obvious from their expressions that Calhoun and Lemke did not agree or share any of Chamberlain's excitement. But for Jason Richter, this seemed like an important moment. The war on terrorism, it seemed, was preparing to enter a newer, deadlier phase – right here in the United States. And he was going to be part of it!

'I'm asking for your full support,' Chamberlain said earnestly. 'The President will back you up all the way. I appreciate your time and attention, and I'll give you any information and constant reports on our progress. Thank you for being here.'

Jeffrey Lemke read over the letter, even running his fingers over the President's signature to see if it was real. He then looked at Jason and the CID unit and nodded. 'The bureau will give you all the help we can, Robert,' he said, 'but this is definitely a difficult time to be standing up a unit like this. We're still reeling from the attack on Kingman City – I need all my people to hunt down those responsible.'

'And now you have a new interdiction and direct-action unit to help you,' Chamberlain said. 'But it's got to be done, and I'm determined to do it – in fact, I'll gladly sacrifice whatever political future I have to get it done.' He extended his hand to Lemke and affixed a sincere, direct gaze. 'I'm counting on your support, Director.'

Lemke seemed skeptical as he shook Chamberlain's hand. He looked at Kelsey. 'Cooperate for now, Agent DeLaine,' he said. 'Keep in contact with me. I want a daily report.'

'That won't be possible, Director,' Chamberlain said. 'TALON needs to operate on a strictly classified basis. No outside communication unless through me.'

'Then I order Special Agent DeLaine to refuse to cooperate at all with this operation,' Lemke said. 'The National Security Council will not be allowed to use Bureau assets or data without full disclosure and reporting. No argument.'

Chamberlain looked at Lemke as if he was going to try to pull rank on him, but instead he nodded. 'Done. Full disclosure. I'd like it directly between Agent DeLaine and your office.'

'My staff will arrange the proper report format and . . .'

'Your office *only*, Director,' Chamberlain said. 'This is not for your staff. This is disclosure, Jeffrey, not approval or consultation. You can go up to the Justice Department with any concerns, but not to your staff.'

'Mr Chamberlain, I *guarantee* I will be going to the Justice Department with this,' Lemke said sternly. But he nodded. 'Fine. Kelsey, my direct line only, okay? I'll give you the number.'

'Yes, sir.'

Donna Calhoun shook Chamberlain's hand warmly, then gave him a hug. 'I'm proud of you, Robert,' she said as they embraced. 'God knows the shades of Kingman City are counting on you. This is a difficult thing you're attempting. Thank you for your courage.'

'I won't let you down, Madam Secretary, I promise,' Chamberlain told her softly. 'I will avenge your loss.' He escorted her and Lemke to their waiting limousines and watched as they drove off.

After the second limo departed, Chamberlain turned toward Richter, Jefferson, and DeLaine; he hung his head, and actually seemed to look emotionally weary. He looked up, straightened his shoulders, took a deep breath . . . and then clapped his hands enthusiastically. 'Well,' he said in a loud, energetic voice, 'now that the bullshit is over, let's get to work.'

Richter's mouth dropped open in surprise; Chamberlain noticed it. 'You don't think I really give a shit about Calhoun's dead sister and brother-in-law in Kingman City, do you, Major?' he asked incredulously. 'You deal with these bureaucrats and politicians in whatever terms they understand and respond to. Calhoun is this sweet, sensitive liberal ex-U.S. federal prosecutor from Houston who couldn't hurt a flea. Her wealthy real estate developer husband gave ten million dollars to the party and bought his wife a Cabinet position so he could continue screwing his friends' wives in peace.

'The wild card in the deck is Jeffrey Lemke,' Chamberlain went on, turning back to the others. 'He knew an awful lot about you, Major, and that is troubling.'

'Why, sir?'

'He got wind of this meeting and found out who the principals were,' Chamberlain replied. 'That took initiative, curiosity, and attention to detail.'

'And you don't approve of those traits in an FBI director, sir?' DeLaine asked sarcastically.

Chamberlain turned to the FBI agent and affixed her with a crocodile smile. 'He undoubtedly got the information from you, Agent DeLaine, or somebody close to you in your office,' he said. 'Director Lemke is indeed a capable young man, willing to spy on his own staff to get answers. That could become a liability.' He stepped closer to DeLaine, searching her eyes for any sign of weakness or sorrow for Lemke's fate – and not finding any. He smiled at that realization. 'It doesn't matter. Within a week, all of you will be at your new base, setting up your new unit.' He kept his gaze fixed on Kelsey DeLaine's green eyes. 'You and the lovely Special Agent DeLaine are going to be the cocommanders of Task Force TALON, Major Richter. You are going to employ CID and any other high-tech gizmos you can devise to hunt down the perpetrators of the attack on Kingman City and any other terrorists around the world that threaten America.'

He turned to Sergeant Major Jefferson. 'The sergeant major has already procured a base of operations for you in New Mexico. The commanding general at Fort Polk has been advised to give you all the manpower and support you need. I want you set up as soon as possible. You will use all your skills, expertise, and training, plus an extra helping of guts and audacity, to hunt down the terrorists that attacked Kingman City and bring them to justice – or destroy them. Either works for me.

'Now I know that this is not the typical chain of

command, being organized and run by an NCO, but Command Sergeant Major Jefferson is the most experienced person I know to train and organize this task force,' Chamberlain went on. 'I warn you not to get in his way – I've seen the man eat two-star generals for breakfast. You will treat him as you would myself at all times, is that clear?' He didn't wait for a response. 'Sergeant Major Jefferson.'

'Sir!'

'Take charge of Task Force TALON immediately.'

'Yes, *sir*.' Chamberlain walked away to his limousine without saying another word to anyone, leaving Jason and Kelsey alone with Jefferson and the CID unit. 'Agent DeLaine, Major Richter, Dr Vega, listen up,' he began. 'Time is critical now. Our objective is to organize and set up a base of operations to train and support TALON's weapon systems, collect and analyze intelligence data, and begin to conduct antiterrorist operations. Within three days we need to be in place, and within ten days we need to be set up and operating.

'I have already sent a forward field deployment team to our base of operations to help get set up,' Jefferson went on. 'In fact, they have been working since yesterday. They're not familiar with FBI procedures or the CID technology, so you need to bring them up to speed as soon as possible. That means getting your supplies out to New Mexico right away.' He handed them both cellular telephones. 'Speed-dial zero-zero-one for me, ask, and I'll get it for you. You already have transports and men to help you move. Agent DeLaine, a cargo aircraft will be here at Andrews ready to take you and your gear tomorrow. Major, the plane will arrive at Alexandria ready to take your gear the day after. Be on it. Questions?'

'What "gear" do we take, Sergeant?' Jason asked.

Jefferson's eyes widened in anger, and he stepped up to Jason and stood nose to nose with him. They were of just about equal height, but Jefferson's sheer physical presence suddenly made Jason feel very small. 'Major Richter, sir,' he said between clenched teeth, 'I realize you are an officer, but it appears it is necessary for me to teach you something you should already know. I am not a sergeant, I am a *sergeant major*. That is something recruits learn within days of starting basic training. I hope it doesn't take you as long to learn it.' He glared once more at Richter, then went on to all of them: 'Bring everything remotely connected to CID or to any of the other devices you've set up in this warehouse,' he said. 'You can take your whole lab if it'll fit in a C-130 Hercules. Our priority will be deploying and utilizing the CID units in the field in the quickest amount of time. I understand you have two prototypes – bring both of them. Bring as many parts and partial prototypes as you can as well.'

'How do we know who or what to bring?' Kelsey asked.

'Bring everything you can get packed and ready in two days – we'll sort it out when we get to Clovis,' Jefferson said. 'The critical stuff needs to go on the plane; other things can be shipped by truck if necessary.'

'Clovis?'

'New Mexico. Cannon Air Force Base. Your new home for a while.' He detected that they were trying to think of anything they needed to ask, and the tall Marine was determined not to give them the opportunity. 'That'll be all, folks. Be at Cannon in three days, or I will come back and make life exceedingly unpleasant for you.'

He then looked directly at Jason and, addressing them

all, 'One more thing: in my unit, you will conform to all military discipline, dress, and appearance standards – clean shaven, clean uniform, and most important, you will conduct yourself in a professional military manner at all times, and that means inside your toy there as well as outside of it. We are not in your world now, sir – you're in *mine*. Questions?'

'Just a comment, Sergeant Major.'

'What is it?'

'It would've been helpful if I was briefed on what you intended to do here, Sergeant Major,' Jason said. 'If I had known that you were thinking about using the CID system to form an operational unit . . .'

'Major, I report to the National Security Adviser, and he reports only to the President of the United States and Congress, not to you,' Jefferson said. 'He doesn't need to ask you "pretty please" before he decides to do something. He confers with the President, gets the go-ahead, and acts. That's his job. I expect you to shut up and do yours, sir. Clear?'

'Yes, Sergeant.'

'That's Sergeant *Major*, sir – don't make me remind you again. Anything else for me, sir?'

'No, Sergeant Major.'

'Then may I *strongly* suggest you get a damned haircut and don't let me see you in a dirty uniform again, sir. Now move out.'

Sergeant Major Jefferson departed immediately, leaving Jason, Ari, and Kelsey together alone with the CID unit. 'Wow, dude,' Ari said to Jason. 'You're in the FBI, man. You're a G-man. Awesome.'

'You are *not* in the FBI any more than I'm in the freakin' army,' Kelsey said sternly. She opened the new cellular phone and dialed. 'As far as I'm concerned, this is an FBI operation – you two and your gizmos are support, nothing more. The key to the success of our unit is intelligence, not how fast or how high this thing can go.' She said something on the phone, then turned back to Richter and Vega distractedly. 'Listen, I have a lot of work to do, and so do you. I think it would be a good idea to pack up the robot here and start heading back to wherever Fort Polk is . . .'

'Louisiana.'

'. . . and be prepared to teach my staff all about CID here. But I don't anticipate we'll be using it right away.'

'Why not?' Jason asked. 'You still prefer to go up against the bad guys with just your little pistol there?'

'The key to a successful investigation, Major, is information – timely, accurate intelligence data, carefully analyzed and strategized,' she responded. 'We decide exactly what level of support we need once we've studied the suspects and determined their size, strength, composition, and . . .'

'That's easy, Special Agent DeLaine – they're bad guys, not suspects, and they got their hands on a nuclear device,' Jason said. 'If we find them, we should go in and shut them down. CID was developed to do that with speed and power. What else is there to do?'

'Folks, I don't have time to teach you every aspect of a successful investigation while we're standing here,' Kelsey said impatiently. 'I have lots of work to do, and so do you. I'll meet up with you in New Mexico. Goodbye.' She turned her attention to the cellular phone, dismissing them.

'Wave bye-bye to the nice FBI agent, El Cid,' Jason said. The robot turned toward Kelsey and waved a massive mechanical right hand. Kelsey ignored it. Jason whispered something else to the robot, and it raised its arms and shook its hips in her direction. *That* she couldn't ignore. She rolled her eyes and shook her head in exasperation and headed for the exit.

Ari gave the command to retire, and the robot folded itself up so she and Jason could pick it up and stow it in the back of the Humvee. 'How soon can you break down the lab and get it ready to move, Ari?' Jason asked.

'No sweat, J,' Vega responded. 'My boyfriend broke up with me, so I got nothin' better to do than work in the lab. This is just freaky, dude, *freaky*. We're going to be this top-secret bad-guy hunting posse. Awesome!'

'Maybe.'

'Maybe what, man? You think we're being scammed or somethin'?'

Jason went into the cab of the Humvee and punched instructions into a small palm-sized computer. Moments later several unusual-looking devices appeared: two large devices that looked like giant cat-sized cockroaches crawled down the walls of the warehouse and over to them; and a trash can–sized device with a ducted fan propulsion system, mechanical arms, and a large telescopic sensor underneath slowly flew over. 'I don't think we're being told the whole story.'

'You mean that dude Chamberlain? He is for sure one scary-assed bad boy. I mean, schizoid.'

'He's smart, Ari,' Jason mused. 'So why would he pick me for this job? I'm just an engineer. I haven't been in the field since . . . well, I've *never* been in the field, unless you count Officer Candidate School or Aberdeen Proving Grounds. And what about DeLaine?'

'I think that Chamberlain guy has got the hots for

her.' She glanced at Jason and smiled. 'I see you checking her out too, J. You like her too? Want her to put you in handcuffs and interrogate you?'

'She's an intelligence officer, and obviously the director thinks she's competent,' Jason said, ignoring Ari's remarks, 'but I don't get the feeling she's an experienced field agent either. It looks like Chamberlain picked two newbies to run this task force. Why would he do that?'

'That grunt is gung-ho enough for all of us put together.'

'Jefferson – well, that's easy: he's Chamberlain's spy. He'll keep a close eye on us for the boss, keep us in line.'

'Well, you and me are the gadget guys, J, and Kelsey DeLaine, the G-babe, will work the intel side,' Ari said. 'The grunt will keep everybody in line, and Chamberlain will take all the credit. Sounds pretty simple to me.' She slapped Jason excitedly on the shoulder. 'And we get to take El Cid out into the world and take down some really evil characters. I love it!'

Jason retrieved one of the 'cockroaches' and plugged it into a computer terminal built into the front cab of the Humvee. It immediately gave him a list of cellular phone calls and radio transmissions that had taken place in the past hour. 'FANBOT Two is still outside?'

'Roger,' Ari said. 'It'll follow Chamberlain for another fifteen minutes or so, report on where he goes and where he stops, download his phone calls, then head on back.' She looked over Jason's shoulder at the intercept log. 'His phone is scrambled, so we can't hear what he's saying, but we can pick up the numbers he's calling.'

'Some of them we can't, apparently,' Jason said. 'Completely blank numbers and EINs.'

'Bizarre,' Ari said. 'I thought we had every domestic and international ID code programmed into our computers. He's got a bunch that we've never scanned before.'

'Well, he *is* the National Security Adviser,' Jason mused. 'He probably talks with military and government leaders and spooks all over the world. Still . . .'

'Give me and the kids a few days and we'll break out the EINs on those calls,' Ari said. 'The numbers might take a while longer.'

'See what you can do,' Jason said. 'If he's got untraceable codes then he can probably change them quickly, so it might not help us, but maybe it'll give us clues on what kind of technology he's using to block his codes from our scanners.'

'I'm on it, J.'

Jason scrolled through the list of intercepts until he came across a call from Kelsey's new cellular phone, the one given to them by Chamberlain. Clicking on the item opened up an audio media playback window:

'G-3, Cortez.'

'Hi, Rudy. It's me. Meeting's over.'

'New phone, Kel? I didn't recognize the caller ID.'

'Got it from Chamberlain himself. I'll fill you in when I get there, but I'm going to need your help. They're sending me TDY to New Mexico. I need to build a special access server so I can get into my files on the road and search the Bureau's intelligence database.'

'What for?'

'It's an antiterrorist project being run by the White House. But get this: they're pairing me up with this complete Army nerd from Louisiana.'

'That's harsh, man,' Ari said.

'Shh.'

'Him and his even geekier sidekick have developed this . . .
cyborg . . .'

'Who's she calling a geek?' Ari protested.

'Shut it, Ari.'

'Cyborg? You're kidding me, right?'

'It's a robot that he can climb inside and it runs and jumps
like a bat out of hell and carries cannons on its back and folds
up into a suitcase.'

'Bullshit.'

'I saw it myself, Rudy. It's pretty incredible. But the NSC
thinks that we're going to zip around the world in this thing
breaking down doors and mowing down terrorists.'

'You're shitting me. This will screw up years of investigative
work.'

'I think it's all some big power play by Chamberlain. Don't
worry – I'll squash the cyber-Rambo wannabes. Anyway, I'm
supposed to help set up this task force.'

'No way the director is going to approve you getting involved
with this.'

'The director was here, Rudy. He's not totally convinced, but
he gave me the go-ahead.'

'Kingman City has got everyone flustered and running
around like chickens with their heads cut off. This is bullshit.'

'I know, I know. I'll be in major cover-my-ass mode, and
I'll need to protect the director's six too. Fortunately the army
guy and his flunky are barely one or two generations more
advanced than a lab rat.'

'Flunky! Who's she callin' a flunky?'

'Shh!'

'Aren't they all?'

'I'll make sure I'm in charge. I just need you to help me get
a secure server set up so I can get into my files, and back me
up in case things start going south.'

'No sweat, Kel. If the boss signed off on this, getting the server set up will be a piece of cake. You'll be able to test it from home tonight. You going to use satellite DES?'

'I'll likely be moving quite a bit, so yes, I'll access it via satellite.'

'Got it. Everything will be optimized for secure satellite downlink. Won't be as fast as what you normally get but it'll be available anywhere except the Poles.'

'I want to scan for that downlink setup routine,' Jason said.

'No prob, J,' Ari said. 'I'll find out where she lives, set up the Cockroach to monitor, capture the authentication codes, and have it broken in a day or two. Maybe less, if it's a standard satellite encryption routine.' Jason nodded.

'Where they sending you?'

'Clovis, New Mexico.'

'Bring sunscreen.'

'Anything else on GAMMA?'

'From Brazil – no. But Kingman City, yes. TransGlobal headquarters in San Francisco received a tape, supposedly from GAMMA, warning them to evacuate Kingman City. The tape was never listened to – never even left the fucking mailroom.'

'Oh, shit. Thousands of people might . . . might have died for nothing.'

'The voice was in English but electronically altered – we might not be able to voiceprint, but we should be able to pick up speech patterns and nuances that can help us build a profile.'

'Did GAMMA leave warnings in Brazil?'

'Yep. Every time. Other places in South America too – other TransGlobal targets too. The latter messages were electronically altered too. We should be able to detect the frequency of the device that alters the voice and come up with a manufacturer.'

'I tell you, Rudy, this task force shit better not be a waste of our time, because I think GAMMA is in Brazil plotting another attack, and we need to break them up and get them behind bars before they bring another nuke into the U.S.'

'Amen.'

'Hey, didn't Chamberlain used to be an exec with TransGlobal Energy?'

'I think so.'

'That could explain why he wants this task force and robot thing chasing after these terrorists. Maybe he still has an interest in TransGlobal.'

'Aren't these guys supposed to divest themselves of any financial interest in public companies before they take public office?'

'Yeah. Let's get someone to check on that.'

'Sure. Well, I better get busy. Talk at you later, Kel.'

'Thanks, Rudy. Later.'

Jason sat back in complete surprise. 'Holy shit, the FBI might be on their trail already,' he said. 'We have to find out where in Brazil they're talking about, and we have to get down there as fast as we can.'

'As soon as I break that encryption routine, J, I should be able to look in her files and find out what she has on this GAMMA,' Ari said. 'Or maybe once she sets up in New Mexico, she'll let you look at her goodies . . . and then maybe she lets you look at her files.'

'Slim chance of either happening, Doc,' Jason said. 'Have your guys break her satellite downlink as quickly as they can.'

'You got it. Uh . . . dude, is there any chance we'll get in deep shit by crashin' into the FBI's computer system?'

'Maybe. But as far as I know, this is what I was told to do – by the fucking National Security Adviser himself.'

'Sweet,' Ari said excitedly. 'I'm in but I'm in, man.'

Cascavel, Paraná State, Brazil
A short time later

Originating in the lushly forested highlands of western
Paraná near the Paraguay border, the Piquir River was
the last of the 'living' rivers of Brazil, untouched and
unspoiled, once nourishing millions of acres of rain
forests and providing food, drinking water, transportation, and a livelihood for thousands who lived along its
banks. Some of the towns and villages there had existed
for centuries, and its people lived much as they had for
the past four generations. As unbelievable as it sounded,
it was said that some of the inhabitants who lived along
the river had no implements or devices built before the
turn of the twentieth century, and some had never before
even seen a light-skinned man or woman.

That changed with a single vote of the Third District
Regional Federal Tribunal of the Brazilian Federal Court
in São Paulo, when it overturned a protective order by
a lower court and allowed the construction of the
Cascavel Nuclear Power Project. Despite protests by a
number of environmental and natives' rights groups –
and, it was said, bolstered by lavish gifts and bribes – the
court gave the final go-ahead, and within minutes of the
decision the first trees were being bulldozed.

Cascavel was actually planned to include seven state-
of-the-art reactor facilities; each of the seven plants was
larger than any nuclear power plant in the United States
– 1,500 megawatts each, for a total of 10,500 megawatts
capacity. Designed to serve not just Brazil but many of
Brazil's neighboring countries – Paraguay, Argentina,
Uruguay, and even Chile – it was by far the largest nuclear
power project in South America and one of the largest in

the world. Once completed, each facility was to employ five hundred workers, although only a fraction would be from the state of Paraná – engineers, technicians, and security would mostly be from outside the country.

In order to provide cooling water for the facility as well as power to serve the new towns begun during construction until the plants came online, a hydroelectric dam was built on the Piquir River, which took just over two years to complete. Six hundred meters wide and two hundred meters tall, the plant had four turbines and produced over four hundred megawatts of power. Thousands of natives were employed – some human rights groups charged they were 'shanghaied' – to build the dam, and many perished under the difficult, 'round-the-clock' working conditions. Then, to add insult to injury, when the dam was completed, the Piquir River ceased to exist . . . along with hundreds of villages within fifteen kilometers of its banks, some that had existed for centuries. Almost overnight, thousands of inhabitants lost their homes, and millions of acres of rain forests were destroyed.

The newly formed lake was called Repressa Kingman, named for the president of the American company, TransGlobal Energy Corporation, which built the dam and was working on the nearby nuclear power plant as prime contractor for the Brazilian Ministry of Energy. At the dam's activation, Harold Chester Kingman himself was on hand, and was hailed by energy and commerce ministers from four nations as the benefactor – no, as the *savior* – of the entire region.

As they stood there atop the gleaming concrete and steel monstrosity, the corrupt politicians and indifferent, unfeeling, uncaring builder could – if they bothered to look – see where the villages, graveyards, churches, schools, and lands of the natives once were. They were covered by twenty meters of water now. In the winter, when the rains slowed and the river's level went down, it was possible for some families to visit the graveyards of their ancestors and to actually search for their possessions.

The next year the natives again made their way to the bare banks of Repressa Kingman to mourn their loss and try to recover anything of value they could find, but a riot broke out and several private security officers employed by TransGlobal Energy were killed, along with dozens of natives. Days later, the same district courts that opened the way for construction of this facility ordered a halt to the annual procession, and they authorized the state military police, the *Polícia Militar do Estado*, or PME, to enforce the ban.

The atmosphere in the area surrounding the Cascavel nuclear power plant project today was just as tense as it was that first day. 'It looks like they've deployed another two hundred PME troops around Unit One,' Jorge Ruiz, Ph.D., said, peering at the Cascavel construction site through a pair of brand-new high-tech binoculars. 'And I see more armored cars too – perhaps another dozen surrounding unit one alone. There might be another hundred troops in them.'

'Unit One is scheduled to be powered up soon,' Manuel Pereira, Ruiz's student and friend, said as he looked through his own binoculars. 'Second anniversary of the Repressa riot, Unit One's activation – I would say that is reason enough for more jackbooted storm troopers, no?'

'Maybe, Manuel,' Ruiz said, lowering the binoculars

and slipping his rimless spectacles back on his nose. 'It sure seems like an unusually large buildup of forces just for the anniversary of the Piquir massacre. But I'm definitely the wrong guy to ask.'

In a million years he never would have thought he'd have found himself discussing military tactics, Ruiz mused for the umpteenth time that week. Tall, thin, with black curly hair and long, delicate fingers, Dr Jorge Ruiz was anything but an outdoorsy, gung-ho military type – but circumstances had a way of changing everything and everyone, most times not for the better . . .

Jorge Ruiz was born in Abaete, Brazil, one hundred and sixty kilometers northwest of Belo Horizonte, the capital city of the state of Minas Gerais. Raised in a Catholic orphanage, adopted by a rancher father and a teacher mother, Jorge and his two adoptive sisters and one brother grew up with the best of everything. In the summer they lived in a small home in Abaete proper, but for most of the rest of the year they lived in a ranch about twenty kilometers outside of town, where they raised Spanish Barb and Mangalarga Marchador horses, turkeys, large floppy-eared Indubrasil cattle, and large blue and white peacocks that were trained like watchdogs.

As a high school student, Jorge received a foreign exchange student scholarship and was sent off to attend school in rural upstate New York. Although leaving his Brazilian family was hard, leaving his American family was even harder – he wept like a baby from the moment he was dropped off at the airport almost until landing in Rio de Janeiro. He vowed right then and there he'd return to the United States.

After attending just two years of college in Belo Horizonte, studying agribusiness to follow in his father's footsteps, he received a student visa, moved to the United States, and five years later received his bachelor's degree in agricultural science, a master's degree in agricultural and environmental education from the University of California at Davis, then a doctorate in global environmental and energy policy from Stanford University. He traveled throughout the United States for the next five years, accepting a number of fellowships and chairs to teach and publish his thoughts on the role of multinational corporations in the development of environmental laws and energy policy.

As much as he loved the United States, his last position, chairing the Georgetown University McDonough School of Business's Emerging Nations Fellowship, began to change his view of the multinational corporations' role in the third world. Governments, he found, could be coerced or convinced by the people to better their economies and societies – but the large multinational corporations developing around the world were like stateless dictatorships, virtually unaffected by any codified laws or by the will or desires of their employees. They answered to only one code: greed. Their wealth was enormous and growing every year, and they remained almost completely above the law. If a nation changed its laws to make a situation unfavorable to a corporation, they simply moved to another country where laws were lax or more favorable. The Internet, satellite communications technology, overnight delivery, and high-speed international travel made such moves easy and rarely caused an interruption in business.

Moreover, Ruiz began to be more and more disturbed

by the noise, waste, pollution, chaos, and gross excesses of life in the United States – and how the American lifestyle was quickly spreading around the world, especially to his native Brazil. Bound and determined not to see his beloved native country turn in that direction, he decided to return home to see what good his first-class education, training, and experience could do. He immediately accepted a teaching position at the Universidade Federale de Minas Gerais in Belo Horizonte, and was soon named dean of the College of Environmental Studies. Ruiz quickly became known as one of the world's leading experts on environmental policy and reform.

He was also known as something of a firebrand, a label he didn't foster but didn't reject, either. Almost forty years old, a husband and father of a ten-year-old daughter and six-year-old son, Ruiz still thought of himself as a young long-haired radical student and enjoyed nothing more than hanging out at the student union or in the hallways outside his office, sipping strong thick coffee – half espresso, half sugar, thank you very much – smoking hand-rolled cigarettes, and arguing with his students and other faculty members on the issues of the day. In the summers he would return to his family ranch and there his students and the world press would find him, ankle-deep in cattle shit, having the time of his life working the ranch and arguing with his extended family around him.

But the Brazilian government was not ready to hear his message. Investments in Brazil by multinational corporations like TransGlobal Energy meant much-needed revenues for the government and assured re-election of its political leaders. The more he fought to restrict or control the influence of the big stateless conglomerates, the more ostracized and isolated he became. He was eventually forced to leave his dean's position, and he decided to go home to Abaete to his family's ranch, a move that his detractors encouraged.

But he wasn't ready to be silent. He continued to publish his thoughts and research on the Internet and submitted op-ed pieces for newspapers and magazines around the world. Many others followed him to the farm. The ranch became a sort of campus-away-from-campus for students, intellectuals, analysts, and soon even economic ministers from governments all over the world.

Jorge Ruiz's message was simple: rein in the multinational corporations before they took over the world by eliminating the corporate entity and replacing it with individual ownership, responsibility, and accountability. If businesses lay in the hands of a single man or woman, and each and every action was the responsibility of that one person, those responsible would automatically reduce the size of their business to lessen their liability. Wealth would be shared by more and more citizens; laws could be simplified; and the abuses committed by nameless, faceless paper entities would theoretically lessen.

He attracted many students and even some followers, drawn to Abaete by his simple message, simple lifestyle, and real passion for reform. Jorge would hire some of his students on at the ranch, exchanging work for lessons. The classes and lectures soon became an even bigger part of life on the ranch than cattle and horses, and some of the students were hired to be librarians, administrators, graduate assistants, and even security personnel. The ranch and its teaching, lecture, and publishing offices soon became known worldwide as the *Grupo do Abaete de la Movimento Meio Ambiente*, or GAMMA, the Environmental Movement Group of Abaete.

But Ruiz was not destined for a quiet, peaceful life in rural Minas Gerais.

A hydroelectric dam was under construction on the São Francisco River about forty kilometers north of the ranch. Once completed, the dam would supply electricity to a bauxite mine and aluminum processing plant outside Abaete – but it would also flood almost eight hundred square kilometers of the valley, force the relocation of thousands of citizens, and poison the river downstream with strip-mine and factory pollutants. Ruiz opposed the construction and filed numerous lawsuits to stop it.

One night, masked men invaded his home, poured gasoline in the living room, and set it afire. While his wife collected the children from their rooms, Jorge tried to put out the flames. He was almost overcome with smoke and just managed to crawl outside before the house his family had lived in for five generations burned to the ground.

He found out later that morning that his wife and children never made it out, but were overcome by the smoke and perished in the blaze.

Several days later, the security office of the dam's construction company, a subcontractor of TransGlobal Energy Corporation, was dynamited, killing a dozen men inside. The letters 'GAMMA' were written in blood-red paint six meters tall on the partially completed dam face itself. An announcement sent to media outlets all over the world via the Internet stated that the acronym stood for *Guerra Alliance de la Movimento Meio Ambiente*, or the Environmental Movement Combat Alliance, declaring war on multinational corporations that polluted the environment and exploited the working people of the world.

Jorge Ruiz was of course the main suspect in the blast.

Many saw him as a modern-day Zorro – one man battling the forces of evil around him, no matter how big or powerful. Even in an age of worldwide concern about terrorists claiming to be freedom fighters or patriots, many all over the world cheered him on, supporting him at least with their hearts and words if not their hands or wallets. But Ruiz was nowhere to be found; he was believed to be deep in hiding or perhaps executed by TransGlobal Energy's rumored death squads.

Instead, here he was, several months later, crawling on his belly in the mud about a kilometer from Repressa Kingman. He and Manuel had been out there for a week and a half, studying the security setup and inching their way – literally – toward various parts of the dam, then inching their way back out. They had been hounded almost every day by ground and air patrols, which got steadily heavier and more persistent every day. But their timing had been perfect, and they managed to avoid giving in to panic as they covertly made their way back to their observation post.

Their mission was successful despite the dramatically added security because of two factors. First and foremost was Manuel Pereira's skill in the field. He was a former Brazilian army infantryman – every able-bodied man in Brazil had to go through army basic training at age eighteen or after graduating from high school, then had to join a local state military police reserve unit until age forty; Pereira chose to spend three years in the regular army in an American-trained Special Forces infantry unit before joining the reserves. He knew how to move silently, knew how to search for sentries and signs of pursuit. Pereira showed the same joy of teaching Ruiz about moving, hiding, and reconnaissance as Jorge did of professing his love of the environment.

The second reason for their success was heading in their direction at that moment; Manuel spotted them several hundred meters away: three members of the *Policia Militar do Estado* of the state of Paraná, the PME, armed with submachine guns and pistols, driving an old American open-top Jeep that sputtered and coughed down the dirt construction road.

As it was in the days of military rule, the central government was concerned more with antigovernment insurgents and Communist infiltrators rather than with external threats. In Brazil there were few municipal police departments: law-enforcement duties were handled by the PME, which were locally directed by state public safety officials but organized, trained, and administered by the Brazilian armed forces. Here in Cascavel, as in most of the country, the local gendarmes were very well armed and trained. Like police officers around the world, many officers in the PME moonlighted as security guards for private companies and even individuals – and the biggest private employer of PME officers in the state was TransGlobal Energy. So it was with these men.

But Brazil is a very big country – the fifth-largest in the world in land area – and without strong supervision from state or federal offices, the PME became virtually autonomous, especially in the frontier and jungle regions, answerable to no one except local bosses, wealthy landowners, or military commanders. Many PME officers had been charged with human rights abuses, and steps had been taken over the years to try to more closely supervise the force and punish the offenders, but in the end the old ways worked the best: patronage, fear, guns, retribution, and payola.

Although these men took money from the Brazilian government to maintain order in Paraná and from TransGlobal to provide private security for the construction site, they *also* took money from a third source: GAMMA. They and a number of others had been recruited by Ruiz's second in command, an ex–oil executive from Russia turned activist by the name of Yegor Viktorvich Zakharov, to simply look the other way when requested.

The PME soldiers stopped their Jeep just a few meters from where Ruiz and Pereira were hiding, at a bend in the construction road that would partially hide them from the guard towers back at the construction site. They were making an awful lot of noise. They searched the area carefully, looking right at the two men hiding in the bushes several times, then returned to the Jeep. Ruiz was then surprised when one of them pulled out a bottle of *cachaça* – liquor similar to rum, fermented from sugarcane juice – and took a sip. Pereira pulled a suppressed .45 caliber IMBEL-GC Pistol-45 from a shoulder holster and aimed it at the men; Ruiz pulled his pistol, a suppressed .380 caliber IMBEL-GC Pistol-380, but did not aim it. He was not yet comfortable with aiming a gun at another human being, although every day in the jungle was slowly but surely changing his mindset.

'Don't turn around,' Pereira said.

The man drinking from the bottle took a shallow swig, passed the bottle, then started taking off his web belt and undoing his fatigue trousers, getting ready to take a piss. 'You two fucks are about two minutes away from getting your asses caught,' he said. 'They brought in more security in armored vehicles. The first patrol is on its way out.'

'We've seen them – they're deploying them over at Unit One, not out here,' Pereira said. 'Why in hell are you out here drinking, *puta*?'

'Because this is outside our normal patrol route – we'll need a reason why we're out so far from the construction site. If they spot us from the towers, they'll see us drinking, and TransGlobal will probably fire us. I wouldn't want to be around when you two get caught anyway.'

'You already have your money and your escape plan,' Ruiz said. 'All we need to know is if our packages are secure.'

'No one has touched your packages,' one of the soldiers said. 'That is our normal patrol route and our responsibility. Don't worry.'

'Then why the hell don't you just get out?'

'Because I want to see it with my own eyes when you set it off.'

'What in hell are you talking about?' Ruiz asked. 'Are you crazy, or just drunk?'

The soldiers looked confused. 'It's not every day you see a nuke go off,' one of the other soldiers remarked.

'Do you wear just sunglasses, or do you wear special goggles?' another asked. 'Are we far enough away here? It looks awful close.'

Ruiz and Pereira looked at each other in total shock. '*What are you talking about*?' Pereira exclaimed finally.

'You guys don't know?' the first soldier asked incredulously. 'Shit no, you don't, because you've been crawling around out here in the mud for the past week. All hell has broken loose in America, and *you* guys are responsible for it. You've just been declared the number-one terrorist organization in the whole fucking *world*, way ahead of al Qaeda, Islamic Jihad . . .'

Ruiz looked at Pereira, his mouth open in surprise. 'What happ . . . ?'

But at that moment, they heard the soldier's radio crackle. The man listened, then responded. 'They're starting to seal up the entire complex, boys, including the dam. I think your stash of explosives down by the garbage pit was found.'

'I thought you said . . . !'

'Fuck what I said, asshole. I secured them the best I could.'

'Damn you!' Ruiz holstered his pistol and turned his binoculars toward the dam. He and Pereira had already hidden about a hundred kilos of high explosives in various sections of the dam, getting ready to blow it up in the next couple days; they had planned to plant another fifty kilos, but that was going to be impossible now. They had no desire to make martyrs of themselves, so the plan was to get safely away first – but now it looked like that was not possible either. Sure enough, he saw several dozen soldiers running toward the dam, with a helicopter starting to move into position. Ruiz turned back toward the PME soldiers. 'Why didn't you tell us . . . ?'

'Because then we couldn't capture you before the dam blew, assholes,' the soldier said. Ruiz turned. Pereira was still pointing his pistol at the first soldier, but the other two soldiers now had their M-16 rifles aimed at them. 'Drop your pistol, Pereira, or my comrades will open fire.'

'You bastard,' Pereira breathed. 'You'll be the first to die if there's any shooting.'

'You won't be able to spend all the money you've been squeezing out of both sides if you're dead,' Ruiz reminded him.

'Don't be stupid, both of you,' the soldier said. 'You

don't want to die out here lying in the mud and bushes – neither do I. I take you in, I get the reward money for capturing a saboteur, I get the hell out of the state, and you have Zakharov and your other supporters spring you from prison. Everyone keeps a clear head and we get out of this alive.'

'The TransGlobal Energy security forces won't let us live,' Pereira said. 'They'll interrogate and torture us, then dispose of us.'

'I've notified your buddy Zakharov to arrange with the PME and the state tribunal to take you into custody right away – TransGlobal won't get their hands on you, as long as you do everything I say.' He looked overhead. One of the TransGlobal Energy security force helicopters that had been patrolling the northwest face of the dam was now slowly heading in their direction. 'They'll be watching everything we do, and if you resist, they'll likely kill you. Do as I say, and I will stay in control of this situation. Now drop the guns and let's go.'

'Jorge?' Pereira asked in a low voice. 'I think I can tag at least two of them . . . you might be able to get away . . .'

'No,' Ruiz said. 'We tried. Put the gun down.' Pereira reluctantly dropped his pistol.

The PME soldier radioed to the TransGlobal security chief that he had two prisoners and was going to take them to the security force headquarters in Cascavel. The helicopter kept on approaching, very slowly, staying at least fifty to sixty meters away. They could now see a TransGlobal security officer sitting in the helicopter's open right-side doorway, wearing sunglasses and a headset, with what appeared to be a hunting rifle with a large telescopic sight affixed, safely pointing out the door but not upraised or aimed at anyone on the ground.

'He will not hesitate to shoot you in the head if you resist, Ruiz,' the soldier repeated. 'Those TransGlobal sharpshooters are damned good, I must admit. Now, first, hand over the detonators to the explosives you set on the dam.'

'Your greed has destroyed you,' Ruiz said. One of the other soldiers had climbed behind the wheel of the Jeep and started it up; the other lit up a cigarette, cradling his rifle in his arms.

'Shut up and hand them over, Ruiz,' the leader said. He nodded to the third soldier, then motioned with his head toward Pereira. 'Handcuff that one and search him.' The soldier nodded, then slung his rifle over his shoulder as he took a deep drag of his cigarette and reached in a rear pocket for handcuffs.

Pereira used that moment of distraction to move. The first soldier may have been anticipating his move, because he had the gun trained on him the entire time, but Pereira was quick and managed to get a hand on the pistol . . . but he wasn't quick enough to keep him from firing. Pereira was hit in the right shoulder. He cried out and rolled to his right, but he didn't go down. Instead, he grabbed the second soldier's rifle out of the front seat. Struggling through the pain, he flicked off the safety and tried to level it at the first soldier, but he had lost all strength in his right arm.

'Too late, Pereira,' the first soldier said with a smile. The helicopter was hovering, now less than forty meters away. The shooter in the door had already raised his rifle and was taking aim. Pereira thought about trying to dive atop Ruiz before the gunner took them both out, but just then he saw the gunner's body buck and a puff of smoke jet from his rifle's muzzle . . .

. . . and the first soldier's head disappeared in a cloud

of red gore. The heads of the two other PME soldiers disappeared seconds later. Three head shots, three kills, from forty meters away, in about three seconds. Whoever was in that helicopter was a damned good shot, Ruiz thought.

The gunman in the door motioned for Ruiz and Pereira to follow, and then the helicopter translated to a wide spot in the construction road a few hundred meters away. Ruiz supported Pereira as they trotted over to it. The gunman was aiming his rifle toward them, scanning over their shoulders for any sign of pursuit. As they approached, the gunman took his sunglasses off . . .

. . . and when Ruiz saw that it was none other than Yegor Viktorvich Zakharov, a wave of relief washed over him: saved once again by Yegor Zakharov, the guardian angel of GAMMA.

The sharpshooter helped Pereira into a seat in the helicopter and fastened his seat belt for him. '*Muito obrigado*,' Ruiz shouted over the roar of the helicopter's jet engine. Instead of trying to respond over the noise, Zakharov motioned with his right thumb as if pressing a button – he was telling Ruiz to detonate the explosives. 'But they are not all planted yet!' he shouted.

'Are you crazy?' Zakharov asked, shouting. In a flash of motion, he raised his Dragunov sniper rifle to his shoulder, aimed toward Ruiz, and fired. Ruiz felt as if he had been slapped in the face by a red-hot paddle as the muzzle blast pounded him . . . but he wasn't hit. He looked over his shoulder just as another TransGlobal Energy Security Force Jeep, with a headless driver behind the wheel, careened into a tree about seventy meters behind him. 'Blow whatever you got out there and let's get the hell out of here!' Zakharov shouted. His voice was serious, but he was smiling, like a father admonishing his young son for swearing moments after scoring the game-winning goal.

Ruiz needed no more prompting. He withdrew a small detonator from his pocket, punched in an unlock code, and hit a red button, holding the unit aloft to be sure its radio signal got out cleanly. But Zakharov wasn't going to wait. He shouted, 'Either it will work or it won't, Jorge. Let's go!' then lowered his rifle and grabbed Ruiz by the front of his shirt, pulling him headfirst into the chopper. His feet had barely left the ground before the helicopter lifted off . . .

. . . and the helicopter was barely a kilometer away when the first charge went off, followed quickly by three more. Ruiz and Pereira had hidden four twenty-five-kilo charges on various parts of the dam, designed not to cause a catastrophic failure – they would not have been able to hump in enough explosives to do that, unless they were nuclear devices – but to weaken the structure enough that work on the reactor units would have to be stopped while the dam was inspected and repaired. That could take months, maybe years, and cost TransGlobal millions – hopefully.

Ruiz looked at the dam as best he could while he fastened his safety belt and donned his headset. 'I couldn't tell if all the charges went off or if the face was damaged,' he said. 'All that work for nothing.'

'You got out with your skin and struck a blow for our cause – that is enough for now,' Zakharov said casually, lowering his Dragunov.

'I thought you said those PME guys were trustworthy, Zakharov,' Pereira said angrily.

Yegor Viktorvich Zakharov safetied his sniper rifle, removed the magazine, and ejected the live round from the chamber, leaving the action open. 'I did say that, Manuel – but as we all know, money speaks louder than words,' he said in very good Portuguese, laced with a thick Russian accent, like *percebes* – boiled barnacles – served on fine china. 'There is more money than law, authority, morality, or evil out here in western Paraná these days. I guess we just didn't come up with the right amount of it, and TransGlobal did.'

Jorge Ruiz sometimes wished he had the life experience and real-world wisdom of men like Pereira and Zakharov, not just his ivory-towered view of right and wrong. He was right, of course – Yegor Zakharov was most often right, at least when it came to operations like this.

Yegor Viktorvick Zakharov was a former Strategic Rocket Forces brigade commander within the Eleventh Corps, the Black Raiders of the Napoleonic Wars and World War Two fame, headquartered in Kirov, four hundred and eighty kilometers east of Moscow. Large, barrel-chested, and square-jawed, he was a very imposing figure and seemed to be the archtypical Soviet warrior. He was a trained military pilot and an expert marksman, as he'd demonstrated just now and quite often to their men; he was also a weapons expert, intimate with everything from pistols to nuclear weapons and everything in between. He liked to drink straight vodka but would make do with strong Brazilian *agua ardente*; he had a grudging liking for American whiskey because it made him feel that he was absorbing some secret or clue to the American psyche with every bottle he consumed. Zakharov loved his women as much as his alcohol and, although a husband and father of two sons and a daughter who lived somewhere in the Caribbean, was never without a woman or two in the evenings.

During the Cold War, Zakharov commanded seven

regiments of medium- and intermediate-range surface-to-surface missiles, including the SS-12, SSC-1 cruise missile, and SS-15 mobile ballistic missile, all capable of carrying high-explosive, chemical, biological, or nuclear warheads. His assignment, in case of a massive attack by NATO forces against Moscow, was to blanket Eastern Europe with missiles to stop any thoughts of occupying Russian territory – a modern version of the 'scorched Earth' policy used by the Black Raiders in their campaigns against Napoleon and Hitler.

With the collapse of the Soviet Union and the advent of more and more onerous arms-control agreements, it was made clear to Zakharov that after twenty-two years his services were no longer required by his beloved country, so he took what was left of his measly pension and went into the growing private sector. He became a security officer with the giant Russian oil company KirovPyerviy, one of Russia's largest private oil companies outside Siberia. He rose quickly in status, power, and wealth, and soon became a vice president. Many believed he would enter politics, but as an ultranationalist his views were not very popular with the Russian Duma, which sought a more centrist leader whom they could use to extract partnerships and favorable financing agreements with the West. Zakharov continued to be an outspoken critic of Russia's growing rapprochement with the West in general and the United States in particular.

Then, the unthinkable happened: the Russian government, which – as was true for all oil and gas companies in Russia – was the principal shareholder in KirovPyerviy, sold its shares of the company to the American oil giant TransGlobal Energy Corporation. Although Zakharov had overnight become a multibillionaire from the value of his own shares in the company, he was outraged and felt betrayed. A foreign company – an *American* company in particular – owned a majority stake in a large Russian oil firm! It was the very thing he had been warning the Russian people about for years, but he never truly believed it would ever come to pass.

It was too much to stomach. Zakharov dumped his shares and sold all of his belongings in his hometown of Kirov. It was widely known that he had many residences and mistresses all over the world, particularly in South America and Southeast Asia, but he had virtually disappeared overnight . . .

. . . until one day, about a year after he left KirovPyerviy, Yegor Viktorvich Zakharov mysteriously appeared in Ruiz's base camp near Porto Feliz, about ninety kilometers northwest of São Paulo, and pledged his personal, financial, and moral support for Ruiz's guerrilla organization. He admitted he used contacts and resources within the Russian Eleventh Corps, along with his skills and intuition as a security officer and military man, to locate Ruiz and his GAMMA organization. But he tried to assure Ruiz and his followers that he was not here to spy on them but to offer his services and support to the cause.

At first everyone was wary and believed him to be working undercover for the government – until they saw Zakharov kill a *Policia Militar do Estado* officer with his own hands on a raid near Macae. The usually cold, indifferent Brazilian state military police would not favor an undercover agent killing one of their own, even a highly placed informant – there appeared to be no doubt that he was tapping into his own connections and resources to assist GAMMA. Slowly but surely, Ruiz was won over. Zakharov was charismatic, powerful, wealthy, and committed to the cause of breaking down all multi-national corporations. His focus of course was on TransGlobal Energy, the company that financed the corruption of the Russian government and the betrayal of the Russian working class, but he participated in all of Ruiz's operations with equal zeal.

Since his sudden arrival, GAMMA quickly had plenty of skilled, highly effective men and women working in various operations, mostly involving direct attacks on security forces belonging to large corporations – men and women who weren't afraid to get their hands bloody. They were much different than the usual 'tree-huggers' who belonged to GAMMA: they knew explosives, sabotage, intimidation, and even darker arts, but they seemed to be genuinely dedicated to the cause and devoted to Zakharov and, therefore, to Jorge Ruiz and GAMMA. They also brought extremely useful, incredibly detailed, first-class, near-real-time intelligence information. Many were Russian, but men and women of action from all over the world followed Zakharov. The leadership of GAMMA did not change, which suited the membership fine. Jorge Ruiz stayed in control and was forever the spiritual and inspirational leader, but Yegor Viktorvich Zakharov quickly became second in command and the man in charge of direct action operations.

There appeared to be a great deal of excitement and energy on the ground as the helicopter set down in their encampment, a remote clearing in the forest about sixty kilometers from Cascavel. The men and women were busy breaking down the camp and packing up, ready to scatter and head to their temporary base, but something else was definitely stirring – Ruiz could feel it, even before they touched down. He looked at his trusted friend

Manuel Pereira with concern. 'I like seeing our people happy after a successful mission, Manuel,' he said on the interphone, 'but this is rather unusual.' Zakharov glanced at him and smiled but said nothing and continued idly checking his rifle.

'They could not have heard about Cascavel, Jorge,' Pereira said. 'We are under strict comm security. Something else has happened.'

'I could use some good news,' Ruiz said cheerfully. Pereira glanced at Zakharov; he nodded but offered nothing else.

They were being congratulated and thumped on the back and shoulders from the moment the chopper touched ground. Ruiz wanted to ask what had them so excited, but a stern glare from Zakharov scattered the crowd. 'I want the camp ready to roll in ten minutes – that's how long it will take for the first PME helicopters to arrive if they successfully tracked us,' he told his aide in Russian. A tall, powerful, steel-blue-eyed former Russian army captain by the name of Pavel Khalimov, he barked an order in Portuguese.

Zakharov led them to his tent, which was always the last to be taken down and the first to be set up in a new forward operating location. He poured a shot of chilled vodka for each of them – despite their austere living conditions when in the field, Zakharov *always* had chilled vodka – offered them a slice of salted cucumber already prepared beside the bottle, then raised his glass. '*Za vashe zdarov'ye*!' he said, and downed the vodka in one gulp, chasing it with the cucumber. 'Another successful mission. Well done!' Ruiz did the same.

Pereira took a tiny sip, nibbled at the cucumber, then took a big drink from his canteen. 'Something has happened,' he said, looking at Zakharov carefully. 'The men are jubilant like I have never seen them before. A few are scared.'

'Yes, something has happened,' Zakharov said casually. He cast an amused glance at the Brazilian ex-soldier. 'But would it kill you to drink to our success like a man and not a sissy, Sergeant Pereira?'

'And the PME pigs that betrayed us said something about being too close to the dam and never having seen one before,' Pereira went on, ignoring Zakharov's request. 'They weren't talking about watching a few satchels of Semtex go off.'

'Who cares what those traitors were saying, Manuel?' Ruiz asked curiously. He hated to see any discord between his senior officers, but he wondered what in hell Pereira was trying to get at. Zakharov didn't look perturbed or worried – but then again, he never did. 'They were getting ready to arrest us and turn us over to TransGlobal's storm troopers – they were just blathering.'

'Were they, Zakharov?' Pereira asked. 'Or were they talking about something else?'

Zakharov hesitated, adopting a faraway expression as he poured himself another shot of vodka. Now Ruiz was getting very concerned. 'Yegor . . . ?'

'Harold Kingman has been very seriously hurt today, *tavarisch*,' Zakharov said, a satisfied smile on his face. 'We have won a major victory and advanced our cause tremendously.'

'What are you talking about, Yegor?' Ruiz asked.

'It means, Jorge, that he went ahead and did what he said he could do – he attacked a TransGlobal plant in the United States itself,' Pereira said ominously, carefully watching Zakharov for any sign of evasion or contradiction. 'He has been telling our soldiers that he could attack Kingman on his own soil, in his own back-yard, with weapons of mass destruction – apparently now he has done so.'

Ruiz looked first at Pereira, then at Zakharov. 'Is this true, Yegor?'

'What I have done is take the fight to the enemy,' Zakharov said easily. 'I showed that Kingman and his lackeys in Washington are not immune to attack in their own land.'

'You mean . . . you attacked a TransGlobal facility *in the United States* . . . ?'

'You did not expect us to just keep on attacking facil-ities in South America, did you, Jorge?' Zakharov asked with mock surprise. 'Harold Kingman cares nothing for the people of other nations, least of all in South America. You are just sources of cheap labor and land to him. If you want to get the attention of men like him, you need to hit him where he'll *really* feel it and where more people will be able to witness his defeat – and there is no better place to hit a man than right where he lives.'

Ruiz was stunned. He knew of course that he would one day have to take his fight to his beloved America – he fully expected to die there, either in a gunfight with American police officers or killed while in prison by one of TransGlobal's hired assassins, perhaps a prison guard or another inmate. And Yegor Zakharov had always said that he was going to get Kingman where he lived – Ruiz always believed he was just bragging, although he also knew that if anyone could do it, Zakharov could. But attacking Kingman in the United States was something Ruiz only prayed he'd live long enough to do.

'Well,' he said a bit hesitantly, 'I think congratulations

are in order.' He raised his shot glass, and Zakharov refilled it. '*Za vashe zdarov'ye.*'

'*Spasibo*,' Zakharov responded, draining then refilling his glass. Without looking, he said to Pereira, 'You still won't drink with us, Sergeant?'

'I would like a debriefing on the attack in the United States, Zakharov,' Pereira said.

'And I would like you to show a little more respect, Sergeant . . .'

'I am not a sergeant any longer, Zakharov, and from what you have told us, you are no longer a Russian colonel, either,' Pereira said acidly. 'So shall we stop with the military lingo?'

'Very well, Pereira,' Zakharov said. 'But I don't appreciate this treatment I'm getting from you. I'm sorry about those PME turncoats, but there was nothing I could do about them – once a traitor, always a traitor. I came to cover your withdrawal, and I'm damned glad I was there when they pulled guns on you.'

'So are we,' Ruiz interjected, trying to defuse this suddenly tense situation.

'I am not talking about Cascavel, Zakharov,' Pereira said, 'although I have many questions about that incident as well . . .'

'Oh, really? Such as?'

'Such as how you happened to be there at the exact moment those soldiers tried to capture us.'

'I was covering your withdrawal, Manuel, I told you,' Zakharov said. 'We back each other up on every mission . . .'

'You weren't planned to be at Cascavel.'

'What difference does it make, Manuel – he rescued us, we're still alive, and that's it,' Ruiz said, more forcefully this time. 'If he was working with the PME, why would he have killed all three of them? Why would he even have risked his life to go to Cascavel?'

Pereira fell silent. Zakharov smiled broadly. 'Two good questions, eh, Manuel?' he asked. 'I could have made a deal with those PME soldiers and split the reward money with them. There is a reward of one million reals for you two, you know – dead or alive. Does that not deserve even a little "thank you," Pereira?'

'Thank you, sir,' he said quickly. 'Now, about the attack in the United States . . . ?'

Ruiz shook his head and started to speak, but Zakharov raised a hand to him. 'It's all right, Jorge. Manuel is a volunteer, a good fighter, a dedicated member of our cause, and a senior member of the GAMMA leadership – he has earned the right to ask questions.' Zakharov put down the vodka and took a seat. 'I had been planning an attack in the United States for many months. I assembled a corps of loyal soldiers, helped procure disguises, vehicles, materials, and false documents, and executed the plan when I determined that the conditions were most favorable. It appears that the operation was successful.'

'Which was?'

'The destruction of TransGlobal's oil and natural gas transshipment facility and oil refinery in Houston, Texas.'

' "Destruction?" ' Ruiz asked. 'Are you saying you *destroyed* the facility? You *destroyed an oil refinery*?'

'How did you do this?' Pereira asked immediately. 'That would require tens of thousands of kilos of high explosives, with dozens of trained men to plant them over a long period of time. And Kingman City is one of TransGlobal's largest and most secure facilities in the United States – approaching that plant with the manpower it would have taken would be almost impossible . . . unless . . .' And at that, Manuel Pereira stopped and looked aghast at Zakharov. The Russian's expression told him that his guess was true. '*Nao . . . nao . . . impossivel . . . inacreditavel . . .*'

'What is it, Manuel?' Ruiz asked. 'What are you saying? Why does it matter how Yegor pulled it off? It is a great victory for our cause! A major refinery and shipment facility right in the United States – striking at the heart of the global multinational corporation's organization has always been our biggest objective. He has . . .'

'Do you not see what Zakharov has done, sir?' Pereira asked incredulously. 'He has ensured that the wrath of the entire American law-enforcement machine and probably their military as well will rain down on us!'

'I'm not afraid of them, Manuel,' Ruiz said confidently, although casting a puzzled glance between his two closest comrades. 'The more they fight, the more attention will be drawn to our cause. They will know that . . .'

'You do not understand, Jorge,' Pereira said in a low, fearful voice. 'Zakharov used some sort of a weapon of mass destruction in Kingman City.' He stared accusingly at Zakharov. 'What was it? A firebomb? A tanker truck loaded with explosives? A . . . ?' He saw Zakharov's eyes glitter, and his eyes widened in shock. '*Nao* . . . you used a *nuclear weapon*?'

'Is . . . is this true, Yegor?' Ruiz asked, after turning a stunned expression toward the Russian.

'You are being a bit overdramatic, aren't you, Manuel?' Zakharov asked with a glint of humor in his eyes.

'*Overdramatic*? You destroy an American petroleum complex with a nuclear weapon, and you accuse *me* of being "overdramatic"?'

'We have discussed this many, many times in the past,'

Zakharov said, his voice becoming a bit edgier. He poured himself another shot of vodka. 'We explored the use of weapons of mass destruction – weapons developed and produced by the very companies we are seeking to hold accountable! – in our attacks. I told you I might be able to get one or more of these weapons and that I would do so, at my own expense, if the opportunity presented itself and if it was operationally safe to do so. I believe the reason you accepted my offer to assist you in your struggle was *precisely* because I know how to procure and use such devices.'

'We never spoke about using one in the United States of America . . . !'

'We most certainly did, Manuel, and precisely for the reasons you just outlined – it would be impossible to attack any facilities in the United States and do any significant damage without high-yield weapons of mass destruction,' Zakharov argued. 'Now, whether you actually did not believe that we would ever accomplish such an attack is your failing, not mine. Do not punish me because I took the initiative, based on our discussions and goals. The cause is just, the reasons adequate, the opportunity clear, and the losses and consequences acceptable; so, I acted. That is what a good soldier does. Is that not correct, Sergeant?'

'Stop calling me that, Zakharov!' Pereira snapped. 'And stop trying to include me in this insane scheme of yours! I had nothing to do with it.'

'Wait, Manuel, just wait a minute!' Ruiz interjected. His head was still swirling in confusion. 'We have got to think about this. We need to . . .'

'Comrades, the deed is done, the enemy engaged,' Zakharov said casually. 'You wanted the fight taken to the doorstep of the enemy – I have seen to it. In the end, the method doesn't matter one bit. Yes, the Americans and perhaps the world will shriek and hide with horror and call us monsters, but it will also call attention to our cause.' Pereira remained defiant, angrily staring at Zakharov; Ruiz still looked confused and frightened. 'Is this not what you wanted, Jorge? Do you want to strike out at the company that murdered your wife and children, or not?'

'Zakharov, do not . . .'

'Yes . . . yes, I do,' Ruiz said weakly. 'I have dedicated my life to seeing that corporate murderers like Kingman and TransGlobal Energy are destroyed. But to use a nuclear weapon . . . my God, I never believed it would ever happen. The devastation must be horrible, absolutely horrible . . .'

'Trust me, Jorge, the devastation is the same with a high-explosive device as with a small nuclear device,' Zakharov assured him with a fatherly pat on the shoulder that Pereira thought completely emotionless and insincere. 'Look at the effects of American firebombing campaigns in Germany and Japan and their napalm attacks in Southeast Asia: millions killed or maimed by nothing but gasoline and incendiary devices. A cluster bomb the size of a baseball, or a bullet the size of a pea, kills just as surely and just as gruesomely as a nuclear device. Are we going to cease our campaign and surrender because we happen to use a weapon that creates "more bang for the buck"? I think not.' He looked at Pereira and added smugly, 'Or maybe I am wrong, Manuel? Do you think I was wrong?'

'All of our attacks have always been discussed, planned, and coordinated in advance,' Pereira said. He had to grudgingly admit that Zakharov was making a good point here: what exactly was the difference? Dead is dead, no matter how it happens. But it infuriated him

to see Zakharov's smug expression as the Russian realized that Pereira was weakening. Zakharov was just too
clever and too . . . efficient was the only word. Pereira
went on. 'We prepare leaflets and broadcasts to warn
innocent civilians to leave the area; we try to minimize
the impact of our attacks to the environment and the
land. *We are not murderers*, Zakharov – at least we were
not until today! We are supposed to be defenders of the
oppressed, not slayers of them!'

'Come down from your heavenly perch in the clouds
and join the real world, Manuel,' Zakharov said. 'All of
our attacks have killed innocent persons – the only way
not to do so would be to expose members of our group
to capture. But I will have you know that the brave
patriot who executed the operation in Texas *did* send a
warning message to a local radio station and *did* in fact
try to warn men and women around the TransGlobal
facility away – he even tried to warn a TransGlobal security officer of the attack.'

'How in hell do you know that, Zakharov?'

'I kept in constant communication with our man and
monitored his movements at all times,' Zakharov
responded. 'After all, he was carrying a very valuable
weapon, one not easy to replace, and I wanted to make
sure he carried out his assignment exactly as planned. He
did a superb job. He had befriended several security
personnel at the facility and got to know them personally,
so before he set off his device he tried to warn them to
get away from the area. They did not, of course – Harold
Kingman would have had the man skinned and boiled
alive if he had left his post and survived when others left
behind perished. Our man was under orders not to try to
give such a warning if he felt it would jeopardize the

mission, but I left it up to him. He both issued a warning and accomplished his mission. As for the taped radio message, I do not know. He was supposed to have delivered it the same day as the attack, but it was a weekend and perhaps the lazy Americans didn't bother to open it.'

'All right, all right, everyone *relaxe*,' Ruiz said. He was obviously relieved that his two comrades were starting to find a middle ground here, which allowed Ruiz to focus on the ramifications of this very unexpected, horrifying news. 'There's nothing we can do right now. We're all tired, and we need to rest and think.' Zakharov didn't look tired in the least, and his rather exasperated expression confirmed it, but he said nothing. 'I suggest we all go to safe houses as planned while our camp is broken down and moved, then meet in a few days' time after we get a chance to assess the American reaction to the attack and decide how it will affect our future operations.'

'Let's make it one day,' Zakharov said. 'We need to best decide on how to capitalize on this successful event.'

'Let's make it a *month*,' Pereira spat. 'You think you can just march into another American city *now*, after an attack with nuclear weapons? Every soldier and law-enforcement officer in the country will be out looking for us. The Brazilian government will hand us over or kill us just to show they're cooperating with the United States.'

'Everyone will be running scared,' Zakharov said confidently. 'Yes, law enforcement will be mobilized – they'll scoop up all the usual suspects, make a few hundred arrests, and declare victory. After a short time, things will return to normal, except more Americans will stay in their homes, watch the world from the comfort of their television sets, and fret over the losses in their investment portfolios.'

'Easy for you to say,' Pereira said. 'Anyone with colored skin will be considered a suspect.'

'*Bastantes! Aquele é bastante*!' Ruiz said wearily. 'I do not want to argue about this again. We will use all of our best information and resources to determine the best time to meet again. Until then, we will all keep a low profile, gather as much data as we can about our targets all over the world, and come up with recommendations. When it is safe to do so, we will meet and decide on a plan of action.' He grasped both Zakharov's and Pereira's hands in his. 'There is much work to be done, *meus amigos bons*. Colonel Zakharov has struck a mighty blow for our cause, but the fight is not yet over, and I feel it will become more difficult. We must be strong and united until our common enemy is brought down. *Sim*?' When he did not receive a response from either of them, he grasped their hands tighter. 'Agreed?' Finally Pereira and Zakharov nodded and shook hands. '*Muito bem*. Good luck to you, my friends. May God be with you both.' Pereira endured a stern glare from Zakharov's aide Khalimov, but he was accustomed to that – and the aide was not so tough without his boss nearby, Pereira knew, so he didn't concern himself with the big Russian.

'That peasant Pereira deserves another helicopter ride, Colonel – I would be happy to show him the sights of, for example, the Atlantic Ocean, about two hundred miles offshore,' Khalimov said.

Zakharov thought for a moment, then: 'Track him to his safe house – somewhere in São Paulo or Santos, along the wharves I think. When he's safely inside, contact our man in the PME and have him arrested. They can publicize his capture, but then I need for Pereira to try to escape or try to kill a guard, at which time the people of Brazil should be spared the expense of securing, trying, and incarcerating him.'

'*Da, rookavadeeteel*,' Khalimov said, grinning. '*Ya paneemayoo*.'

'I want to meet with our strike leaders at the farm first thing tomorrow night.'

'They will be there, sir,' Khalimov said.

Zakharov smiled and nodded. With Pereira out of the way and Ruiz scared out of his wits, the operation was looking better and better all the time. Zakharov gulped another shot of vodka, disappointed as ever that his favorite drink got so warm so quickly in this damnable forest, then headed out to his waiting armored sedan.

About an hour later, Yegor Zakharov's car pulled off the main highway into São Paulo onto a two-lane road that twisted through farms and patches of forest. After another thirty minutes' drive, he turned down a dirt road and a few minutes later approached a comfortable-looking adobe farmhouse with a red tile roof, an expansive walled courtyard in front, and a barn and a maid's quarters in back. The car drove immediately into the barn, and the doors were quickly closed by men armed with machine guns. Khalimov got out of the driver's seat, withdrew a submachine gun, and carefully kept guard while several men approached Zakharov's car. The men saluted as Zakharov emerged from the sedan.

'Report,' the ex-Russian Strategic Rocket Forces Colonel ordered.

'All secure, sir,' one of the men reported. 'No unusual activity in this area, and the *commandante* of the local PME barracks reports no unusual movement or strangers in the area. Radio traffic is routine.' He handed Zakharov transcripts of local radio and telephone conversations.

'The airspace?'

'Last PME patrol aircraft flyover was yesterday, sir,' the man reported. 'Photos and identification are in the report. One American Keyhole-class photoreconnaissance satellite over our area – its orbit is elliptical, optimized for the northern hemisphere, but obviously it can be adjusted quickly to scan our area. Next flyover will be in six and a half hours.'

Zakharov nodded. The lower-altitude intelligence satellites were easy to avoid or spoof – it was the high-altitude satellites and the unmanned long-range drones that were the real threat. The best tactic was to avoid all exposure as much as possible – change codes, shift frequencies, alter timetables and travel routes, and move from place to place as much as possible to cover their tracks.

Zakharov dismissed the security men and stepped outside to a shaded patio to get out of the hot sun. Pavel Khalimov, his submachine gun now hanging on a snap-cord around his neck so he could quickly raise it, approached him, holding a portable satellite phone. 'He has called twice now, sir,' he said simply.

'Let him call. It is far safer for him than it is for me.' But at that moment the phone rang. Zakharov swore under his breath and motioned for the phone. 'Have you ever heard of communications security?' he asked in Russian, after engaging the security circuits.

'Just a friendly warning – stay out of the United States for a while,' the caller said in Russian. The voice was being altered with an electronic scrambler – it changed every few seconds from a high-pitched whine to a very low-pitched moan, so much so that it was impossible to decipher even if it was male or female. 'The FBI, CIA, and every American military investigative unit will be . . .'

'Yes, yes, I've heard it before,' Zakharov snapped. 'Listen, you wanted TransGlobal to bleed, and now they're bleeding. You think anyone was going to pay attention to attacks in Panama or Egypt?'

'Just a word to the wise, that's all, you big asshole,' the voice said affably. 'Every government agency is going to be on the lookout. We don't want to spoil the big finale. Everything is on schedule and going according to plan – just don't blow it now by being too anxious. Concentrate on the African and European target list I've already given you. Stay out of sight for a few weeks.'

'Stop telling me what to do, *zalupa*!' Zakharov shouted. 'If you had the guts to do what I have done, you would have done the same. You know damned well that Kingman's base of power is the United States. You want him destroyed, my friend, then you go to America.'

'You did a fine job, Colonel,' the caller said. 'I'd hate to have such a fine career cut short. Once again, a friendly word of advice: stay out of the United States.' And the call was terminated. Fifteen seconds from start to finish – even when angry and wishing to chew one of his subordinates out, Zakharov thought, the chief of the Consortium maintained the strictest communications security. The most sophisticated eavesdropping systems in the world – TEMPEST, Petaplex, Echelon, Enigma, Sombrero – couldn't intercept, lock, and triangulate a satellite call in less than fifteen seconds.

But he had to grudgingly hand it to him: the head of the Consortium, known to Zakharov only by his code name *Deryektar*, the Director, was one cold-blooded son of a bitch. He had money, lots of it, and he wasn't squeamish about where to spend it as long as whatever happened furthered his objectives.

Fuck him, Zakharov thought. He was running scared. Yegor Viktorvich Zakharov had just become the greatest and most deadly terrorist in the world – he wasn't about to run and hide now.

'What is the plan now, Colonel?' Khalimov asked.

'A few days to rest while you find Pereira's safe house,' Zakharov replied. Operational security procedures, instituted by himself – Ruiz was not tactically smart enough to set up such rules – detailed that individual members of GAMMA did not know where the others' safe houses were located. They used blind phone, letter, and e-mail drops to communicate while in hiding, then set up a different meeting location every time to plan the next operation. 'I need to find out what the Americans will do and plan a course of action. What are your thoughts, Captain?'

'Security will be extreme,' Khalimov said. Pavel Khalimov had been an aide-de-camp and tactician for Yegor Zakharov for many years, and he had learned to trust his opinions and expertise implicitly. 'Penetrating even local or private security or law-enforcement patrols will be difficult. We may have more success at European or Asian targets, although they will be substantial as well.'

'Our benefactor said the same,' Zakharov said. He paused for a moment, deep in thought. Then: 'Very well, we continue as planned. The last time America was attacked within its own borders, it lashed out mostly at terrorists overseas – the nation's leaders did not have the stomach to combat terrorists on its own soil. It is too politically incorrect, too unpopular with their constituents. They set up a few security measures here and there, mostly in airports and a few docks and border crossings. But Americans are so enamored of personal freedoms, their precious Bill of Rights, that they would rather allow an entire society to be threatened with death or horrible injury by weapons of mass destruction than inconvenience their citizens with more exhaustive searches and investigation. Stupid.'

'Our mission is proceeding as planned,' Khalimov said. 'We anticipated the American government instituting severely increased security measures after our first attack – in fact, we were *hoping* for it. Most of our forces are already in place and waiting for the American people's patience to run thin.'

'Exactly. When that happens, we will strike the final blow.' Zakharov fell silent for several long moments, then said, 'I want the next attack in the United States to make the one in Houston look like a campfire, Pavel,' he said finally. 'We will continue our overseas operations as planned – but it will be nothing compared to what will happen in the United States.'

Chapter Three

Cannon Air Force Base, Near Clovis, New Mexico
Four days later

Jason Richter kicked off the rough green wool U.S. Air Force-issue blanket and balsa-wood-like starched sheets. Sunlight was streaming through uncovered windows – not just through the glass, but around the edges of the window itself where the wood and masonry trim was crumbling away. The open barracks was divided into rooms with simple cinder-block walls that had no doors and didn't even extend all the way to the ceiling; being a field grade officer, he was actually given a cubicle of his own. He was careful to shake his sneakers on the floor to be sure no poisonous spiders or scorpions had crawled inside before he slipped them on to head to the open bay latrine.

'Let's hit it, Ari,' he said as he passed Ari Vega's cubicle across the building from his. All of the other cubicles, about thirty of them, were empty. Her cubicle had no doors on it either, but Ari never insisted on separate men's and women's facilities – if you couldn't handle a woman in the lab, the field, or the latrine, she had always said, that wasn't *her* problem.

'Shit, J,' Ari murmured, 'what time is it?'

'Almost seven-thirty.'

She was still wearing the black fatigue trousers and olive drab T-shirt she had been wearing for the past three days, ever since their demonstration at Andrews Air Force

Base. Ari had long, wavy, dark hair, an olive complexion, and a very sexy body, but she always had her hair up, rarely used makeup, and kept her body hidden under bulky clothing; Jason had only seen her with her hair down maybe a handful of times in two years of working closely together. 'Seven-thirty? We just hit the rack three hours ago!' Not unexpectedly, things ran late yesterday: the transport planes were delayed by weather and mechanical breakdowns, so they were late getting loaded up in Alexandria, which meant they got in very late to Cannon Air Force Base, the eighty-seven-thousand-acre military installation in eastern New Mexico. To top it off, there were no helpers or offloading equipment to help them at Cannon, so they had to unload the plane themselves by hand. 'My brain doesn't start until eight, man. I'm skipping breakfast. See you later.' Jason was too tired to argue.

The water in the latrine's shower was ice cold, and when the hot water started, it was as brown as the dirt outside. Jason let it run, hoping it would eventually clear, but he ended up showering under an adjacent head in cold water because it never did. He shaved in cold water, put on the same set of fatigues he wore the day before, brushed the dirt and sand off his boots as best he could, found his fatigue cap, and headed outside.

They were set up in Field Exercise Support Facility Twelve, located about thirty-two kilometers west of Cannon Air Force Base in a restricted area known as Pecos East. Two large rickety-looking steel hangars perpendicular to one another faced a large concrete parking ramp. Long shafts of grass grew through numerous cracks in the tarmac. Obviously the facility had been used recently, but judging by the gang graffiti and empty beer cans they found everywhere they guessed it had not been used for any military purposes. The air was warm and breezy, with thunderstorms already building to the west. The terrain was flat, flat, flat, and Jason could probably count the number of trees he saw on one hand.

Jason found the chow hall, a broken-down-looking place called the Tumbleweed Dining Facility with cracked windows and peeling paint everywhere, but it was closed. He swore to himself and made his way across the dusty curbless street to the front of the center hangar. A steel door that appeared to have been pried open with a crowbar several times bore the familiar sign that read, RESTRICTED MILITARY FACILITY, AUTHORIZED PERSONNEL ONLY, followed by a long paragraph of legalese and finished with, USE OF DEADLY FORCE AUTHORIZED. He pressed a button to an intercom box beside the door, and moments later he heard a buzz and pulled the door open.

'Unit, ten-*hut*!' he heard. A lone Air Force security guard in desert camouflage fatigues, web belt with sidearm, and black Security Forces beret snapped to attention behind a gray metal desk. A bank of security camera monitors was set up on a desk to his left; a gun locker and radio recharging stand was on the right. 'Welcome to Task Force TALON, sir,' the guard said. He was rather short and perhaps a little on the pudgy side, with horn-rimmed glasses strapped to his head with an elastic band, but he seemed professional, enthusiastic, and friendly. 'May I see your ID card, please?' Jason fished it out for him. The guard studied it for a moment, took down some information from it, and returned it. 'Thank you, sir. I'm Staff Sergeant Doug Moore, in charge of security here at Area Twelve.' He handed Jason a folder. 'Inside you'll find gate codes, your flight line badges, maps of the base, and other information. Is Dr Vega with you?'

Jason found the flight line badge on a neck strap and put it on – he had a feeling he was going to use it quite often here. 'She should be along shortly.'

'Very well, sir.' His look of surprise obviously told Jason that he didn't know Ariadna was a woman – she liked using her more male-sounding nickname 'Ari' so she could see the surprised look on the faces of the men when they discovered she was a woman. 'I'll notify the rest of the staff that you've arrived.'

'Don't bother – I'll find them. This way?' Jason pointed to the only other door. He retrieved his flight line badge and swiped it in the card reader, entered a code, and the door popped open.

The hallway inside was dim and narrow, with a decades-old linoleum floor and bare walls. Jason remembered he was here last night, looking for the bathroom, but he didn't remember much from that long night of transferring equipment from their C-130 Hercules transport plane out at Cannon into a couple tractor-trailers and then making the hour-long drive out to Area Twelve. But he followed vehicle and cargo-handling noise to another locked steel door, entered his codes, and entered.

Containers, boxes, and equipment were strewn all over the hangar, but in the middle of it all were the two Humvees Jason and Ariadna brought out to Cannon, the working prototype they had used in the demo in Washington and another they were using to test upgrades. Jason had to show his badge to a security guard before he could check the Humvee – yes, two CID units were on board, they hadn't been disturbed, and both were fully charged and ready to go. The first CID unit was the operational prototype; the second, like the other Humvee, was used to test enhancements to the weapon system. Two more upgraded units were just a few weeks from being ready – after Kingman City, Jason was sure that timetable was going to be stepped up. Jason went over to check on the second Humvee . . .

. . . and found a guy in a plain gray lightweight jacket, khaki slacks, shooter's yellow sunglasses, and outdoor all-terrain shoes sitting in the driver's seat. He was taking notes on the various switches and controls, and he had the computer access panel open. 'Who are you?' Jason asked.

'Who are *you*?' the guy challenged him. 'No one's allowed near these vehicles!'

'They're *my* fucking vehicles,' Jason snapped.

The guy scrambled out of the driver's seat. He was a good three inches taller than Jason, square-jawed and athletic – he definitely looked like he could take care of himself. He withdrew a leather wallet from a breast pocket and flashed a gold badge and ID card that said 'FBI' on it. 'Special Agent Bolton, FBI.' He stood right in front of Jason, blocking his view of what he was doing inside the Humvee. 'Step away from the vehicle.'

'I told you, it's *my* Humvee,' Jason said. 'What were you doing in there?'

'And you are?'

'Major Jason Richter.' He lifted up his flight line badge and stuck it in Bolton's face. 'I'm commander of this task force.'

Bolton grasped the card, read it, and nodded, after giving Richter a quick and apparently none-too-favorable appraisal. 'Okay,' he said, 'you're cleared.'

'I asked you, what were you doing in my Humvee?'

'I asked him to take some notes for me.' Jason turned and saw Kelsey DeLaine walking toward him. The guards did not ask to see her badge, Jason noticed. 'I wanted to know the difference between the two vehicles, and since you weren't around to ask, I had Agent Bolton go in and check. Carl, Jason Richter, U.S. Army. Jason, Special Agent Carl Bolton.'

'Agent Bolton should leave his paws off things he knows nothing about,' Jason said pointedly.

'Carl Bolton is the Washington director of the advanced technology office of the FBI,' Kelsey went on, ignoring Jason's warning. 'He has a master's degree in electrical engineering and a Ph.D. in advanced computer architecture. He might know more about the systems in there than you do.'

He might indeed, Jason thought – he had heard of this guy before, but had no idea he worked for the FBI. But he was still in a peeved mood, and he'd only been awake for twenty minutes. 'Then he should know better than to touch anything he's not intimately familiar with, especially switches that can activate weapons.'

'I assure you, Major, Agent Bolton didn't touch anything – he was simply taking notes.'

Jason stepped around Bolton, reached into the cab, and closed the computer terminal's access cover – he couldn't remember if he had left that cover open or not, but he assumed that Bolton had opened it. 'Oh yeah? Maybe Agent Bolton would like it if I took a look around inside his suitcase – I promise I won't touch a thing. Is that okay, Agent Bolton?' The big engineer scowled at him but said nothing.

'Problem here?' Jason looked up and saw Command Sergeant Major Jefferson approach. He wore a slightly boyish grin, but those eyes . . . his eyes pierced through Jason's brain like a white-hot poker. Despite the crocodile smile, those eyes said only one thing – you are dog meat to me, sir. 'Good morning, sir. Any problems?'

'Good morning, Sergeant Major.' Jefferson nodded but said nothing. 'I was just warning Agent Bolton here about the dangers to himself and others – especially himself – if he gets near my equipment without letting me know first.'

'Slept in this morning, I see,' Kelsey said to Jason with a trace of humor in her green eyes – her rather gorgeous green eyes, Jason had to admit. He ignored her, mostly because she was too damned perky and together to be for real.

Jason turned to Jefferson instead. 'I want everybody kept away from the Humvees until I've had a chance to brief everyone on their operation,' he said. 'It's too dangerous.'

'Yes, sir,' Jefferson responded.

'Next item, Sergeant Major: are all the showers screwed up like mine is?'

'If you mean is the hot water not on and do the pipes need flushing out: yes, sir. This facility was mostly shut down when we arrived – there wasn't time to get everything up and running.'

'That's unacceptable, Sergeant Major,' Jason said. 'I realize the urgent nature of our mission, but piss-poor planning on the White House's part shouldn't become a hardship on our part – there'll be plenty of time for that when we get on the road. I want you to find every available unoccupied transient or visitor's quarters available at Cannon, divide our crew into shifts, and send them over there for rest, a shower, and a meal.'

'We can't spare the time or the manpower,' Kelsey DeLaine interjected. 'We need to be up and running in less than six days.'

'Agent DeLaine, I don't care what Chamberlain said – I'm not going to have bone-tired soldiers working around my equipment,' Jason said. 'Everyone here understands the urgency of our mission, and we'll all work as hard as we can. But CID works because my directorate is careful, deliberate, and we don't make bonehead mistakes. I'm going to keep it that way. Sergeant Major, see to the crew rest rotation schedule, and have someone out at the air base get our facilities fixed ASAP.'

'Yes, sir.' Jason was relieved to see Jefferson's scowl had lessened a noticeable bit – obviously his way of showing his approval – as he turned to issue orders.

'Next item: What time does the chow hall open, Sergeant Major?'

'The chow hall here at Facility Twelve is closed, sir,' Jefferson replied. 'Because of the THREATCON ALPHA security alert, all civilian contractors without at least a Confidential security clearance are prohibited from entering this area. Hours had to be severely cut for all support services. We've requested MREs and box lunches until we can get hot meals prepared again.'

'That won't work either, Sergeant Major.' He thought for a moment; then: 'Is there a Pizza Hut near Cannon?'

'I do not know, sir.'

'Sergeant Major, in all your years of experience, do you know of *any* military installation in the continental United States that does *not* have a Pizza Hut right outside the front gate?'

Jefferson glared at Richter as if he was trying to decide

if the man was pulling his leg or not. 'There are usually an abundance of civilian fast-food restaurants within a very short distance of the entrance of every CONUS military base that I am aware of, sir,' he replied with a deep threatening voice, obviously warning the young major to get to the point quickly and not to fuck with him in front of all these outsiders.

'And are there any restrictions to the movement of properly credentialed military persons on and off the base?'

'Not at this time, sir.'

'Then I want you to find a vehicle and a couple of men and pick up as many pizzas as you think we'll need for all the personnel here for lunch and dinner,' Jason said. He pulled out his wallet and handed him a credit card. 'That should take care of it. Make mine pepperoni and sausage. And scout around to find out what other restaurants are nearby – even I will get sick of pizza.'

Jefferson blinked in surprise, but his voice never wavered: 'Yes, sir,' he responded. He motioned for a soldier working nearby to make the arrangements.

'It's understandable that you want to be fed and clean, Major,' Kelsey said impatiently, 'and I think it's cute how you're trying to take charge here like this, but we really don't have time . . .'

'Agent DeLaine, as I said, I don't want tired, hungry, cranky people working around my weapon systems,' Jason said. 'You may think it's "cute" that I'm trying to look out for the men and women who are stuck out here, but even us Officer Candidate School "ninety-day wonders" learn to take care of our people first. I assume if my latrine and meals were screwed up, everybody else's is too. Am I wrong? Did you have a hot shower and breakfast this morning, Agent DeLaine?'

'No, but we . . .'

'Sergeant Major, did *anyone* here have a hot shower and hot meal here this morning?'

'No, sir. None of the personnel that arrived last night had either. I cannot speak for the base personnel assigned to us by the Air Force.'

'There you go – an invitation to disaster,' Jason insisted. 'Any other complaints, Agent DeLaine?' He didn't give her an opportunity to answer. 'Good. Next item: I want coffee, and I want a target,' Jason said.

'A target?'

'Coffee first, and then I want to find out who and what to hit first,' Jason repeated. Kelsey looked as if she was ready to protest again, so he turned back to Jefferson. 'Sergeant Major, where's the damned coffee?'

'Right this way, sir,' and he headed off toward a small office inside the hangar.

'Hey, wait a minute!' Kelsey protested. 'We need to have a meeting first! We have a staff to organize. We need progress milestones, a timetable, set up a daily report . . .'

'Why don't I leave that up to you?' Jason suggested over his shoulder to Kelsey. 'I think all we need is some fresh intel and a plane that'll get us to wherever the bad guys are. CID will do the rest.'

Jefferson led the way to the coffee – actually an old metal percolator half-full of boiling water on an even older hot plate, with Styrofoam cups and packets of instant coffee from MRE kits strewn about – but stopped before entering. 'I think Special Agent DeLaine is right, sir,' he said. 'We've got a mixed task force here – civilians, military, Army, Air Force – that has never trained or fought together before. We should take the time to organize and plan strategies before we head off into the field.'

'How many agents and soldiers were we given, Sergeant Major?' Jason asked.

'I have a support staff of three, a security staff of six, plus two Special Forces instructors here with me, sir,' Jefferson replied. 'We have two staff officers, one from the Marine Corps and one from the Air Force. Agent DeLaine has one FBI intelligence officer with her.'

'Doesn't seem to me that we have anybody to plan or train with.'

'The typical procedure, sir, is to build a game plan – a TO&E, or Table of Organization and Equipment – and then requisition the personnel, weapons, and equipment we'll need to execute the plan,' Jefferson said evenly, like an impatient teacher explaining an important point to a rambunctious teenager. 'We can't move forward without a plan. I believe Mr Chamberlain is prepared to give us anything we need to make this task force mission-ready. But we have to tell him what we need first, and the best way to do that is to sit down and make some decisions.'

'The "typical" procedure,' Jason repeated. He could see that Sergeant Major Jefferson was unaccustomed to being questioned as to how things should be done. Jason turned and motioned toward the C-130 and his two Humvees in the hangar. 'I believe we have everything we need right there, Sergeant Major,' he said. 'Let's load it up and get the bad guys.'

Sergeant Major Jefferson took in a lungful of air and looked for all the world like he wanted to start barking at Richter; Kelsey quickly interceded before he did. 'Let's try it our way, okay, Jason?' she asked. 'This is our first full day here. Let's come to an agreement on how we want to proceed, come up with a workable plan, then upchannel it to Chamberlain. If we're together on the plan, it'll stand a good chance of getting approved.' Jason looked as if he was going to keep arguing, so Kelsey let her voice rise a bit. 'I think the sergeant major and I have a bit more experience in organizing, training, and employing a task force than you do, Major. Try it our way for now, all right?'

Jason saw Ari enter the hangar, now wearing a dark blue warm-up suit, still a little groggy, and decided he wasn't going to get much help from her yet, so he nodded. 'Okay,' he said. 'Let's go meet with the staff and talk.' He endured Jefferson's exasperated scowl as they exited the little office and headed for the conference room in the main hangar.

Two officers already in the room got to their feet and called the room to attention when Jason walked in. Kelsey took the head of the table; Sergeant Major Jefferson sat on her right. As expected, the two officers stared at both Kelsey and Ari, not expecting two women to be involved in this project. 'As you were, guys,' Jason said. He stepped over to the first guy and extended a hand. 'Jason Richter.'

'Frank Falcone,' he responded, shaking hands. He was an Air Force captain, mid- to late twenties, with very close-cropped hair to mask his early baldness. He was of above average height, maybe a little on the heavy side, and walked with a noticeable limp. 'I've been assigned as your operations and intelligence officer.'

'Your second in command, sir,' Jefferson said. 'Special-operations experience during Operations Enduring Freedom and Iraqi Freedom.'

'Fifty-seven sorties in central Asia in MH-53Js,' Falcone said, 'and sixteen in the Iraqi theater before I took an SA-7 in the face.'

'That how you got the limp?'

'The crash took out most of my left thigh and hip,' Falcone said. 'I was in Walter Reed and various other hospitals for eight months. After rehabilitation and recertification, I went to Air Force Special Operations Command Headquarters at Hurlburt Field for three months in plans and operations before being assigned to the task force.'

'First Lieutenant Jennifer McCracken, sir,' the woman next to Falcone, a Marine Corps lieutenant, said. She was shorter than Richter, with ear-length straight brown hair, thick glasses, not athletic-looking but sturdy – a female Marine who didn't look too feminine but didn't want to look like one of the guys either. She had a firm handshake – a little too firm, Jason thought, as if she thought she had something to prove to her temporary army boss. 'Logistics officer, Headquarters Battalion, First Marine Division, Marine Depot Twentynine Palms. I'll be your adjutant and logistics officer.'

'As you can see, sir, we had to double up on your typical staff assignments because of time constraints,' Jefferson pointed out. 'I think we can overcome any difficulties we encounter.'

'You three represent three more staff persons than I'm accustomed to,' Jason admitted. He turned to Ari, who was making faces as she tried to drink a cup of the instant coffee. 'This is Dr Ariadna Vega, the lead design engineer and team leader at the Infantry Transformational BattleLab, Fort Polk, Louisiana. She is also my adjutant, logistics assistant, cleanup gal, and chief cook and bottle washer. Take seats and let's get going.'

As they sat, Kelsey DeLaine asked, 'Mind telling us about yourself, Jason?'

'I think we need to get this meeting started . . .'

'It is started,' Kelsey said. She smiled at his obvious discomfort at being the center of attention and added, 'You look awfully young to be a major in the U.S. Army.'

He rolled his eyes at her, then said, 'There's not much to tell, guys. I come from a long line of career army officers stretching back to the Civil War, but I didn't go to West Point myself because I got accepted to Georgia Tech's engineering program when I was in ninth grade. I got my bachelor's and master's degrees by the time I was eighteen.' That bit of information got a mix of impressed nods and disbelieving glares from the others in the room. 'But my dad is a retired army colonel and really wanted me to join up, so I enrolled in OCS. That's about it. I've worked at the Army Research Lab for the past three years. Any questions? Comments?'

'It was pretty awesome, what you did in Kingman City, sir,' Falcone said. 'What other units have you been with? What kind of special-ops training have you had?'

'Uh . . . well, none, Frank,' Jason replied rather sheepishly. 'I got my master's and doctorate degrees at Georgia Tech and Cal-Poly San Luis Obispo, then went on to Fort Polk and the Army Research Lab, working in weapon system engineering and development. I did a year at the Armed Forces Industrial College in Washington and a year as project officer at Aberdeen Proving Grounds, working on various projects.' No one said anything after that. He shrugged, then motioned to DeLaine. 'How about you, Kelsey? Been a G-Man for long?'

Kelsey gave Jason an evil scowl but got to her feet. 'Thank you, Major. Welcome, everybody. I'm Special

Agent Kelsey DeLaine. I'm the deputy director of intelligence, FBI Headquarters, Washington, D.C., second in command at the FBI's intelligence headquarters, which oversees nationwide and worldwide law-enforcement information-gathering, analysis, dissemination, and operations. Before that, I was deputy special agent in charge of intelligence for the FBI field office in London, with a force of twenty-three agents and a staff of sixty personnel. Before that, I was at the FBI Academy in Quantico, teaching classes in intelligence field operations and international law. I have a prelaw and law degree from Georgetown University.'

'The sergeant major said you had something to do with that huge black market weapons bust in London a couple months ago?' Falcone asked.

Kelsey nodded. 'I was the coleader of a joint U.S.-British-Russian task force tracking down terror cells moving into Europe from the Middle East through the Caspian Sea region and southern Europe,' she replied. 'Our task force broke the London cell wide open, which led to the discovery of the black market WMD dealers in London and Washington.'

'I heard that op might have saved both capitals from a nuclear or bio-weapon attack,' McCracken said. 'You confiscated something like seven *billion* dollars in secret bank accounts?'

'More like ten billion, plus those four huge chemical weapon caches that we . . .'

'That's good, Kelsey, thanks,' Jason said. Kelsey rolled her eyes at Richter but took her seat. 'I'm not sure why I was chosen to be in this group, except I have the keys to the gadgets out there in the hangar. Intros over? Good. Frank, get us started. What do you have for us?'

Falcone distributed folders from his briefcase, disguising a smile at DeLaine's expense as he did so. 'This is the latest information we've received on the attack in Kingman City,' he said, 'mostly details about the explosion itself and the extent of the damage. Over eleven known terrorist and extremist groups have taken responsibility for the attack. The FBI is working with the CIA, State Department, and foreign intelligence and law-enforcement agencies to narrow the list down.'

'Any information on this, Kelsey?' Jason asked.

'Not yet,' Kelsey responded. 'We do know that another three dozen or so unknown group or individuals have also claimed responsibility. It'll take time to track down each and every lead.'

'Any guesses? Anyone stand out?'

'I think that's very premature,' she said hesitantly. 'We need more information.'

Jason glanced at Ari, who made an imperceptible nod in return as she sipped her coffee. 'Okay. We don't have a target yet, so we can't ascertain exactly who or what our enemy is yet,' Jason said. 'But Sun-tzu said that in order to be effective in war you needed to know your enemy *and* know yourself. I think it's time to get to know El CID.'

'El Cid?'

'Cybernetic Infantry Device – our little friends in the Humvees,' Jason said. 'I brought two with me from Fort Polk, including the one I used in Kingman City. We have four more in various stages of readiness back at Fort Polk – since we use a spiral development program, we can manufacture units one by one and subsequent units adopt upgrades and enhancements. I expect we'll get one or two within the next month, followed by the rest within six months along with the specialized Humvees and other support equipment. Our goal should be to train someone to use CID number two and have him or her up to speed.'

'I thought of that,' Kelsey said. 'Carl Bolton has volunteered to train in the second unit.'

'Carl? Really?'

'He's the perfect choice,' Kelsey said. 'He's a career FBI agent, graduated top of his class in the academy, and has degrees in engineering and computers.'

And it would give you someone on the inside on my side of the task force, Jason told himself. 'Actually,' he said, 'I was thinking of . . . Staff Sergeant Doug Moore.'

'Who?'

'Sergeant Moore, the Air Force Security Forces guard assigned to this area.'

'You mean, the guy at the front desk?' Kelsey asked incredulously. 'The short fat guy with glasses?'

'He's of average height and maybe a little on the husky side, but not fat.'

'I think Carl would have a much better understanding of the technology than the staff sergeant,' Kelsey said. 'We don't have time to train someone in all the intricacies of haptic interfaces. Carl has researched that technology for years. He's also a marathon runner and open water SCUBA diver – I think he would do better physically and endurance-wise inside CID than Moore. I vote we train Carl Bolton in the second CID unit and use Sergeant Moore in the next units that arrive.'

'A "vote," huh?' Jason looked at the people around him. Apparently the feds were ready to vote; the military men and woman looked confused and hesitant but seemed to be willing to follow along if a vote was called for. 'I've got a better idea – a trial run.'

'Trial run?'

'A contest, a challenge,' Jason said. 'It'll give us a good opportunity to look over the units, see what they're capable of, and show how easy it is to operate. How does that sound?'

'I don't know . . .'

'Let's give it a try, shall we?' He got to his feet and headed for the door. 'Sergeant Major, have Sergeant Moore relieved at his post and have him report to the Humvees.'

'Yes, sir.' Jefferson looked at Richter with a quizzical, skeptical expression as he departed.

A few moments later, while Bolton and Sergeant Moore watched, Jason and Ari unloaded the two CID units and lined them up beside one another. 'CID is programmed to respond to coded voice commands,' Jason began. 'But for this exercise, Ari will program the units to respond to a voice command from myself, Ari, or any person aboard.' He motioned to the two rectangular hunks of composite material. 'Their names are Troy and Moffitt.' Jason paused, looking around to see if there was any reaction from the others. 'You guys don't get it? Troy and Moffitt?' No reaction. 'No one ever saw *The Rat Patrol* TV show?' Still no reaction. 'Okay, we'll just use CID One and Two. The command to get it to unstow is "activate," and then give it the command "pilot up" to open up the access hatch. Go for it.'

Bolton stepped forward and stood in front of the first unit. 'CID One, activate,' he shouted in a drill-sergeant-like voice. The other unit shuddered to life and within moments it was towering over him. Moore did likewise with CID Two, a bit more hesitantly but he got the job done.

'Very good. Ari, help Sergeant Moore. I'll show Agent Bolton. CID One, pilot up.' The machine leaned forward slightly, its arms extended backward to act as railings. It bent its left leg then extended its right leg backward; finally, a hatch popped open in the center of its back.

'CID Two, pilot up,' Ari commanded. The second unit did as the first. She hopped up on the robot's right arm. 'C'mon up here, Doug,' she said. Moore carefully, gingerly approached the machine. 'C'mon, Sergeant, it won't bite. Hop on up here.' She gave him a mind-blowing smile, which definitely encouraged him.

Moore stood over the entry hatch and peered inside CID Two. The interior looked like a very comfortable satiny padded pillow, with a half-helmet with breathing apparatus and a large electronic visor near the eyes. The inside portion of the open entry hatches were similarly covered in satiny pads. Ari moved beside him. 'Here's your ride, Doug,' she said. 'Once you're inside, you'll slip the gloved portions on and your feet into braces. Everything will be locked down, so you won't be able to move until the unit powers up, but then you'll be able to move freely. You give the command, "CID Two, lock me in," and the hatch will close. Everything will be automatic from there on out.'

'It looks like I'll be squished in there pretty tightly.'

'Yes you will, but it won't feel like it once power is applied,' Ari said. 'You'll be able to move perfectly normal. Just be careful – the kinesthetic algorithms in the software should keep you from hitting yourself and breaking sensors with your limbs, but they take time to adapt to your movements. Move slowly at first until you get the hang of it. Ready?'

Moore faced the open hatch, both hands on either

side, but he didn't go in. 'Will I be able to breathe and talk normally?'

'Sure. It'll be like wearing a motorcycle helmet. Your breathing will be a bit restricted but you'll get used to it. There will be a lot of symbology and messages flashing on your visor but you'll be able to see just fine. Ignore them for now – we'll teach you what it all means later.'

Moore looked down into the place where his head needed to go like a young child staring down into a pool before jumping in for the first time from a diving board. 'I . . . I've never been on a motorcycle before.'

Ari sensed the growing fear in Moore's voice. 'Hey, Doug,' she said gently. He looked up at her. 'It's okay if you don't want to do this. The major just wanted everyone to see how easy it is to run this thing. He thought you'd do it no sweat. But if you'd rather not, it's cool.' Moore said nothing, but nodded numbly and looked back down inside the machine again, not moving in either direction. 'You have a call sign, Doug? All you Air Force guys have call signs.'

'No.'

'How long have you been in the Air Force, Doug?' she asked.

'Eight years.'

'Gonna hang in there for twenty?'

'Yes.'

'What else do you like to do?'

'I like being in the Security Forces,' Moore said. 'Security, patrol, law enforcement, weapons.'

'I mean, what do you do for fun, relaxation?'

He looked up at her, a little embarrassed, and shrugged. 'I read up on tactics and procedures, practice on the range – you know, study all there is to know about my job.'

'You like guns?'

'Sure I do.'

She could see his eyes brighten. Aha, she thought, he's paying attention to me and not the CID. 'What kind of guns?'

'Every kind,' he replied. 'I know a lot about hand-guns, rifles, machine guns, cannons – you name it. I even reload my own ammo.'

'I'm a little afraid of guns – no, I'm a *lot* afraid of guns,' Ari said.

'There's absolutely nothing to be afraid of,' Moore said. This was definitely the chattiest he's been, Ari thought. 'They're tools, implements – just like CID Two here. The more you learn, the better you feel about them.'

'What does your wife think about guns?'

His expression turned embarrassed again. 'I . . . I'm not married.'

'Me either.' He looked up at her, and she affixed another mind-blowing smile on him with her enticing red lips. 'Hey, would you teach me how to shoot a gun?'

His face practically exploded with glee. 'Sure!' he replied enthusiastically. 'Most girls I know hate guns. They don't want anything to do with them.'

'Well, I'm not a *girl*,' Ari said, giving Moore a playful slap on the back of the head, 'and I'm definitely not like most *women*, Doug.' His use of the term 'girls' told her a lot: this was a guy who didn't have much of a life outside the Air Force Security Forces. He was afraid to try new things – not a good choice for someone picked to use CID for the first time. But Jason wanted him for this demonstration – she'd have to see if she could make this work. 'Besides, I work for the army – I'm around guns all day. I don't hate guns, and maybe I'm not afraid of them, but I do respect them. I don't pick them up and fire them myself. But if you teach me, maybe I won't be afraid.'

'You won't be, I promise.'

'It's a date, then,' she said. She nodded toward the interior of the CID unit. 'Now, what about this thing, Doug? It's no biggie if you want to get down. I'll do the demo with Bolton over there, wax his ass, and then when you get off you and I will go out to the desert and you can teach me about guns.'

Ari could see the transformation on Moore's face when she said the word 'date' – he felt as if he was ready to take on a band of nuclear terrorists all by himself. 'Let me give it a spin,' he said resolutely.

'You sure?'

'Yeah.'

She gave him another smile and a pat on the cheek that melted his heart completely. 'All *right*, Doug. Wait until you see the weapons we have for this thing – it'll blow your mind. Climb on in and let's get started. Breathe normally and try to relax until we get the power on.'

Slowly, gingerly, Moore eased his legs into the interior of CID Two. He paused about three-quarters in until his boots found the braces, then slowly lowered himself inside. He gave Ari one last worried smile, received a smile of encouragement in response, then lowered his face into the helmet so his entire body weight was resting inside the body supports. His arms withdrew inside the machine and slipped between the smooth padded coverings until his hands found the rough gloves inside; then he slipped his fingers in. He tried to flex his fingers and move his head but everything was frozen solid, and a thrill of panic crept up his spine. He was blind, almost deaf, and the padded interior molded itself to his body so well that he felt as if he were floating in a sensory-deprivation chamber.

'Okay, Doug,' he heard Ari say. 'You have to give the command to close the hatch.'

'Ahh . . .' He didn't think he could do it. It was hard to tell which way was up. He knew he should be almost upright, leaning forward a little, but he felt horizontal, maybe even past horizontal, a little head-down. It was starting to get warm, and he hated the feel of his own breath on his face and going back into his own nostrils. Where's the air in this thing? Wasn't it dangerous to breathe your own exhalation? Isn't that mostly carbon dioxide, and it's bad to . . .

'Hey, Doug? We're waiting, tiger. Go for it.'

'Okay. Okay . . .' He took a deep breath and found it exceedingly hard to get a full lungful of air. I better do it, he thought, or I might puke in here. 'CID Two, lock me in.'

It was silent for what seemed like a long time – then, suddenly he heard a whirring sound, and the hatch closed behind him, pressing his body deeply into the padding. Now it was *really* difficult to breathe. Moore subconsciously tried to raise himself up, but he was squished in tight. He couldn't move, couldn't breathe, couldn't see, couldn't hear . . . He realized with a roar in his ears and tightness in his chest that he was suffocating! *Suffocating*! This is what it felt like! Holy shit, he screamed to himself, I've got to get out of here! How do I get out? Ari never told me how to get out! What if I'm dying? What if there's a malfunction and they can't tell I'm smothering in here! What do I . . . ?

'Relax, Doug,' he heard Ari say. 'Don't get up too quickly. Relax.'

Cool air rushed into his lungs. He felt his body weight on his left leg – not uncomfortable or heavy, but it felt weird after feeling so weightless for what seemed like a long time – and found he was able to straighten his legs and lower his arms with ease. He could see just fine – maybe a bit of distortion, like looking through a window with a bit of glare on it, but not bad. He saw symbology floating across his vision, popping up here and there, like a stock market ticker that appeared and reappeared almost randomly. He brought his hands up to his face . . .

. . . and saw the biggest, meanest clawlike fingers he had ever seen. *It was the robot's fingers, not his*! He flexed his fingers and saw the robot's fingers flex the same way . . . but they were *his* fingers he was moving, not the robot's . . . but the robot's fingers were moving, he was *watching* them move . . . !

'How do you feel, Doug?' Ari asked, stepping in front of his field of view. 'Be careful touching your visor or sensors with your fingers or trying to rub your eyes – your fingers will go right through those sensors.'

'What's happening?' he asked. 'I mean, I feel okay, but I feel weird. Am I still in the robot? I remember I was panicking a little, and I wanted to get out.'

'Un . . . believable,' he heard Kelsey DeLaine gasp. She stepped in front of him, a look of absolute wonderment on her face. It reminded Moore of how passersby looked at auto accidents or criminals getting arrested. 'How do you feel, Sergeant?'

'I feel just fine, ma'am,' Moore said. She reached out a hand to him, and he reached out . . . except it was the robot's massive hand that touched hers. He dared not close his fingers over hers. 'I . . . I can feel you, Miss

DeLaine. It feels like I'm touching you . . . but I'm not, am I? It's the robot touching you, isn't it?'

'It certainly is, Sergeant,' Kelsey murmured. She backed away. 'Try moving around a little.' He raised his arms over his head and did a deep-knee bend, and he saw the FBI special agent's eyes grow wide in absolute amazement. 'You . . . you look like . . . like *you*, like a real person moving, but it's this huge robot moving around!'

'I feel perfectly normal, ma'am,' Moore said. He stood up quickly. There was a very slight but noticeable pause in his body reaction from when he thought about moving and when he actually moved, but he was completely free and unhindered. 'I feel a little slow, like I've had a couple beers and I'm just starting to get a buzz, but I feel perfectly normal otherwise.'

'Good to hear it, Sergeant,' Jason Richter said. 'The fabric inside the CIDs is actually an electroconductive material attached to thousands of fiber-optic sensors over your entire body. They collect muscle and skeletal movement, combine the inputs into a computer, analyze them a few hundred thousand times per second, and translate the data into microhydraulic motion commands in the exoskeleton.'

Moore looked around and saw the second CID unit also experimentally moving around, looking at its hands and feet in surprise – and yes, Doug could tell that the robot was 'surprised' by its body language. He stepped forward . . . and suddenly his left foot banged against his right leg, and he tripped and stumbled forward. Kelsey DeLaine scrambled out of the way in sheer terror. 'Are you okay, Sergeant?' she asked.

'I feel like I don't know where my feet are,' he responded.

'The computer will put in a kinesthetic compensation between how much your limbs move and how much they *need* to move,' Ari said. 'You have to move around a little more so the computer can make the corrections.'

Moore stepped around carefully, flexing his arms and taking bigger and bigger steps. 'I think it's working,' he said, but at that moment a foot hit his leg again. 'I still feel pretty clumsy in this thing.'

'Don't pretend you're the Tin Man from the *Wizard of Oz* or a robot from one of those old-fashioned sci-fi movies,' Ari said. 'The key is to walk like a human being and let the system correct your movements. Don't fight it – eventually you two will start working together instead of against one another.'

Moore didn't – couldn't – move. It was as if he could feel every little hydraulic actuator moving, exactly opposite his own movements. It was decidedly uncomfortable, like swimming against a riptide, realizing you were being carried out to sea. 'I think I'm done with the demo,' he said nervously. 'This is not for me.'

Ari stepped toward Moore so only he could hear. 'The secret, Doug, is not to think in terms of a normal human body,' she said. 'We've matched it so well that you might think you're simply *you* – maybe even a step or two slower. That's not the case. CID has capabilities that far exceed a normal human being. You may not feel you do because we've designed it to make carrying around a robot on your back virtually effortless. But you're not human anymore – you're a CID, a Cybernetic Infantry Device. You're not Doug Moore – you're Superman. Remember that.' Heartened, Moore started to pace around the hangar a bit, eventually working up to short, gentle hops and even a quick set of jumping jacks.

'The exercise is simple, gents,' Jason said. 'This is a race.'
He pointed to the far end of the parking area in front of
the hangars, about a hundred and fifty meters away. 'You
will both start over there. First person to make it to the
northwest access gate on the other side of the range area
wins. It's less than two kilometers, on the other side of
the hangars, across the road, past the service buildings and
the shooting range – shouldn't take too long. Let's do it.'

Moore thought this was all a little silly, but he followed
Bolton across the parking lot. There was an expanse of
sandy earth on either side of the access ramp, followed
by the parking ramp and hangar complex. There was a
gap behind the hangar to the left and a much larger
vacant area to the right – there was plenty of room to
run. Beyond the hangars was the main street, followed
by more buildings spaced fairly widely apart. Moore knew
this area well and would have preferred the left side
because it was a shorter distance to the northwest access
gate, but he'd be fine going to the right. Besides, this was
stupid. So what if he lost this race? He wouldn't be . . .

'Go!' Richter shouted.

Bolton took off like a sprinter, and Moore couldn't
believe how fast he was moving – in a flash he was at
the parking ramp, effortlessly racing around the perpendicular hangar. He seemed to get the hang of the cyborg
just fine. For some reason, Moore was afraid to run for
fear of banging or tripping on his robotic legs.

'Remember what I told you, Doug!' Ari shouted. 'Go!
Catch him!'

Moore started to jog after Bolton, who was already
starting to disappear around the south hangar – but
instead, he stopped, looked around, then actually took
several large steps backward toward the taxiway.

'What's he doing?' Falcone asked.

'He's gonna try being Superman,' Ari said. He did. Moore turned, ran toward the parking apron in front of the hangars – and then leaped into the air. To their surprise, he bounded all the way to the top of the hangar!

'Holy shit!' Kelsey exclaimed. 'I don't believe it!' Jason gave Ari an exasperated smile and shake of his head – he knew she encouraged him to do that, and it worked.

They could hear the loud 'WHUUMP!' as Moore hit the hangar roof, but thankfully he didn't come through it. He took two steps and leaped off the other end, clearing the street outside and almost landing atop the Tumbleweed Dining Facility. Moore caught a glimpse of Bolton, just fifteen meters ahead of him. He was running toward the entry gate to the shooting range about fifty meters to his left. This time, Moore didn't hesitate – he ran right for the four-meter-high wooden fence surrounding the outdoor shooting range, crashing through it with ease, and just kept on running. Seconds later, just as Bolton made it through the access gate, Moore was crashing through the fence on the other side of the range, and he made it to the finish line well ahead of the FBI special agent.

'*Waa-hoo*!' Falcone shouted, as he ran through the decimated wooden fence. '*Did you freakin' see that?* He didn't even slow down! And I can't believe he leaped on top of that hangar *in one jump*. That has to be ten meters high!'

'We're going to have to repair those fences, sir,' was all Jennifer McCracken could say. Richter looked at Jefferson, who wore a stony expression – he imagined he could see a slight nod of approval, but couldn't be sure.

'I suppose you're going to say,' Kelsey DeLaine said as she joined Jason a few moments later, 'that you intend that the way Sergeant Moore performed was the way you intend the CID units to act in the field, right, Major?'

'That's exactly right, Kelsey,' Jason said. 'These two guys just covered two kilometers through varied quasi-urban and open terrain in less than a minute. They're better than Humvees, Kelsey – they can go over an obstacle as well as through or around it. And they can do the same with a three-hundred-kilo weapon pack on.'

Ari ran over to Doug Moore, yelling and jumping in celebration. 'Great job, Doug!' she shouted happily. 'Man, you were *awesome*!' She showed him how to dismount from the machine, helped him climb out, and gave him a big hug when he was back on the ground. 'How do you feel, tiger?' she asked. He smiled, nodded . . . then turned away from her and promptly vomited on the ground. 'That happens to everyone the first time in CID, Doug,' she said. 'It's like astronauts trying to walk after being in space – it feels too weird.' She gave the orders for the machine to stow itself, then put an arm around Moore's waist and helped him back to the hangar, while Jefferson had a couple of soldiers carry CID Two back to the hangar.

Bolton took his machine back to the hangar, exited it with help from Richter, and folded it. 'How did it feel, Carl?' Kelsey asked as Jason and Ari stowed it back in the Humvee.

'It's fine – if you want to go crashing through walls all the time,' Bolton replied. He shook his head. 'It works amazingly well, but it's not suited to our needs, Kelsey.' Sergeant Major Jefferson walked over to them to listen in. 'I think you know what I'm talking about, Sergeant

Major,' Bolton went on, immediately including the army veteran in his review. 'In some situations, it would be great having something like that leading the way. But if Chamberlain or Richter thinks we can form an entire unit of those things, he's sadly mistaken.'

Jason and Ari heard their interchange and quickly went to join them after attaching the folded CID unit to its power and diagnostic umbilical in the Humvee. 'It seems pretty effective to me, Carl,' Kelsey said. 'Sergeant Major? Your thoughts?'

'It's a bull in a china shop, ma'am,' Jefferson said flatly, giving Richter a suspicious glance. 'I've been training Army Ranger and other Special Forces units for a decade and a half. There's a *reason* why they don't use stuff like this: it's too cumbersome, too expensive, too unresponsive, and too difficult to support and maintain. Special-ops teams require maximum stealth, mobility, adaptability, and minimum support, hassle, and complexity. CID is everything special ops is not. As Agent Bolton said, it certainly is impressive; as a support device, it might be useful.'

'*Useful*?' Jason exclaimed. He shook his head, smiling in frustration. 'CID is a revolutionary technology that makes its wearer powerful, nearly invincible, and as effective as a light armored or missile squad, and the best thing you can say about it is that it's *useful*? C'mon, Sergeant Major, give me a break.'

'With all due respect, Major,' Jefferson shot back, 'I was assigned to this task force by the White House and Pentagon to build a military team designed to travel around the country and around the *world* pursuing terrorists, not to test and evaluate new technology. We've already wasted half a morning playing with these toys . . .'

'*Toys . . . ?*'

'. . . and I agree with Special Agents DeLaine and Bolton that we can be using our time more effectively if we concentrate on building a more conventional special-ops force, composed of highly skilled operators from both the FBI and military. Obviously the President's National Security Adviser is enamored of your devices there, sir, but I don't really think he expected us to build an entire unit around CID.'

'Then why did he place me in command of Task Force TALON?' Jason asked.

'He placed *us* in command, Major,' Kelsey said, making a point of using Richter's rank similarly to Jefferson to make it obvious she was siding with the sergeant major. 'Look, we're supposed to get this unit up and running in a week and a half. Now we could spend the next three months studying how to use CID and another three months designing a training program for the field, or Sergeant Major Jefferson and I can work together with you to develop a standard special ops-capable unit and then as we go we can find ways to merge CID into our activities. It'll just take too long if we try to do it the other way around.'

Jason looked over at Ari, who was still sitting with Moore as he tried to recover from his experience. She shrugged and turned her attention back to the Air Force sergeant. This was definitely turning into an 'us-versus-them' scenario, Jason thought. He felt like arguing some more in an almost desperate attempt to try to make them realize what kind of power and capability he was placing in their hands – but it didn't seem like it was going to work.

Richter shrugged. 'Okay, guys,' he said. 'We don't have

any experience organizing or leading special-ops or intelligence units; we're just lowly engineers. I'll do whatever I need to do to help the team.'

'Hey, Jason, let's not have that "lowly" stuff – everybody's valuable on this team,' Kelsey said. Frankly, she didn't really expect too much static from the eggheads, although she was ready to jump down Jason's throat and shut him up quick if he did any more whining. She was surprised at the incredible capabilities of the CID units, but Jefferson was right – it would simply take too long to try to integrate those machines into an effective special-ops unit. They had work to do, and Richter was just not up to the task of organizing and training a light-quick-reaction fighting force. 'If we start thinking like a team, we'll start fighting like one. Right, Sergeant Major?'

'Absolutely, ma'am,' Jefferson responded smartly.

'Agreed, Jason?'

'Sure,' Jason said. 'What should we do first?'

'Let's put away the robots and grab some coffee,' Kelsey said. 'Everybody, take ten and then meet at the conference room.' She grabbed Bolton's and Jefferson's arms and took them with her on the way back to the conference room.

'Looks like the Fee-Bee has taken charge here, Jason,' Ari observed.

The meeting was already underway by the time Jason and Ari arrived at the conference room. 'Lieutenant McCracken,' Kelsey was asking, 'I assume you have some basic Table of Organization and Equipment documents we can use to get us started?'

'Of course, ma'am,' McCracken responded.

'Explain how it's organized if you would.'

'Yes, ma'am,' McCracken responded. 'The basic organization of every Marine unit, from the smallest platoon to the largest division, is the same: a command element, a support element, and one or more operations elements. A platoon is usually composed of a command element, a support element, two machine gun or mortar squads, and two security squads. Each squad is composed of four to eight Marines; the command and support elements have roughly the same number, depending on the mission, making each platoon number between twenty-four and forty-eight Marines.'

'Very good,' Kelsey said. 'That's about the same setup for an FBI field unit, so we're already on the same page. I move that we adopt that Marine infantry platoon TO&E for our first Task Force TALON field unit, have the sergeant major get the men and equipment out here ASAP, and start training right away. We can tweak it as we get more intelligence information about our target; I can see that we would need some specialized nuclear-chemical-biological weapon detection, decontamination, and neutralization equipment, for example. Any thoughts?'

'Just one – we don't need any of that stuff,' Jason said. 'Two full-up CID units on one, preferably two, Humvee platforms are all we need. In about a month I can have all our weapons packs out here and have two CIDs trained and ready to go. Give me a C-130 and I can deploy anywhere in the western hemisphere in two days.'

'We've been through this already, Major,' Kelsey said, the exasperation evident in her voice. 'We're very impressed by CID, but we'd be wasting too much time learning how to use it and *then* learning how to employ it in the field. We've got the basic setup already drawn up and ready to go – no sense in reinventing the wheel here.'

'If it's so logical, why do you think Sergeant Major Jefferson or Chamberlain didn't already have a platoon out here waiting for us?'

'That's argumentative, Major, and not very constructive,' Kelsey said pointedly. 'Any other objections?'

'What are Ari and I supposed to do while you guys are out playing army?'

'Major Richter, I expected a lot more cooperation and contribution and a lot less attitude from you,' Kelsey said. 'National Security Adviser Chamberlain invited you here because he was obviously impressed by CID and thought it could make a contribution. I think it's up to you to find out how best to utilize your technology. But we've decided that a basic infantry platoon is the best organizational unit to start with. Once the task force is set up and running, we'll be looking to you to let us know how we can integrate CID with it, most likely in a support role. In the meantime, I think you could be extremely helpful in setting up and organizing the command and support elements.'

That was a not-too-subtle blow-off, Jason decided, but he wasn't going to protest – besides, it was the answer he was hoping for. He nodded, and he and Ari took their seats and remained mostly quiet for the rest of the meeting.

Jason soon had to grudgingly admit that Kelsey DeLaine was a good organizer and an effective leader, well tuned to her audience and not afraid to challenge others for their opinion, commitment, or compliance. She didn't tolerate any sidetracks. By the time the meeting was over in less than an hour everyone, including him, had a full list of things to do and a very tight and strict timeline in which to get them done.

'You run a pretty tight ship, Special Agent DeLaine,' Jason said after everyone else except Ari and Bolton had left the room.

'Thanks. Ten years in the Bureau, most of it in organizing operations, surveillance missions, and joint task forces such as this will do it.' She stopped shuffling the notes before her and looked at Richter. 'I feel we got off on the wrong foot, Jason. I know you're proud of CID – justifiably so . . .'

'I sure am.'

'But I'm concerned about meeting Sergeant Major Jefferson's and National Security Adviser Chamberlain's deadlines for organizing a fully mission-ready unit,' Kelsey went on. 'I'm sure CID is incredibly effective and useful, but I don't know anything about it, or you, or the technology behind it. If it doesn't work, or we can't build a fighting unit around it, we'd have to start all over, and by then another American city could get attacked. I just don't want to take the chance.'

'I hear what you're saying, Kelsey,' Jason said. 'But Ari and I *do* know how to use CID, and we're here. We're ready to teach all of you, even Sergeant Major Jefferson, how to use it. You just have to trust us.'

'Not that argument again, Richter,' Bolton moaned. 'It's time to get off that old song.'

Kelsey held up a hand to Bolton. 'I think you know where we're coming from, Jason,' Kelsey said. 'CID is your pride and joy, and you want to see it in action. The sergeant major and I have experience with setting up small-unit special-ops task forces. That's our background and training. When under the gun like this, we simply fall back on our experience and training. We're not trying to exclude you – in fact, after a while, we might have nothing but a platoon full of CID units in this . . .'

'That's what I've been trying to tell you, Kelsey – with CID, you don't *need* a whole platoon of soldiers to do the job,' Jason interjected. 'Don't you get it? Chamberlain chose us because he saw the potential for a rapid-reaction force that can swing into action *now*, not a month or two from now until we get thirty guys out here, trained, and equipped for what we want to do. I think he chose CID because we're ready *now*.'

'Jason . . .'

'If you want to organize a platoon in the traditional sense, fine – the command and support elements make total sense,' Jason went on. 'But you don't need sixteen Marines to form the operational elements, because I guarantee that two CIDs have the same fighting power and self-defense capabilities of four Marine mortar or rifle squads. Plus, we're *here*, ready to go.'

Kelsey looked at Jason for a long moment, thinking hard. 'I don't know . . .'

'Both of you, stop right now,' Sergeant Major Jefferson interjected. He regarded Kelsey for a few moments, making it clear that he didn't believe her. 'Special Agent DeLaine: Why, may I ask, are you not going to utilize Major Richter's weapon systems?'

'I'm just not familiar enough with them, and I feel we don't have the time to fully integrate that technology into the task force's mission,' Kelsey responded. She glanced at Jason, then added, 'I just don't trust him yet, that's all. We should prepare a TO&E for a standard infantry platoon, configured and customized for joint military–FBI tactics, rapid deployment, and special-operations missions. We feel we can be on time and fully mission-ready within the allotted time frame.'

'Major?' Jefferson asked, without turning his eyes away from Kelsey. 'You agree?'

'No, Sergeant Major, I don't,' Jason replied. 'But I'm willing to defer to Special Agent DeLaine's and your experience and cooperate with your plan. I'll be sure to make suggestions at every relevant point on how CID can enhance and improve the task force's effectiveness.'

Jefferson turned and faced Richter, and he looked none too pleased. 'Well, suddenly you two seem to be all sweetness and light together,' he said acidly. 'It had better stay this way, or I will shit-can both of you and see to it that you are both assigned to an office in the farthest reaches of Greenland or northern Uzbekistan, where you can threaten and cajole each other twenty-four-seven until I can successfully get you drummed out of your respective services. Do I make myself clear?'

'Yes, Sergeant Major,' they both responded.

'Hoo fucking-rah,' Jefferson said in a low, menacing voice. 'I am going to meet with the base commanding general, and I'm going to brief him on our activities here and then do nine holes of golf. Being a good subordinate army NCO, I will lose to him by two strokes, which I hate doing, so I will be in no mood for any bullshit. By the time I return, I want the TO&E transmitted to my laptop for my review and approval. And it had better be complete, or I will come back out here and shove that aforementioned laptop down both your throats piece by piece. Have I made myself understood?'

'Perfectly, Sergeant Major.'

Jefferson then turned to DeLaine and said, 'The President's National Security Adviser did not assign Richter,

Vega, and their equipment here just to watch you do your own thing. If you don't know how CID works, then I strongly suggest you take the time to learn. I'm not telling you how to run your task force, but when we give you tools we expect you to use them unless you decide they're no good. Can you do that, Special Agent DeLaine?'

Kelsey hesitated just long enough for Jefferson's eyes to widen in anger before replying, 'Of course, Sergeant Major.'

'Do you have anything else you wish to tell me, DeLaine?' he asked suspiciously. 'Speak now, because if I leave this room and you two still have a problem that needs to be addressed, and you don't inform me of it, I will hold you personally responsible for the outcome. Do you have *anything* to say to me, Special Agent DeLaine?'

She took another glance at Jason, returned her gaze to Jefferson, and said, 'We'll take care of it, Sergeant Major.'

Jefferson nodded, his expression still angry but willing to let them try to work it out together. 'I'm holding you to it, DeLaine,' he said. 'Major Richter, do you have anything to add?'

'No, Sergeant Major.'

'Now stop your squabbling and get to work,' Jefferson said. No one dared move or even blink until the Army Ranger departed.

'Well, that was enjoyable,' Jason deadpanned. He turned to Sergeant Moore. 'You did good today in CID Two, Doug. Still want to train with us in the CID?'

'Yes, *sir*!' Moore said enthusiastically.

'You're a stand-up guy, Doug – and besides, you fit perfectly into CID Two. Meet up with Ari in the Humvee; she'll run your orientation program.'

'*After* we go out to the range to learn how to shoot,' Ari added.

'You still want to learn how to shoot, Dr Vega?' Moore asked, surprised. 'I thought all that was just to get my mind off climbing into CID Two.'

'As long as we're all being honest here: yes, it was to take your mind off CID,' Ari admitted. 'But I really want to learn how to shoot – all the other army guys I know are too busy or too married to take me out to the range. As long as you stop calling me "Dr Vega" and "ma'am," we're still on. Start me off small and light, then work up to the bigger stuff – I want to learn to shoot every weapon we might have in the field, even the really big cannons. Okay?'

'Yes, ma'a – I mean, okay, Ari,' Moore said excitedly. He looked like a kid again as he excused himself and headed off to get ready.

'Looks like you made his day . . . again,' Jason observed. 'That kid has a lot of strength. You helped bring it out. He's going to turn into a real asset.'

'You got it, J,' Ari said. They walked together to the first Humvee. Ari showed Moore how to check the CID unit's self-test and self-repair functions by simply examining rows of green lights. 'CID One is in good shape, J,' she announced.

Jason nodded, lost in thought; then: 'I think I'll take it for a spin,' he announced.

Ariadna shook her head with a smile. Jason spent a lot of free time with the CID units. She always thought it was a little creepy, like he was getting addicted to wearing the robot, or he was losing touch with humanity – maybe even reality. 'You need a hobby, J,' she said to him privately after Jason and Doug Moore carried the

CID unit out of the Humvee and Moore moved out of earshot.

'I've got all I can handle right here.'

'That Special Agent DeLaine is kinda cute, don't you think?'

'You going to ask her out?'

'*Ojete*!' Ari exclaimed. 'No, jerk, I mean you.'

'So that's what you mean by "hobby"? You mean, I need a woman.'

'You catch on quick for a Ph.D.,' Ari said. 'You do find her cute, don't you?'

Jason shrugged. 'She's okay. But she's not my type. We're too different. And don't give me that "opposites attract" bullshit either.'

'Hey, I don't believe in "opposites attract" either, boss,' Ari said. 'That's why I think you two make a cute couple. You're exactly alike.'

'Bull.'

'You're both stubborn, you're both pros, and you're both married to your jobs,' she added. 'You each need to find somebody to share your lives with.'

'You know, I always thought you and me would make a cute couple. What do you say?'

'What? You mean, you and me, *dating? Sleeping together?* No offense, J, but that would be like frenching my grandfather.'

'*Grandfather* . . . !'

'You're a nice guy, J . . .'

'Uh oh – the kiss of death sentence: "You're a nice guy . . ." '

'You are, when you're not being an asshole, like now,' Ari said. 'But you and I are like brother and sister. Now if we were stuck on some deserted island for, like, a year . . .'

'A *year*!'

'. . . and I started climbing the trees going crazy and all, then *maybe* I'd give you a try. But otherwise . . . c'mon, J, I can't even think about it. Let's change the freakin' subject before I start having nightmares.'

Jason nodded toward the young Air Force tech sergeant. 'What about you and Sergeant Moore?'

Ariadna smiled despite herself and shrugged. 'He's kinda cute, and innocent, and like you said I saw some strength in him this morning. You never know . . .'

'Why do I get the sudden image of a shark circling around a young sea otter pup?'

'Screw you, Doc,' Ari said with a smile and a laugh. 'Get in and shut up, all right?'

Jason unfolded the CID unit and climbed in. After he exercised the cybernetic unit for a few minutes, Jason backed into the side of the Humvee and then stepped away moments later with the forty-millimeter grenade launcher weapon pack attached to the CID's back. 'This is the grenade launcher pack,' he explained to Moore. 'The pack contains thirty-two rounds, normally eight rounds each of high-explosive, infrared marker flare, tear gas, and flechette grenades, depending on the mission; we've only got smoke rounds in there now for training. The firing system interfaces with CID's laser targeting system, and rounds are selected by either voice commands or an eye-pointing menu system in the electronic visor. The barrel can swivel one hundred and eighty degrees so you don't need to be facing the target to attack it.'

'If you're going to fire grenades out there, sir,' Moore said, 'I'll call in for range clearance. Go out to the Charlie Range controller's pad and give me a call. After that, you can go and do anything you want.'

'Want us to follow you out to the range?' Ari asked. 'We can fire up the radar, maybe test out the datalinks?'

'Maybe later,' Jason said. 'I just want to run around a bit, pop off a few grenades, clear my head.'

'Nerd,' Ari said to the man in the fearsome-looking robot before her. The robot pointed to its crotch area, then turned and ran off.

The main part of Cannon Air Force Base was typical of most American air bases, about four thousand acres in size, but Cannon was fortunate in that it had a large tract of vacant land to the west called Pecos East, or R-5104 on aviation charts, about eighty-five thousand acres total, in which Task Force TALON was located. The airspace above Pecos East was restricted from the surface to eighteen thousand feet above ground level. The Air Force performed a wide variety of training exercises on these ranges, including bombing, aerial gunnery, close-air support training, ground-based air defense deployment simulations, and joint forces operations. A number of targets had been set up throughout the range by the Air Force. Some were nothing more than large bull's-eyes painted on canvas and supported by poles, but others were very realistic models of buildings, armored vehicles, mobile missile launchers, cave entrances, and even oil refineries.

It took about ten minutes for Jason to run the eight kilometers out to the range controller's station for R-5104 Charlie, which was nothing more than a large concrete parking area, large enough to park two helicopters plus a number of trucks, painted Day-Glo orange and with a large black 'X' on it so fighter jocks wouldn't mistake it for a target. After checking in with Moore and getting thirty minutes' time in the range, Jason started exploring the range area by jogging around – except in his case, he was casually 'jogging' at almost forty kilometers per hour.

Okay: DeLaine was cute, for an FBI agent, he thought as he sped around the range, jumping over targets and the occasional coyote. And maybe he and Kelsey were more alike than he cared to admit. But the problem with old, established, bureaucratic institutions like the U.S. Army and the Federal Bureau of Investigation was they were slow to adopt new ideas and concepts. The 'gray-beards,' as Jason called them, liked everything neat, tidy, and under control.

How was he going to get any information on the terrorists if DeLaine was going to dig in her heels like this?

He had been jogging around the range, 'attacking' targets he found with his smoke grenades and testing his jumping and vertical leaping abilities, for almost twenty minutes when he heard, 'Jefferson to Richter,' on CID's secure communications system.

'Go ahead, Sergeant Major.'

'Say location.'

He quickly checked his satellite navigation system, then responded: 'Charlie Range, four hundred and seventy-five meters southeast of the range controller's pad.'

'Roger that. Hold your position.'

He landed from his last jump and froze. 'Okay. What's going on?'

'Just hold position, sir.'

A few minutes later, Jason noticed a small helicopter appearing on the horizon to the east. He switched to a higher magnification and saw that it was a sand-colored Marines Corps AH-1W Cobra gunship helicopter. 'Is that you in the Cobra, Sergeant Major?' Jason asked.

'Affirmative.'

'Shall I meet you at the range controller's pad?'

'Negative. Hold your position.'

'Roger.' Okay, Jefferson, what are you up to? he thought.

'Okay, Major, let's see what you can do,' Jefferson radioed a few moments later.

'Okay, Sergeant Major,' Jason responded. 'What am I supposed to . . . ?' But he was interrupted . . . because seconds later a 'LASER' warning came over CID's threat warning system, telling him that he was being illuminated by a targeting laser. Then, moments later, just as Jason was about to ask Jefferson if he had hit him with the laser, the Cobra gunship opened fire from about two kilometers away. Jason saw the puffs of smoke coming from the nose Gatling gun and felt the pounding of shells on the hard earth beneath his feet milliseconds later, and he leaped away just as the shells walked their way to the exact spot in which he had been standing just a fraction of a second earlier.

'Good move, Major,' Jefferson radioed. 'Our ammunition is just plastic frangible shells and shouldn't hurt you, but let's pretend they're armor-piercing shells – three hits and you're out. There are three large "enemy vehicles" marked with green Xs in Charlie Range. Find them and destroy them without getting hit by more than three shells. Let's go.'

This is *fun*, Jason exclaimed to himself. He started running in the same direction as the Cobra helicopter and behind it. The desert floor was hard-baked with a lot of mesquite, snakeweed, and mesa dropweed, and he had no trouble racing through, around, or over it. As the Cobra gunship turned, he turned with it, keeping easily

on its tail and away from its guns. Once the Cobra tried
a steep sliding turn to reverse course, but Jason simply
ran underneath it at speeds exceeding thirty miles an
hour.

When the Cobra tried a hard turn to quickly spin
around to bring its guns down on Jason, he fired two of
the smoke grenades at the chopper. *'Hey, what the hell was
that?'* Jefferson shouted as the rounds whistled uncomfortably close.

'You didn't say anything about me not firing back,
Sergeant Major.'

'You wanna play rough, Major? I'm your Ranger,'
Jefferson said. He stood on the gunship's antitorque
pedals and accomplished a simultaneous spinning-
twisting-diving turn and raked the ground with machine
gun fire at where he anticipated Jason would be, and
very nearly got him. But as skillfully as Jefferson made
the Cobra dance, Jason made the CID robot move faster.
At one point, Jason found the second 'enemy' vehicle,
an old World War Two-vintage American M61 tank. He
fired a smoke grenade to mark its location, jumped on
top of it, and leaped into the air – very narrowly missing
punching the Cobra helicopter at his apogee.

The demonstration was over in less than ten minutes.
He had found all three vehicles with no problem whatsoever, and the Cobra gunship's bullets only came close. A
few minutes later, Jefferson landed the gunship on the
range controller's pad. Jason dismounted from CID and was
introduced to the commanding general of Cannon Air Force
Base, who had been seated in the gunner's seat. Jason
fielded a few questions from the general, and then Jefferson
excused himself so he could talk with Jason privately.

'Very impressive, Major,' Jefferson said after the Air

Force general was back over by the chopper. 'I think perhaps Special Agent DeLaine might be a little premature in her opinion of CID.'

'I agree, Sergeant Major,' Jason responded enthusiastically. 'Why don't you go back to base and tell that to DeLaine and Bolton so they'll get off my case?'

Jefferson's eyes turned from light blue to thundercloud dark blue in an instant, and he stepped closer to Richter so he was almost nose-to-nose with him. 'I was ordered to get this task force ready for battle,' he growled, impaling Jason with an angry stare, 'and if you think I'm going to let anything or anyone interfere with that, you are sadly mistaken. The safety and security of the United States is in peril, and I will not let some childish spat between two wet-behind-the-ears jerk-offs threaten my country or my government. I will *crush* you under my boots first *before* I turn you over to a court-martial.' He fell silent, scanning Jason's eyes carefully for several long moments; then: 'I think you've spent too much time in the lab, Major. You think you're in control because in your little world of computer programs, simulations, and mathematical equations, you might be. Out here, you're being nothing but an irritant.' Richter said nothing in response.

The big Ranger looked Richter up and down again, then sneered at him. 'Look at you: Major What-Me-Worry. You're a lab rat, Richter, nothing but a transistor head.' Still, Jason had nothing to say. 'Why don't you tell me what you're really thinking, Richter? You've got to give a shit about something; everything around you now can't be neat and tidy and orderly like it is in your laboratory or on your design computers. What does your finely tuned brain *really* want to tell me?' No reply.

Jefferson sneered again. 'C'mon, you're a big tough army officer.' He glanced over at the CID unit. 'Or are you? Maybe you're not shit unless you're humping that big hunk of metal there. Go on. Speak freely. Now's your chance.'

Richter looked as if he might say something, but after a few moments he simply caged his eyes. 'I have nothing else to say, Sergeant Major,' he said finally.

Jefferson backed away and nodded, eyeing Richter suspiciously. 'Very well, Major,' he said. 'You're on the hook for this now. Mess it up, and your military career is over.' He nodded to the CID unit. 'Good job with your robot, Major. If DeLaine still decides not to use it, I think it would be a big mistake. But as long as you two are working together, whatever you decide is how we'll play it.'

'Okay, Sergeant Major.'

'But if either one of you are stonewalling or holding back, and I find out about it, there will be hell to pay,' Jefferson warned. 'Those are *my* feelings. That'll be all. Carry on.'

'Yes, Sergeant Major,' Jason responded. Jefferson saluted, waited until his salute was returned, and strode to the Cobra gunship, and he was off minutes later.

'Are we ever going to catch a break, Troy?' Jason asked the robot as he gave the order to prepare for uploading. He climbed in and activated the unit. Power was down to about fifty percent, plenty to make it back to the task force area at full speed.

Chapter Four

Cannon Air Force Base, New Mexico
That evening

That night, Jason and Ariadna had dinner in a mesquite barbecue restaurant at the Clovis Municipal Airport's general aviation terminal. Because the nation's airspace was still shut down, business at the airport was terrible – but the food there was outstanding. As they feasted on spicy ribs, enchiladas, and barbecue beef sandwiches, Jason nodded at Ari. 'You look different somehow,' he said.

'Oh?'

He looked closer. 'Is that an olive drab T-shirt you're wearing under your blouse?' he asked.

'So what?'

'Where'd you get a . . . oh, I see. Doug gave you his T-shirt too?'

'We fired over three hundred rounds today. Doug said I shouldn't wear nice stuff because of the oil and powder residue that comes off the weapons. He gave me a couple of his T-shirts. We're going to practice tomorrow too.'

'What piece of *your* underwear did you trade for the T-shirt?'

'You're a degenerate.'

'What kind of gun are you practicing with?'

'Forty-five-caliber SIG Sauer P220, the best semiauto in the world,' Ari said. 'He showed me how to clean it, hold it, shoot it, even holster it.' She opened her blouse and withdrew the SIG from a shoulder holster, pointing it toward the wall. 'Beauty, isn't it?'

Jason's eyes bugged out in surprise as if she had shown him a nuclear fuel rod. 'Christ, Ari! You had it on you this whole time? Isn't that illegal?'

'In New Mexico it's legal to carry a concealed weapon without a permit as long as it's unloaded,' Ari said. 'Here.' She opened the action with a loud *cha-chink*! which garnered no reaction whatsoever from the diners around them, as if everyone expected to see handguns at restaurant tables all the time. She inspected the chamber. 'It's unloaded, but always check it yourself.' She handed it to Jason, who looked at the empty chamber. 'No, J, *never* put your finger on the trigger!' she snapped as he wrapped his hand around the butt end.

'But you said it was unloaded, and I looked myself and *saw* it was unloaded!'

'Doug says *always* treat a gun like it's loaded,' Ari said sternly. She pushed the gun's muzzle away from her as he started to turn it toward her. 'And never, *ever* point a gun at anyone.'

'But it's *empty*, for Christ's sake. There's not even a clip in it!'

'Doesn't matter – and it's a "magazine," not a "clip." A clip is a device that holds a number of rounds; a magazine is a box that feeds rounds into a chamber.'

'It's the same thing.'

'Sure – like EDO and FPM memory chips are the same thing.'

'No – those are *totally* different.'

'You are such a nerd, Major,' Ari admonished him playfully. 'We spent more time on gun safety today than anything else, and I learned so much.'

'Oh yeah? What else did *Doug* say?' Jason asked, emphasizing the sergeant's name like a grade-schooler does to a friend on Valentine's Day.

'Grow up, J. Doug says pretend there is a laser beam emanating from the muzzle at all times, and if it hits anyone they will die. If you can't point it in a safe direction, point it at yourself. You *always* treat a gun like it's cocked, locked, and ready to rock unless you personally verify it otherwise.'

' "Cocked, locked, and ready to rock" – what in hell does that mean?'

'Jesus, J, I thought you were in the army! Which army might that be – Captain Kangaroo's army? Didn't you ever learn how to handle a gun?'

'Seven years ago at OCS, a nine-millimeter Beretta, for one week.'

'You're pitiful.'

'Why are you carrying it around?'

'Doug said I should get used to carrying it,' Ari said. 'I'm going to get my concealed carry permit for New Mexico. I spoke with Kelsey and asked her to help me get a federal carry permit, but after this afternoon I don't think she'll give me the time of day. I might have to go to Jefferson.'

'What do you want to carry a gun for?'

'Wake up, J,' Ari said. 'The terrorist threat is the highest it's been since 9/11, and we're right in the thick of it. I'm surprised you aren't carrying a weapon. You're active-duty military – Chamberlain can probably get you authorization in a snap.'

'I'm here to employ CID, not shoot it out with bad guys with pistols,' Jason said. 'I think I impressed Jefferson out there in the range today. He asked me again about the argument between me and DeLaine.'

'You both clammed up when he asked you together – makes sense that he'd want to ask you individually too.'

'Yeah, but what was most interesting: I don't think Jefferson told Chamberlain anything except us having a disagreement about something other than CID.'

'So?'

'So it means that maybe Jefferson isn't spying for Chamberlain after all,' Jason said. 'If he was, and Jefferson then finds out we're tapping FBI servers and satellite datalinks, he'd have us kicked off this project so fast our heads would spin. Jefferson is a fossil, but one thing's for sure – he has a personal code of conduct, and he follows it to the letter, no matter who he's talking with. He may be Chamberlain's shill, but his loyalty is with the task force.'

'He probably figures you'll shoot yourself in the foot anyway – no need to rat you out,' Ari said.

'You're the one who'll shoot herself in the foot, once you start carrying bullets in that thing.'

'You pansy – guns are perfectly safe once you learn a few basics on gun safety and learn how it works,' Ari said, holstering the weapon. 'I've field-stripped this gun and put it back together three times today, and the third time the gun was under a towel – I did it by *feel*. It's one hundred percent safe even with a round in the chamber. Hundreds of police units and dozens of nations use this gun as their primary sidearm.'

'To tell the truth, Sergeant Moore seemed a little like a mama's boy the first time I met him.'

'He got this gun *from* his mother, as a birthday present.'

'Doug gave you the gun he got from his *mother*? Sounds like you two are engaged to be married already!'

'Bite me, J.'

A woman walked up to the table, notepad in hand. 'Anything else I can get for you guys?' she asked.

'Just the check, please,' Jason said, finishing off the last of his barbecue sandwich.

'Nothing else at all? A doggie bag, a refill on your sodas – or how about a damsel in distress that was rescued by a robot knight in shining armor?'

Jason's eyes bugged out in surprise, and his eyes snapped up at the waitress – only to find Kristen Skyy standing there, smiling at him, pretending to be a waitress with a reporter's steno book in her hands. She was wearing a faded leather bomber jacket, a gray scarf, faded blue jeans, snakeskin boots, and an Albuquerque Isotopes minor league baseball team cap, obviously dressed to look like one of the locals. 'Hi there, Major Jason Richter, Dr Ariadna Vega. Good to see you two again.'

Jason got to his feet and gave Kristen a hug, and she returned it with a kiss on his cheek very close to the corner of his mouth that sent a shiver of electricity through his entire body. He led her to his side of the booth as Ari moved over to let him sit beside her. 'This is quite a surprise,' Jason said after he and Kristen locked eyes for a few moments after they were all settled in – long enough that no one noticed Ariadna's amused grin as she watched the two unabashedly gazing at one another. 'What a coincidence. What in the world are you doing here?'

'Are you kidding me, J?' Ari interjected, rolling her eyes in mock disbelief at Richter's apparent naiveté. 'This is no coincidence. She tracked us down.'

Kristen looked into Jason's eyes, trying to figure out if Richter was baiting her or not; she decided not to test him. 'Yes, I did track you down,' she said with a smile. 'Hope you don't mind. I should have called, I guess, but when I got the information I decided to come right away.'

'How did you find us?'

'I have my sources,' Kristen said. 'But I assure you, it wasn't hard. My producers don't even really have to lie – they usually mention that they work for Kristen Skyy or SATCOM One News and that's enough. But most of the civilized world saw us together on television, and they might figure we're already an . . . item?'

'And you want to know more about CID?'

'Of course,' Kristen said. 'Your technology is simply amazing. It could revolutionize not just armed combat but policing high-crime neighborhoods, search and rescue, relief activities . . .'

'Sounds like the usual spiel from our public affairs office,' Ari said suspiciously. Kristen shrugged, admitting the fact. 'What's the real reason you're here?'

Kristen smiled at him and nodded, apparently deciding to tell him everything – she obviously figured Ariadna would challenge her on anything she thought might be spin. 'My sources say that the White House is planning on starting a secret terrorist-hunting unit, in response to the Kingman City attack,' Kristen said. 'They're preparing some sort of major antiterrorist policy statement, and they want this secret unit ready to go once the President makes the announcement.

'Now, if I was going to build a secret military anti-terrorist force, I'd start with CID. You're not at Fort Polk anymore; the Army Research Lab says you're on temporary duty but they won't say where, and not available for interviews. But while we're at Fort Polk's visitor's center waiting to talk to someone who can tell us more about you, one of my staff members observed two civilian tractor-trailer trucks, which looked like they were loading gear up from the building where your office is. The trucks are from a moving and storage company in Shreveport, and they headed north on Interstate 49 toward Shreveport – Barksdale Air Force Base, I'm guessing.

'I have a source who's an Air Force reservist, flies A-10 Warthogs out of Barksdale, and he tells me that each of the trucks had two twenty-foot steel army camo cargo containers that were loaded aboard an Air Force C-130 transport. He says that Base Ops said the C-130 was heading to Cannon Air Force Base but was not accepting space-available passengers. I head out to Cannon. I can't get onto the base and public affairs won't talk to me, but the locals tell me about the secret test ranges west of the base, almost as secret and well guarded as Area 51 in Nevada. They also say this place is a popular hangout for Air Force types. We've been watching it for a couple days now. Suddenly – poof, here you are.'

'You'd make a good intelligence officer – or spy,' Ari said. Jason looked at her but with a weird expression – not anger or exasperation, but with surprise at her comment.

'I'm a good investigative TV journalist, which most times is the same as being a spy,' Kristen said. 'Anyway, here we are. So, what can you tell me?'

'Not anything more than what you know right now,' Ari said. 'We're here. Sorry you came all this way just to learn that.'

'Are you involved in a secret government antiterrorist unit?'

'If we told you, it wouldn't be "secret" anymore, would it?'

'This conversation is strictly off the record,' Kristen said. 'It's deep background, nothing more.'

'Does anyone ever buy that line?' Ari asked. 'It doesn't mean a thing except what you reporters want it to mean.'

'What it means, Dr Vega, is that I would never use anything you told me in any article, not even if I "quoted unnamed sources," ' Kristen said. 'I would use your information as a stepping-off point to finding information from other sources. It lets me know if I'm getting warmer or colder, that's all.'

'And it's guaranteed never to get back to the source, huh?'

Both Jason and Ari could see Kristen Skyy finally putting up her professional's steel-curtain defensive shield. 'No, Ari, I can't guarantee anything,' she said stonily. 'But many times it protects a person who has something to say and badly wants to say it. Information is purposely leaked all the time in exactly this way. The press gets the story it wants, and the government or groups get the information they want disseminated without revealing the source – namely, themselves. Governments, businesses, organizations, and individuals take advantage of the constitutional and professional protection the press can provide. I have kings and terrorists alike agree to make deep background comments every day.'

'So you just broadcast any information you receive from unnamed sources?'

'Of course not,' Kristen retorted. 'We realize why the information is being leaked: it's propaganda, pure and simple. We always double- and triple-check information we receive with other sources. I've already received deep background information about a new government military antiterror unit being considered; you are one of the corroborating sources. I'll need another couple sources to verify *your* information, and on and on it goes. But I'll go to prison before I reveal my sources.'

Ariadna was obviously unconvinced, and she scowled a little at Jason when he didn't decline Kristen's request. What's the matter with you? Jason? she asked him silently. 'We'd better go, J,' she prompted him, none too subtly.

'Wait,' Jason said.

Ari couldn't believe it. 'We can't talk to her, J,' Ari said emphatically. 'We're already in hot water.'

'Oh?' Kristen asked Jason, her eyes dancing. 'Stirring up trouble, are we?'

'Hold on, Ari,' Jason said. He turned to Kristen, his expression earnest and troubled at the same time. 'Here's the deal, Kristen: we have information on a possible terror cell that might be responsible for Kingman City . . .'

'Jeez, J . . .' Ari breathed.

'. . . and we can't verify it – the various government agencies won't share intelligence with us,' Jason went on. 'We have the technology we need to move on this group right now, but we need verification of the group's existence, location, and strength.'

'And you want me to get it for you?' Kristen asked. 'You have any information to go on?'

'Yes.'

'But you can't do it yourself?'

'There appear to be . . . political roadblocks.' He spread his hands and added, 'And I obtained some of this information by surreptitious means.'

'You scientists and your five-dollar words,' Kristen said, smiling. 'You mean you stole some juicy information but you can't verify it and you certainly can't ask the people you stole it from to do it.' Jason smiled like the cat caught with the bird in its mouth. 'Fair enough. What's in it for me?'

'A piece of the action,' Jason said. 'Exclusive firsthand coverage of the first American high-tech joint civil-military antiterrorist assault force in action.'

'Jason!' Ari exclaimed. 'You can't *invite the media* along on a secret mission – especially when it's not authorized!'

'It'll be our mission,' Jason said. 'CID alone.'

'Sounds very tempting,' Kristen said.

'I'll bet it does!' Ari interjected. 'It could also land us all in prison.'

'Not if we get the bad guys,' Jason said. 'Kristen, you have to promise me that if you can't or don't help us find the terrorists, then you sit on all the information you gather on us and our other units and their missions forever – no "deep background," no anything. It stays with you to the grave.'

'Unless I get information from other sources . . .'

'That's not good enough,' Jason said. 'I don't want to blow any chances for the powers-that-be to find the terrorists and go after them their way. You either help us to close in on the terrorists, chase them out of hiding or plant them six feet under, or you forget we ever had this conversation.'

'You sound like you don't trust me, Major,' Kristen said playfully. 'I'm hurt.'

'That's the way it's going to have to be, Kristen,' Jason said seriously, but inwardly he was thinking: boy, I'll bet that smile opens a lot of doors for her. She still appeared as if she wanted to argue. 'You'll have front-row seats to the future of war fighting, Kristen,' he added. 'You saw CID in action once in Kingman City – but you haven't seen *anything* yet.'

It didn't take any more convincing. 'I'm in, Jason,' she said, extending a hand. Jason shook it. 'Tell me what you got.'

'Two words: GAMMA and Brazil.'

Kristen looked surprised, then skeptical. 'Oh, for Pete's sake, that's it? That's all you have? And I was getting pretty excited there for a minute!'

'Who is GAMMA?' asked Jason.

'GAMMA is a radical environmental terrorist group formed in central Brazil years ago that opposes what they call oppressive multinational corporations, mostly big oil, and specifically TransGlobal Energy,' Kristen explained. 'But they're small potatoes, Jason. They've harassed TGE for years, mostly in South America – recently in fact. But they take great pains to avoid human casualties – I don't believe GAMMA would ever use a nuclear weapon, even if they had access to one. And they haven't been responsible for any activities north of the equator that I'm aware of.'

'Our intel says otherwise.'

'Are you sure you're getting reliable information? You sure no one's feeding you bogus information just to throw you off the trail of the real terrorists?'

'Like I said, we obtained this information by ourselves, our own means – it wasn't contained in a briefing or field report.'

'If you think it's so good, why don't you stay plugged in to this source?'

'Someone blew the whistle on us, and we had to shut down or be cut out completely.'

'I'm surprised you weren't busted, given the security climate around the country these days,' Kristen observed. 'The feds would just as soon throw you in jail first and *then* investigate, just to be on the safe side.'

'We've managed to keep it in-house for now, but if we kept the pipeline open and got caught again, they would definitely lock us up and throw away the keys,' Jason said. 'Can you help us?'

'Well, you sure didn't give me much to go on,' Kristen said, 'but I do have pretty good sources in the Brazilian paramilitary, the PME, which is their combined municipal police and interior military. Problem is, when they find a terrorist group, drug smugglers, poachers, insurgents, or anyone else stepping outside the law – or on their own turf – the PME tends to interrogate, torture, kill, display, and claim victory – they rarely jail anyone, and they don't share too much information outside their provincial headquarters.'

'You seem to know a lot about them,' Ari observed.

'I go to Brazil a lot, and I don't just hang out at Copacabana or Ipanema,' Kristen said. A brief image of Kristen Skyy strolling down the famous clothing-optional Brazilian beaches in nothing but a thong and suntan oil flashed in Jason's mind, but he forced it away – unfortunately not fast enough to keep Ari from elbowing him in the ribs. 'Fact is, if you have a PME officer on your side, especially a Colonel, you are completely safe from anyone and you can do pretty much whatever you like.'

'Something tells me,' Ari said, 'that you've charmed your way into the hearts of a lot of officers.'

If Kristen Skyy was stung by that remark, she didn't seem to care. 'International broadcast journalism isn't like sitting in a lab all day and having your professional life judged by lines of computer code, sister – it's about taking chances, running hard, and not being afraid to take a few shots in the gut to get the story,' she said. 'I get the big fish because I'm thorough and fair, not because I sleep around or hand out bigger bribes than the next guy.'

'Being rich, famous, and beautiful doesn't hurt.'

'Dr Vega, in places like Brazil and most of the *real* world, the men in charge are richer and more powerful than the presidents of most countries in the world – including the United States – and they suck rich, famous, and beautiful women dry and discard them every week. I would be just another trophy on their walls if I was just a news whore.'

She turned to Jason and went on: 'The only way we're going to get information from the PME commandants in the provinces is to give them something they don't already have. They're already as wealthy as they want to be in their own regions: they *are* the federal, state, and local government; they can have any woman or any politician they want just for the asking. You can scare them, but they'll turn on you faster than you can take a breath as soon as you're out of sight. About the only thing of yours they may want is your robot.'

'Then let's not get information from the commandants,' Jason said. 'Ari's right, Kristen: you're rich, famous, and beautiful. That might not impress the commandants, but speaking as a lowly field-grade officer, it impresses the hell out of me. I'll bet there's a lot of young bucks down there who would love to talk to Kristen Skyy of SATCOM One News and give her anything her heart desires.'

'Maybe.' She gave Jason another mind-blowing smile and nodded. 'I'll see what I can do.'

'Once you find them, we'll need transportation,' Jason said. 'We'll need a plane big enough to carry a Humvee.'

'We're a satellite news organization, Jason, not the Air Mobility Command,' Kristen said. 'Why can't the army fly us down?'

'If your information is timely, accurate, and action-able, and if I can convince my bosses that we should act, then maybe they can,' Jason said. 'But I'm assuming no one will believe us or that no one will support us even if they do believe us. SATCOM One must have jets that fly all over the world all the time that carry thousands of pounds of equipment . . .'

'Sure – for the VIPs going on vacation or for coverage of the World Cup, not for me,' Kristen said. 'But I do have fairly ready access to a medium jet that can make it around Central and South America with very few customs hassles – assuming the airspace in the United States isn't shut down and I can fly it out of the country. It can carry a crew of two, six passengers – that means you two and four for me – and all the cargo and supplies we can carry. One full day of flying to get to Brazil, maybe two depending on weather. That's the best I can do until I have something juicy to show my boss.'

'That'll do nicely,' Jason said. 'We won't be able to take our Humvee, but it'll give us practice in using CID with minimum ground support on a rapid-reaction mission.'

'And my photographers and I will have total access to all your activities, right?'

'As soon as we load up our equipment in your plane, yes,' Jason said. 'But we get a look at your information first. If it's good, we're on.'

'How are you going to get your stuff off the base?'

'Heck, that won't be hard – they're ready to kick us

off already,' Ari said wryly. 'All Jason needs to do is something asinine – like talk to the news media about what we're doing, right, J?'

Jason turned away from Kristen and fully toward his friend and colleague. 'Listen, Ari, I need you with me on this,' he said. 'If you're not, I'll stop this and we'll go back to helping DeLaine and Jefferson do whatever it is they want to do.'

'Riddle me this, J – why are you doing this?' Ariadna asked. 'You told me that the powers-that-be were impressed with CID – I think they'll put us online eventually. Why do you feel the need to step out like this?'

'Because I don't trust anyone I'm working with,' Jason replied. 'I don't know why, but I just don't feel like anyone's being straight with us. Do you?'

'I don't know, J,' Ari said. 'I'm just an engineer – same as you. I'm not a soldier or a spy. I write computer code to instruct computers to design futuristic weapons. I do it for the U.S. Army because I love my country and I think my designs can help, and because they pay me a lot of money to work hard for them. I don't get paid to worry about who's pulling the strings or whose agenda is being played. What is it with you, J? It's not just distrust. You seem unhappy, or dissatisfied, or paranoid, or *something*. What is it you're looking for, Jason?'

The army major sat back, his eyes adopting a faraway look for several long moments. He looked back up at Ariadna and shook his head. 'I've been working on CID for three years, Ari – it's almost the only thing I've done in the army,' he said. 'I was so damned proud, of our gear as well as myself, when we were able to save those people at Kingman City. I felt like we could take on the world. Almost immediately we get the call, and it's like my dreams suddenly came true: they wanted us to fight.

'But then I look at the players involved, and I know they don't want the same things I want,' he went on. 'I don't know what it is exactly, but it's as if they don't want to fight the terrorists, like they have their own secret agenda . . .'

'And you don't, J?' Ari asked.

'Me? Hell no. I told you what I want: to use my technology to get the terrorists . . .'

'And when the powers-that-be don't put CID at the tip of the spear, all you want to do is squawk and pout and break off and link up with a reporter and do your own thing,' Ari said flatly. 'Who's not being the team player now?'

'I . . .' Jason stopped, looking at Ariadna's accusing expression, then away. He stayed silent for several moments; then shook his head. 'Sure, maybe I'm pissed. I know CID works, and I proved it can do some good. I *want* it to do some good.

'But the army or the powers-that-be could've taken CID away from us and used it however they wanted,' Jason went on. 'They didn't: they put us in charge. That makes it personal. I want to win, Ari. No matter who else is involved or what they really want out of this thing, *I want to win*. CID can do it. I don't think they want us to succeed. I'm going to do everything I possibly can to win.'

Ari looked at Richter with a serious, concerned expression, and her smile didn't return. She put a hand on his shoulder and nodded. 'Okay, J. I don't know if what you're doing is legal or right or even smart, but I think your heart at least is in the right place – even if your brain maybe isn't. But one thing's for sure: we're a team. We have been ever since you showed me your drawings for CID three years ago. If you want to do this, then I'm with you.'

Jason smiled, nodded, then leaned over and gave her a kiss on the cheek. 'Thanks, Ari.'

'Sounds like a discussion that needed to happen,' Kristen said. She wrote some information down on a business card and handed it to Jason. 'That's a secure e-mail address, although how secure it is from the government I'm not sure.'

'We'll check it. If it's secure, we'll send information on how you can contact us.'

'Good.' She got to her feet. 'I'll be in touch, guys.' Jason slid out of the booth as Kristen walked away; he looked back at Ari, who rolled her eyes and waved him on with mock impatience, like a school chum urging a buddy to slip a valentine to the prettiest girl in school who just walked by. He hurried to catch up to her.

It was clear and slightly cool outside, with the fresh smell of a late-afternoon thunderstorm and welcome rain on the desert still lingering. He looked for her but couldn't see a thing in the gloom of the dark street outside the terminal and restaurant.

'She seems to care quite a bit about you.' Jason turned and found Kristen standing in the shadows beside the terminal building, stubbing out a half-smoked cigarette.

'We're friends,' Jason said, walking to her. 'We've worked side by side for many years.' He stepped close to her. 'Isn't there anyone you've worked so closely with that you tell them everything, even if it's not work-related?'

'You mean, other reporters? Hell no,' she said.

'No. I mean friends. Someone you've known for a while, shared something of yourself, opened up to a bit.'

He could hear Kristen's leather jacket rustle as she shrugged. 'Maybe. I don't remember. So many cities, so many assignments, so many persons you get thrown together with to get the job done. It all kinda gets jumbled together. Boyfriends don't hang around too long if they don't like being second banana to the job.'

'Sounds lonely – like you're never by yourself, but always by yourself at the same time.'

'It is.' As if she was afraid she was opening up too much, she straightened her shoulders. 'But it's exciting, and it pays well, and once in a while I get to do something really cool . . .' She patted his chest playfully and added, '. . . like work with Superman.'

He took her hand in his. The toughness she tried to portray instantly melted away. She used her other hand to pull him to her, and they kissed. The friendly kiss turned into a long, passionate one.

Jason didn't quite know what happened next, except that she had slipped her rental car keys into his hand, then the keys to her room at the Clovis Inn just a few minutes later when they pulled up, and then they were in each other's arms and undressing one another. They didn't do much talking that night either.

Hours later, she kissed him good-bye and dropped him off again at the airport terminal. Ari had caught a ride back to the base on her own, as he knew she would do. Partners to the last, she knew it would not look right for a world-famous investigative reporter to be dropping off the commander of a secret military task force at the gate to a military base late at night.

Pecos East Training Range,
Cannon Air Force Base, New Mexico
Several days later

The eighteen commandos who formed the operational strike members of Task Force TALON, along with Kelsey DeLaine, Carl Bolton, and Sergeant Major Ray Jefferson, were assembled on a weapons-training range in a special area of Pecos East shortly before dawn. With them were six specialized vehicles resembling narrow, fat-tired, high-tech dune buggies they had nicknamed the 'Rat Patrol,' designed to fit inside large transport helicopters or small fixed-wing transports. Out in the distance was a group of buildings they were going to use for target practice as a warm-up for their big training exercise later that morning.

Standing apart from the other task force members were Jason Richter and Doug Moore, both mounted inside Cybernetic Infantry Device units. Richter had a grenade launcher backpack, while Moore wore another backpack that launched small observation drones called GUOS, or 'Goose,' short for Grenade-Launched Unmanned Observation System. The two CID units were not really part of the morning exercise, but were allowed to use the range and targets after the rest of the task force were finished.

Again, Jason thought ruefully, Kelsey and the sergeant major still weren't interested in merging CID's capabilities with Task Force TALON. What an incredible waste.

The other members of Task Force TALON were busy checking their weapons, equipment, and radios, and were now standing before a short platform awaiting their final briefing. 'Okay, ladies and gents, listen up,' Sergeant Major Raymond Jefferson began. 'Welcome to Task Force

TALON's first field exercise. Our first objective this morning is simple: get used to moving and communicating as a team.

'Our primary means of tactical transportation on our missions will be by helicopter, which is why we've chosen to use the "Rat Patrol" dune buggies for fast ingress and egress,' he went on. 'There are three men per vehicle. Each vehicle is fitted with a machine gun or M19 grenade launcher. Top speed is about a hundred kilometers an hour. They're designed for rough terrain but they're nimble and top-heavy with the guns mounted on their pedestals, so be careful your first time out and get the feel of steering and handling these things on uneven ground.

'In about an hour we'll bring in a couple of MH-53 Pave Low special-ops helicopters and try a helicopter assault on a simulated oil refinery out on the range, but right now we're going to get the hang of riding and attacking from the dune buggies by attacking that small group of buildings out there. Hop in, try some turns and fast starts and stops, then spread out and try firing on the buildings from the buggies and on foot. Charlie Range is heavily instrumented, so we'll have multiple cameras on all players and will be able to do an intensive debrief later on. All communications, weapon hits, and player movements will be recorded. We'll have some time to iron out procedural problems later on, so let the glitches happen. Questions?'

The officer in charge, Jake Maxwell, nodded toward Richter and Moore. 'What are the CIDs' roles today, Sergeant Major?'

'They are here to observe,' Jefferson responded. 'They will test-fire their grenade launchers after you are finished. Sergeant Moore in CID Two will use his drones when we move on to the second phase.'

'I'd like to watch those things in action,' one of the commandos said. 'Why don't they come along with us and see if they can keep up?'

'We can wax your ass, Yonker,' Moore said with his electronically synthesized voice.

'In your dreams, robo-toy . . .'

'Can it,' Jefferson interjected. 'CID tactics will be merged with the task force once a training syllabus has been drawn up and approved. Any other questions?' There were none, so he turned to the others beside him. 'Ma'am?'

Special Agent Kelsey DeLaine stepped up before the team. Unlike the others, she and Special Agent Carl Bolton wore black FBI fatigues and headgear instead of the high-tech pixilated fatigues worn by the commandos. 'Welcome to our first field training exercise,' she began. 'This will be the first of many exercises we'll do to fine-tune our daytime procedures; then, we'll advance into night exercises and finally some urban terrain training. Our team members come from all segments of the special ops and tactical law-enforcement community. You are all superstars in your own units – now, we need to see what it will take for us to work together as a team.' The troops appeared very anxious to get out into the field to prove what they could do. 'Be careful out there. Lieutenant Maxwell, take charge.'

'Yes, ma'am,' army First Lieutenant Jake Maxwell, the TALON platoon leader, responded. Maxwell looked impossibly young, but he was an experienced Army Ranger and special-operations commando. He turned to his platoon and asked, 'Any other last-second questions?' He waited only a few heartbeats, but no one said anything. 'Okay, mount up and let's do it. Follow me.'

As Kelsey moved off, she said over her shoulder, 'Major, Sergeant, we'll meet you over at the oil refinery.'

'I thought I'd do some target practice with the team,' Jason said. 'I'll bet CID can move faster and shoot better than the guys on those buggies.'

'We're trying the GUOS drones today,' Kelsey said. 'We'll try assaults later. See you there.'

The commandos loaded into their buggies, started them up, then lined up in a column behind Maxwell. They started out on a paved road up to maximum speed for a few miles, then took the buggies off-road, first on a dirt road and then cross-country. The gunners stayed seated for the first few minutes off-road, but soon Maxwell directed the gunners to take their places up in their braced mounts behind the weapon pedestals to get the feel of riding while standing. Soon the buggies were racing across the open range at full speed. A few of the buggies had to stop because the gunners got jostled a little harder than they expected, and several had some scary moments when the drivers took a few turns too tightly and they threatened to roll over, but it did not take long for all six vehicles to stay in a tight column while racing full speed across the desert with the gunners standing behind their weapon mounts.

'Pretty damned impressive,' Kelsey DeLaine said as she watched through binoculars. 'Looks like they've been doing this for years.'

'These guys are pros, ma'am,' Jefferson said approvingly. 'They'll be up to speed in no time. Shall I send them over to the target buildings?'

'Absolutely,' Kelsey said. 'I'm anxious to see how well they shoot while moving.'

Jefferson made the radio calls, and the buggies headed

south toward a small group of metal and plywood target
buildings located in a circular berm made of sand, rock,
and dirt dug up from the desert. The buggies lined up at
a range of fifty meters and began firing smoke rounds
into the buildings from the grenade launchers mounted
on the back of the buggies and from the M203 grenade
launchers carried by the commando riding in the
passenger's seat. They moved out to one hundred meters,
then two, and finally three hundred meters. After firing
several rounds from stationary positions, the buggies
lined up and began firing from fifty meters with the
buggies traveling just twenty kilometers an hour, gradually stepping up the speed.

'Amazing,' was all Kelsey could say after the exercise
was completed and they had assembled to talk about
their performance. 'My hat's off to you guys. You were
up to sixty kilometers per hour and consistently making
hits. Well done.'

They had a fifteen-minute break to check their
weapons and equipment and brief the next portion of
the morning exercise. DeLaine, Bolton, and Jefferson
were picked up by a UH-60 Black Hawk helicopter and
taken out to the next exercise target area, and minutes
later two massive MH-53 Pave Low III special-operations
helicopters approached their location. The rear cargo
ramp lowered, and the loadmaster and crew chief
emerged and waved them in. Three dune buggies fit in
the cargo hold of each of the big choppers with room to
spare. The flight was not very long, and the cargo ramp
remained lowered as they dropped to low altitude and
sped in toward the landing zone.

The two massive MH-53 Pave Low III special-ops
helicopters stirred up an immense cloud of dust as they

translated from racing just a few meters above the desert floor at ninety knots to zero airspeed in just a few seconds. Within seconds the high-tech dune buggies drove off the choppers into the dust storm kicked up by the massive rotors. Their objective was about five kilometers in the distance, just outside the reach of simulated 'enemy' rocket-propelled grenades or shoulder-fired antiaircraft weapons: a small compound, thirty-six acres in area, with oil derricks, pumps, tanks, and electrical control buildings, built to resemble a small oil-pumping facility. Normally they would deploy and fight at night, but this was their first practice and it gave them an opportunity to take it a little easy until they got the hang of using their new vehicles.

Even with fat tires and wide stances the buggies were top-heavy with the gunner and their weapon situated above the driver, and it made for some exciting moments when the drivers executed all but the gentlest turns. Bouncing across the open desert in the buggies demanded a lot from the gunners. They rested against a metal back brace and wore a harness attached to the weapon stand, but they were still wildly bumped and jostled around while racing at nearly a hundred kilometers an hour. Aiming the weapons while moving at more than thirty kilometers per hour was nearly impossible. But at a slower speed or while stopped, the gunners did an incredible job and showed off their marksmanship skills, hitting practice targets with great precision even from as far as a hundred meters.

Kelsey DeLaine, Carl Bolton, and Sergeant Major Jefferson watched the six buggies approach and then encircle the 'facility' through high-powered binoculars. They were inside the 'oil terminal,' watching the task force as they started their raid. 'I thought Crenshaw was going to lose it for a second there – he took that last turn a little sharp,' Kelsey commented. 'But they're doing great. Twenty-one minutes to surround the compound and hit all the perimeter targets – not bad.'

'I'd sure like to see it done in less than fifteen,' Bolton commented.

'This is their first time out, sir – they're not pushing those buggies too hard yet,' Jefferson commented. 'A few more days and they'll be moving at top speed.'

'I hope so, Sergeant,' Bolton said. 'Otherwise we'll have to rethink this whole "Rat Patrol" idea.'

'They'll get better, sir,' Jefferson insisted.

'I still think we can parachute or sneak in some snipers and have them take out any Stinger air defense sites first,' Bolton argued. 'Then the choppers can move in closer.'

'It takes time to put snipers in position properly, sir,' Jefferson said. This was an old argument, and he was tired of making it. 'Our mission profile calls for a light, rapid-response force. It could take days to move three or four snipers into position.'

'Then what about getting Cobra or Apache attack helicopters to launch precision-guided weapons from outside Stinger range? A Hellfire missile has three times the range of a Stinger . . .'

'It's only twice the range, sir, not three times,' Jefferson interjected. 'But the main reason is that the support necessary for even one Cobra or Apache helicopter is enormous – we would need our own C-17 transport, maybe two, and probably double our personnel.'

'We were lucky to get two MH-53s and the buggies sent out here,' Kelsey admitted. 'If we can get additional funding or get a change in our operational profile, then perhaps we can get some attack choppers.'

'If we changed our profile to include things like helicopters, ma'am, we're losing the thing that makes us distinctive and gives us an edge – our speed and flexibility,' Jefferson said. 'We'd be just another Marine or Army Ranger mixed light infantry–helicopter company.'

'Then I suggest we practice more and get our times down, Sergeant,' Bolton said, 'before the White House disbands us in favor of some grunt unit.'

'Yes, sir,' Jefferson responded, making the 'sir' sound more like 'cur.' Sergeant Major Jefferson was unaccustomed to civilians telling him what to do while training his men, especially civilians that rarely, if ever, picked up a gun or rode in military vehicles.

There was an uncomfortable pause for a few moments; then, Kelsey keyed the mike on her walkie-talkie: 'Okay, Sergeant Moore, let's give the Goose a try.'

'Yes, ma'am,' Staff Sergeant Moore, mounted inside CID Two and positioned near the helicopters' landing zone, responded. He turned toward the oil compound and issued a command via an eye-pointing system inside his helmet. There was a loud *pop*! and a projectile, resembling a long bowling pin, fired from the unit's backpack. When the projectile reached fifteen meters' altitude, a set of long thin wings popped out of its body, a small jet engine started, and the projectile flew up and away like a tiny jet plane. A few moments later, Moore launched another. The projectile was a GUOS, or Grenade-Launched Unmanned Observation System, nicknamed 'Goose,' a remotely operated drone with a tiny camera on board that sent back pictures to a ground observer team or to the CID pilot from as far as forty kilometers away and four kilometers' altitude.

'Two Geese away, both in the green,' Moore reported. No one responded to him. 'They should be on station in five minutes.' Still no reaction. 'Ma'am, I think CID could've reached that compound and taken out those perimeter targets faster than the buggies.'

'After the task force gets it down in the buggies, maybe we'll give it a try,' Kelsey said noncommittally, turning to the portable surveillance monitor set up in her Humvee.

'Or maybe not,' Bolton said under his breath.

'Ready to activate random gunfire, ma'am,' Jefferson said.

'Do it,' Kelsey responded. Automated emitters inside the compound would fire laser beams outside, which would be scored as small arms fire with the Multiple Integrated Laser Engagement System. The emitters were just distractions, added to enhance the realism of the exercise.

All of the officers observing the exercise were just simply amazed at the precision and accuracy of the 'Rat Patrol' dune buggy gunners. They were indeed getting better by the minute: after just two complete orbits of the perimeter, Sergeant Moore reported, 'Ma'am, I see smoke coming from every defensive position. They did it. Every Stinger site and machine gun nest destroyed by TALON.'

'Those guys are incredible,' Kelsey said. 'Congratulations, Sergeant Major.'

'Thank you, ma'am,' Jefferson responded. 'But that was only phase one. These guys work best on the ground.'

The six dune buggies surrounded the oil refinery, and

twelve Task Force TALON commandos in pixilated desert camouflage fatigues, Whisper Mike communications headsets, Kevlar helmets, safety goggles, gas masks, and M-16 rifles fitted with the MILES direct fire training system modules dismounted. The six dune buggy drivers moved their vehicles away from the perimeters, then configured the pedestal-mounted weapons on their vehicles to fire remotely from the driver's seat. The twelve commandos joined up into three groups of four and began to approach the refinery at preselected entry points. Each commando carried an M-16 rifle with a retractable stock to make it more compact, along with pouches of ammo and gas grenades; one commando in each team had an M203 grenade launcher attached under his rifle for additional firepower.

Maxwell was the first to break radio silence: 'TALON, One,' he radioed, 'look sharp, I just found a booby trap. Claymore mine with a fishing-line trip wire.' Each team leader checked in, acknowledging they heard the warning. Maxwell disarmed the Claymore – a smoke grenade, not a high-explosive mine – and proceeded on. Several more traps were discovered on their way in. The more they found, the sharper their attention became. This was just a first exercise, sure, but at least Kelsey DeLaine and Ray Jefferson were making it interesting right off the bat!

They made it to the perimeter fence without tripping any of the five mines they discovered. The barrier was a simple three-strand electrified enclosure, typical of those used for farm animals. Fearing the fence might be wired to set off an alarm or an explosive if cut, the teams decided to slip under the lower wire – until they spotted the trip wires on the other side, less than a centimeter aboveground, attached to more smoke bombs. 'Good setup here, Kelsey,' Maxwell said on his comlink.

'Thank you,' Kelsey acknowledged. 'Continue.'

After a short discussion, the teams decided to jumper the electrified fence wires, then cut them. No alarms or booby traps were set off, and they were able to disarm the Claymores inside the compound. The flat desert floor made it easy to spot more trip wires and booby traps set up inside the fence. One team member was able to move up to a mechanical dog – actually a wooden box on legs with ultrasonic emitters and a speaker that would emit barking sounds if activated – and disarm it without it detecting his presence.

'Pretty amazing,' Kelsey said off the air to Special Agent Carl Bolton seated beside her. 'Thirty minutes after launch and they've reached the inside of a well-guarded and booby-trapped oil refinery without setting off one noisemaker. They'll be done in five minutes.'

'They're the best of the best, that's for sure,' Jefferson said. He made a few more notes, but he had precious little to debrief the team so far. 'They're acting like they've trained together for years.'

'This is better than I hoped,' Kelsey said. 'If we can find another twenty guys to bring out here like this, we'll be operational in plenty of time with an entire platoon ready for action, with one in reserve.'

'I'm just glad we're not screwing with that CID thing,' Bolton said, completely ignoring Doug Moore standing almost right beside him in CID Two. 'We'd still be sitting in a classroom learning how each and every microchip fits together. Do those eggheads really think it's that important to learn *how* that stuff works? Those briefings are the most God-awful boring things I've ever been to.'

'It's impressive, but Richter and Vega are just out of their element,' Kelsey said, trying to be upbeat. 'They're not helping themselves, that's for sure. We made the right decision by deferring their participation for now.'

'Definitely,' Bolton said. He focused in on the refinery again. 'They've started the search. Moore?'

'The Gooses are on station,' Doug Moore reported. He was watching the imagery from the GUOS unmanned aerial vehicles through his helmet's electronic visor. 'Imaging infrared sensors active . . . I've got the three TALON elements in sight . . . Team Three, CID Two, hot contact, one o'clock, eleven meters . . . Team Two, no contacts . . . check that, Team Two, I've got a stray blip at your three o'clock, fifteen meters. Might be residual heat from a timer or chemical package.'

'Checks,' the TALON team leader radioed back. 'Demo charge with a mechanical timer. Deactivated.'

'Roger that,' Moore acknowledged. 'Team One, stop, stop . . .' But it was too late – a robot 'terrorist' swung around on a mechanical pivot and fired a MILES laser beam. One commando was hit in a nonlethal spot: his backup 'killed' the 'terrorist' with a three-round burst. 'Sorry about that, One.'

'If you can't help them out, Moore, then terminate and let them do their job,' Bolton complained.

'It had an infrared shield on it,' Maxwell reported. 'Very clever, hiding it from the Goose's sensors. We would've completely missed it and it would've hosed us if the Goose hadn't warned us. I'm starting to develop a fondness for our little Goose friends up there, Kelsey.' Bolton shook his head but said nothing.

In less than ten minutes, assisted by Doug Moore and the GUOS drones, the task force had 'killed' more than

a dozen 'terrorists' and deactivated six demolition charges
and booby traps set up in various parts of the complex.
'Excellent work, guys, excellent,' Kelsey said. 'Mission
accomplished. Let's head back to the training area, get
cleaned up, and . . .'

'Something's happening,' Doug Moore in CID Two
suddenly interjected.

'What?'

'GUOS Two has detected a high-speed vehicle
approaching,' Moore said, studying the downloaded
images in his electronic visor. 'It's Major Richter, ma'am.
He's . . . *watch out*!'

Suddenly there was a tremendous '*Craashh*!' and CID
One burst through the outer perimeter fence. Several live
Claymore mines exploded, but Richter kept right on
coming. He ran through the avenues in the complex at
a very high speed, firing smoke grenades at all of the
already-attacked targets. Several MILES laser guns
opened fire on him, scoring hits. The Task Force TALON
commandos were stunned at how fast the CID unit was
traveling and how accurate it was launching grenades.

'Knock it off, Richter,' Kelsey radioed, waving at the
smoke wafting in her direction. 'The exercise is over. Stop
before you run over someone.' But Richter kept right on
going, running faster and faster, dodging around pipes
and tanks with incredible speed while firing in all directions. Once all the targets were destroyed, Richter stood
triumphantly in the center of the complex, raising his
hands and jumping from foot to foot like a huge robotic
Rocky Balboa on the Philadelphia Museum of Art steps.
'What a hot dog. Bring it in, Jason.' He turned to
acknowledge an imaginary crowd, swatting at a steel pipe
still left standing, then turned again, still dancing . . .

'*Watch out*!' Moore shouted. The steel pipe had been holding up a steel tank on a short steel pedestal, and when Richter broke the pipe the tank teetered over and crashed on top of him. '*Major*!' Moore shouted from within CID Two, running up to Richter.

Helped by CID Two, Richter got CID One to its feet and came trotting up to where Kelsey, Bolton, and Jefferson were standing. It unloaded its backpack and assumed the 'dismount' stance, and Jason Richter climbed out a few moments later. He immediately began examining the robot's left side. '*Jason*! What did you do?' Kelsey shouted as she stepped quickly over to him. 'Are you all right?'

'I don't know,' he said. 'I lost everything for a moment there.'

'You know better than to just run out onto a live fire range without getting clearance from the range supervisor!' Bolton shouted. 'You did this on purpose to screw up our exercise and turn attention to your CID stuff.'

'Hey, Bolton, you can kiss my ass,' Richter retorted angrily. 'I thought you guys were done and it was my target.'

Kelsey felt bad that the CID unit was damaged, and she was impressed that it had assaulted the complex so quickly and so effectively. Fortunately no one got hurt, and the task force had already done pretty well on their morning training. It was a good first exercise, despite the unwanted intrusion. She walked over to where Richter was examining the robot's back. 'What happened to it, Jason?' she asked.

'Cracked an access panel,' he said worriedly. 'The primary hydraulic power pack is leaking. It's more maintenance than I can do here – I might have to take it back to Fort Polk.'

'How long will it take to fix it?'

'I have no idea – maybe a couple days, maybe a week.'

'Take all the time you need,' Bolton interjected sourly. 'Maybe we'll get some work done around here for a change.'

'Button it, Carl,' Kelsey said. 'All right, Jason, you and Ariadna can head on back.'

Jason nodded dejectedly. 'Okay. There's an Army Research Lab C-130 here from Fort Polk right now – I'll just hitch a ride with them. I don't want to stow the CID because of the break, so I'll just walk it into the cargo bay.'

Kelsey nodded. This was the first real sign of emotion she had ever seen from Jason Richter – it should've come as no surprise to her, she thought, that he reserved his deepest feelings for a machine. 'Sorry about your robot, Jason,' she said. 'Get back as soon as you can. We'll use CID Number Two as scheduled.' Jason nodded, shot Bolton an angry glare, which did nothing but increase the size of the smirk on his face, climbed back inside the robot, started it up, picked up his grenade-launcher backpack, and trotted back toward the task force base, moving a little awkwardly.

Bolton shook his head as he and Kelsey watched the robot run out of sight. 'I thought that thing was more sophisticated than that,' he remarked.

'I thought it did pretty well – a lot better than a Humvee, dune buggy, or helicopter could,' Kelsey said. 'But I'm glad we decided not to go with it right now. That should get us off the hook with Jefferson for us not wanting to use it, too.'

'It looks like a wounded raccoon hobbling away,' Bolton observed. 'Maybe he won't interfere with our training for a while.' He turned to speak with the commandos as they returned to the range controller's pad. Kelsey watched the CID unit trot away for a few more moments. It did look rather pitiful. Richter's pride and joy, brought down by a small grenade. This is not going to look good in front of the brass, she noted.

Back at the task force training area, Ariadna was shaking her head as she watched CID One trot up and saw Jason dismount. 'I got the call from Doug,' Ariadna said. 'I can't believe you broke CID One.'

'It was an accident.'

'What were you doing in the middle of that training exercise?' Ari asked.

'I wanted to see how well I could find all the targets,' Jason said. 'I was watching the GUOS downlinks the whole time and found a couple mines the task force didn't.'

Ari shook her head, then stepped closer to Jason and asked, 'Okay, J, what's going on? Why did you go over there?'

Jason looked at his partner for a few moments, then shook his head and replied, 'Because I was pissed they didn't invite us out there for the first field test,' he said. 'I wanted to show him that we don't need all those dune buggies to do our job – CID can do everything they can do, and better.'

'That wasn't a very smart move, doofus,' Ari said. 'You could've gotten yourself killed.'

'We've shown many times how impervious CID is to grenade and heavy weapons fire,' Jason said. 'The tank falling on me was a lucky shot. I wasn't worried.'

'You're crazy, that's why – you're too stupid to be worried,' she replied, trying to keep her tone of voice lighthearted but serious at the same time. 'Don't do it again.'

'Yes, Mom. I'll be careful.' Ari shot him an exasperated glance and began examining the damaged compartment. Jason's cell phone rang, and he stepped away to answer it while Ari hooked up a portable monitoring unit and recharger from the Humvee. Jason made sure his special encryption routine was running before checking the caller ID readout and replying: 'Kristen? How are you? I haven't heard from you in a while.'

'I'm fine, Jason,' Kristen Skyy responded. He could hear a great deal of airplane noise in the background. 'Listen, I have a hot lead, and we need to move as quickly as possible. I have a jet ready to take us to Brazil, but we have to leave this morning.'

'*This morning*?' Jason exclaimed. 'I don't know . . .'

'My source tells me he's got a lock on one of GAMMA's head guys,' Kristen said. 'But they've been moving around every couple days. We need to be down there *tonight*. I got us a plane that can take us to Brazil in seven or eight hours. We'll arrive at Clovis airport within the hour. My pilot says if we can leave in the next hour, we can be down at São Paulo shortly after sunset.'

Jason threw his mind into overdrive as he tried to work out the logistics. They barely had enough time. They had to grab as much supplies and ordnance as they could and go immediately. 'I'll be there, Kristen,' Jason said. 'I'm not sure how I'll manage it, but I'll be there. Gotta go.' He hung up.

'It doesn't look too bad, J,' Ariadna said as Jason went

back to her. 'Failed main hydraulic power pack. The secondary power pack picked up the slack.' She showed him a slightly damaged access panel on the robot's back approximately where the left kidney would be. 'The hydraulic lines look okay thank God, but the fiber-optic connector needs replacing. I think I might have the parts I need, but I need a good two or three hours.'

'Can you fix it?'

'I can fix a rainy day, as long as it's in my lab, J,' she said confidently. 'But in the field, reliably enough for combat? Maybe . . . probably . . . yes, I think so. I have to take apart the left data bus assembly to change the fiber-optic cable – that's practically the whole left side's electronics. It's not difficult, just time-consuming work.'

'Do we have a spare?'

'Spare power pack – sure. Spare access door – no,' Ari replied. 'Looks like the entire left edge of the panel is cracked – we won't be able to secure it tightly. We don't have any equipment for making repairs to composite structures here. I'll need the material, a frame, an autoclave . . .'

'Can we secure it in place temporarily?'

'I think I might have some duct tape,' Ari quipped. 'Why? You're thinking about finishing the exercise with the rest of the task force?'

'That call was from Kristen,' Jason said. 'She has information on that terrorist group GAMMA. They located one of its leaders, in São Paulo, Brazil . . .'

'*Brazil*?'

'They move around a lot, and her source says our only chance to grab him will be tonight.'

'Why don't we get the FBI or the locals to do it?'

'Because it's *our* job, Ari,' Jason said. 'If Kristen knows where this guy is, maybe the locals do too, and he's free because he's working *with* the locals. We need to get down there.'

'Not with CID One. He's down for repairs. You'll have to take CID Two.'

'There's no time to pull him out of the exercise,' Jason said. 'We need to be airborne with all the gear we can take in less than an hour. Kristen is bringing a jet to Clovis to pick us up.'

'Are you sure about this, J?' Ariadna asked. 'This may look like we're stealing the CID unit. We could end up in prison for this . . .'

'And we could end up catching a major GAMMA commander and learning a lot about their next attack,' Jason said. 'We've got to try it. We still have one good power pack. We can't have everything perfect. I want to move on Kristen's hot intel. Let's do it. We'll load our gear; tell the crew we'll be ready to go in half an hour.'

'You want to take CID One into battle with just the secondary power pack?' Ariadna asked. 'If that one goes out, CID One will turn into a sixteen-million-dollar lawn ornament.'

'We have to chance it,' Jason said. She still looked skeptical. 'I'll contact Jefferson. If he absolutely forbids us to go, we'll stay. But we've got to get moving or we won't have any options.'

'I hope you know what you're doing, dude,' Ari said as she hurried off to pack some equipment. She loaded up a portable test system, a case of tear gas, and smoke grenades for the grenade launcher backpack – the only weapons she could find that she had ready access to – plus the GUOS drone backpack with six drones and some tools and spare parts to work on the CID unit, and within minutes they were in a truck heading out to Clovis Municipal Airport. Meanwhile, Richter got on his secure cell phone to Sergeant Major Jefferson. The phone conversation was very short: his instructions were simply to 'stay put.'

At the airport, a Bombardier Learjet 60 business jet was parked outside the general aviation terminal being fueled. Jason hugged Kristen Skyy and resisted giving her a kiss, but she gave him one anyway. 'I thought you couldn't get us a cool ride, Kristen,' he said.

'You have no idea how many chips I had to cash in to get this,' she responded. 'You got the rear baggage compartment for the CID unit – if your dimensions were accurate, it should fit.'

'I won't be able to work on it in the rear baggage hold, J,' Ari said.

'What's wrong?' Kristen asked.

'We had a little accident,' Jason said. 'It'll be okay. Hopefully we won't be going into battle.'

'Is it serious?'

'Could be, but CID has redundant systems so it should be okay.' Jason admitted to himself that his tone wasn't all that positive; Kristen obviously noticed it but said nothing. 'Was it difficult getting clearance to fly with all the security precautions in place?' he asked.

'It took a few phone calls to Washington from the CEO of SATCOM One to get us just from Teterboro to here,' Kristen said, 'but it was surprisingly easy to get clearance out of the country. We're nonstop to Manaus, Brazil, where we'll meet up with some company agents who'll take care of customs formalities. We'll also pick up a PME officer who'll talk on the radio for us as we head to the rendezvous point.'

'What do you trade for no questions asked at customs?' Jason asked.

'The one thing more valuable than money, booze, gadgets, sex, or drugs: American press credentials,' Kristen said. 'Six-month work permits for SATCOM One, unlimited entry and exit into the U.S., and no monthly check-ins with Homeland Security as long as their status can be verified by the network. Government officials will sell them for tens of thousands of dollars each.'

It was a tight fit, but the folded CID unit just fit in the rear baggage compartment. The jet's cabin was choked with equipment but was still comfortable enough. Kristen had brought a sound engineer and a cameraman, and they had more gear than Richter and Vega. Minutes later they were loaded up, and the pilot received his clearance to depart. 'We have to wait,' Jason said after Kristen was told by the pilot they were ready for takeoff.

'We can't wait, Jason,' Kristen said. 'It'll almost be dawn by the time we get there as it is.'

'We need clearance from our supervisor,' Jason said.

'I thought *you* were the commanding officer.'

'I've never commanded anything more than a four-person laboratory or project office,' Jason said.

'Are we waiting for the same person who gave you your "political roadblocks," as you put it before?'

'Not quite,' Jason said. 'This guy doesn't believe in "political roadblocks" – if there's a roadblock, he'd prefer to smash it in . . .'

'Which is what he's going to do with our heads, once he finds out what we're doing,' Ariadna said.

'So you're talking about Special Agent Kelsey DeLaine then?' Kristen asked. Jason and Ari looked surprised –

they had been careful not to mention the names of any other Task Force TALON members around Kristen Skyy. 'I did a bit more checking and put two and two together. A combined military and FBI task force – very, very cool. DeLaine is one of the Bureau's up-and-comers, but she's not known for fieldwork – she's an administrator.' She paused, looking at Richter carefully. 'Interesting pick of persons to lead this task force. I would've expected a few more hairy-armed snake-eating "Rambo" types to go after nuclear terrorists.'

'Me too,' Jason admitted. 'But we have CID.'

'Why not give my information to Special Agent DeLaine and the rest of the task force? Why not do it as a team?'

'Because she won't act on it, and they'll shut down our source of information and most likely throw me in jail for involving the press in a classified government program,' Jason said. 'Then the terrorists get away, the task force gets shut down or reshuffled, and no one wins except the bad guys.'

'You don't trust her to share information or support your task force, is that it?'

'She would probably form an FBI task force herself to go down there and get the bad guys.'

'What's wrong with that?' Kristen asked. 'The goal is to get the terrorists, right? We could use all the help we can get.'

'This might not be the best way to do this,' Jason said, 'but we're going to do it anyway because we have actionable information and the means to respond.'

Ariadna sat beside Jason and lowered her head confidentially toward his. 'This would be a good time to head to Fort Polk, J,' Ari said quietly. 'We haven't done anything really wrong yet, and CID One is *really* broken.

Once we step off this plane in Brazil, we're swimming in deep shit.'

'What do we do with Kristen's hot tip?' Jason asked. 'Should we just ignore information like she says she's got?'

'We pass it on to DeLaine and the rest of the task force,' Ari said.

'We're pressing on,' Jason said immediately. 'Do the best you can with the replacement power pack and re-attaching the door once we reach the target.' Ari looked at him carefully, silently questioning his judgment, but nodded and fell silent.

But Jason could feel her concern, and she knew after years of working together that Ariadna was rarely wrong. He pulled out his secure cellular phone and pressed some buttons.

'Go ahead, Jason,' Kelsey responded moments later.

'I need to talk with you, Kelsey,' Jason said.

'We're in the middle of a briefing. Can't it wait?'

'No.'

Kelsey sighed and said something to the others in the room with her. 'Okay, go ahead.'

'I saw something on SATCOM One News about a connection between a terror cell in South America and the attack on Kingman City,' Jason said.

'I saw it too,' Kelsey responded after a noticeable pause. 'We're still checking, Jason,' Kelsey went on. 'The Bureau's got nothing to go on yet.'

'Kelsey . . .' Jason paused a moment, then went on: 'Kelsey, I've received some information about a group calling itself GAMMA that might have had a . . .'

'*Have you been tapping my computer and phone conversations, Richter?*' Kelsey blurted.

'No, I haven't,' Jason said.

'Then where did you hear about GAMMA?'

'It's no secret, Kelsey . . .'

'Where did you hear about a connection between GAMMA and Kingman City?'

'My source doesn't want to be revealed just yet,' Jason said, 'but I think it's good information, and I have enough that I think we should act on it. This group GAMMA was involved in Kingman City – how, I'm not sure yet. But my source may know where one of its leaders may be hiding in the next few hours. But they only stay put for a day at the most – we've got no time to waste if we want a chance to catch him.'

'How specific is your information?'

'Location down to one or two harbors; time, down to twenty-four hours.'

'One or two *harbors?*' Kelsey asked incredulously. 'It would take hundreds of men to search an area that size, and another hundred to secure it. There's no way we can . . .'

'Two CID units along with the Goose drones can do it alone,' Jason said.

'In that short a time span? Impossible.' But as soon as she said that, she knew that it was certainly doable – they had spotted several small targets inside that oil refinery complex during their training exercise without any trouble.

'It's possible, and we've got no time to waste,' Jason urged. 'I've drawn up a plan. I'd like to take the team and both CID units and go down to South America to . . .'

'South America! You can't just blast off to another country with a task force just like *that*.'

'We can, and we have to. It can't wait.'

'No way, Jason,' Kelsey said. 'If you have actionable

information, you need to present it to Chamberlain, Jefferson, and the rest of the task force. We'll verify the information and draw up a plan.'

'It can't wait,' Jason said. 'In twelve hours it'll be too late – we need to head down there *now*. I've got a plane standing by that can take us to Brazil tonight.'

'*Brazil*?' She paused. Then she said, 'Where are you now, Richter? Where's Dr Vega? You're not . . . ?'

'I'm sure Jefferson can get us clearance,' Jason said. 'C'mon, Kelsey, we need to move on this. Trust me.'

'Who's your source, Major?'

'I can't reveal it just yet . . .'

'So you can't trust me either, huh?' Kelsey asked accusingly.

Jason hesitated for a few moments, then he continued. 'A well-known international TV correspondent got me the information, and has a high degree of confidence in its accuracy,' he said. 'She's laid the groundwork for us to . . .'

'*She*?' Kelsey interrupted. 'A well-known *female* international TV correspondent . . . ?'

'You'd recognize her immediately,' Jason said. 'I've spoken to her on condition of complete anonymity . . .'

'You've *spoken* to her? About the task force? About CID . . . ?'

'Yes.'

'Have you ever heard of the concept of keeping a secret, Major?' Kelsey asked hotly. 'Obviously not, because you seem to violate it every chance you get. What did you tell her about us?'

'She made contact with me and gave me information on this terror group,' Jason said. 'She thought we could act on the information. All she wanted in exchange was to get exclusive access to our activities and . . .'

'*She* made contact with *you*, huh . . . wait a minute, wait a minute . . . that TV reporter you rescued in Kingman City . . . Skyy, Kristen Skyy, SATCOM One News. Jesus, Richter, she'll blow our organization wide open in no time! We'll have an army of reporters camped outside the front gate and flying overhead from now until doomsday! We won't be able to go to the latrine without a camera crew taking pictures of it . . .'

'That's not going to happen.'

'Richter, you've blown it big time, and you are in a world of shit,' Kelsey said. 'I suggest you get your butts back here immediately and report everything you've been up to with this reporter.'

'What about the information on GAMMA?'

'If her information pans out, then we'll use that source again in the future.'

'But we may miss our opportunity to . . .'

'That's the way it goes, Major,' Kelsey said. 'Sources are verified by receiving a certain quantity of validated information, and most times their information is validated by something bad happening. Once we take the task force off the base, we expose ourselves to counterespionage forces and a lot of official and unofficial scrutiny. We can't take that risk until we're fully operational. We need to . . . hey, why am I bothering explaining all this to you? You're a lab rat. You go off and do whatever you feel like doing anyway . . .'

'I'm a *what*?' Jason asked angrily. 'What did you call me?'

'I meant you're an engineer, not an operations guy, and you obviously don't care about operational procedures or protocols,' Kelsey said. 'What do you care about security, coordination, or teamwork? Apparently not much. I suggest . . . no, I *order* you to report back here immediately!'

'Maybe I should go to Jefferson directly.'

'You just can't learn to be a team player, can you, Richter?' Kelsey asked acidly. She shrugged. 'Go ahead. You'll look like an ass. He'll tell you the same thing I'm telling you. Now discontinue all contact with anyone outside the task force and *get back here on the double!*'

'We're missing an important opportunity here, Kelsey . . .'

'I strongly advise you to cut off this contact with Kristen Skyy or whoever you've been talking to,' Kelsey said sternly. 'The information may be useful and even accurate, but you're risking the safety and security of everyone on the team. Cut it off.' And she terminated the connection.

Back at the conference room at the training base, Carl Bolton stepped up to Kelsey, scanning her surprised expression. 'What in hell did he want? What was all that about Kristen Skyy?'

'He said he had information on a GAMMA leader hiding out in Brazil,' Kelsey said breathlessly, her mind racing.

'GAMMA! Did he say anything about . . . ?'

'He mentioned a connection between GAMMA and Kingman City.'

'*Shit!* That *bastard*!' The other task force members looked at Bolton curiously, wondering what he was so riled up about. They didn't trust either Richter or DeLaine very much yet – Sergeant Major Jefferson was their leader, no matter what the organizational chart said – but they trusted Bolton even less, if at all.

'Carl, you have got to get updates from all our researchers and investigators and get an update on the whereabouts of all the known GAMMA leaders,' Kelsey said. 'Richter's source claims to have one localized.'

'*How* localized?'

'Pretty damn close. He wants to take the entire team down there to grab him, including both CID units.'

'He's smoking something,' Bolton said dismissively.

'He might be on his way down there right now with the CID unit he was riding in this morning.'

'Is he *crazy*?' Bolton exclaimed. 'Who authorized that?'

'I don't think anyone did.'

'Richter has lost his mind,' Bolton said. 'Jefferson will strangle him.' He fell silent for a moment; then: 'Who in hell could he be talking to? Our sources haven't come up with squat yet.'

'Call Washington and have Rudy get us an update, *fast*,' Kelsey said. 'If Richter got his hands on something, we need to find out right away. Hit up our sources in SATCOM One in New York and Washington. If they won't talk, threaten to arrest them.' Bolton pulled out his secure cell phone and made the call. 'And one more thing: have someone keep an eye on Richter. If he tries to leave the base, notify Sergeant Major Jefferson and us right away.'

'It'll be my pleasure,' Bolton said.

'What did she say?' Ariadna asked Jason when he hung up the phone.

'She said get our butts back to the training area.'

'Did you tell her you're working with Kristen Skyy and SATCOM One News?'

'Not by name, but she guessed who it was.'

'What about Jefferson?'

'He said "stay put." '

'We're in deep, deep dog doo, J,' Ari said seriously. 'We'll be thrown off this task force so fast it'll make your head spin. We need to head back to the base right *now* and forget all this.'

'Maybe that's what we *should* be doing, Ari, but I still feel we need to be moving on Kristen's information,' Jason said. They noticed a blue Air Force sedan with flashing yellow lights roaring up the street toward the general aviation terminal – followed by a Security Forces Humvee. 'We'll find out soon enough.'

'Gee, I wonder where we'll be sleeping tonight – in a jungle in Brazil chasing down terrorists, or in a federal prison cell?' Ariadna asked absently. 'And I wonder which would be worse?'

Richmond, California
That same time

After all the delays and endless paperwork, the job of unloading the cargo vessel *King Zoser* was finally underway, with a long line of flat-bed trailers waiting to pick up the oil-derrick parts. One by one, massive overhead Takref/Gresse container cranes picked up the parts and pipes and placed them on the trailers, where armies of workers secured the parts to the trailers with chains. As they worked, U.S. Customs Service inspectors, augmented with Army National Guard soldiers with military working dogs, looked on, occasionally asking to look inside the pipes or recheck a serial number.

Captain Yusuf Gemici looked and felt immensely

relieved as he watched Boroshev's heavy equipment being loaded aboard the trailers. American National Guard troops watched the pumps as they were chained in place, but they made no move to check them. No sign of any law-enforcement activity whatsoever, just normal, albeit heightened, port security and customs scrutiny. He couldn't wait to get on with his voyage and . . .

Just then, a U.S. Customs Service officer who was sitting in a Humvee nearby stepped out of his vehicle, said a few words on a walkie-talkie, stepped quickly over to the pumps being chained onto the trailer, and started examining the lead tamper-evident seals on the safety wires on the sealed flanges. What in *hell* . . . they went to precisely the pump that had Boroshev's mysterious delivery in it! Gemici fished out his cigarettes and lit one up to help steady his nerves . . . but as he looked away, out the port side of the ship toward the west into San Pablo Bay, he saw the Coast Guard patrol boat *Stingray* approaching them, just a few hundred meters away now, with the skipper watching him through binoculars and with two Coast Guardsmen on deck with M-16 assault rifles. Another customs service interceptor speedboat was a bit further north, officers lining the rails on both sides watching carefully for any sign of anyone trying to jump overboard and escape.

Gennadyi Boroshev came strolling up to him a few moments later. 'Do you see this?' Gemici shouted. 'The Americans are looking at your damned cargo and will be arresting us any second! What the hell have you done? What is in those pumps? Tell me!'

'Relax, Gemici,' Boroshev said, lighting his own cigarette. 'You'll have yourself a heart attack.'

'I will not relax! You had better tell me, dammit!'

'Shut up, you fucking old hen, or I will shut you up permanently,' Boroshev said. A white van without windows drove up to the cargo on the pier, and several men in protective MOPP suits emerged with detectors in hand. Armed officers started appearing, M-16 rifles in hand; Boroshev looked behind him and saw several Coast Guard seamen lining the rails with M-16s drawn as well. 'If they find anything, we're fucked. But they will not find anything.'

One of Gemici's crew members ran up to the captain. 'Sir, the Coast Guard and the harbormaster wish to speak with you.'

'May Allah help me, I am going to be arrested . . . !'

'If they wanted to arrest you, fool, you'd be in hand-cuffs by now,' Boroshev said. 'Go see what they want. Be cooperative, and stop babbling like a damned monkey.' He didn't trust Gemici one bit to keep his cool, but it didn't matter – the more nervous he seemed, the more the damned American customs officers would think they were on the right trail.

'*All hands, the smoking lamp is out, waste disposal in progress,*' the loudspeaker announcement said. Boroshev stubbed out his cigarette and kicked it over the side. Christ, the air would stink of shit and diesel for the next eight hours, even though offloading the waste would only take one hour.

He wanted to stay and watch Gemici, but he had to act natural in case he himself was being watched, so he left and filled out logbooks in the engine room for several minutes, had a bite to eat, then returned to the rail. It took over an hour of sweating, hand-wringing, gesturing, and pleading from Gemici, and a careful search by the customs investigators, but finally they packed up and departed. 'They questioned me about radioactive residue on those pumps!' Gemici said when he returned to Boroshev up on deck. 'They said they detected radioactive residue! Those pumps are going to be confiscated!'

'They will hold them until the owner comes looking for them, and then they will have no choice but to release them,' Boroshev said.

'But the residue . . . !'

'Do not concern yourself over "residue," Captain – they can't arrest anyone for "residue," ' Boroshev said. 'There are dozens of good reasons why large machinery parts like that would trigger radioactive detectors, and they know it.'

'But . . . he said *radioactive* residue . . . !'

'You old fool, shut your mouth and go about your business!' Boroshev snapped. 'Your job here is done. You have been paid for your work – now get out of my face.'

Boroshev tried to look calm and collected, but inwardly he was still nervous. They apparently *did* detect something, but obviously at levels far below what they needed to confiscate the entire vessel and crew. That meant they had no concrete evidence, which meant so far their operational security was good. He had made it. He'd given himself only one chance in ten of pulling it off, but he'd done it.

The customs officials were now going over each and every piece of machinery being offloaded – it would take several more hours to accomplish, maybe the rest of the day. The Coast Guard vessel *Stingray* was still off the starboard side, but the crewmen on the rails no longer had their rifles at port arms. Most of the crew of the *King Zoser* was on the port rail, watching the U.S. Customs Service inspectors and National Guard soldiers doing their work. Almost all other work aboard the cargo ship had come to a halt . . .

. . . except for the task of unloading tons of trash, sewage, gray water, and contaminated oil and diesel into a garbage barge that had pulled alongside, which was going on at the stern. Boroshev watched the inspections going on at the bow . . . but out of the corner of his eye, he was also making sure offloading the ship's waste was going smoothly as well. There were no uniformed customs officers over there, just contract workers making sure nothing was dumped in the harbor. When that was done and the announcement came that the smoking lamp was lit again, he smiled and lit up another cigarette.

Mission accomplished, he thought happily. Mission accomplished.

Clovis Municipal Airport, New Mexico
That same time

'I'd say we have a major problem here, folks,' Sergeant Major Ray Jefferson said wearily. He had everyone standing out on the ramp beside the Learjet, with Air Force security vehicles surrounding them. The rear cargo hold was open, and Jefferson went back and looked inside, saw the folded CID unit, and shook his head. 'I'm going to take extreme pleasure in seeing that all of you spend the next twenty years or so in a federal prison, breaking big rocks into little ones.'

'Sergeant Major, I'm prepared to explain why we're . . .'

'*Shut your fucking mouth, Major Richter!*' Jefferson exploded. 'There is no possible explanation on earth for this. You're absent without leave; you left the base with classified government property without permission; you conspired to use classified government property in an unauthorized manner. That's only for starters. I'm not a damned lawyer, but I'm pretty sure all of you could grow very old in Leavenworth before you ever see the light of day again.' He took an exasperated breath. 'Are you absolutely insane, Richter, or just a damned idiot?'

'Sir, if you'll allow me to . . .'

'*I said shut your fucking mouth, Major*!' Jefferson shouted again. 'You have no right to be heard, sir. You have no explanation for any of this, and I'm not going to waste my time and energy listening to whatever nonsense you've dreamed up.

'I'm going to give you the courtesy of telling you what's going to happen to you now, Major,' Jefferson went on. 'You will be taken into custody by the Army Criminal Investigation Command. They will take you to Fort Belvoir, where you'll be booked and formally charged. You will undoubtedly be interrogated by the FBI and CIA as well as the Defense Intelligence Agency. Eventually you'll be tried and no doubt convicted of dereliction of duty, espionage, conspiracy, leaving your post, absent without leave, trafficking in classified government property, conduct unbecoming, and any other charges we can think of. Dr Vega, as a military employee in a highly sensitive position in the Army Research Laboratory, and therefore subject to the Uniform Code of Military Justice, you will face the same charges and specifications and will probably face the same fate.'

'Sergeant Major, just listen to Major Richter for a . . .' Ariadna began.

'*You will shut up now, Vega*!' Jefferson shouted.

'That's uncalled for, Sergeant!' Jason interjected.

'For starters, sir, it's "Sergeant Major" – I earned those stripes on the field of battle, and I better damn well be addressed properly,' Jefferson said angrily, a vein impressively standing out on his forehead now. 'Now, did you just back-talk me . . . ?'

'I said, talking to Dr Vega like that is uncalled for, Sergeant Major,' Jason said. 'As her immediate supervisor, she was following my direction. I'm the one responsible here.'

'You think that's going to make any difference, Richter?' Jefferson asked incredulously. 'You are *both* going to be put away for a very, very long time. Don't expect me to be cordial or polite to either of you. You're criminals, thieves – nothing more, nothing less. There is no explanation, excuse, or defending one another anymore. Enjoy your last night of freedom here, because once we arrive in Virginia, you will be in federal custody probably for the next twenty years, or longer. Fun's over.' Jefferson looked over at Kristen Skyy and added, 'Miss Skyy, your plane and all your equipment will be impounded by the CIC, and you will be taken into custody by FBI agents and . . .'

'Like hell I will, buster. One phone call and the weight of the world will be dumping on you so fast it'll make your head spin.'

'That's why you won't be allowed to make a phone call, Miss Skyy,' Jefferson said matter-of-factly. 'You and your crew will be held in federal custody as material witnesses, which means segregated from all other persons and prohibited from contacting anyone until you are formally charged. When that happens will depend on your cooperation in our investigation. As you know, in the current security condition, we have the power to hold you as a material witness indefinitely.'

'I hope you like plenty of media exposure, Sergeant Major,' Kristen said angrily, 'because you're going to be experiencing a shitload of it if you try any of that stuff, I guarantee it. My network knows I'm here; they're expecting me to check in daily, and if I don't they'll call out the dogs looking for me – and the first place they'll go is to your bosses in the Pentagon and the White House. When they find out you've *kidnapped* me, you'll be in really deep shit. Your career will be over.'

'We're way beyond threats here, Miss Skyy – we're into high-level military espionage and illegal transfer of military secrets,' Jefferson said. 'Haven't you been reading the papers or watching TV? There is no First, Fourth, Fifth, Seventh, and Eighth Amendment protection for spies, terrorists, or conspirators. After 9/11 and Kingman City, the American people will gladly put people like you away for good.' Jefferson's cellular phone rang; he glanced at the caller ID number, gave Jason a scowl, and walked away to answer it.

Jason saw two Air Force Security Forces men photograph the CID unit inside the Learjet, then carry it out and set it on the ramp. He looked at Ariadna and tapped his wrist, and she looked at him with an 'Are you damned sure you want to do this?' expression. 'Kristen, how sure are you of your information?' Jason asked.

'Doesn't matter now anyway . . .'

'Kristen, I need to know if your information is any good,' Jason said seriously. 'We're risking our careers over this – maybe our lives, if those Security Force guys get too rambunctious here in a moment.'

Kristen's eyes narrowed fearfully at that remark,

darting back and forth between the guards and Jason apprehensively. 'Lieutenant Alderico Quintao is one of my best sources in South America,' Kristen insisted. 'I've known and used him for about three years when I covered terrorist activities in Brazil, even before GAMMA was created; he's got connections in every nation that shares a border with Brazil; his family is politically connected and wealthy. If he said he knows GAMMA's whereabouts, I believe him. What difference does that make now?'

'I hope you're right, Kristen.' He lifted up his sleeve, revealing a large square wristwatch, and pressed several buttons. 'We're about to start a ruckus.'

Suddenly they heard excited voices shouting near the CID unit. They looked over – and saw the CID unit unfolding itself. Jason looked over at Jefferson, but he was still talking on his cell phone, looking out toward the runway with a blank look on his face, a finger in each ear to block out the unidentified noise behind him. Most of the Air Force Security Force officers were armed, but they were too stunned to pull their weapons and just scrambled to stay out of the machine's way.

'Get the plane loaded up again and ready to fly,' Jason said to Kristen. The CID unit walked straight over to him. 'CID One, pilot up,' he said, and the machine assumed the boarding position. In a few moments, Jason was inside, and the robot really came to life.

What in hell is going on here? Jefferson thundered. In a flash, Jason stepped over to him, and before Jefferson could react, he was trapped in the robot's strong mechanical hands. One robotic hand was wrapped around each of Jefferson's arms, and Jason held him just high enough so he was dangling in mid-air and couldn't wriggle free.

The Security Forces readied their weapons, but didn't point them at the robot for fear of hitting the Ranger. 'Put those damned guns down!' Jefferson shouted to them. To the robot, he yelled, 'Is that you in there, Richter? You are in big fucking trouble, asshole! Let me go immediately or I will bust your ass all the way to Antarctica and back!'

'Sergeant Major, as I tried to tell you, I have actionable evidence of the whereabouts of the terrorist group that planned and executed the Kingman City attack,' Jason said, his electronically synthesized voice firm and unwavering. 'They're in Brazil. Kristen Skyy knows where they are, and her confidence in her source is high.'

'Really? And since you've spent a few quality hours with Miss Skyy in Clovis, your confidence in *her* is very high as well, eh?'

Jason told himself that he should not have been so surprised to learn that Jefferson knew about his evening with Kristen. He swallowed hard within his composite armor shell but managed to reply, 'Yes, sir, it is,' his embarrassment evident even through CID's electronic circuitry.

'You sure you're not thinking with your dick instead of your brain, Richter?'

'I believe Kristen's information is accurate, sir.'

'Put me down, dammit!'

'We are going to depart with Kristen's camera crew,' Jason said. 'You will tell the Security Forces not to interfere and to authorize our departure.'

'You are not the one giving orders here, Richter . . . !'

'But I can be, Jefferson,' Jason said. 'I will destroy those Security Force vehicles if you give me no other choice.'

Jefferson knew he could do it too – better try to talk

him out of this, he thought. 'I said put me down, Major,'
Jefferson said, a little softer this time. 'That's an *order*. I
will not repeat myself.' Jason paused for a moment, then
lowered Jefferson to the hangar floor and released him.
'Have you got any fucking idea of what you're doing,
Major? Or is this your idea of how an officer in the U.S.
Army is supposed to behave?'

'Sir, if you tell me that you believe that Task Force
TALON is everything it appears to be and that it is being
managed and supported in the best way possible by
everyone involved, then I will gladly step down, turn
over all of the CID technology to you and Special Agent
DeLaine, and accept any punishment you give me
without another word,' Jason said. It was indeed a rather
shocking and otherworldly sight to see – a huge three-
meter-tall cyborg talking, gesturing, and expressing itself
so earnestly and emotionally, resembling some weird
alien creature with very humanlike mannerisms.

'Richter, I don't give a shit about your fears, concerns,
or frustrations,' Jefferson said, 'and I am not one bit
impressed by your admonition or offer of surrender,
redemption, or cooperation. I care about only one thing:
getting Task Force TALON functioning as quickly and as
efficiently as possible. Your job, your *duty*, is to follow
orders and support the efforts of your commanders and
superior officers to the absolute best of your abilities, or
get the hell out of the way. Now which is it going to be?'

'Sir, just tell me you believe we're not being played
for fools, and I'll obey your orders to the hilt.'

'I'm not going to tell you anything except obey my
orders, *now*, or find yourself relieved of duty and facing
judicial punishment,' Jefferson said. 'You had better learn
right here and now, mister, that in my command there

are no assurances, guarantees, hand-holding, kissy-face, or group hugs – there is only me and everyone else. I give the orders, and you obey them. It's that simple. What is it going to be, Major?'

The cyborg stood silently for a moment, and Jefferson thought he saw its shoulders droop and its arms go limp, as if in surrender . . . and then suddenly those huge mechanical arms reached out and grasped Jefferson's arms in a steel-like grip once again. Jefferson was so surprised at the trap-quick movement that he gasped aloud.

'*Put him down, now*!' a Security Force officer shouted, his M-16 rifle raised.

Jason turned and with unbelievable speed went over and, with Jefferson still in his hands, lifted one of the Security Force Humvees up with his right foot and over-turned it. In another blur of motion he dashed over to a second Security Force officer and simply bumped him, sending him flying onto his back, bruised but unhurt. Just as Jason turned toward a second officer, ready to put him down, Jefferson shouted, 'All right, all right, *stop*.' To the other officers he said, 'Lower your weapons.' They did as they were ordered. 'Happy now, Major? You think you can fight off all of the Air Force Security Forces? Is that how you want to play this?'

'*This* is how we're going to play it, Sergeant Major,' Jason said, his electronic voice as firm as the CID unit's composite structure. 'We are going to follow Kristen Skyy's intelligence and pursue the leads we have. If we find nothing, we will fly back to Washington or Fort Leavenworth or anywhere you wish and turn ourselves in. But I've come this far because I believe I'm doing the right thing, and I'm not going to stop now.'

'What do you think you're going to do with me,

asshole: kill me?' Jefferson shouted. He was glad to see Richter wince at the very notion of killing anyone – it was that obvious, even inside the CID unit. 'Or maybe you're going to carry me around like a doll while you chase through the jungle?'

'If I have to, sir, I will,' Jason replied. He turned toward the plane. 'Kristen?'

'Fuel truck's on the way, and the pilot is filing our flight plan as we speak,' she replied. 'We're getting clearance to depart right now – we'll be ready to go as soon as we're fueled. What about Sergeant Major Jefferson?'

'He's coming with us,' Jason said. 'Get some nylon ties to secure him.'

'That won't be necessary, Major,' Jefferson said.

'Sorry, sir, but I don't trust you to cooperate with us.'

'Your mission has been authorized,' Jefferson said. 'Apparently the name Kristen Skyy gets you instant credibility these days. The National Security Adviser authorizes us to proceed to São Paulo only to observe and assist in her investigation. We must be accompanied by local police or paramilitary forces at all times, and we are not authorized the use of force.'

Jason immediately put Jefferson back on the ground, then dismounted from the CID unit . . . and as soon as he did, Jefferson had him by the collar and pulled the young Army officer nose to nose with him. 'Now you listen to me, you sniveling chickenshit little *worm*,' Jefferson snapped. 'If you ever touch me again, in or out of that machine, I will break your scrawny little neck like a *twig*. I won't prefer charges; I won't report you; I won't write up one letter of reprimand or letter of counseling – I will simply *kill you with my bare hands*. Do you read me, Major Richter?'

'Yes, Sergeant Major.'

'You think you're the big tough crusader riding off with your lady-love to thwart the evildoers and save the world? You are an officer in the United States Army, so start thinking and acting like one! You will follow my orders and behave like an officer, or you will find yourself cooling your jets in the stockade – after I finish kicking your damned ass.' He tossed him away from him, then turned to the others. 'Let's get this show on the road, people. Mount up.'

Chapter Five

Porto do Santos, State of São Paulo, Brazil
Later that evening

Jorge Ruiz was a farm boy, but Manuel Pereira was a wharf rat. Born and raised in the bustling port city of Santos, on the South Atlantic coast southeast of São Paulo, Pereira loved the sea and loved the hardworking, hard-playing, no-nonsense life on the docks. The rules were simple: you worked, you supported your family, and you gave thanks to Jesus at the end of the week . . . the rest was up to you. Drinking, smoking, whoring, fighting, whatever – as long as you took care of the first three first, just about everything else was *boa vida* – the good life.

Although he joined the army and loved being a ground soldier, he would always be drawn to life on the docks. He loved the smell of the mountains of burlap bags of coffee or boxes of bananas on the wharf awaiting loading onto the rows and rows of ships from all over the world, the scent even overpowering the big diesel and oil engines; he loved the power and brutish efficiency of the cranes, tenders, tugs, and barges, all fighting for position and attention like bees in a hive; and he especially loved the grimy, gritty resolve of the men and women who worked the docks. Loading hundreds of tons of produce aboard a ship in just a couple hours might seem impossible for most men, but the workers did it day in and day out, in any kind of weather, for laughably low wages.

They griped, groused, swore, fought, threatened, and complained every minute, but they got the job done because it was their way of life and they loved it.

Sometimes Pereira wished he could go back to the hard but fulfilling life of his boyhood. The people of the docks taught him how to be a man. It was not an easy tutelage, nothing he would ever want to experience again, but something he could look back on and be proud of how he got through it, proud of how well he learned and adapted, and anxious to pass along his knowledge and experience to his children.

'Manuel?' Pereira turned. His wife of two years, Lidia, stepped into the room, breastfeeding his son, Francisco. 'Should you be sitting in the window like that?'

'You're right,' he said, and moved his chair back into the shadows. They lived in a little two-room fourth-floor tin and wood shanty over the Onassis Line Southeast Pier, one of the busiest and oldest sections of the Porto do Santos. Almost five thousand families lived in this roughly one-square-kilometer shantytown, the home-made wood and tin cottages stacked and jumbled atop one another like thousands of cockroaches in a box. He knew he should be more careful – it would be ridiculously easy for the *Policia Militar do Estado* to scan hundreds of windows in just a few seconds from the harbor, an aircraft, or a nearby wharf.

But Pereira felt very safe here among the other shanties and thousands of people all around him. There was no question that one third of his neighbors would gladly turn him in for the reward he knew was on his head – but he also knew that the other two thirds of his neighbors would avenge him on the spot, and the next morning the informant's body would be found floating in the harbor, minus his tongue and *testículos*. The people here were permitted to destroy themselves, not assist the government in destroying others; everyone survived by helping their neighbors, not ratting them out. Justice was swift and sure here on the docks – and justice belonged to the people, not the government, as it should.

Lidia sat on the arm of his chair, bent down, and kissed her husband deeply. 'My sexy little chief of security,' he told her after their lips parted.

'I am nothing of the kind,' she said. 'But I will be your nagging bitching wife if that is what it will take to keep you alive.'

Manuel smiled hungrily. Sniping at each other was how their love game usually started, and it delighted him. Lidia was barely one generation removed from her native Bororo Indian relatives from the interior, people who both lived off the land and worshiped it, people who were spiritually attuned to the forest, the wildlife, and the very vibrations of the interior regions. The Bororo, especially the women, were fiery, brash, and emotional – the three things that Pereira most desired in women. They lived for one thing: attracting a mate and having as many children as possible before age thirty. Most Bororo women were grandparents by age forty-five.

Manuel had met her while he was in the army, in Mato Grosso state. Lidia's nineteen-year-old husband was a drug smuggler; she had just turned twenty, mother of a seven-year-old son and a three-year-old daughter. Manuel had never met the daughter . . . because he had accidentally killed her when the husband used her as a shield during a pursuit when they tried to serve a warrant on the husband.

Manuel was devastated by the daughter's death. He had, of course, seen many dead children in his military career – children were an inexpensive and highly disposable commodity in most of Brazil, especially the interior. Even so, Manuel would never have knowingly raised his weapon against a child. But he was also struck by the way Lidia handled her grief. She didn't blame the military as he expected – she put the blame squarely where it belonged, on her husband and on herself for allowing her *bastardo* husband to have any contact at all with the children, especially with drugs, large amounts of cash, and wanted criminals around. She was a tough, strong, principled woman, yet she tore herself apart with grief.

She also knew that no other man in her tribe would have her now: she'd lost a child, and as the only surviving family member was therefore responsible for the deaths of her husband and child and for outsiders coming into their village. Manuel could see the hatred building already in the villagers' faces. If she didn't commit suicide shortly after the funeral, she would either be gang-raped and turned into a lower-caste prostitute or servant, or driven out of the village. She would soon be nothing but a walking ghost.

Manuel attended the child's funeral, a half-Catholic, half-animistic ritual cremation, then stayed to question the widow. Bororo Indians usually don't cooperate with outsiders, much less with the authorities, but Lidia was ready to break that code of silence in order to rid her village of the drug smugglers. She became his secret witness, then a confidential informant – then, rather unexpectedly, his lover. They had their first child secretly – having a bastard child by someone outside their tribe was strictly forbidden and would have resulted in death for the child and banishment for her – and then he sent for her shortly after he left the PME. They were married in the Roman Catholic Church just days after she received her first communion.

Although native women were usually scorned by the mixed-race Euro-Indians of modern Brazil, Lidia wisely adapted herself: she became a Catholic, learned modern Portuguese and even some English, and taught herself to mask her own native accent. But more important, she discovered how not to belittle herself in the eyes of other Brazilians. Life on the docks of Porto de Santos became just another jungle to her, and she quickly made it her home.

While his son sucked hungrily on her right breast, Manuel opened Lidia's white cotton shirt and began to suck her ample milk-swollen left breast. 'Maybe I will be your baby now, Mama,' he said. 'Go ahead and nag – I'm not listening anymore.'

'Leave some for your son, you greedy pig,' she said in mock sternness, but she did not move out of his hungry reach. The sensation of both her son and her husband nursing her was one of the most sensual experiences she'd ever had, and she felt the wetness between her legs almost immediately. She reached down and felt him beneath his cutoff canvas trousers, stiff and throbbing already, and she gasped as his left hand slowly lifted the hem of her dress and inched its way up her thigh. '*Ai, ai, mon Dios,*' she moaned as she spread her legs invitingly. 'Let me put Francisco down, and then you may have all you wish, you big baby.'

'I think we are both happy right where we are, my love,' he said, reaching higher and finding her wet mound.

'If I fall off this chair it will be your fault, bastard.'

'If you fall off the chair I expect you to fall on me, lover,' he said, 'and then I guarantee you will not be slipping off.'

'You filthy horny pig, you are disgusting,' she said breathlessly as she grasped him tighter through his trousers. He chuckled as he suckled – they both knew that Indian women were a hundred times hornier than any normal Brazilian male, which said a whole lot for the men in Brazil. 'How dare you touch me there when you know your son might walk in on us at any moment?'

'I always thought Manuelo should learn from the best,' Manuel said.

'*Carajo,*' she gasped as she thrust her hips forward, impatiently driving his fingers toward her and pressing her breast tightly into his face. 'Filthy horny bastard. You would shamelessly put your fingers into your wife's *chumino* and continue to suck her breasts while your son watched? You are a monster.'

'I would do whatever I felt like to my wife and take great delight into pleasuring her any way I chose,' he said, roughly scraping his beard against her nipple.

'Pig. Fucking whoring pig.' There was only one other place where his beard felt better on her body than on her breast, and she couldn't wait until he rubbed it down there. Thankfully she knew that Manuelo would probably not be home until dinnertime – they had at least an hour of privacy before the baby would awaken and her oldest son would return home. Her fingers started fumbling for the buckle on his belt. 'Let's see if this is really yours or if you just had a banana in your pocket this whole time, you filthy whoremonger.'

He moaned again as she worked on his belt . . . but

then he heard steps on the wooden stairs outside, rapid-fire running steps, and his body froze. Lidia detected the change immediately, got to her feet, and wordlessly retreated to a curtained-off area of the second room with the baby. Manuel was on his feet, an automatic pistol that was hidden in the chair cushion behind his head in his hand. He quickly stepped over to the window and peeked outside. It was his son, Manuelo, running up the stairs past his shanty. Manuel lowered the gun and was about to call out to his son to ask him where he was going, but something – a tenseness in his nine-year-old son's young body – made him stop. Something was wrong. Something . . .

'I said *stop*!' he heard. Manuel ducked low. A PME officer ran up the stairs and grabbed Manuelo by the back of his neck. 'Don't you run away when I tell you to stop, asshole!'

'I'm sorry, sir, I didn't know you were talking to me, sir,' Manuelo said. Pereira was proud of his son for staying cool and polite – the PME liked nothing better than to beat up on young orphans and street urchins to keep them in line. Politeness and showing respect went a long way toward survival in Brazil, especially if you were a kid.

'Who else would I be talking to, the damned fish?' the officer yelled. Pereira didn't recognize him – he must be from outside São Paulo state. 'What's your name, boy?'

'Carlos, sir.' Carlos was his Catholic confirmation name, a lie that he could easily pass off as an honest mistake if questioned later. It was an unwritten code word in the shantytowns that you used your middle or confirmation name when being questioned by police, so your neighbors could support your lie for you. 'Carlos Cervada.' 'Cervada' was his mother's 'Portuguesed' Bororo name – again, only a half-lie.

'You're lying. Your Indian name is Diai. You go by the name of Manuelo, in honor of your whore mother's new husband.'

'I'm not lying, sir. I was taught never to lie to the police.'

'Shut up, bastard! You are lying, I say. Where do you live?'

'Right up there, sir,' Manuelo said, pointing.

'Where?'

'Right up there, sir. I'll show you. My mother is there – can you see her?'

'I see a hundred women up there, boy,' the officer said. 'Is your father at home?'

'My father is working, sir.'

'Where does he work?'

'At the docks, sir, for the Maersk Line. "Constant Care." That's what they say all the time. I don't know what it means, but . . .'

'You're lying, boy. Your father is a deserter and a terrorist.'

'I'm not lying, sir. I was taught never to lie to an officer. The PME is here to help us. We must all do as the PME officers tell us. The PME is our friend. Isn't that right, sir?'

'Where is your mother? Point her out to me.'

'*Direita lá, senhor*. Right there, sir,' Manuelo said. '*Mamai*! It's me!' As expected, at least six or seven women waved back. 'See? There she is!'

'You had better not be lying to me, boy, or I'll beat you so badly you'll wish you were dead. Now take me to her, *imediatamente*!'

'Yes, sir, right away, sir.' Manuelo scrambled up the steep steps, and the PME officer had to hustle to keep up with him. 'Not much farther, sir.' He was leading him away from his father, giving him the precious seconds he needed to get away. 'We're almost there . . .'

'Slow down, *bastardo*!' the officer said. But that was Manuelo's cue to bolt. He actually accelerated up the last flight of stairs, ran down a catwalk, and reached a ladder leading up to a roof of the lower tier of shanties. '*Stop*! I order you to stop!' the officer shouted. Pereira was proud of his boy for reacting so fast . . . but out of nowhere, another PME officer grabbed Manuelo just as he started climbing up the ladder.

'*Nao!*' Pereira shouted, and he raced up the stairs toward his son. The first PME officer, turned and pulled out a walkie-talkie to report making contact with his quarry. The second PME officer had grabbed Manuelo by the ankle, pulled him off the ladder, and was holding him with his arms pinned behind his back, making the boy cry out in pain. Like an angry lion, Pereira went up the stairs after him.

'Stop, Pereira!' the first PME officer shouted. He had drawn his sidearm and was pointing it at him. The second PME officer started dragging Manuelo toward the first officer, making Pereira freeze. 'We just want you for questioning, that's all,' the first officer shouted. 'No need for . . .'

At that moment there was a loud 'BOOOM!' from below. Lidia Pereira had appeared in the doorway of her shanty with a sawed-off shotgun and had aimed it at the second PME officer holding her son. The second officer cried out and let go of Manuelo, who immediately ran toward his father.

'*Puta*!' the first officer shouted, and he turned, aimed, and fired four shots. Lidia Pereira ducked behind a wall but the flimsy and half-rotted plywood could not stop a bullet. She screamed and slumped to the floor.

Clutching his son and momentarily forgetting all about the PME officers moving in from all directions, Manuel Pereira headed back to check on his wife. She had been hit in the left thigh and grazed in the left rib cage. 'Lidia!' he shouted. 'Hold on. I'm going to get you out of here.'

'I'm all right, Manuel,' she gasped. There was a large bloody hole in her leg, but thankfully the bullet that had hit her chest had not pierced her lung. 'Take Manuelo and go.'

'Sergeant Pereira is coming with us, Mrs Pereira,' the first PME officer said. Two other PME officers grabbed Manuel and handcuffed him behind his back. 'I think we'll take his son too, to ensure his cooperation.'

'Cowardly bastards . . . !'

'It is you who is the coward, Pereira, hiding behind your son and making your wife fight your battles for you. Get them out of here.' As neighbor women came to help Lidia, Manuel and his son were taken away by the PME. Several neighbors came out of their homes and looked on, and for a moment it looked as if they might try to take the Pereiras away from the PME, but more armed officers showed up and kept the crowd from getting out of control.

They were loaded into a PME van, but instead of being driven out of the harbor area to PME headquarters in São Paulo or Santos, the van detoured into an older, more isolated section of the waterfront. Garbage trucks were unloading onto huge piles of trash, while bulldozers were pushing the piles onto conveyor belts, which led up to garbage barges ready to be taken to nearby island landfills. When the PME van came inside, the entry lane was closed off; within a half hour, all of the trucks and the bulldozer operators had gone.

Manuel Pereira and his son were finally taken out of the van and over to one of the garbage piles, both still in handcuffs. Manuel didn't need to ask why they were taken there – he knew all too well. Moments later, he saw Yegor Zakharov's aide, Pavel Khalimov, and then he was certain. 'So, the colonel didn't have the guts to do this himself, eh?' he asked. 'I knew he was a coward.'

'The colonel doesn't have time to take out the trash,' Khalimov said idly. The big Russian looked at Pereira's son, smiled, put away the silenced pistol he was holding, reached down to an ankle sheath, and flicked open a switchblade knife. 'I had planned this to be quick, but now I think we'll have a little fun first. Let's see how the big tough Brazilian soldier boy does when he sees his son die before his eyes.'

'I was sure you'd bugger him a few times first – you *are* into little boys, aren't you, Khalimov?' The Russian killer's smile dimmed, and Pereira saw him swallow hard. 'Or did your boss tell you not to bugger the victims before you killed them? Afraid you'd leave DNA traces behind that would lead back to him? I get it.' Pereira turned to his son and said, 'This is Captain Pavel Khalimov, son. He rapes and kills young boys for fun, like that old one-eyed Colombian Feliz down on Pier Seventy-seven did before you and your friends took care of him. What do we do to perverts like that, son?' Manuelo expertly shot a glob of spit into Khalimov's face. 'Very good, son. That's exactly what we think of corn-holing faggots like Khalimov here.'

The big Russian flicked the switchblade in a blur of motion, opening up a deep gash on Manuelo's left cheek. The boy screamed like the child he was but quickly silenced himself and started swearing in Portuguese. Blood gushed down his face, and very soon the boy's face began to turn pale. 'I suppose you would call that a badge of honor for your bastard child, eh, Pereira?' Khalimov asked. He stepped forward, grasped Manuelo behind his neck, and pulled him around so he could face his father. The boy kicked, clawed, and pulled, but it was obvious his strength was quickly leaving his young, thin body. 'Say good-bye to your son, Pereira,' the Russian said, raising the knife. 'Maybe I'll pay a visit to your big-titted young wife after I dispose of you and see if she needs consoling.' Pereira screamed over the noise of the nearby bulldozers as Khalimov drew the knife across . . .

Suddenly a massive shape and a blur of motion obscured Pereira's view. He and his PME captors were pushed roughly backward by a metallic bar or tool of some sort. Manuelo screamed again, and the father screamed in unison, unable to see or do anything in the confusion. Machine gun fire broke out – Khalimov's guards, no doubt – so close that Pereira thought he could feel the bullets whizzing past his ears, and he instinctively curled up into a ball to present the smallest and most innocent-looking target for the gunmen. A shotgun blast rang out, completely destroying Pereira's hearing.

He hated himself for thinking it, but he prayed that last shot, directed at the last spot where he thought Manuelo had been standing, would quickly end his suffering.

Just then, in the midst of another barrage of machine gun fire, Pereira was suddenly airborne, lifted by the back of his trousers and hurled through the air. A split-second later he landed, hard, on the concrete wharf again – and when he opened his eyes, he was face-to-face with his son, Manuelo, who was looking at him with tear-filled but overjoyed eyes, holding a blood-covered hand over his facial wound. 'Manuelo . . . my God, Manuelo . . . !'

Then, between the gun blasts, he heard a strange but very loud and clear electronically synthesized voice in English. 'Help the boy, dammit. Get him out of here.'

Pereira pressed his hand over his son's face to staunch the blood and to cover his young body with his. He looked up just in time to see . . . well, he had no idea what in hell it was. It moved like a man but looked like something out of a science-fiction movie, with segmented body parts, wide back tapering down to a slim waist, bullet-shaped head, and weirdly articulating limbs. It didn't move like any machine he had ever seen, but it obviously was some kind of human-looking construct. He heard machine gun fire and then saw sparks and flying pieces of shattered lead fragments as the bullets bounced off the machine; a barrel like a short grenade launcher atop a large box on the machine's back swiveled around and fired a projectile of some sort. The acidy, stinging scent of tear gas reached his nostrils, making it instantly hard to breathe, and Pereira instinctively scooped up his son in his arms and scrambled to his feet, moving away from the gas and hoping he didn't fall off the wharf into the harbor.

The robotlike thing sprinted away so fast that Pereira couldn't believe what he saw. More bullets ricocheted off its smooth metallic skin. A PME officer would move out of hiding, afraid of the approaching machine, and before he could take two steps the machine was on him, knocking him unconscious with a single blow to the head with an armored fist. The pattern was repeated twice more: a soldier or one of Khalimov's men would shoot, the robot would rush him, the gunman would bolt, and the thing conked him out.

Out of the clouds of gas a PME wheeled armored vehicle appeared, firing its twenty-three-millimeter machine gun mounted on a roof turret at the robot. The robot sprinted diagonally away, far faster than the gunner in the turret could follow, and in moments it had dodged back and jumped atop of the APC. One massive hand reached down to the machine gun barrel, and with a quick jerk the barrel bent, then snapped. The robot then pulled the gunner out of the gun turret and tossed him to the pavement, aimed the barrel of his shoulder-mounted grenade launcher inside the vehicle, and fired. Within moments acidic smoke began streaming from the turret and all of the APC's crew members abandoned the vehicle, coughing and gagging as they threw themselves outside as fast as they could. With the APC stopped, the robot stepped off, reached down to the bottom of the armored car's body, and effortlessly lifted the vehicle over onto its side, putting it out of action.

Yop tvayu mat! Khalimov swore to himself as he dashed for his Land Rover SUV a few meters away and opened the locked steel case in back. What in hell *is* that thing? He remembered something about the Americans developing a powered strength-enhancing exoskeleton that could carry weapons and give its wearer incredible physical ability, but he never thought he'd ever see one, especially not down here in Brazil! This had to be reported to Zakharov immediately – but first it had to be stopped before it rolled over both his security men and the PME officers he had hired to help him find Pereira. The thing was strong and obviously bulletproof, but it didn't look that massive.

He had just one choice of weapon and just one chance to knock this thing out.

Through the thinning clouds of gas Pereira saw Khalimov raise what looked like a rocket-propelled grenade launcher or LAWS rocket and aim it at the robot. *'Olhar Para fora! Tem um foguete!'* he shouted, but he was too late. The projectile hit the robot squarely in the back on his left side, and it went flying as if hit by a wrecking ball. When the smoke cleared, the robot was lying face-down, blackened and smoldering like a half-burned piece of firewood. It looked like a smashed toy, but Pereira could see a small rivulet of purplish fluid and a wisp of smoke leaking from its back near where the projectile exploded and thought about the irony of a bleeding machine. Was it blood, or could it be . . . ?

. . . and at that moment, to Pereira's astonishment, the robot began to slowly get on its feet. It was obviously wounded, moving much more stiffly and not nearly as smoothly and gracefully as it had been just moments ago, but it was now moving toward the Russian.

Khalimov swore in Russian, dropped the spent LAWS canister, drew his pistol, and fired. The robot tried to pursue him but appeared to be suffering a serious malfunction, because it was now moving very slowly and clumsily. Khalimov holstered his pistol and ran over to one of the nearby running bulldozers, jumped in, and steered it toward the robot. The machine managed to keep from getting pinned under the front blade by hanging onto it, but Khalimov didn't care. He steered the bulldozer over to the edge of the wharf, set the throttle lever to high, and jumped off just before the bulldozer, with the robot still clinging onto the blade, tumbled into the harbor. He looked over at Pereira, wanting to finish the job he had been assigned, but by then Manuel had retrieved a PME assault rifle and had just loaded a fresh magazine in it, so the Russian turned and sprinted away. In moments he sped off in his Land Rover with two PME sedans accompanying him.

'*Jason*!' Ariadna shouted. Vega, Skyy, and Jefferson, all wearing bulletproof vests, helmets, goggles, and gas masks, sprinted over to where the bulldozer had gone into the ocean.

'*Follow me*!' Jefferson shouted. He leaped aboard the garbage barge closest to the scene, lowered the conveyor belt that had been loading trash onto the barge, and unclipped the cable. Swinging the arm out over the gunwale, he fed out a length of cable, kicked off his boots, grabbed the end of the cable, and jumped into the harbor where bubbles were still rising. Ari dashed over to the barge and stood by the controls. A minute later, Jefferson surfaced. '*Go*! Raise him up, *now*!'

It was an immense relief to all of them to see the CID unit pulled from the ocean. He was unceremoniously laid facedown into a pile of garbage, and Ariadna was beside him immediately. 'That round hit him right in the damaged power pack access door,' she said. 'He lost the entire hydraulic system.' She used a Leatherman pocket tool to open a tiny access panel on the unit's waist, punched in a code on a keypad, and the entry hatch opened up on the CID unit's back. 'Help me get him out of there.'

But it wasn't necessary, because just then Jason pulled

himself out of the flooded CID unit. He coughed, then vomited seawater, looking as white as a sheet, rattled but unhurt. 'Shit, what *was* that?' he said after they took him away from the worst of the tear gas still wafting around the wharf. 'I feel like I got hit by a train.'

'It was a LAWS rocket fired from about fifteen meters,' Ari said. 'We thought you were toast. Then you got run over by a bulldozer and pushed into the ocean.'

'The sensors went blank when the rocket hit – all I got were warning messages about the hydraulic, electrical, and environmental systems failing,' Jason said. 'I had just enough power to lift the blade or whatever was on top of me, then everything went out. I was okay until the water covered my face. Thirty more seconds and I was a goner.' He looked up at Jefferson and raised a hand, and the Ranger shook it. 'Thank you for saving my life, Sergeant Major.'

'Don't mention it, Major,' Jefferson said. 'I'm glad you're in one piece. I saw that LAWS round hit and thought we'd be spending the next few days picking up all the pieces. That's one hell of a machine you built.'

They went back to look for Pereira. The Brazilian was trying to get away in the confusion and battle, but he couldn't move very fast while still handcuffed and with an injured boy in his arms. They found him a few minutes later, hiding in some wooden shipping pallets. '*Relaxe, relaxe,*' Kristen Skyy said in English-accented Portuguese. She pressed a handkerchief over the boy's facial injuries while Jefferson found a handcuff key and released them both. 'The boy is hurt.'

'*Quem esta? Pode me ajudar?*'

'I'm a reporter. *Televisao,*' she replied. She was wearing a dark blue bulletproof vest with the letters 'TV' in white cloth tape on both front and back; a blue Kevlar helmet with similar letters front and back; yellow-lensed goggles; a gas mask hanging under her chin; blue jeans and combat boots. 'Yes, we can help you.'

Through his watery vision, Pereira could see four persons carrying the immobile robot to a waiting PME panel van. *'Quem é aquele? O deus, o que é ele?'*

'Amigo,' Kristen said. She put his hands back on his son's face. 'Help the boy.' She went over to the van and watched as they loaded the machine into the back. Her cameraman and soundman were right behind her, recording everything.

'Is that him?' Jason asked after the CID unit was loaded up.

'Yes,' Kristen said. 'Manuel Pereira, former Brazilian army commando, GAMMA second in command. His family lives somewhere in this shantytown. I assume that's his son – he's supposed to have at least one son around that age.'

'Who was trying to kill him?'

'The men in uniform are PME officers,' Kristen replied. 'Manuel Pereira is wanted by the PME – more accurately, he's wanted by TransGlobal Energy, and that's good enough for the Brazilian government.' She motioned toward an unidentified man in civilian clothing lying unconscious on the wharf. 'But these guys, the ones not in uniform and the one who fired that LAWS rocket and drove you into the drink – I don't know who they are. They might be *Atividade de Inteligencia do Brasil*, the Brazilian Intelligence Agency, which reports to the President of Brazil, or maybe they're CIA.'

'That's easy enough to check,' Jefferson said, pulling out his cell phone.

Jason, Kristen, and her crew went over to Pereira. *'Fala Ingles,* Manuel?'

'Um pouco. A little.'

'Quem o atacou? Who attacked you?' Pereira paused, still ethnically and morally hesitant to rat on anyone even after everything that had happened. Kristen motioned to the boy and asked in broken Portuguese, *'Quem atacou seu filho, Manuel?'*

Rephrasing the question to include his son changed everything – one look down at his son's deeply scarred, blood-covered face, and the hesitation was gone. 'Captain Pavel Khalimov,' Pereira said. 'He is soldier with Yegor Viktorvich Zakharov, GAMMA's second in command.'

'I thought you were second in command of GAMMA?'

'No more. Zakharov is military leader now.'

'What about Jorge Ruiz?'

'I think Zakharov in charge now,' Pereira said. 'Jorge want only to warn of *poluicao,* of *corrupcao* – Zakharov, *nao.* He is *violencia, guerra, poder.* GAMMA is no more.'

Kristen looked at Jason in surprise; then, after making sure her cameras were rolling, asked, 'Did Zakharov have something to do with Kingman City, Manuel? Did Yegor Zakharov plan and carry out the nuclear attack in the United States?'

Pereira closed his eyes, lowered his head, then nodded. *'Sim,'* he said. *'Terrivel. Desventurado.* He must be stopped. He is very powerful, *importante.'* He swallowed hard, then looked away. *'Desculpe.* I am sorry. Zakharov is not GAMMA, GAMMA is not Zakharov. Jorge wants only *paz, respeito, esperanca.* Zakharov wants only *violencia.* I never trust Zakharov. Jorge only trust him.'

'Onde e Zakharov *agora?'*

'*Nao sabe*,' Pereira replied. 'After we attack Repressa Kingman, we hide, move around.'

'*Pode falar* Jorge Ruiz?'

Pereira's eyes returned to Kristen's. '*Sim*,' he replied. 'I can call. *Telefone segredo*.'

'Does Zakharov know this secret phone number?'

'*Sim*,' Pereira said. 'We must hurry. *Pressa. Jorge está no perigo grande*.'

Pereira, his son, wife, and baby were taken away with Richter, Vega, Skyy, her film crew, and Jefferson into their waiting PME armored van. As they sped off to their waiting helicopter at São Paulo International Airport, Pereira called their secret drop number. '*Nao resposta*,' he said. '*Eu comecei somente sua máquina da mensagem*. He will call this number when he receives my message.'

'If Zakharov doesn't get to him first,' Jefferson said. 'His assassin Khalimov found Pereira – Zakharov might know where Jorge is hiding.'

'*Onde esta* Jorge Ruiz?' Kristen asked Pereira.

'Hiding. We move many times.'

'But do you know where he might be most of the time?'

Pereira hesitated, then nodded. '*Sua quinta*, his farm, *em* Abaete, Minas Gerais,' he said finally.

'I know where it is,' Kristen said excitedly. 'I covered Ruiz during one of his human rights rallies there. Abaete is where GAMMA was started. It's less than two hours north of here by jet.'

'The government seize his farm, move his family's gravesite, and sold it, but the new owners allow him to visit and hide there. He . . . *como você diz* . . . *torna-se re-energizado* . . . strong, refreshed, there. Maybe he go there.'

'We need to get there as quickly as possible, Sergeant Major . . .'

'We're going to need authorization to operate outside São Paulo state first,' Jefferson said. 'I'm not going to start a war down here.'

'We're working with the PME to . . .'

'Don't even go there, Major,' Jefferson said. 'I've seen how the PME operates: each officer hires himself out to the highest bidder, and no one even thinks twice about switching sides whenever it suits them. I was authorized to travel to Brazil to assist the authorities to capture and question Manuel Pereira, not to fly around the entire country getting into gunfights with government troops. We're not going anywhere else except back to the States.'

'But Jorge Ruiz will be dead by then.'

'From what Pereira has said, he might be dead already – and even if he's not, his organization has been corrupted and taken over by this Zakharov guy,' Jefferson said. 'I'm not going to risk the future of Task Force TALON chasing after a guy who might not be a factor in the attacks in the United States.' He glanced back at the van following them, the one carrying Richter's and Vega's CID unit. 'Besides, Major, Doctor, you two have some repairs to do. Or did you forget that your robot back there had to be pulled off the bottom of the harbor with a crane?'

'Then send Task Force TALON, Sergeant Major,' Jason said. 'You've got a platoon of top-notch troops back at Cannon ready to go – why not get clearance for them to deploy? We can act as their advance team and scout Ruiz's farm in Abaete. They can bring CID Two along with some *real* weapons.' He made a quick mental calculation in his head; then: 'They can be here by dawn. We can be in Abaete and scope out the farm at night and brief the team before they go in.'

Jefferson thought for a few moments, then nodded

and opened his phone. 'I'll request the clearances and get the rest of the team loaded up and moving south,' he said. 'But we don't do anything until we get permission from the White House. We were authorized to fly to São Paulo, period. We stay here, or we head back to the States.'

Over Kingman City, Texas
A short time later

'My God,' the President breathed. 'I can't believe it . . . I simply can't believe it.' He sat back in his seat in a Marine Corps UH-60 Black Hawk helicopter, one of three orbiting over the blast site in a sort of aerial 'shell game' to confuse any attackers that might want to shoot the President's helicopter down. None of the helicopters had any presidential markings – they resembled the military helicopters that had been orbiting the area since shortly after the blast occurred. He shook his head numbly. 'A nuclear terrorist attack on American soil. It's simply incredible.'

'I think we've seen enough,' the President's chief of staff, Victoria Collins, said, taking an apprehensive glance outside. 'Perhaps we should head back, Mr President,' she said nervously.

'Suck it up, Vicki,' they heard, just barely audible above the roar of the helicopter's rotors.

Collins turned angrily to the third passenger in the President's compartment. 'What did you say, Chamberlain?'

'I said, "Suck it up, Vicki," ' National Security Adviser Robert Chamberlain said in an exasperated voice. 'It means, we're here to gather information and get a firsthand sense of the destruction here, not to soothe your sensibilities. It means as bad as you feel now, there are thousands of Americans down there who are *suffering*. So suck it up, Vicki!'

'How dare you talk to me like that?'

'I dare, Miss Collins, because you want to cut this important inspection short because your delicate little tummy can't stand the sight of a nuclear blast just a few thousand meters away. I dare, Miss Collins, because somebody needs to tell you to put aside your fear and queasiness and *do your fucking job.*'

'All right, that's *enough*,' the President interjected. 'This is no time to be sniping at each other.' The President picked up the intercom and spoke to the pilot, and in fifteen minutes they were on the ground at Houston-Hobby Field. After a few more meetings with military, state, and federal investigation, security, and disaster relief officials aboard *Air Force One*, the President and his staff were airborne once again, heading back to Washington.

Aboard *Air Force One*, the President and his advisers were assembled in the large conference room. Only Chamberlain and Collins were with the President – the rest of the Cabinet and military advisers were present via secure video teleconference, dispersed to various safe Continuity of Government locations around the northeast and mid-Atlantic region for their security. The President first turned to General Charles Lanier, Chairman of the Joint Chiefs of Staff. 'Update on our defense response, General?'

'Fully implemented, sir,' Lanier replied. 'Complete shutdown of all major civil and commercial air, sea, and land gateways. Full mobilization underway of all National

Guard and Reserve units to help secure the borders, ports, petro-gas facilities, chemical plants, and major utilities. All current air and coast defense units are on full alert, and we're adding three new air, coastal, or border defense units per day. In less than two weeks we'll be on full war-time continental defense configuration. We've gotten an average of one thousand new enlistments per *hour* since Kingman City in active, Reserve, and Guard branches, and there's no letup. The American people are responding like nothing we've seen since World War Two.'

'Everyone is going through normal background screening and training though, correct, General?' Chamberlain asked.

'Yes, of course,' Lanier responded. 'Our backlogs are long but we're ramping up and increasing our capability every day. We're not cutting corners, just increasing capacity, slowly but surely.'

'Good. What about inspection routines?'

'Ramping up slowly but surely as well, sir,' Lanier said. 'Reserve Forces units are working with Homeland Security agencies to set up one hundred percent cargo inspections.'

'Donna?'

'We're already up to eighty percent of all air cargo and twenty percent of all sea cargo being inspected before entry,' Secretary of Homeland Security Donna Calhoun responded via video. 'There's a tremendous backlog of containers, but many shipments were stopped after Kingman City, so the disruption was already mitigated. I'm thankful for the quick Reserve Forces mobilization.'

'George?'

'Same with the prosecutors and the FBI,' Attorney General George Wentworth said. 'We're getting thousands of applicants for positions and lots of retired and former employees returning every day. The offices are bursting at the seams and it looks like total chaos out there, but the people are hunkering down and getting the job done. Everyone knows we're under attack now, and they're doing everything they can to help. I want to congratulate Mr Chamberlain for proposing that call for volunteers, sir – we were ready when we needed to be. I'd hate to think of the mess we'd be in now if we didn't have that big influx of volunteers after you made your speech.'

'I add my thanks as well,' the President said. 'Now, I need some clearheaded opinions on what to do next. Let's hear it.'

'Whoever did this has to *pay*, Mr President, and pay dearly,' Chamberlain said bitterly. He turned to Collins and asked, 'What about the President's proposal of asking Congress for a declaration of war on terrorism, Vicki?'

'The status is still the same, *Bob*,' Collins shot back acidly. She turned to the President: 'It's still being staffed, Mr President. The White House, Justice, State, Defense, and congressional counsels have been meeting for weeks with no consensus.'

'What's the holdup?' Chamberlain asked.

'Simple: we don't have anyone to declare war *on*,' Collins said. 'You can't legally declare war on an *activity* or a *concept*. Even Israel has never declared war on organizations such as the Palestine Liberation Organization or Hezbollah, no matter how deadly they are. You can only declare war on another *nation*.'

'You of course have read that in the statutes, Miss Collins?'

'It's not in the law, Mr Chamberlain, but it's common sense and logical,' Collins said.

'State agrees,' Secretary of State Christopher Parker chimed in, speaking via secure videoconference from a Continuity of Government location in Virginia. 'Organizations that operate within a particular country take on the legal status of that country. Countries like Libya and Syria sanctioned and even supported groups we considered "terrorists" for many years. The U.S. can declare war on that country in retaliation for something an extremist organization does while operating there, but it is incorrect to declare war on the organization itself.'

'Justice does not agree,' Attorney General George Wentworth interjected. 'The invasion of Afghanistan to eliminate the Taliban and al Qaeda was a combat operation against a terrorist organization . . .'

'But the Taliban was never considered the legitimate government in Afghanistan,' Collins argued, 'and we certainly did not "declare war" on either the Taliban or al Qaeda . . .'

'What about Hamas in Libya and Lebanon, al Qaeda in Afghanistan and Iraq . . . ?'

'*Making* war and *declaring* war are two different things, Mr Chamberlain, and you know it,' Collins interjected. 'The President has full authority to take action against anyone or anything that threatens the peace and security of the United States, within the limits of the War Powers Act. But if the President wants authority and funding to pursue terrorists around the world for the next ten years, he needs an act of Congress.'

'In your *opinion*.'

'In my opinion, yes,' Collins said, 'but so far the staff concurs.'

'You concur because it's the safest and most politically nonconfrontational path, not because it's *right*,'

Chamberlain admonished. He turned to the President and went on, 'Mr President, I believe you can act at any time. The rumors have been circulating for weeks that you intend to do this: TV commentators have been examining the issue from top to bottom and I haven't seen one roadblock presented yet . . .'

'Except the fact there's no legal precedent for it,' Collins interjected. 'Mr President, let the staff do their job. Delay your decision awhile longer. Let us keep the topic alive with hints, rumors, and questions, and let the press and the pundits address the questions for us.'

'And how many more attacks do we have to endure like this before we act, Miss Collins?'

'What about *your* Task Force TALON?' Collins asked with the same acidity with which Chamberlain queried her. 'That was supposed to be the prototype antiterrorist unit, sweeping out around the world hunting down the bad guys, and as far as anyone knows they're still sitting on their hands in New Mexico.'

'They are most certainly not "sitting on their hands" . . . !'

'My last report tells me that there is a significant policy and leadership rift between the people you chose for that unit,' Collins said. 'I've been told that half the unit doesn't even train together and there is almost constant infighting because of a general disagreement on how the unit should be organized, led, and deployed.'

'Where are you getting this information, Collins?' Chamberlain asked. 'Have you been briefed by either myself or Sergeant Major Jefferson . . . ?'

'That's not important. What *is* important is if the information is accurate or not. Is it?'

The President looked at Chamberlain, silently ordering

him to answer. Chamberlain shot Collins an evil glare, but nodded toward the commander in chief. 'There has been some . . . friction between the military and non-military elements, Mr President,' he conceded. 'That was expected and it is being cleared up as we speak.'

'Robert, everything hinges on that team being ready when I go before the congressional leadership to announce my intention to ask for a declaration of war against terrorism,' the President said, the concern evident in his voice. 'We have to be ready to act as soon as I get the vote, and I mean out the door and in action, not just "ready" to get started. What's the problem?'

'It's the first dedicated full collaboration between the military special-ops community and federal law enforcement, sir – there were bound to be difficulties in establishing set procedures, tactics, chains of command, and exchange of intelligence,' Chamberlain said. 'We're attempting something that's never been tried before: one command that controls both civil and military personnel, rather than two separate entities that attempt to work together but in fact have completely different priorities and procedures.'

'They're all professionals, and they're all federal employees – they know how to follow orders, don't they?' Collins asked. 'Just *tell* them to get their asses in gear and get the job done!'

'It's not as simple as that, Miss Collins,' Chamberlain said. 'They *are* professionals, and the last thing they need is an unelected bureaucrat from Washington with no military or intelligence training telling them how to do their jobs . . .'

'Then maybe we picked the wrong man to form this task force,' Collins interjected.

'I serve at the pleasure of the President, same as you – he can remove me at any time and for any reason,' Chamberlain shot back at her. 'But it goes to show how little you know of how experts work . . .'

'Experts? Mr Chamberlain, correct me if I'm wrong, but you picked a young female FBI agent with very little field experience, and a young army major with absolutely *no* field experience, to lead this task force . . .'

'I picked a dedicated group of professionals with unique talents to head this task force, Miss Collins,' Chamberlain said resolutely. 'I have every confidence in their abilities.' An Air Force communications officer dropped a message in front of him. While glancing at the message, Chamberlain went on, 'It'll just take time to get them ready for action. They will . . .' His facial expression became more and more disbelieving as he read, until finally, he said, 'Excuse me, Mr President, let me take care of this.' He picked up the phone and dialed a number, his voice shaking slightly as he gave the communications officer the number.

As he was speaking on the phone, Secretary of State Parker took a message handed to him by an aide: 'Mr Chamberlain, I've just received a message from the foreign minister of Brazil that I think you should know about . . .'

'I'll be there in a sec, Chris.'

'What is going on, Chris?' the President asked.

'Sir, the Brazilian foreign ministry wants to know why we've sent a strike team *with an armed robot* down to Brazil to kill federal military police forces.'

The President turned to look at Chamberlain . . . but the National Security Adviser was already sitting with his

mouth agape in surprise as he listened to his aide's report.
'Robert . . .'

'Tell them to *get their asses back here*, on the double!'
he hissed into his phone.

'*Mr Chamberlain!*' the President shouted.

'Do it!' Chamberlain snapped into the phone, then
hung up. He took a deep breath, then said, 'Mr President,
I've just received a report from my aide, Sergeant Major
Jefferson. He is in São Paulo, Brazil, with elements of
Task Force TALON.'

'*What?*' the President exclaimed. 'Who in hell authorized this?'

'I did, sir, on my own initiative,' Chamberlain replied.

'Explain.'

'The cocommander of the task force, Major Richter,
received information from a highly reliable civilian source
of the location of a senior member of a terrorist group
known as GAMMA that may have been responsible for
the nuclear blast in Kingman City,' Chamberlain
explained. 'Without prior authorization, Major Richter
prepared to take one of his robotic units, what he calls
a CID, or Cybernetic Infantry Device, down to Brazil to
capture this suspect. Sergeant Major Jefferson intercepted
the major before he could depart.'

'So how did they end up in Brazil?'

'I verified the information Major Richter had with
Kristen Skyy's producers and top executives at SATCOM
One News in New York,' Chamberlain went on. 'The
information was good, so I authorized the investigation.'

'With a damned *armed robot*?'

'No, sir. I told Sergeant Major Jefferson this was to be
an investigation only. They apparently decided to bring
their manned robot weapon system with them.'

'Are they *crazy*?' Secretary of State Parker exclaimed. 'What in hell is going on with this unit of yours, Chamberlain? Are they out of their minds?'

'Under whose authority did he think he was operating, Chamberlain?' chief of staff Collins asked heatedly. '*Yours*?'

'I wasn't privy to his decision-making logic, Miss Collins,' Chamberlain said distractedly.

'Oh, *great* . . . !'

'In any case, the task force did find this terrorist leader, who had been captured by government troops . . .'

'And our guys fought with the Brazilian army?'

'The troops were apparently trying to kill the terrorist leader, not arrest him, on orders of an unidentified foreign fighter,' Chamberlain said. 'I'm unclear as to the details, but the bottom line is that the task force captured the terrorist second in command.' To the President, he went on: 'Sir, they are now requesting permission to pursue leads that might result in the capture of the terrorist leader himself. They are requesting that the rest of the task force deploy to Brazil to assist.'

'Not only should they *not* deploy – they should all be *court-martialed*!'

'For what, Collins – doing their jobs?' Chamberlain asked. 'They said they had concrete evidence linking this terror organization with the blast at Kingman City, and they acted. That's exactly what they should be doing. I may not agree with them doing this without coordinating with me, but at least they acted.'

'That's enough,' the President said. 'Robert, make sure the task force members stop what the hell they're doing and await further orders. No other contact with local law enforcement or the Brazilian military until I give the word. Brief State and Justice right away on the task-force members down there and their capabilities – especially that robot thing that's tearing the place up.'

'Yes, Mr President,' Chamberlain said, picking up the telephone and looking immensely relieved.

To the Secretary of State, the President said, 'Chris, speak with the Brazilian Interior Ministry about getting our guys official sanction while they're down there before the world press thinks we've just started an invasion of Brazil.' He paused for a moment, then added, 'And talk to him about getting them permission to hunt down terror suspects down there. If our guys are pursuing the ones who planned and carried out the attack on Kingman City, I want full cooperation.'

São Paulo, Brazil
A short time later

Ray Jefferson closed his cell phone. 'That's it,' he said. 'We've been ordered to stand down and await further orders. No other task force deployments authorized.'

'This could be our only hope to capture Ruiz before Khalimov gets him,' Kristen Skyy pointed out.

'We've exceeded our authority as it is,' Jefferson said. 'Mount up and let's get out of here before more PME troops arrive and they decide we've broken the law – which I'm sure we've done.'

Jason Richter hesitated. Then, he turned to Kristen: 'Do we have enough fuel to get to Abaete, Kristen?' he asked.

'Sure.' Kristen saw the look on Jason's face, and her own expression turned serious. She shrugged and added, 'Maybe *just* enough. We should stop there to refuel.'

Jefferson shot an angry glance at Richter. 'Major, I warned you . . .'

'Sir, Abaete is north of here,' Jason interjected quickly. 'We need to make a fuel stop as we head northbound, don't we? Abaete is just as good a place to stop as any.'

'There's a restaurant at Abaete Regional Airport that serves the best *churrasco* – Brazilian barbecue,' Kristen said with a twinkle in her eye. 'You boys will love it.'

'You clowns got it all figured out, don't you?' Jefferson asked irritably – but he nodded: it was exactly the excuse he was looking for. 'All right, mount up. And get that CID unit fixed as best you can, Dr Vega – I have a feeling we're going to need it.'

Abaete, State of Minas Gerais, Brazil
That evening

'I see you chose to disobey orders and stop in Abaete after all, eh, Sergeant Major?' Robert Chamberlain remarked via their secure cellular phone.

'Yes, sir,' Sergeant Major Ray Jefferson replied. He knew that their cellular phones had a GPS tracking system that continuously broadcast their exact position; he would have reported their stopover point in any case. 'I can explain.'

'It'd better be good.'

'Sir, Kristen Skyy's information has been dead on so far,' Jefferson said, 'and we have every reason to believe our captive's information is good too. We already have a large quantity of intel on this terror group and its links to Kingman City – there was no way we could simply overfly this location on our way north without checking it out.'

'Sergeant Major, that's just not good enough to send a classified military strike team into a sovereign nation and have them blasting up the place,' Chamberlain said. 'I don't have any clearances for you yet. The Brazilian government has authorized you to be in the country with PME escorts, but you have no authority to go out searching for Ruiz or the Russians or anyone – you must turn over all information you have to the PME immediately or your authorization to be there will be revoked and you could be arrested if you have any weapons on you at all. If you get caught, the U.S. government can't protect you. Make this just a fuel stop and get out of there as quickly as you can.'

'Sir, we have a Brazilian military police officer with us who has procured landing rights and authority for us to travel with our equipment, including the CID unit . . .'

'He can't authorize you to take the CID unit into battle.'

'No, sir, but he hasn't said we *couldn't*.'

'Playing fast and loose with the rules now, Sergeant Major? Doesn't sound like you at all.'

'As I said, sir, I believe we're close to making a very large break in the terrorist organization that attacked Kingman City,' Jefferson said. 'I think it bears investigating.'

There was a long pause on the line; then: 'Is the CID unit operational?'

'They're still working on it, sir, but I think it's down permanently. It took quite a beating in São Paulo – I'm still amazed Richter survived it. But the robot is definitely broken.'

'Probably just as well – I can't imagine the shit-storm if you used that thing again down there without authorization.' There was a momentary pause. Then: 'Very well, Sergeant Major. I'll try to expedite getting you some kind of official clearance to be there, but for the time being you're going to have to rely on Miss Skyy's press credentials and whatever authority your PME officer has to get close to this Jorge Ruiz character, if he's still alive. Try to avoid any contact with any more of the local gendarmerie. Grab Ruiz if you can, collect any intel on this GAMMA organization you can find, and get back here on the double.'

'Yes, sir.'

'I don't need to tell you that most everyone in the White House wants your head on a platter right now,' Chamberlain went on. 'You should have stopped the team from going to Brazil. If Kristen Skyy had truly actionable information, we could have gone through official law-enforcement channels, grabbed those GAMMA operatives, and maybe even enhanced international relations. You could win this battle and still lose the war by getting the task force canceled and yourself and your team members kicked out of the service – or worse.'

'I understand, sir. I had a decision to make, and I made it. In light of the attack on Kingman City, I felt it was the only option I had.'

'I hope you're right, Sergeant Major, but I wouldn't count on too many happy moments for you and your people once you get back to the States,' Chamberlain said seriously. 'Just remember, until I get you some kind of emergency authorization, you're down there on your own. If you leave that airport, I can't protect you.'

'I understand, sir.'

'I don't think you do, or if you do I haven't changed your mind,' Chamberlain said with a slight bit of sardonic humor in his voice, 'so I'll say it one more time: I *strongly* suggest you bring your team back to the States ASAP. Let the FBI, CIA, and INTERPOL handle GAMMA, Ruiz, and Khalimov. You received the information I sent on Khalimov and Zakharov?'

'Yes, sir.'

'Then you should know, Sergeant Major, in case you haven't figured it out, that you're playing with some very, very bad dudes out there, and I don't believe you're equipped right now to handle them,' Chamberlain went on, his voice showing astonishment at Jefferson's lack of reaction. 'We're not sure what Zakharov's game is – he's pretending to be a big supporter of GAMMA but we think he's got another agenda. But there's no doubt at all about Captain Pavel Khalimov: he's a trained military and government assassin, linked to hundreds of killings around the world over the past eighteen years for the KGB in the Soviet years, for the Russian Internal Security Service, and lately as an assassin for hire. If he's got PME troops on his payroll, he'll be unstoppable.'

'I understand, sir,' Jefferson repeated, 'but again, the opportunity to grab the head of this terror group and find out exactly who was responsible for Kingman City is paramount. We have to try.'

'I could order you not to do it.'

'Yes, sir, you could,' Jefferson said. 'I believe Kristen Skyy would still demand to go.'

'You could force her to stay.'

'Yes, sir, I believe I could, and I believe her flight and production crews would not fight me on this,' Jefferson said. 'But then Jorge Ruiz would probably be killed. . . .'

'You told me you think he's dead already.'

'We don't know for sure, sir,' Jefferson said. 'It's only logical to think that Pereira would be a secondary target and Ruiz the primary, but perhaps Khalimov went after Pereira first in São Paulo because he's the harder target and more of a threat to Zakharov. I don't know. But Abaete was on the way, we're here, and I think we should proceed.'

'Kristen Skyy won't be able to save Ruiz even if he is alive.'

'But if I and a few PME troops go along with her, sir, we might get lucky.'

'It's too risky. We have all the intel we need, Sergeant Major. We don't need Ruiz . . .'

'Yes, sir, but it would sure be helpful if we had him,' Jefferson said. 'I have no intention of letting this get out of hand, Mr Chamberlain. We'll be careful, sir.'

There was a very long pause on the line; then, in a very reluctant voice, Chamberlain said, 'I don't like it, Sergeant Major, but I agree that this is an opportunity we can't pass up to get the guy who masterminded the attack on Kingman City. I'll advise the President of what you intend to do and try my best to sell him on the idea. If there's anyone who can take on the likes of someone like Pavel Khalimov, it's you.'

'Thank you, sir,' he responded, but the connection was broken before he got all of the words out. He closed the flip and rubbed his eyes wearily. 'Major Richter.'

'Yes, sir?' Richter replied. He and Ariadna Vega were both leaning inside the CID unit with tools and flashlights; an electronic diagnostic device was attached to an access panel, with several rows of readouts flashing red numerals. Their jet was parked by itself on an isolated part of Abaete Regional Airport's parking ramp, about three hundred meters from the terminal building. A blue plastic tarp was slung over the rear fuselage near the open baggage compartment to hide the CID unit from observation, but this section of the ramp was pretty deserted. The PME officer traveling with them had spoken to the local PME patrols, and together they were keeping everyone away. One local PME soldier roamed around the aircraft itself, while two more in a U.S. military surplus Jeep patrolled the ramp area, chasing away curious onlookers.

'Any progress?'

'A little,' Jason replied. 'We've replaced the hydraulic power pack, but seawater has damaged a lot of other circuitry so we can't test it yet. We have no idea how long it will take to get it dried out and going again. Maybe not until we get it back to Fort Polk.' Ari looked at Jason with serious concern all over her face.

'Well, you gave it a try, Major, Dr Vega,' Jefferson said. 'Mr Chamberlain is still advising us to return to the States.'

'Just "advising" us? Sir, he's not *ordering* us to return now?'

'He was on board *Air Force One* before and was reacting to the news of us being in Brazil,' Jefferson explained. 'Now that he understands we're on the trail of the oganization that might have been responsible for Kingman City, he's backed off.' Jason nodded; Ari's concerned expression only darkened. 'So it's up to us. He has not gotten us any official government support – he says most of the White House still wants us in prison.'

'But he's not ordering us to return anymore,' Jason observed. 'It sounds like he's secretly urging us to press on, sir.'

'That would be my guess as well, Major,' Jefferson said. 'However, Chamberlain maintains that without the CID unit, we could be in real trouble without backup. I agree with him: it's too dangerous. We should leave it to the PME, State Department, and CIA to get those guys.'

'It may be dangerous, Sergeant Major, but you're not making the decisions here,' Kristen Skyy said. She and her crew had been unloading her equipment into an old panel van she procured from the airport manager with a lot of cash and a little womanly schmoozing. 'It's *my* plane, *my* crew, and *my* story. The locals will protect you and the plane while you're here. I'm taking my crew and going out to Ruiz's farm to try to locate him.'

Jason climbed down off the CID unit. 'Khalimov will certainly be out there, waiting for you,' he said, stepping over to her. 'Don't go. The sergeant major's right: it's too dangerous.'

'This is the hottest story of the decade, maybe even of the *century*,' Kristen said. 'The story is out there, not here at this airport. I'm going.' She noticed the look of extreme concern on his face and smiled appreciatively. 'Hey, don't worry. I've been in lots of dangerous places before – I don't think a farm in Brazil will be one of them.'

'Kristen . . .'

She reached out, touched his face, and smiled. 'Hey, look at me – I've got a man worried about me. That's a nice switch.' She motioned to the PME officer from São Paulo, now behind the wheel in the van. 'I've got my friend Alderico there too, so I don't think we'll have any trouble if we run into any local PME.'

'What's your plan, Kristen?' Jason asked.

'I want to make contact with the farm's new owners

and see if anyone else other than the PME has been sniffing around,' she replied. 'I intend to look around first, do a little surveillance, and check it out carefully before I go in. That farm is surely under twenty-four-seven surveillance by several Brazilian and other government agencies . . .'

'And Zakharov and Khalimov,' he reminded her.

She held up a pair of night-vision binoculars, and tapped her chest indicating her bulletproof vest. 'Standard issue stuff in our line of work. Don't worry about me. I suggest you be ready to blast off as soon as I radio you – I might be high-tailing it out of there.'

Sergeant Major Jefferson drew his forty-five-caliber Smith and Wesson pistol from its holster on his right hip, checked the safety was on, then holstered it again. 'I'm going with you,' he said.

Kristen looked at the big Ranger and nodded. 'Good. Let's go.'

Jason looked surprised. 'You *want* him to go with you?'

'Hell yes. Do you think I'm stupid? I'll take as many guns as I can with me.'

'Then I'll go too,' Ariadna said, unholstering her SIG Sauer P220. Kristen was about to ask if she knew how to handle it, but Ari checked that she had a round chambered in the gun and reholstered it almost as fast and as expertly as Jefferson. Kristen nodded, impressed, and made sure she got a bulletproof vest, one with the letters 'TV' outlined in tape on it.

'Ari . . . !'

'I'm no use here until all that seawater is dried up inside the CID unit, right, J?' Jason looked at her carefully, not believing what she was saying. '*Right*?'

'Yes, right.'

'Then let's do it,' Kristen said.

'*Eu irei protegê-lo*. I will go and protect you,' Manuel Pereira said.

Kristen nodded, and a PME officer gave him a bullet-proof vest, a beat-up looking shotgun, and a box of shells; he loaded his gun quickly and stuffed the remaining shells into his pockets. To Jason, Kristen said, 'The flight crew can watch over you and the plane and make sure the PME doesn't try anything. It'll take us no more than twenty minutes to drive back from the farm. When we radio you, have the crew fire up the engines and taxi to the hold line – we'll go right to the end of the runway and jump on board so we can be off the ground as soon as the door's shut.'

Everyone headed to the van to load up; Jason grasped Ariadna's arm before she climbed inside. 'Keep your damn fool head down, Ari,' he said.

'I will,' she replied. She looked at him carefully. 'Do you have any idea what you're doing, J?'

'Let's go, boys and girls,' Jefferson prompted them.

Jason shrugged. 'I'll get back to work on El CID,' he said. 'Wish me luck.'

'Just get it fixed, J,' she said seriously, and climbed inside the van. Jason immediately returned to work on the crippled robot, working as fast and as hard as he could.

Less than thirty minutes later, they passed over a cattle grating and four-strand barbed-wire fence with a white-washed wooden archway over the driveway. Kristen scanned the area with her night-vision equipment – nothing seemed out of place. A dog barked in the distance – typical of any farm – and a peacock screeched, a bird often used by Brazilian farmers like watchdogs. 'This is it,' Kristen said. 'My crew and I are going in. I've contacted the new owners, and they've agreed to meet with us off-camera, although they say they have nothing to say about Jorge Ruiz or GAMMA.'

'Did you detect any kind of duress?' Jefferson asked.

'They were definitely nervous when I mentioned Ruiz,' Kristen said, 'but it also seemed to me they were accustomed to doing interviews about Ruiz and GAMMA – rather, giving interviews but *not* talking about Ruiz. They did invite us inside, though. He's a retired federal judge; I think I've met him before.'

'Think Ruiz is here? Think they're protecting him?'

'There's only one way to find out.' She turned to Pereira. 'Manuel, *onde nós encontraríamos* Jorge? Where would we find him?'

'*Cemetery da sua família* . . . his family cemetery, the place of the *sepulturas*, the gravesites, before the government dig them up,' Pereira replied. 'The graves are no longer, but the *Rocha da Paz*, the Rock of Peace, is there. That is Jorge's place of prayer.'

'That's the *last* place you should go – if the PME or Khalimov is here, that's exactly where he'll be waiting for us,' Jefferson said. 'Manuel and I will scout it out. We'll meet up with you in the farmhouse.' The Ranger took their short-range FM walkie-talkie, keyed the mike, engaged the 'HOT MIKE' locking switch keeping the mike button depressed, tested it, and told Ariadna to hook it on her pants out of sight. 'I'll be able to hear everything you say, so if you get in trouble I'll know. You're a producer or an assistant; you're from Mexico; you speak Spanish and not much Portuguese; your English is very poor. Got it?'

'*Si, señor,*' Ari replied weakly.

'You want to give me your gun? If they find it on you, they'll likely make it very difficult for you – it'll be harder to convince them you're just a journalist.'

Ari swallowed hard, but shook her head and smiled bravely. 'I'll keep it. *¿Una muchacha consiguió protegerse, no?* A girl's gotta use protection, right?'

'How will we know if *you're* okay, Sergeant Major?' Kristen asked.

'Manuel, how long to get to the cemetery from here?'

'*Não muita hora.* Ten, fifteen *minutos.*'

'Give us no more than thirty minutes to scout out the cemetery,' Jefferson said. 'If you don't hear from us, assume we've been captured or killed, and get the hell out. Get on the jet and blast off – don't try to set up a rescue mission or talk to the PME, just get out of Brazil.'

'Make it forty-five,' Kristen said. 'Thirty minutes is not enough time for me to . . .'

'Thirty minutes, Miss Skyy,' Jefferson maintained, 'or you're risking your life and that of your crew and Dr Vega. I would take it personally if any of you are hurt because you stayed to ask one last question or took one last "reaction" shot.' Kristen noted the big Ranger's stern voice, remained silent, and nodded.

'Shouldn't we all scout out the farm first before we go in?' Ariadna asked.

'You're a film crew from the United States here to do a piece on Jorge Ruiz and GAMMA – why would you be skulking around the place first?' Jefferson asked. 'Let us do our recon, and you do your interview. Forget that we're out there.'

'Okay,' she said, handing him her night-vision goggles. 'You'll need these.'

'Thank you.' Jefferson turned directly to Kristen and

said, 'I know this is your job and your career, Miss Skyy, but these men are killers, and no story is worth your life or the lives of your crew or Dr Vega. Pavel Khalimov is a military-trained assassin for hire. If you suspect anything is wrong, turn around and get out. Is that clear?'

'I've done interviews with genocidal dictators, mass murderers, mobsters, gang-bangers, and every kind of human scum that's ever existed – most times on their own turf,' Kristen said. 'My crew and I have been shot at dozens of times; my cameraman Rich there has pieces of a camera still embedded in his eye socket after a bullet missed his head and his camera was shot out of his hands while he was filming. We'll be careful, Sergeant Major – but we're here to get a story, not sightseeing. The story is learning the whereabouts of, or perhaps rescuing, Jorge Ruiz. If I can't do that story, I'll get out – but not before.'

Jefferson looked at her grimly, then glanced at Ariadna. 'Her attitude the same as yours, Doctor? You still want to go with her?'

'*Si*,' Ari said. '*Usted dos es los comandos, no yo*. You two are the commandos, not me.'

'All right, let's do it,' Jefferson said. They checked their watches, and he and Pereira disappeared into the darkness at a fast trot.

'Here we go,' Kristen said, and they drove ahead toward the farmhouse. After about a kilometer on a bumpy gravel road, they came across a corral with two horses, a two-story barn, a small adobe cottage, and a low rock wall surrounding a very nice pink stucco single-story house with a tile roof. An older couple had been on rocking chairs on a tile-covered patio seated beside a low fire pit, and they got to their feet as the van approached. Two men who appeared to be farmhands approached the van, one in front left and one from the right rear, both carrying small-gauge shotguns – useful for scaring off coyotes or shooting snakes and not much else.

Kristen emerged from the front passenger seat. 'Are you Miss Skyy?' the old gentleman called out from his patio.

'*Sim,*' Kristen replied. '*Eu sou* Kristen Skyy, SATCOM One News. *Senhor e senhora* Amaral?'

'*Sim,*' the gentleman replied. 'That is Jose, and the other is Marco. They are my men. Who else is with you, *menina?*'

'My crew, Rich, Bonnie, and Ariadna,' Kristen replied. She motioned to the PME officer behind the wheel of the van. '*Tenente* Quintao is here just as an escort, not in any official capacity. He is from São Paulo. He won't interfere.' The worker named Marco opened the van's side door, stepped away, and waved the others out; the PME officer wisely put his hands atop the steering wheel so the first farmworker wouldn't get too nervous.

Amaral saw the cameras and recording equipment and waved his hands. '*Nao câmeras, nao retratos,*' he said.

Kristen nodded to the cameraman, who put his camera back in the van – then, while the sound person Bonnie and the PME officer screened him, Rich put the camera up onto the glare shield pointing toward the farmhouse and turned it on. Thankfully the dome light didn't work and Marco, intent on watching Kristen, didn't notice. '*Nao retratos,*' Kristen said. She held up her palm-sized digital recording device. 'I would like to use a recorder, but it is only for my own personal use – I will not broadcast your or your wife's voice. *Nenhuma transmissão de suas vozes, aprovação?*'

Amaral nodded and waved for them to come up to his patio. His wife had a pitcher of cold *guarana* fruit juice and a bowl of *salada de fruta* on a small table between them. There was only one chair, but Rich and Bonnie were accustomed to melting away into the background while Kristen worked. One of the farmhands, Jose they assumed, stayed somewhere behind them in the darkness on the other side of the rock wall; Marco was nowhere to be seen. *'Obrigado vendo nos hoje à noite, senhor, senhora,'* Kristen said, taking a sip of the sweet green fruit juice.

'You may speak English, Miss Skyy,' the man said, 'although your Portuguese is very good.'

'Muito obrigado,' Kristen said. 'I believe we've met, *senhor*. You were a federal judge when Jorge Ruiz had his environmental workshops here, no?'

'I do not know where Jorge Ruiz is,' Amaral said quickly. 'I have not seen him in many years.'

'But you do allow him to come back, don't you, *Advocado*?' Kristen asked. 'You know he comes and visits the site of his family cemetery, the *Rocha da Paz*, don't you?' Both the Amarals' eyes widened in fear, and they shook their heads – but it was obvious in their faces that they knew. Kristen held up a hand. 'Don't be afraid, *senhor*. We are not here to capture Jorge – in fact, we are here to help him.'

'We know nothing of Jorge Ruiz,' Amaral repeated woodenly. His wife shook her head, afraid to speak but anxious to support her husband's claim.

'Has the PME or any agents of the government or of TransGlobal Energy come out here searching for Jorge, sir?'

'Muitas vezes. Many times. They think he still come here. I have not seen him in a very long time, since the days of his *faculdade ambiental*, his environmental college, here.'

'Do you believe Jorge Ruiz is a terrorist?'

The gentleman sighed deeply, then nodded somberly. 'The police, the TransGlobal Energy corporation, they did terrible things to him and his family,' he said. 'I believe his mind was *torcido*, twisted, by the violence. Any man would be filled with such horrible anger to see his wife and children burned alive in his own house.' But he shook his head. 'But even this does not excuse his actions. Revenge is one thing: continued violence all over the country, possibly all over the world – this is not right.'

'You have heard of the nuclear bomb attack in the United States?' Amaral and his wife nodded fearfully. 'Do you think Jorge could plan and carry out such a thing?'

'*Nunca!*' Amaral retorted. 'Yes, Jorge and his followers have killed a few corrupt police, foreign security officers, and bureaucrats when he bombs dams and bridges – and yes, he has even killed innocent bystanders, for which he must answer to God and to the law. But Jorge would never, *ever* consider using a nuclear weapon! It is against everything he holds sacred.'

'I have reliable information that Jorge Ruiz's organization, GAMMA, orchestrated both attacks.'

'I refuse to believe it,' Amaral insisted. '*Nao*. Jorge is strong-willed and dedicated, but he is not an *assassino louco*. Now you must leave.'

'Judge Amaral . . .'

'*Nao*. You are like all the others . . . you believe what you wish to believe to sell your papers and be on television! Marco! Jose! *Vindo aqui*! These people will be leaving now.'

*   *   *

Guns at the ready, Jefferson and Pereira approached the old gravesite, about a hundred and fifty meters east of the farmhouse. A few cows snorted and mooed in the darkness as they moved along, but except for a few lights at the farmhouse, it was completely quiet and still.

Jefferson listened intently to the walkie-talkie broadcast from the others as they moved. 'Sounds like Skyy has just about worn out her welcome,' he whispered. Pereira could not understand him, but looked at him with an inquisitive glance. 'We must hurry,' Jefferson summarized. 'Hurry. *Rapido*.' He hoped Pereira knew enough English and his pidgin Spanish to make himself understood.

Through the night-vision goggles, Jefferson could finally make out the rock at the old gravesite, a huge boulder about the size of a large desk, with a bronze plaque embedded into the face . . . and, to his surprise, there was a man kneeling before it, his hands clasped atop the rock, his head bowed in prayer. He wore a simple farmer's outfit of coveralls and frayed, muddy knee-high boots. 'There's someone there,' Jefferson whispered. '*Un persona* over there.'

'Jorge?' Pereira asked excitedly.

'I don't know,' Jefferson said. '*No sé*. He's praying. Praying.' He didn't know the Spanish word, and Pereira didn't seem to understand him, so Jefferson made the sign of the cross on himself with the muzzle of his .45 pistol. 'Praying.'

'*Deve ser* Jorge!' Pereira said excitedly, and he trotted past Jefferson.

'No!' Jefferson hissed.

But it was too late – Pereira rushed past Jefferson

before he could stop him. 'Jorge!' he said in a quiet voice. '*É você?*'

'Manuel?' the man replied, half-turning toward him and rising to his feet. '*Eu não posso acreditar que é você!* I can't believe it's you!'

'Jorge, we must get you out of here,' Manuel said, stepping quickly over to him. 'Khalimov is after us. He tried to kill me and my . . .'

Through the night-vision goggles Jefferson saw the man move, but it was too late to call out a warning. Just as Manuel reached him, the man spun, kicked Pereira's legs out from under him, pinned his bad arm behind him, and ground his face into the dirt so he couldn't cry out. 'At least now I get a second chance to finish the job, Manuel,' Pavel Khalimov said. Pereira struggled, but Khalimov had the loop of a nylon handcuff already around one wrist and was about to pull the other wrist through the loop . . .

'Hey, asshole.' Khalimov looked up at the unexpected American voice – and the steel toe of a leather combat boot caught him squarely in his right temple, knocking him unconscious.

'I believe Jorge's innocent, Judge Amaral,' Kristen insisted. 'Please believe me. I believe he's being used as a scapegoat by one of the men in his organization.'

'I know nothing of any of this . . . !'

'You were a federal judge here in Minas Gerais, *senhor*,' Kristen said. 'You were involved in almost everything that happened in Jorge Ruiz's life since he returned from the United States. You presided as he built the environmental and human rights forum here in Abaete and founded GAMMA – I believe you even assisted in projects that helped grow that institution, such as expanding the regional airport and improving the roads so more people would come here from all over the world. You know him as well as anyone . . .'

'I said *go*!' Amaral shouted. 'Marco! Jose! *Onde estão você? Vindo aqui* . . . !'

'Judge Amaral, I have information that one of Jorge's lieutenants, a man by the name of Zakharov, engineered the nuclear attack in the United States,' Kristen said quickly. 'I don't believe Jorge knew about this attack beforehand. I believe this man did this under the name of GAMMA without Jorge's knowledge or authorization. I don't know why he would do this, but . . .'

'I know nothing of this Zakharov!' Amaral cried out. 'Jose! Marco . . . !' He peered into the darkness, obviously wondering where his men were. '*Vindo rapidamente! Eu necessito-o* . . . !'

'*Espera, pai,*' they heard in a soft voice. Kristen turned . . . and saw Jorge Ruiz himself appear out of the darkness around a corner of the farmhouse.

'Jorge, *nao* . . .'

'*Todos endireitam, pai,*' Ruiz said. He clasped Amaral on the shoulder and gave Amaral's wife a kiss on the forehead, then turned toward the others. 'Kristen Skyy from SATCOM One,' he said in a soft, almost accent-free voice with a tired but sincere smile. 'Nice to see you again. It's been a long time.'

'I'm glad to see you're alive, Jorge,' she said. 'Why did you call Judge Amaral "father"?'

'Because he *is* my father, my natural father,' he replied. 'He used his position to keep the adoption records secret, but he shared them with me after my adoptive parents' murder.'

'And he used his position as a federal judge to get this land when the government seized it,' Kristen said, 'knowing he could protect you and tell you when the PME had it under surveillance?'

'*Sim*,' Jorge said. 'But after the attack in the United States, the whole world will have this place under careful watch. It is too dangerous for them to be here. I came back to warn them to leave.'

'You shouldn't have come here,' Kristen said. 'You are in serious danger. A Russian by the name of Khalimov was ordered to assassinate Manuel Pereira in Santos. I believe he'll be after you next.'

'Is Manuel dead?' Kristen looked at Ariadna, then feigned a disappointed expression; Ruiz immediately interpreted it as a 'yes.' 'I am so sorry,' he said. 'He tried to warn me about Zakharov and Khalimov. I thought it was just *competição*, Zakharov being a colonel and Manuel only being a sergeant. I thought . . .'

'Zakharov is a colonel?' Kristen asked. 'A *Russian* colonel?'

'The questions can wait, Kristen,' Ariadna said. 'Let's get out of here.' She pulled the walkie-talkie from her jeans. 'I hope you guys can hear me . . .'

'Now, who might you be talking to, *menina*?' a strange, heavily accented voice asked. Out of the darkness behind Ruiz walked Amaral's two farmhands, Jose and Marco, with their hands on their heads, their shotguns nowhere in sight, followed by two men with silenced automatic pistols aimed at their heads. They were followed by a huge barrel-chested, square-jawed man in a dark hunting jacket, dark pants, and gloves, carrying an immense sniper rifle. 'We must get acquainted. I insist.'

The *Policia Militar do Estado* Jeep approached the SATCOM One News jet in its isolated spot on the parking ramp at Abaete Regional Airport and stopped beside the outer perimeter guard, driver-to-driver as cops on patrol did all around the world. If the inner guard stationed by the jet had been paying any attention, he might have noticed two bursts of light inside the second Jeep, but he was standing behind the tail of the jet, a few meters away from the little blue vinyl tent erected there by the American engineers working on their device, having a cigarette and staring out across the ramp toward the terminal building, wishing he was inside having a beer.

The oncoming Jeep shut off its headlights, then briefly flashed its amber parking lights a few moments later, not enough to get the inner guard's attention. Unseen by the lone guard, a man dressed completely in black, hidden in the brush just outside the airport perimeter fence, slipped through a cut already made in the chain-link fence, lay flat on the ground at the very edge of the tarmac about fifty meters from the jet, and raised his sniper rifle. The scope's light-intensifying optics showed the lone guard in clear detail in the sniper's crosshairs, his body illuminated only by his cigarette . . .

A few moments later, one of the men in the oncoming Jeep heard *'Dal'she'* in Russian in his headset. 'The last guard's been eliminated,' he told the driver. 'Let's go.' They dismounted from their Jeep and walked toward the vinyl tent quickly, trying not to appear rushed or excited, their Beretta M12 submachine guns with sound suppressors affixed slung behind them, readily accessible but out of sight. There was a dim light on in the cockpit, probably from a reading light. The entry door was open, and there appeared to be a light on somewhere inside the cabin. There was a powerful light on under the blue vinyl tent in the back of the plane, and they could see some instrument with blinking red lights and an occasional electronic tone, and what appeared to be a lone individual sitting on a chair inside.

The two men drew their weapons as they approached the jet. One crouched beside the open entry door, covering the interior, while the other stepped quickly around the left wing tip, his weapon trained on the tent. Once he was in position, the first assailant near the entry door said in English, 'This is Sergeant Cardoso, *Policia Militar do Estado*, Minas Gerais. I need to speak with the pilot, please.'

'Just a sec,' a voice said from inside. 'He's in the lavatory.'

'It's important,' the first assailant said.

'Okay. Stand by.'

The second assailant crouched low so he wouldn't be seen by anyone inside through the windows and followed the trailing edge of the left wing, ready to fire. He had strict orders not to shoot the plane itself because the boss was going to fly it out of there tonight, so he didn't want to fire toward the left engine, which was partially obscured by the tent. He could see and hear the jet moving as someone stepped down the aisle. Now he was almost at the fuselage, and he could see enough of the engine out the tent's front opening that he knew he wouldn't hit it. The footsteps behind him were louder – the pilot or whoever was inside was almost at the entry door. He could see the blinking test equipment, the canvas camp stool, and now the open baggage compartment door . . .

. . . but there was no one underneath. '*Huyn'a*!' he swore in Russian into his headset. '*Poostoy*!' He moved toward the tent – no one there at all. There was a duffel bag on the camp chair with a jacket placed atop it to make it look like a person sitting in the chair! '*Bayoos shto nyet*!' He dashed around it toward the tail, aiming his rifle back at the entry door, waiting for whoever it was to come out . . . and then realized that his comrade was gone.

He heard a rustling sound and quickly aimed his rifle at the sound. It was the lone PME guard who had been stationed near the plane, the one he *thought* had been shot by his sniper, kneeling beside the unmoving form of the sniper out at the edge of the pavement! The guard got to his feet and started looking around, unsure of which way to run. The Russian aimed at him and set the fire-select switch to three-round burst . . .

. . . when suddenly his Beretta submachine gun flew up and out of his hands before he could squeeze the trigger. He turned and saw a massive dark figure standing beside him . . . then a blur of motion, just before he felt the blow to the side of his head. His vision was obscured by a curtain of stars, then nothing.

Jason Richter, inside CID One, destroyed the Beretta submachine gun with one quick twist of his robotic hand as he made his way to the entry door. 'Captain!' he shouted. The pilot appeared from behind a seat, a pistol in his hands. 'Get this thing ready to fly! If anyone else comes near this plane, kill them!'

'Hey! Where are you . . . ?' But the robot was

completely out of sight before the pilot could even get out of the plane.

'Yegor!' Ruiz exclaimed. 'What in hell is going on? Release those men! What are you doing here?'

'Weren't you listening, Jorge? I'm here to kill you,' Zakharov replied matter-of-factly. The two men with Zakharov pushed the farmworkers toward the Amarals and made them kneel down, hands on their heads. Zakharov went over to Ariadna and took the walkie-talkie away from her. 'But first I'm going to learn a little more about your new friends here. Miss Kristen Skyy of course needs no introduction. Who is this lovely lady in the bulletproof vest?'

'*Mi inglés no es tan bueno, señor,*' Ariadna said.

'*Absurdo. Pienso que su inglés es excelente, señorita,*' Zakharov said in very good Spanish. He quickly searched her and immediately found her pistol. 'Reporters these days are armed very well, I see – body armor *and* a pistol. Who are you?'

'I . . . I'm with Kristen,' Ariadna said in English. 'SATCOM One News. You must be Yegor Zakharov . . . Colonel Yegor Zakharov.'

'Kristen Skyy's bodyguard? Lover? What?'

'Producer.'

'Producer. Ah, I see. And who were you talking to?'

'Our security officer, in the van.'

'If you are speaking of Lieutenant Quintao, I'm afraid he won't be answering you,' Zakharov said. 'He wasn't very trustworthy anyway – I found him nearly asleep behind the wheel. I believe I taught him a valuable lesson: never fall asleep on guard duty.' He stepped toward Ariadna menacingly. 'But he did not have a walkie-talkie with him, just a video camera. So who were you talking to?'

'I have some questions for you, Colonel Zakharov,' Kristen interjected. 'Let's you and me talk. She isn't in charge of this crew: I am.'

'Oh, believe me, Miss Skyy, we *will* be talking together, quite extensively,' Zakharov said. 'But I know you very well already, of course; and you have two people over there that, if I may hazard an observation, look like members of your production crew. I would even venture to say they are not armed. But you were armed, *menina*. And pardon me, but you do not look like a journalist to me. Now, who are you?'

'I told you, Colonel, I'm a . . .'

The butt end of the Dragunov sniper rifle flashed in a blur of motion, and in the blink of an eye Ariadna lay on her back on the stone patio floor, blood streaming from her mouth. 'It is going to get very, very ugly for you, *lagarta*, unless you talk,' Zakharov said. 'It is a simple question: who are you?'

'Bastard!' Ariadna swore, wiping blood from her mouth. She was unable to speak for several moments, dazed from the blow; then, she replied weakly, 'Vega. My name is Vega.'

Zakharov's eyes widened in surprise – it was clear that he recognized the name. 'Well, well, what a pleasant surprise,' he said. 'Dr Ariadna Vega?' It was Ari's turn to look shocked. 'I am surprised to see you here. You are not at all what I expected. A female civilian scientist and electrical engineer working for the United States Army – I expected either a tattooed dyke or an ugly one-hundred-and-fifty-kilo nerd with glasses as thick as icebergs.'

'What are you talking about, Colonel?' Kristen asked.
'Do you know her? What's going on here?'

'We will have our conversation soon, Miss Skyy,'
Zakharov said in a menacing tone. 'For now, please do
not interrupt us.' He withdrew a military walkie-talkie
from underneath his coat and keyed the microphone:
'*Kapitan? Zayaveet. Ana zdyes.*' To Ariadna, he said, 'We
did not expect you to accompany Miss Skyy, so it created
a little confusion out at the airport.' Ari's eyes widened
in fear. 'Oh yes, we located your jet and your friends at
Abaete airport, and they should be well taken care of by
now. The PME was not very cooperative at first, but we
convinced them quite easily of how much we wanted to
greet our visitors from New Mexico.' He keyed the mike
button again: '*Kapitan? Zayaveet!*'

'If you're trying to call Captain Khalimov, Colonel,
don't bother – he's right here.' Half-hidden by a corner
of the farmhouse, Sergeant Major Jefferson emerged with
his pistol aimed at Khalimov's head. 'Now drop your rifle
and order your men to drop their guns.'

'I suggest you drop *your* weapon before there is a
bloodbath here,' Zakharov said casually, aiming the
captured pistol at Ariadna. 'We have you outgunned.'

'*Não exatamente*, Zakharov,' Manuel Pereira said, using
his commando skills to remain hidden in the darkness
although he was less than a dozen meters away. 'And if
there is to be a bloodbath, you will be the first to die.
Eu garanto-o.'

'Manuel!' Ruiz shouted. 'Thank God you're alive.'

'Do it, Zakharov!' Jefferson ordered. 'Drop your
weapons, or I'll blow this fucker's head off, and Manuel
will do the same to you.'

'You mean, all that's standing between my seven

hostages and you is Captain Khalimov there? *Ya huy na nivo palazhyl.* Here's what I think of that.' In a blur of motion, Zakharov pocketed the pistol, swung the Dragunov sniper rifle up, and fired. Khalimov screamed and flew backward, the round hitting squarely in his chest like a hammer.

The ensuing battle took only seconds, but the carnage was enormous. Zakharov immediately sprinted to his right and took cover behind the van. His two gunmen fired bullets into the heads of the two Brazilian farm-workers, killing them instantly. One of them turned his gun toward Kristen Skyy and fired. Kristen screamed, took a couple of steps toward Jefferson, then dropped to the ground. The Russians died moments later when Pereira fired two three-round bursts from Khalimov's submachine gun and made perfect hits.

Zakharov fired a round toward the corner of the farm-house where Jefferson was, making him duck for cover, then retrieved Ariadna's pistol from his pocket and fired at where Jorge Ruiz had been standing near the Amarals. At the first shot, Ruiz turned, ran at full speed, and body-tackled his parents, sending them and himself over the other side of the short stone wall surrounding the patio. Kristen's crew members leaped over the wall themselves, disappearing into the darkness.

'*Stop*!' Zakharov shouted from behind the van. 'Stop or I'll kill Skyy and Vega!' Ariadna was still too dazed to move – she had simply curled up in a fetal position when the bullets started flying over her, with her hands over her ears and her eyes tightly closed.

'Give it up, Zakharov!' Jefferson said. 'You're not going anywhere!'

'And neither are you!' Zakharov said. 'I knew about

your jet at the airport, and I had everyone there executed. The jet and all your equipment is mine.'

Jefferson found he had stopped breathing – could he be telling the truth? 'Bullshit!' he finally shouted. 'Pereira! Flank that bastard and kill him!'

'If I even suspect he's moving against me, I'll kill her.'

'If you kill Vega, I'll spend the rest of my life hunting you down!' Jefferson said. 'Pereira! Get that son of a . . . !'

At that moment, a military helicopter appeared out of nowhere, a bright Nightsun searchlight sweeping across the patio. '*Uyedu na-hui*! About fucking time!' Zakharov swore to himself. He pulled out a portable radio, keyed the mike button, and said in Portuguese, '*Este é Zakharov. Escute acima*! Target one on the northwest corner of the farmhouse; target two somewhere in the weeds west of target one; targets on the move on the east side of the farmhouse. *Mate-os todos*!'

The Nightsun light zeroed right in on Jefferson, and a gunner aboard the helicopter opened fire with an assault rifle. Jefferson ducked out of the way just in time and ran behind the farmhouse. Pereira switched his submachine to full automatic and swept the sky with bullets toward the helicopter until the magazine was empty, then ran out toward the highway. The helicopter wheeled right and maneuvered in that direction to follow him.

'*Nao*!' Zakharov shouted in Portuguese. '*Comece outro*! Get the other one! I want target one!' The helicopter wheeled hard right again and started searching for Jefferson. Switching to Russian, Zakharov shouted, '*Keptan! Pashlee! Tyepyer*!' Pavel Khalimov rolled painfully onto his back to catch his breath, then rolled again and struggled to his feet, rubbing the spot in the center of his chest where the sniper round had impacted his bullet-proof vest. He half-collapsed on the hood of the van that Zakharov was hiding behind. 'Are you all right, Captain?' Zakharov asked.

Khalimov wiped half-dried blood from around his left eye, but nodded. 'It feels like my sternum is broken, Colonel,' he gasped, 'but I can travel and fight.'

'Serves you right for getting yourself captured, Captain,' Zakharov said, only half-joking. 'Next time you do that, I'll aim higher.' A switchblade appeared in Zakharov's hand out of nowhere; he cut Khalimov's wrists free and gave him the pistol. '*Kyem?* Who is he?'

'He is military,' Khalimov replied. 'Older, but very well trained.'

'Jefferson. United States Army Ranger. *Bardak*,' Zakharov swore. 'Looks like our airport team failed.' He raised his walkie-talkie to his lips, keyed the mike button, and asked in Portuguese, 'Where are the ground units?'

'Pulling onto the ranch now, Colonel,' the helicopter pilot responded.

'I want every one of those *bastardos* captured and executed!' Zakharov shouted. 'No one is to be left alive, do you understand?'

'*Compreenda tudo, senhor*. We have one of them in our sights now.'

They looked over and saw the helicopter stabilize just a few dozen meters away, the Nightsun searchlight focused on the east side of the farmhouse. The door gunner opened fire with several three-round bursts. The helicopter descended until it was less than ten meters aboveground, and the door gunner opened fire again.

From that range, Zakharov thought, he could not miss. 'Well?' he radioed. 'How many did you hit?'

'Uh . . . *senhor, nos temos um problema aqui,*' the pilot radioed back. Both Zakharov and Khalimov turned toward the target being highlighted by the searchlight . . .

. . . just as a strange figure leaped up onto the roof of the farmhouse! It was larger than a man, standing over three meters tall, but it moved with amazing agility and speed. The helicopter swooped down, almost right over him, the door gunner firing on it in full automatic mode now. '*Shto yobanyy eta?*' Zakharov shouted.

'That's it! That's the robot I reported to you, sir,' Khalimov said excitedly.

'The one that was supposed to be broken?' Zakharov shouted. 'The one that you were *supposed to have captured at the airport*?'

But the assassin didn't have a chance to answer because seconds later, just as the gunner stopped to reload, the robot leaped off the farmhouse roof and flew right into the helicopter's open door. Moments later the door gunner flew headfirst out of the door, and thick smoke started streaming from inside the helicopter. The robot figure leaped clear of the aircraft as it started to spin uncontrollably; Zakharov helped Khalimov run away when the craft crash-landed just a few meters from where they had been.

'My . . . God,' Zakharov breathed. 'I've never seen anything like it!'

'They must have repaired it on the way here from Santos,' Khalimov said. 'I crushed it under a bulldozer and dropped it into the ocean!'

'No, I was told that it was inoperative just *before* we came out here!' Zakharov roared. 'That's the last time I listen to intelligence information from someone who's sitting on their ass thousands of miles away.' At that moment, heavy-caliber machine gun fire erupted, followed by a racing diesel engine and then a loud explosion. 'Let's get out of here before something else goes wrong, Captain.'

A squad of six Jeeps raced up the gravel driveway to the farmhouse, with three PME soldiers and a gunner on board manning a fifty-caliber machine gun mounted on a pedestal in the back. The Jeeps were fitted with searchlights, operated by the soldier in the passenger seat. Three of the Jeeps veered off the road to the east and started their pursuit as the soldiers spotted Ruiz, the Amarals, and Kristen's crew members running down into a grassy gully. The gunners took aim on Ruiz and . . .

. . . at that moment a huge figure landed on the hood of the lead Jeep, reached out with a hand, and snapped the machine gun off its pedestal with one twist. Using the forty-kilo machine gun as a club, the figure smashed the Jeep's steering wheel and driver's side instrument panel with a single tremendous blow, then jumped off and ran after the second Jeep. Jason ran beside the second Jeep and swung the machine gun again, destroying the windshield. The driver and passenger ducked just in time to avoid the weapon, but the driver lost control and flipped the Jeep over.

The third Jeep wheeled left to try to run the robot over while the gunner tried to draw a bead on him. Just as Jason was going to make a leap that would take him on top of the gunner, a warning indication flashed in his electronic visor: less than thirty minutes of power remaining. Moments earlier it said he had over an hour of power remaining. Something was happening: he was losing power at a tremendous rate, probably due to a short-circuit somewhere caused by being immersed in seawater. At this rate, he could be out of the fight in just a few minutes – he might not even have one more jump. And there were still three more PME Jeeps out there.

Heavy-caliber bullets began peppering his composite armor shell as the Jeep barreled toward him. Jason crouched down into a ball, making himself as small a target as possible, but the Jeep kept right on coming. As it hit, Jason extended his arms, letting the vehicle slide up and over him, then shot to his feet. The Jeep did two complete rolls, spilling PME soldiers in all directions, before landing upside-down several meters away.

Thankfully, the other soldiers in the PME Jeeps saw what had happened to their comrades and stayed away, firing their machine guns from long range. Jason picked up a tire that had come off the last Jeep and threw it at one of the Jeeps about fifty meters away, caving in a windshield and showering the driver and passenger with glass. After that, the PME soldiers lost the desire to fight and sped away out of sight. Jason made sure they were safely away, then went over to the group of escapees in the gully. 'Are you all right?' he asked.

'*Sim, agradecimentos a você,*' Jorge Ruiz said.

'Stay here until I find out if there are any more soldiers nearby,' Jason said, and ran off in the direction of the farmhouse. He found Jefferson, Kristen, and Pereira helping Ariadna up. 'Ari, are you okay?'

'Yes, I'm okay,' she replied, giving him a crooked grin. 'I see you got El CID working. Thanks for the "help." You can help pay for my new set of teeth.'

Jason scanned the area quickly with his on-board millimeter-wave radar. 'I see two persons rendezvousing with those PME Jeeps that bugged out of here. I'm going after them.' But he took just a few running steps in that direction before stopping.

'Don't let them get away, Major!' Jefferson cried.

'One vehicle is racing away at high speed, and the others are heading back here,' Jason said. 'I'll be lucky if I have enough power to get you guys back to the airport.' They saw the robot's massive shoulders slump dejectedly. 'I can't leave you guys alone out here. Let's get back to the airport. I'll radio the jet to be ready for takeoff.'

The van had been hit by gunfire but was still operating. They removed the body of Lieutenant Quintao and laid him next to the bodies of the farmhands and the two dead Russians, then drove over to where the others were hidden. 'Let's go, everyone,' Jefferson said. He looked around. 'Where the hell is Ruiz?'

'*Ido, senhor,*' Judge Amaral said.

'*Gone*?' Kristen's producer Bonnie exploded. '*He can't go*! He's the whole reason why we're here! He's Kristen's story! Without him, she has nothing! Jason, can you . . . ?'

'I see him,' Jason said, 'but I also detect more radio chatter on the PME command channel. There may be other troops coming.'

'Everyone, load up,' Jefferson said.

'Sergeant Major, wait. I can . . .'

'Major . . . Jason, no more arguing,' Jefferson said. Jason was about to argue again, but the approaching troops and the CID unit's status told him that Jefferson was right and he had no choice. They piled into the van and headed off to the airport.

The jet was already at the end of the runway, its right engine idling, the entry door opened. The copilot, carrying a pistol, waved them in. Kristen and her crewmen helped Ariadna into the plane, while Jason dismounted from the CID unit, folded it, and stowed it into the baggage compartment with Jefferson's help. Once everyone was on board, the copilot closed and dogged the entry hatch, the pilot started the left engine . . .

. . . and it wasn't until then that they realized Pereira was gone. 'Where did he go?' Kristen shouted. It was obvious he wasn't on board. 'That was our last hope! The story is ruined!' She turned to her cameraman. 'Rich, please tell me . . .'

'We got some tape,' Rich murmured. 'I haven't checked it yet, but I got the camera, and it was running.'

'Thank *God* . . .'

'And I'll be sure that the film is confiscated by the Defense Intelligence Agency, CIA, and Justice Department upon our arrival,' Sergeant Major Jefferson said. 'It's evidence we'll need to indict Zakharov, Khalimov, and the rest of his gang.' Bonnie looked at him with a stunned expression, but the jet started its takeoff roll and she took a seat, mentally and physically drained, and chose not to argue.

After they were safely established in the climb, Jefferson got up and checked Ariadna. 'How is she?' he asked Jason.

'Bruised and sore, but I don't think she has a broken skull or a concussion . . .'

'I'm fine,' she responded weakly, half-opening her eyes to look at them. 'Thank you for saving me, Sergeant Major.'

'It was pure dumb luck that we're not all dead,' Jefferson said. He looked carefully at Richter. 'Or maybe not. You told me the CID unit was broken, Major.' Richter nodded. 'Why the bogus story? We could've been killed out there. The CID unit could've detected all those killers long before they attacked us. Two innocent people were needlessly killed. Your own engineer was beaten and could have been killed too.'

'I took a chance, sir,' Jason replied. He turned to Ariadna. 'I'm sorry, Ari, but I had to do it.'

'A *chance*? What are you talking about?'

'A chance to give out some false information so we'd draw out the bad guys,' Jason said. 'Everybody but myself and Ari thought that the CID unit was down. That means . . .'

'That means that someone we told about our plan to go to Abaete to hunt for Ruiz without the CID unit ratted us out to Zakharov,' Jefferson said. 'I only told the National Security Adviser, and it was on a secure circuit.' He turned to Kristen. 'Who did you talk to?' he demanded.

'Our executive producer . . . the chief of the news division . . . the president of SATCOM One . . .'

'Jesus . . . !'

'Even I can't just go traipsing all over South America without getting permission,' Kristen retorted. 'The news was sent all the way up to the president's office before we knew it. What did you expect . . . we were just going to whip out our credit cards and pay for this trip ourselves?'

'And how many persons could *they* have told?'

'They don't blab about our movements, Sergeant Major . . .'

'*Who*? How many could have known?'

Kristen glowered at Jefferson and shook her head, but lowered her eyes and shrugged a few moments later. 'Any number of people,' she said finally. 'At least three associate producers and one or two editors just in the television news division; they could have sent funding requests to Finance; they would have gotten in contact with officials in Washington; fact-checkers, researchers, legal guys . . . who the heck knows, Sergeant Major? It's a big organization . . .'

'And over an unsecured telephone,' Jefferson added. 'Half of New York and Washington could have been listening in. I'm surprised there wasn't a news crew out there in Abaete covering the battle live.' He swore silently, then impaled Jason with an angry glare. 'Dammit, Richter, you never should have gotten a reporter involved in this. Task Force TALON has been blown wide open. The whole damned world will know what we've done by the time we get back to Cannon.'

'I don't think it was Kristen or SATCOM One that leaked our whereabouts,' Jason said. 'I think it was someone in Washington – maybe even someone in the White House.'

'How do you figure that, Major?'

'Sir, I didn't trust this whole setup right from the beginning – something smelled from day one,' Jason said. 'This whole thing was doomed to fail right from the start. I'm positive of it now.'

'This task force was formed by the National Security Adviser himself,' Jefferson said. 'Chamberlain has been our strongest and probably our *only* supporter.'

'Then someone in his office, sir . . . or someone right here in this plane, has sold us out,' Jason said. 'Someone involved with the project right from the start . . .'

'The only other ones involved early on have been . . . Special Agents DeLaine and Bolton,' Jefferson said.

'And *you*, Sergeant Major,' Kristen pointed out. Jefferson glared at her but said nothing.

'DeLaine and Bolton were working on the GAMMA angle when we first had the demonstration at Andrews Air Force Base,' Jason said. 'Ari and I intercepted Kelsey's cell phone conversations with her office, before and after the demo, and they talked about Brazilian terror groups then. She never liked me from day one, and she and Bolton have done everything possible to exclude us from their activities. I threw a monkey wrench into her entire GAMMA investigation, something she and her office had been working on for months.'

'Chamberlain certainly would've informed Kelsey of what we were up to in Brazil,' Jefferson said. 'There could be a leak in her office . . .'

'If she hurriedly tried to pick up the pieces of her investigation into GAMMA and gotten operationally sloppy, she could have tipped off sources in the Brazilian government or PME . . . accidentally, I mean,' Kristen said. 'How well do you know this person? Could she be a snitch or on Zakharov's payroll?'

'No way,' Jefferson said. 'She's a well-known and respected FBI agent. She's the deputy special agent in charge of counterterrorism in Washington, for Christ's sake . . . !'

'Doesn't mean she can't be dirty, Sergeant Major,' Ariadna said.

'I don't think it's Kelsey,' Jason said. 'It has to be someone higher up . . .'

'All right, that's *enough*,' Jefferson said. 'We're not getting anywhere arguing about this. Once we get back to the States, I'll have a full investigation launched. We'll find the leak and shut it down, I guarantee it.' He picked up the satellite telephone. 'I'm going to notify Chamberlain's office of our arrival and what happened . . .'

Jason shook his head. 'Sir, what if . . . ?'

'Major, I heard what you said, but I don't have the authority to launch an investigation of this magnitude,' Jefferson said. 'We need the FBI, CIA, Defense Intelligence, Homeland Security, and U.S. Northern Command in on this – Chamberlain will have every investigating agency possible working on this. They're going to work separately, independently, to get answers. No one office or individual can influence every one of them.' No one had enough energy to argue.

Several hours later, shortly after dawn, the SATCOM One jet landed at Cannon Air Force Base in New Mexico, closely monitored by Patriot antiaircraft missile batteries and Avenger short-range air defense units surrounding the entire base. The Amarals were taken away in separate vehicles by the FBI, while the others were piled into Air Force blue Suburbans. Heavily armed Security Force Humvees escorted the passengers to the task force training area. They were met by each and every member of the task force . . . and by National Security Adviser Robert Chamberlain himself.

There was only one way to describe the mood of the place: funereal. Jason never expected a celebration on his return, but he didn't expect so many glum faces either. Chamberlain was obviously here to deliver really bad news.

Chamberlain stepped up to the door of the Suburban as it came to a stop. Sergeant Major Jefferson was the first out of the vehicle; Chamberlain extended a hand and shook his warmly. 'You've had one hell of a time in

South America, haven't you, Sergeant Major?' he remarked, smiling at his own joke. Jefferson said nothing. Chamberlain shook hands with Richter, Vega, Kristen Skyy, and her crew. 'I'm sure you guys are tired, but we need to get the debriefing sessions out of the way as soon as we can. We have teams from my office inside waiting to speak to you.'

'I need to get in contact with my network, Mr Chamberlain,' Kristen said. 'Jefferson wouldn't let us use the phones on the jet – he said it was per *your* order – and . . .'

'The chief of the debriefing team will let you know when you can make calls, miss,' Chamberlain said. 'You won't be unduly inconvenienced, but they have an investigation to run. Your network has been advised that you're safe and that you're in the direct care of my office. Have a little patience while we get all this sorted out, and everything will be fine in a very short time. You will eventually be allowed . . .'

'Excuse me, Mr Chamberlain, but that's not acceptable,' Kristen said. 'We're not allowed to make any statements to any law-enforcement or government agencies without a SATCOM One News attorney present if the incident involves our work. I understand you're in charge of a very important investigation and that it concerns national security, sir, but the network takes our First Amendment rights very . . .'

'Miss Skyy.' Chamberlain now had turned his whole body toward the SATCOM One crew. Kristen was no shrinking violet, but she was clearly starting to wither under the slow but definite change in Chamberlain's mood. 'We've unfortunately gotten off on the wrong foot here. I've apparently failed to make myself clear, and for that I apologize. Let me start all over again, and I'll try to elucidate my thoughts better:

'You are all material witnesses in an investigation into the terrorist attacks on Kingman City,' he said sternly – all traces of friendliness and relief that the team members were home alive were completely gone. 'You will be questioned by various government authorities. You will be held as material witnesses for as long as necessary, and obviously if you refuse to answer, to protect your First Amendment rights or any other damn fool reason, that will just extend the time you'll be held by us . . .'

'You don't have to do it this way, Mr Chamberlain,' Kristen said. 'We can sit down with our execs and attorneys and work together to get you the information you need while preserving freedom of the press. We're all Americans too: we want to see the ones who planned the attacks brought to justice. We can do this without trampling on the Constitution or the Bill of . . .'

'You may be an American, Miss Skyy, but I don't believe for an instant that you care more about America than you do about your network's shareholders, ratings, reputation, or bottom line,' Chamberlain interrupted. 'I used to be a corporate executive, and I know how big companies go into self-protection and disaster-prep mode when the government is involved. I'm not saying that's evil, but it certainly doesn't help the government's investigations. There are lives at stake here, Miss Skyy. Protecting the American people from another attack trumps the press's right to report a juicy story.'

'Mr Chamberlain, I'm telling you, we can work together on this,' Kristen maintained. 'Call my network – they won't shut you out, I guarantee it. We'll agree to sit on the story for as long as necessary until you catch

Zakharov, Khalimov, and whoever is financing or supporting them. We'll turn over every scrap of tape and notes we have to . . .'

'Miss Skyy, every scrap of tape, video, recordings, or notes *will* be turned over to us immediately, or we will take them away from you by force,' Chamberlain said. 'The chief of the investigation team has a briefcase full of warrants for the information, and he has a federal judge standing by ready to issue more warrants twenty-four-seven. I don't need your network's permission or coordination to get the information. And if there's any information that you've already transmitted to your network, that will be turned over to us as well, or we'll shut down your entire network on the spot.'

'Don't do it, Mr Chamberlain,' Kristen insisted. 'You'll have the entire country turned against you once it comes out that you've done this. The world press will condemn you . . .'

'I really don't care about the world press, Ma'am – I only care about the United States of America,' Chamberlain said. 'And you obviously have no idea about the mood of the American people right now. They want to do everything possible to stop this wave of terrorist violence sweeping this country, and they're doing everything necessary to help accomplish that. They're donating their money, time, and most important their full *support* to the cause, and they don't think kindly of folks like you in the press who think they have some special privilege. You have information that can help us protect this country, and you will turn it over to us immediately and completely or we will take away your freedom and your rights as citizens until you do. It's as simple as that.'

He turned to Jefferson, Richter, and Vega: 'Of course

I expect the utmost cooperation from you three. Major, Doctor, you two face very serious criminal charges, but your cooperation in our investigation is more important right now, so you will not be charged with a crime. That means you can be held indefinitely as material witnesses. The criminal charges will be addressed after the investigation is complete, which could take a very long time.

'Needless to say, Task Force TALON's future was in serious question as of the day you three left this base to go off on your own,' Chamberlain went on. 'I haven't been specifically ordered to shut down the task force, but I doubt if the President will allow it to continue if its commanders are found guilty of a crime. I'm afraid it's out of my hands. I'll do everything I can to keep it alive, but I'm sure I've lost all credibility with the White House as far as you're concerned.'

'Sir, we have got to sit down with you and tell you what we learned in Brazil,' Jason said. 'We have information that will prove . . .'

'It's too late for that, Major – you should have come to me immediately,' Chamberlain said wearily. 'We could have taken this right to the White House. In less time than it took you to organize this stunt with Kristen Skyy, we could have mounted a full frontal assault on all the suspects you were after – it would have been fully sanctioned and supported by both the American and Brazilian governments. We could have descended on all those locations at once and set up an airtight trap for those Russians. It would have been Task Force TALON's first and best operation, an example of what a true military-civil cooperative team could do. Instead, you decided to go off on your own, and now we're all paying for your mistake. You blew it, Major – it's that simple.'

He glared at Richter suspiciously, then shook his head sadly. 'This is the most egregious, the most outrageous, the most foolhardy example of abuse of power and authority I've witnessed in all my years of government service. You were America's best hope to track down terrorists all over the world, Major Richter. I trusted you. I wanted this thing to work, and I was hoping that technology like your CID unit would be the key. Unfortunately, you thought you didn't need to work as a team. Not only will you and your fellow teammates, but all of America, pay the price for your lack of judgment. I should have provided better leadership.'

He looked around at all of the assembled task force members and said, 'This training area has now become your detention facility, folks. All of your weapons will be impounded here and used as evidence. You are all material witnesses, and you will be held here indefinitely until our investigation is complete. You will retain your current rank, pay grade, and privileges until formal charges are levied against you. Until then, I expect nothing less than your full cooperation.' And with that, Chamberlain walked away and into his waiting vehicle and drove off.

After he was gone, the others started to drift away, murmuring comments quietly to one another, until eventually only Jefferson, Richter, Vega, Skyy, Kelsey DeLaine, Carl Bolton, Doug Moore, and Kristen's camera crew remained.

Moore was the first to approach Richter. 'I trusted you, sir,' he said simply before he walked away.

Kelsey walked over to them, looked at the wounds on Ariadna's face with a look of concern . . . then turned to Richter and slapped him hard across the face. 'You stupid *jerk*!' she shouted. 'You egotistical ignorant childish *bastard*! You not only destroyed this task force but the careers of each and every person here!'

'You guys still don't get it, do you?' Jason asked. 'This is a setup. We're being framed . . .'

'We're not listening to you, Richter!' Bolton interjected. 'You're nothing but a crazy-ass *flake*. I'd sleep with one eye open from now on if I were you, buster, because folks are going to realize that their lives would be pretty much back to normal if you got yourself fragged.'

'That is *enough*!' Sergeant Major Jefferson shouted.

'Hey, Sergeant Major, I'm not going to listen to a damned thing *you* have to say either!' Bolton retorted. 'You could have stopped Richter before he left the country with the CID unit! Then, when you got your clearance to go to Brazil, you overstepped it by going to chase down that other GAMMA terrorist. You have absolutely no right to be ordering us around. You're just as responsible for us getting shut down as he is . . . !'

'I am still in command of this task force . . .'

'Didn't you hear, Sergeant Major – *there is no task force any more*, thanks to you and Richter! There's nothing here but a bunch of soldiers and engineers in a detention facility!'

'Mr Chamberlain *did not* disband this task force – until he does, I retain command of this unit, and we will continue to organize and train as before, with any equipment and resources we are allowed to have,' Jefferson said hotly. 'If we're not given any equipment to use, we'll use sticks and stones; and if we're not allowed to use those, we'll do PT; but *we will* continue to train.'

'This is bullshit, Jefferson,' Bolton said. 'It's a waste of time. I'm not doing anything you tell me to do.'

'Until I am relieved of command, I am in charge here,' Jefferson said in a low, menacing voice, 'and my first directive is aimed squarely at you, Agent Bolton – if you touch Major Richter or anyone else here with the intent of causing them any physical harm, I will personally beat you to a bloody pulp and hang your carcass on the barbed-wire fence. And if you don't follow my orders *to the letter*, I'll make your existence here at this facility *extremely* uncomfortable. Do I make myself clear?'

Bolton stepped over to Jefferson and stood face to face with him. Bolton was much taller than Jefferson and probably had ten to fifteen kilos on him – it would be a spectacular fight, if one broke out.

But with one look at Jefferson's icy warning glare, Bolton blinked and backed away. 'Tell me, Sergeant Major – why do you give a shit so much about that loser?' Bolton asked in a low voice. 'He hasn't been part of this team since day one; he's succeeded in getting us all canned and ruining our careers. What do you care what happens to him? If he ends up with his teeth pushed in so he can't talk anymore, this whole thing would be over, wouldn't it?'

'Not by a long shot, Bolton,' Jefferson said. 'If that happened, I would be extremely suspicious of the guy who did it. It would make me wonder why that guy would want to make sure Richter was permanently silenced.'

'You think I had something to do with Richter taking the CID unit to Brazil?'

'No, I'm sure that was the major's idea, along with Miss Skyy there,' Jefferson replied. 'But I'm wondering about how we got ambushed so well out there. Someone knew we were coming and tipped off the terrorists . . .'

'And you think *I* did it?'

'I don't know who did it, Bolton,' Jefferson said. 'But until I do, everyone is a suspect – and I'd consider the guy who threatens to bump off Richter the number-one suspect.' Bolton looked as if he was going to say something, but thought better of it and remained silent. 'Now I'm going to repeat my order just one more time: anyone who harms any other person in this facility will deal with *me*. Am I making myself perfectly clear?' Jefferson affixed an angry glare on every face around him, then shouted, 'I said, *do I make myself clear*?'

'Yes, sir!' the others responded loudly.

'Until we receive orders to the contrary,' Jefferson went on, 'we will continue to study our tactics, develop and refine our TO&E, and maintain our training schedule. *Everyone* trains, or they will get to experience the feel of my boot on their ass – and that includes you, Bolton. You will all cooperate fully with the investigators . . .' He turned to Kristen's crew and added, 'and that includes you too . . .'

'Like hell it does, Sergeant Major,' Kristen said. 'We have our orders, same as you, and our orders say we don't speak with anyone unless we have an attorney present. Just tell us where our quarters are – that's where you'll find us.'

'Miss Skyy . . .'

'And don't give me that "boot up my ass" crap, Sergeant Major,' Rich the cameraman interjected. 'I was a Marine – I can dish it out better than I can take it.'

Jefferson knew there was no use arguing with them – he had absolutely no authority over them at all. 'Very well. I'll see to quarters for you. You will be restricted there at all times except as required by the debriefing teams. I'll post a guard if necessary.' Kristen, Rich, and Bonnie could do nothing else but shoot Jefferson evil glares and walk away. Jefferson checked his watch. 'Pass the word along to everyone else: our training schedule resumes after lunch. In the meantime, I want an update on our training and readiness, and I will brief the staff on what we learned in Brazil. That is all. Dismissed.' Soon just Jefferson, Richter, and Vega remained on the parking ramp outside the hangars.

'Sergeant Major, we need to talk about what's happened,' Jason said. 'We need to file a report with the intelligence agencies, the FBI, and probably Interpol or somebody . . .'

'You have your orders, Major.'

'Excuse me, sir, but with all due respect, can you get off your macho command-sergeant-major high horse for a moment here?' Jason asked.

'Don't push me now, Major . . . !'

'Sergeant Major . . . Ray, have you forgotten already?' Jason asked, almost pleading with him to listen. '*We* know *who planned the bombing at Kingman City*! We know there's a terror cell in Brazil that has somehow managed to get their hands on a nuclear device and set it off *inside the United States*!'

'I'm sure that's what we're going to be questioned about over the next several days and weeks, Major.'

' "The next several *weeks*"? Do you think we can afford to waste that much time, sir?' Jason asked. That gave Jefferson some pause. 'Think about it, Ray: we had two witnesses in our hands that made Zakharov as the planner of both attacks. *We had them* – and the National Security Adviser to the President of the United States *just drove away*, leaving us in the middle of nowhere in New Mexico for God knows how long. He's got all the evidence we brought back from Brazil, too – the Amarals and

Kristen's videotape. All that's left is us four, and no one's going to believe us because we're the ones who took the CID unit to Brazil. It's a setup, sir.'

'Major, Mr Chamberlain's actions have more to do with *your* decisions than with what we found or suspect we found in Brazil,' Jefferson said. 'Just stay in your quarters like I ordered. I'll keep on top of things.' He held out his hand. 'And give me that remote control thing for the CID units.' Jason reluctantly handed over the wrist remote control device for the CID unit. 'Try doing it my way for a change, Richter.'

Chapter Six

He had never seen security such as this. Upon checking in for his American Airlines flight from Mexico City to San Jose, airplane salesman and businessman Tom Estrada had to run his finger across a biometric scanner not once, not twice, but *six times* before he was allowed to board his flight, and his carry-on luggage was checked twice by hand. Security was everywhere – heavily armed, visible, and purposely intrusive. During the flight, no one was allowed to leave their seats without notifying a flight attendant first; no one could stand near the lavatories or galleys; and no one could get out of their seats within an hour prior to landing. Fortunately Estrada was a resident alien of the United States, because all nonresident aliens without visas had to surrender their passports to U.S. Customs upon arrival. Around the airport, security was tighter than he'd ever seen – they even had Avenger mobile antiaircraft vehicles and National Guard canine units patrolling the airport perimeter.

After retrieving his car from the parking garage, Estrada took the U.S. 101 North expressway to San Mateo and parked near the Third Avenue Sports Bar and Grill, a small but friendly neighborhood pub that had a surprisingly well-stocked wine list and free wireless Internet access. After ordering a glass of Silver Oak Napa Valley Cabernet Sauvignon and a small order of beef enchiladas and chatting with Grace, his waitress, who was also the daughter of his landlord, for several minutes, he opened up his Motion Computing Tablet PC and got online.

He checked e-mail first as always, and was worried to find a series of e-mails from a specific sender, one with only a scrambled alphanumeric name and domain. The messages from this sender were small digital photos. Estrada had wired his apartment in San Mateo with a security appliance that would take a digital photo of a room in which the appliance detected motion and automatically upload the photos to Estrada's e-mail box. Several of the photos were of Grace herself – he had hired her to clean the place when he was gone and to turn lights on and off randomly to make the place look lived-in – and she and her family were absolutely trustworthy. But some of the photos were of unidentified men wearing suits and ties, searching the place – just hours ago!

'Hey, Grace, thanks for keeping an eye on my place for me,' Estrada said the next time Grace came over to check on him. He handed her an envelope with two hundred dollars in cash in it.

'Thanks, Tom,' the attractive young woman said. She hefted the envelope. 'How much is in here? Feels like a little more than usual. Not that I'm complaining, of course.'

'There's a little extra in there for you. You're on your way to college next week, right? Barnard?'

'Yep. But you didn't have to do that, Tom. I was happy to help out. You're kind of a neat-freak anyway – taking care of your place is a piece of cake.'

'Any problems while I was gone?'

'Nope.' She started to walk away. 'Did you get the message your friend left on the door?'

Estrada's ears buzzed with concern. 'I haven't been by the apartment yet.'

'A guy who said he used to work with you came by looking for you,' Grace said. 'Left a note and his business card on the door.'

Estrada thought of the digital photos he'd just downloaded. 'Small guy, bald, dresses nice but wears dark running shoes?'

'That's him. Glad you know him. I was worried.'

'Worried? Why?'

'Well, he said he knew you, described you pretty well, and thought you lived in the area, but he didn't know exactly where. I thought at first he was canvassing the area, you know, like the cops do on TV.'

Estrada fought to look completely unconcerned. The reason for that was simple, Estrada thought: his postal mail was delivered to the same Arroyo Court address as the other three families that lived there. That meant that whoever it was who had his address was looking for *him*. 'Well, actually, I didn't tell the guy my address when I met up with him a while back – I'm not sure I want to work with this guy again,' Estrada lied, 'but I did describe our neighborhood, so I'm sure he tracked me down.'

'I pointed out your place to him. Sorry. I shouldn't have done that.'

'Don't worry about it, Grace,' Estrada said.

'If he comes around again, what should I do? Should I give him your cell phone number?'

Estrada shrugged nonchalantly, but inside his mind was racing a million kilometers per hour. 'He should have it,' he said casually, 'but sure, if he wants it, go ahead and give it to him.' It didn't matter – it would be shut

down soon anyway. 'Another glass of the Silver Oak Cab
and I'll be ready for the check, Grace.'

'Sure thing, Tom.'

When she left, Estrada pulled out his secure cell phone
and sent an SMS message that said simply, *'Problem with
escrow.'* He then packed up his gear, being careful to shut
down his wireless network adapter so no eavesdroppers
could interrogate or 'ping' the idle system, and shut the
computer down. He tried to look unhurried and relaxed
when Grace came over with the wine and the check, but
inwardly he was screaming at her to move faster. He
downed the wine much faster than Silver Oak deserved,
paid the check, left his usual tip, then departed, being
sure to wave at the staff and the other regulars and, more
important, not to rush.

Just like that, Colonel Yegor Viktorvich Zakharov
knew that his days as Tomas 'Tom' Estrada, helicopter
salesman, were over.

He got into his Ford minivan, carefully pulled out into
traffic, and drove ten minutes to the Bay Area Rapid
Transit station nearest San Francisco International
Airport. Before he left the van in a secluded area of the
parking lot, he took his SIG Sauer P230 pistol from its
hiding place in his seat and stuffed it into his belt.
Executing a well-rehearsed escape plan, Zakharov took
the BART train across San Francisco Bay to Oakland.
Security patrols were everywhere on the BART stations
and on the train, but the guards looked young, tired, and
bored. He panicked a bit and started looking for a place
to ditch his pistol when he saw the signs warning passengers of security inspection stations ahead, but the airport-
like X-ray machines and metal detectors had not yet been
installed.

He got off at the Harrison Street BART station in Oakland and walked five blocks to a small café on Madison Street across from Madison Park. The word 'escrow' in the status message he sent was the clue to the rendezvous location. When Zakharov first mapped out this attack plan, there was a real estate company on Madison Street near this park, in the heart of the city. The park offered good concealment; it was a mostly Hispanic neighborhood, so he wouldn't stand out too much; and there were lots of small, nondescript hotels nearby in case he had to linger. The real estate company was no longer there, replaced by an organic bean café, but it was still a good location. Zakharov found a park bench, kept the café in view, and waited. Two hours and four drunks who wanted to use the park bench to sleep on later, he saw a faded blue Jeep Grand Cherokee drive up to the spot with a magnetic sign on the driver's door of that same real estate company, and he crossed the street and got in the front seat. A soldier that Zakharov recognized was in the backseat, a TEC-9 machine pistol in his hands but out of sight.

'*Kag deela*, Colonel,' Pavel Khalimov said as he carefully pulled out into the late-night traffic. He headed south toward Interstate 880, staying a few kilometers under the speed limit; other traffic zoomed by as if he was standing still.

'*Oozhasna*,' Zakharov said. 'How do you feel, Captain?'

Khalimov rubbed his chest where the bullet from Zakharov's sniper rifle had hit him. 'It was not broken. I will be fine. How was the flight from Mexico City, sir?'

'Terrible. Security coming back into the United States is oppressive.'

'Then it is mostly for show, sir – I had little trouble

getting in,' Khalimov said. Unlike Zakharov, Pavel Khalimov had no secret identities in other countries – he was a Russian commando, plain and simple. He carried no identification, passports, driver's licenses, or credit cards, just a bit of cash. He traveled fast and light at all times. Whatever he needed, he stole – money, weapons, clothes, vehicles, anything and everything. 'Security patrols are concentrating around the larger ports of entry and larger vessels – it is laughably easy to get a small vessel into a small port.'

'Do not get cocky, Captain – it will only get worse,' Zakharov said. He told Khalimov about his Web cam pictures and his housekeeper's encounter. 'We will have to wrap up all operations in the Bay area. My Estrada identity is surely compromised – perhaps the Americans are actually able to utilize those biometric scanners now. If they have perfected the national database to check international fingerprint records, they will eventually hunt down Estrada.'

'The fact that you were not apprehended on the spot here in the United States, even with all the security in place, despite the worldwide dragnet that is certainly out for us, is promising,' Khalimov pointed out. 'I tell you, sir, the American security apparatus is all bark and no bite. The level of scrutiny is extremely low, their level of training and experience is very low except for the most high-profile duties, and already the American people are squawking about the invasion of privacy and loss of their rights. Whatever they set up will not last long. The Americans are simply not accustomed to tight internal security.'

'I feel that is changing rapidly, Captain,' Zakharov said, 'and now is the perfect time to strike. Is everything ready?'

'Yes, sir,' Khalimov replied. 'We added two four-man strike squads as a backup, for a total of six going at the target itself. We have the original twelve squads handling security.'

'Very good. And the devices you will use?'

'The outer security teams will use C-4 with the gasoline in the fuel tanks as accelerants,' Khalimov replied. 'The inner security units will use divided amounts of HMX and ONC. We will have CS gas and high-explosive grenades to use to disperse first responders as well.'

'You will not use units that carry only ONC?' Zakharov asked. ONC, or octanitrocubane, was the world's most powerful explosive – over three times the explosive power of TNT – but was available in relatively small quantities and at vastly greater cost. HMX (High-melting-point explosive), or cyclotetramethylenetetranitramine, was almost as powerful as ONC but was more readily available. C-4, or Composition-4, was the world's most widely used and widely available explosive material, although not as powerful as the other two.

'I felt the risk was too great, sir,' Khalimov explained. 'The mission might not be accomplished if the attack units carrying only ONC were captured. I felt it necessary to have each of the four main attack units have the same destructive power. Unfortunately we were unable to bring in enough ONC for just one vehicle to do the job per squad.'

'And the device itself?'

'Safely delivered and ready for arming, sir,' Khalimov said.

'*Atleechna. Pashlee.* Let's go.'

They drove northbound on Interstate 880 to the Oakland–Bay Bridge. Traffic was very light. It was a good

opportunity to look at the new security measures instituted on California's large bridges and tunnels. The ten
lanes of freeway on-ramps leading to the bridge were
narrowed into three, with Humvees and Bradley armored
vehicles stationed here and there.

'The National Guard forces do not appear to do much
here, sir,' Khalimov explained. 'Every now and then they
will stop a large delivery truck to search it, but gener-
ally the soldiers stay out of sight. They appear to be very
sensitive to rush-hour traffic lines and will open up three
more lanes approaching the tollbooths twice a day for
three hours each time.' He shook his head. 'Ten dollars
cash now just to cross this bridge into San Francisco,
unless you use one of the electronic wireless express-pay
devices. Outlandish. It is twelve dollars now to cross the
Golden Gate Bridge into the city. All of our vehicles have
the payment devices.

'The troops stationed on both sides of the bridge are
lightly armed except for their vehicles. The Humvees
carry fifty-caliber machine guns. There are usually four
on each side, two in the westbound and two in the eastbound sides. The Bradleys are fairly new and represent
the most serious threat. They have a twenty-five-
millimeter Bushmaster cannon with sabot, high-
explosive, and armor-piercing rounds, and a
7.62-millimeter coaxial machine gun. They all appear to
be the M2A1 variant instead of the more capable M2A3
or M3A3 models. They have TOW antitank missile
launchers fitted but I do not believe they carry any
missiles in them – they may still be in storage magazines in the vehicles, but none appear to be in the
launchers themselves. There are usually Bradleys on
either side of the bridge, one on the eastbound and one

on the westbound side. They move them several times daily but that appears to be just for maintenance or crew rotation purposes, not for tactical reasons.'

'A little more than just show, but not a real defense force,' Zakharov summarized.

'My opinion as well, sir.'

They crossed the Oakland-Bay Bridge into San Francisco, then exited the freeway and made their way to the Financial District. The streets at this hour were almost deserted, but the police presence was noticeable. 'Approximately one police cruiser every other city block in the Financial District,' Khalimov said. 'No parking allowed on the streets – everyone must use parking garages, and they are heavily patrolled.' They stopped at a traffic light at Market Street between Main Street and Spear Street. 'The heaviest security is here, at the U.S. Federal Reserve Building. One special police cruiser on each corner; absolutely no cars allowed to park or wait here.'

'But no military forces?'

'I have seen several Humvees down here, sir – I am surprised they are not here now,' Khalimov said. 'There have been news pieces on complaints by citizens about the military presence in downtown San Francisco – they say it affects tourism and scares everyone. Perhaps they took them away.'

'We will not count on that,' Zakharov said. 'We assume the vehicles that are here will be heavily armed military patrols.'

From Main Street, they made their way to California Street and drove up the steep boulevard to Van Ness Avenue, then to Lombard Street and onto the approach to the Golden Gate Bridge heading toward Marin County.

Huge outdoor lights had been set up, illuminating the tollbooths and bridge approaches like daytime. They passed two Bradley Fighting Vehicles here. 'Security appears even heavier on this bridge,' Zakharov observed.

'It is all for the TV cameras, sir,' Khalimov said disgustedly. 'The Golden Gate Bridge is a symbol of the Western United States and the state of California, and they put more National Guard forces out here to show the public they are defending them. But they are no more capable than the ones in Oakland.'

Zakharov looked at his aide carefully. 'You appear more confident than I have ever seen you, *tovarisch*,' he said. 'Perhaps . . . too confident?'

'I am confident of success, sir,' Khalimov admitted, 'but it is not overconfidence. It is disgust.'

'Disgust?'

'This is their *country*, one of their greatest *cities*,' Khalimov spat, 'and they try to act as if nothing whatsoever is wrong. They were attacked with a *nuclear weapon*, for God's sake, and yet they pretend that everything is *ahuyivayush'iy*.'

'As you were, Captain,' Zakharov said. 'Don't let these people's attitudes about their life and society cloud your judgment. Keep fully alert and ready at all times.'

'Yes, sir,' Khalimov said. 'I will. But they are making this seem too easy.'

'Beliefs like that will get us killed, Pavel. I order you to stop it and concentrate,' Zakharov said seriously. 'You thought it would be easy to trap Jorge Ruiz in Abaete, too.'

'Yes, sir. I'm sorry. Don't worry about me.'

They drove across the Golden Gate Bridge to Marin County, struck by the incredible contrast of going from a large cosmopolitan high-rise city to a wooded countryside in just a few kilometers. Just past the Marin County Airport north of Novato on Highway 101, they exited the freeway onto Redwood Highway and proceeded to the Redwood Landfill, then to a side road, stopping near a set of railroad tracks. Khalimov made a radio call using a short-range FM transceiver, and a man with an Uzi submachine gun appeared out of the darkness and unlocked an old, rarely used railroad access gate on the far side of the landfill. Khalimov drove inside to the incinerator facility. Inside an area marked with signs carrying skulls and crossbones that read DANGER HAZARDOUS WASTE DISPOSAL AREA and POS REQUIRED, they were met by a man wearing a respirator and carrying an Uzi submachine gun.

'It is here, sir,' Khalimov said. He handed Zakharov a respirator with a full-face mask and small green bottle of oxygen on a shoulder strap. 'Hazardous waste materials from the piers in Richmond are brought here for incineration. We will move the device immediately after prearming.' Zakharov donned the mask, checked it, and they left the car. Khalimov retrieved a small yellow case from the back of the Cherokee and followed the Russian colonel inside the facility.

Even with the masks on and with positive pressure against his face, the acidy taste and feel of the air was oppressive. The temperature was at least ten degrees Celsius higher inside. Khalimov went over to the back of the facility, where a row of waste collection hoppers were waiting in a row with a chain around them so they could not be used. Khalimov removed a padlock from the chain, and he and his men pulled one of the hoppers out of the row. He unlocked a large lever and pulled it carefully, tipping the hopper. Several liters of thick sludge dumped out. Bolted to the side of the hopper was a device about the size of a small car transmission, wrapped in aluminum foil and plastic. 'It is not petroleum-based oil – the heat from the device might have caused regular oil to burn,' Zakharov explained as he began to carefully cut the foil and plastic away. 'It is a mixture of antifreeze and dry cell battery carbon,' Zakharov said as he dumped the slurry out. 'It makes an excellent homemade coolant and neutron absorption fluid. The foil should have reflected any other stray gamma rays and alpha particles back into the core, and also prevent detection from passive radioactive detection systems.'

They wheeled the hopper out of the incinerator building so they did not have to wear the respirators any longer. Even though it was almost forty years old, the warhead itself was in almost perfect condition, Zakharov noted as soon as he had the protective wrapping peeled away. It was an AA60 tactical nuclear warhead, very common in a variety of Soviet weapons from short-range ballistic missiles and rockets to large artillery shells. Its design was simplicity itself. It was a gun-assembly-type device, with two eight-kilogram slugs of highly enriched uranium-235 on either end of a tube. One slug was surrounded by a shield or tamper that reflected neutrons back into the supercritical mass; the other end of the tube had an explosive charge that would drive the second slug into the other. When the explosive charge was set off and the two sub-critical slugs were driven into one another, it formed a supercritical mass that instantly created a nuclear fission reaction.

This particular warhead had been used on a 9K79 Tochka short-range tactical ballistic missile, what the West called an SS-21 Scarab. The main part of the warhead, the 'physics package,' was simple and required no fancy electronics; the arming, fusing, and firing components were the tricky parts. The keys to deploying nuclear warheads were reliability, security, and safety – three ingredients that were mostly mutually exclusive. These systems had to be bypassed in order to get a nuclear yield, but done in the proper sequence to successfully arm the weapon and create a full yield, yet still allow his men to escape the blast.

Zakharov attached several cables from the test kit to ports on the warhead. 'Watch carefully, Captain,' Zakharov said as he punched instructions into the test kit. 'I am first removing the barometric arming parameters to the warhead – from now on it does not need to sense acceleration or airflow to arm. Second, I have set the radar fusing system to "contact" – as long as the warhead remains inside this container, it will not detonate. Do not touch the warhead or strike it with any hard objects – although the mechanical lock is still in place, any sharp blows may activate the chemical battery and trigger it, and the mechanical lock may not hold. There is a half-kilo of high-explosive material in the warhead that will detonate if the warhead is activated, which will at the very least kill anyone with ten meters and scatter a lot of nuclear debris around. I trust you will drive safely.'

'Of course, sir,' Khalimov replied stonily.

He placed a device in Khalimov's hand. 'Your procedures are simple, Captain. First, remove the mechanical safety lock by pulling this pin. Next, turn on the test kit by turning this key, flip these two switches, and remove the key. Finally, once you are safely away from the weapon but no more than thirty meters away, press and release the red button on that remote. From that moment you will have sixty minutes to get at least five kilometers away from the area. At the end of sixty minutes, the test kit will electronically change the fusing from contact to radar altimeter altitude of three meters. Of course, it will sense the distance from the warhead to the side of the container is only a few centimeters, so it will fuse and detonate immediately.

'Three notes of caution, Captain. One: once you remove the mechanical safety lock, it activates a chemical battery inside the warhead, which powers the warhead,' Zakharov said. 'Since the fuse will be set for contact, any sudden movement or impact on the warhead that creates more than twenty Gs could set it off. It does not have to be a violent action – dropping it or even hitting it with a hand or object hard enough could be enough to trigger it. Have your men out of the building when you pull the pin, be careful to walk away from it, and for God's sake don't slam any doors on your way out.

'Two: you have just five minutes from the time you pull the mechanical safety pin to when you must turn on the test kit,' Zakharov went on. 'After that, the chemical battery will be spent and there will be no way to set off the detonation charge except if you somehow managed to cook off the explosive charge using a blasting cap. The warhead will be all but useless then.

'Third: that remote control device is also a dead man's switch,' Zakharov concluded. 'If you press and hold the red button for more than six seconds, the weapon will detonate when you *release* the button. There is no way to stop the device from triggering after that unless

someone disarms the device while the button is pressed.
The device will also detonate when you move out of
radio range of the test kit, farther than about two kilometers or so, even if you are still pressing the button.
This may help you and your men bargain for escape if
you are caught or discovered. *Vi paneemayetye?*'

'*Da, Colonel,*' Khalimov responded.

The ex-Russian commando was one of the most
emotionless men Zakharov had ever known, he thought.
He nodded approvingly. 'You don't seem too nervous,
Captain.'

'I have worked around dangerous ordnance many
times, sir,' Khalimov said. 'Dying in a high-explosive,
biological, or nuclear blast makes no difference to me –
I am still dead.' He looked at the Russian colonel with
stone-cold eyes and added, 'Besides, I watched *you* shoot
me in the chest point-blank with a Dragunov sniper rifle,
sir. I have already lived and re-lived death many times
since then.'

'Of course,' Zakharov said. 'That's an experience most
humans will never have.' They unbolted the warhead
from the hopper, set it in a case inside one of their soldier's
vehicles, wrapped it securely in the aluminum foil material again, and concealed it all under a carpet and spare
tire. 'It must never leave your sight from now on,
Captain.'

'It won't, sir.'

'Good luck to you, Captain,' Zakharov said. 'We will
see each other shortly. As soon as your operation is
complete, I will arrange to wire the funds to your
numbered accounts in Latvia.'

'Do you anticipate any problems, sir?' Khalimov asked.

'The Director has not been as well informed as I

thought lately,' Zakharov admitted, 'but he has always paid promptly and I have no reason to believe he won't do so again. But I want to be close to him when your mission is complete just to make sure he stays cooperative.'

'Very good, sir,' Khalimov said.

'*Razvjazhite Ad*,' Zakharov said, saluting the assassin and then grasping his right forearm in a brotherly Roman Legion-style handshake. 'Unleash hell.'

'Yes, sir,' Khalimov said confidently, returning the salute and the handshake. '*Ih sud'ba nahoditsja v moih rukah*. Their fate is in my hands.'

Chapter Seven

Cannon Air Force Base, New Mexico
That same time

'We found him!' Special Agent Ramiro Cortez shouted in the phone.

Kelsey DeLaine looked at the time on her cell phone display; about four A.M. local time. 'Who, Rudy?'

'Colonel Yegor Zakharov.'

She was instantly awake, swinging her feet off the lumpy mattress in a flash. 'Talk to me, Rudy,' she said, stepping quickly over to Carl Bolton's room next door and pounding on the rickety door; he was awake and dressed in moments.

'Homeland Security was tracking down citizens, visa holders, naturalized citizens, or resident aliens who recently entered the U.S. from overseas but whose fingerprints collected during customs inprocessing didn't match in the national database,' Cortez said. 'They were focusing on males traveling from South or Central America with advanced degrees or skills such as pilots, chemists, physicists, and so forth, matching Zakharov's general description. There's one guy on a flight from Mexico City to San Jose, California; came in last night – commercial pilot, resident alien, but he has no prints on file.'

Kelsey could feel the excitement rising in her gut – this one sounded very promising. 'Is it him?'

'It's a Mexican citizen and three-year resident alien.

Real documents, not fakes. Has rented a room from a lawyer in San Mateo for the past year and a half.'

'But you faxed Zakharov's picture to customs in Mexico City and San Jose, and . . .'

'Bingo. Positive ID.'

Kelsey punched Bolton's pillow excitedly. 'Did you get an address on him? Did you pick him up?'

'The San Francisco SAC decided to set up a surveillance unit first until he could get an arrest warrant,' Cortez explained.

'If they have his place under surveillance and he hasn't shown up since last night, it means he probably picked up the surveillance and bugged out.'

'But now we got a new identity and hopefully a whole new set of clues as to his whereabouts,' Cortez said. 'He's an aircraft sales rep for a firm in San Jose, named Tomas Estrada, goes by "Tom." He travels frequently to Central America . . .'

'Easy enough to hop on down to Brazil from anywhere in Central America,' Kelsey pointed out.

'Credit cards, frequent flyer account, bank account, all legit and well established,' Cortez went on. 'Commercial pilot, Mexican and U.S. licenses. Speaks fluent English and Spanish. Well known to the airline ticket agents and local flying businesses around the Bay area. They're still checking around to see if Estrada or anyone matching his description has any other places he frequents in the area.'

'An arrest warrant for a suspected terrorist linked to Kingman City should be a slam-dunk for any federal judge these days, for God's sake,' Kelsey said. 'Rudy, I need to get the hell out of here. Hasn't the director met with the White House yet? Chamberlain needs a good bitch-slapping right about now.'

'The meeting is supposed to happen this morning,' Cortez said. 'Don't worry – you'll be out in a couple hours. I've got a jet on the way that'll take you to San Francisco to meet up with the SAC.'

'Are you sending Zakharov's picture . . . ?'

'To every airport, bus, rail, ship, and state police office west of the Rockies – as we speak,' Cortez said. 'If he doesn't surface within twenty-four hours, we'll go nationwide.'

'Go nationwide *now*,' Kelsey said. 'This guy's mobile. If he's a pilot, you'd better include fixed-base operators at as many general aviation airports as you can. He might have his own plane.'

'Good point. I'm on it.'

'Any other clues come up?'

'Nothing, except the Estrada character was legit all the way,' Cortez said. 'Lots of paper pointing to a regular hardworking guy taking advantage of all the fine things our country has to offer.'

'Hiding out in plain sight, you might say.'

'Exactly. This guy's smart, Kel. Real smart.'

'He's a stone killer with his hands on one and possibly more nuclear weapons,' Kelsey pointed out. 'I'm going to talk with Richter and Jefferson again to find out if they can tell me anything else about Zakharov and his henchman, Khalimov.'

'I'm wondering why the guy came back to the U.S.,' Cortez said. 'Why take the risk, especially since he was almost nailed in Brazil?'

'Only two good reasons I can think of,' Kelsey said. 'Either he didn't get paid and he's looking to collect, or . . .'

'He's not finished blowing things up in the U.S.,' Cortez said ominously. 'Or both.'

'Get me the heck out of here, Rudy,' Kelsey said. 'Keep on pestering the director until he sees the President himself.'

'Get packed – you'll be out of there soon,' Cortez said, and hung up.

Kelsey filled in Bolton as she put on her boots. 'Where are you going?' Bolton interrupted her when he realized what she was doing. 'You're not going to tell *them*, are you?' Kelsey stopped in surprise – in fact, that's exactly what she was going to do, and Bolton knew it. 'Are you crazy? No way, Kel! As soon as the director can fix it we're out of here. As far as I'm concerned, the task force is dead. Rudy gave *you* privileged FBI information – you can't share it with anyone outside the Bureau.'

'But . . .'

'But *nothing*, Kel,' Bolton insisted. 'You can't even go out there now asking them questions, because they'll figure you just got some hot information and they'll want to know what it is. I suggest you keep it to yourself, Kel.'

After a moment's hesitation, she nodded and kicked off her boots again. She found it surprisingly hard to roll back into bed. 'Why do I feel like I'm withholding important information?' she asked.

'You don't owe them jack, Kel,' Bolton said from the other side of the hallway. 'This task force thing has been nothing but a royal cluster-fuck from day one, because Richter thought his shit didn't stink. *He* abandoned *us* first . . .'

'He tried to get me to listen,' Kelsey said. 'He told me and Jefferson what he wanted to do.'

'He told you about this hot information he had, sure – and *then* he left the base without any authorization and was getting ready to go to freakin' Brazil . . . !'

'They almost got Zakharov.'

'They almost got themselves killed,' Bolton insisted, 'and they *still* did it without authorization. Why are you defending them, Kel? They screwed up, but it's *our* careers on the line! Just forget about these guys, Kel. By lunchtime we'll be in Washington tracking these terrorists down, and we'll do it the *right* way.'

Kelsey fell silent. If she had any hope of falling asleep again before dawn, she was disappointed.

The Oval Office, Washington, D.C.
Later that morning

Attorney General George Wentworth, National Intelligence Director Alexander Kallis, Secretary of Defense Russell Collier, and FBI Director Jeffrey F. Lemke stepped into the Oval Office and found Robert Chamberlain standing right beside the President of the United States, going over some documents. Victoria Collins was on the President's phone, noticeably apart from the others.

That, Lemke thought, was not a good sign.

'C'mon in, guys,' the President said, standing and motioning to the chairs and couches in the meeting area in front of the fireplace. A steward brought in a tray of beverages and fixed one for each of the attendees according to their preferences. Again, Chamberlain sat on the chair just to the President's right, the chair normally reserved for the Vice President. He took that chair not only because the Vice President was not in Washington – it had been decided after the attack in Kingman City to have the Vice President stay out of

Washington and move locations to ensure the continuity of the government in case of an attack in the capital – but also to highlight the status and power the National Security Adviser held in this meeting.

Robert Chamberlain was in no uncertain terms the de facto vice president – and many in Washington, like Wentworth and Lemke, would say he was more like the copresident.

'Thank you, Mr President,' Wentworth said. 'We have some positive news to report, and a request.'

'Go right ahead, George,' the President said, taking a sip of tea. Wentworth outlined the details of the search for Yegor Zakharov in the San Francisco Bay area. 'Interesting he decided to come to the States,' the President observed.

'Any reasons for that would be speculative, Mr President,' FBI Director Lemke said, 'but I think it was a mistake on his part. It'll make it that much easier to nail him.'

'Robert has been reviewing Zakharov's background with me,' the President said, motioning to the folder he and Chamberlain had been looking at before the meeting began. 'As commander of this Russian tactical nuclear missile battalion, he would certainly know where the warheads were stored, who was guarding them, and who to bribe to get his hands on some.'

'Do you need me to bring you up to speed on Zakharov, Alex?' Chamberlain asked.

'Zakharov was commander of a regiment of short- and intermediate-range nuclear ballistic missiles near Kirov, northeast of Moscow,' Kallis said before Chamberlain could begin. Alexander Kallis had degrees in international relations from Dartmouth and Harvard. He joined the

CIA after receiving his master's degree and quickly rose through the ranks to become a deputy director in charge of policy before being nominated to serve as the National Intelligence Director, the office that combined all the federal, civil, and military intelligence activities of the United States of America. 'After the Intermediate-Range Nuclear Forces Treaty was put into effect in 1988, his unit was deactivated. Zakharov publicly denounced the treaty and was quickly retired.

'He entered politics and joined the new Liberal Democratic Party of Russia in 1990, which was started by ultra-nationalist Vladimir Zhirinovsky,' Kallis went on. 'Zakharov was the party boss in Kirov Oblast, the district in which his unit was headquartered, and was considered a major factor in Zhirinovsky's rise to power and a candidate for a major office in Zhirinovsky's government, perhaps minister of defense. But he obviously saw the handwriting on the wall, because after Zhirinovsky's defeat in 1991, even though Zhirinovsky and the LDPR were still very powerful, Zakharov left politics and became a vice president of a pretty good-sized independent Russian oil company, KirovPyerviy.

'Zakharov became very wealthy, and combined with his military and political following, was starting to enjoy another tremendous surge in popularity,' Kallis said. 'That might explain why the Russian government just a few years ago announced the decision to allow a foreign company, TransGlobal Energy, to acquire a majority stake in a private Russian oil company – and why that company turned out to be KirovPyerviy. Zakharov left KirovPyerviy . . .'

'No, Director Kallis – Zakharov went *berserk*,' Chamberlain interjected, quickly tiring of being upstaged by the youngster Kallis. 'He threatened to blow up his wells, stage a coup, kill the Russian President, kill our President, kill Kingman . . .'

'Did you ever meet him, Mr Chamberlain?' Kallis asked. 'Sounds like you know him pretty well.'

'I met him once, at an energy conference in Scotland,' Chamberlain said dismissively. 'He was full of himself, all right – acted like he still had the Red Army uniform on. We dismissed him as a stressed-out nutcase and figured he'd just drink himself to an early grave, like most of the nouveau riche in Russia.'

'Well, he didn't,' Kallis said. 'He sold off all his shares, took his fortune, and disappeared. He then shows up aligned with GAMMA, an environmental and human rights group based out of Brazil, helping the terrorists bomb dams and energy facilities, most of which belonged to TransGlobal Energy.'

'According to the report from your task force that went down to Brazil, Mr Chamberlain,' Lemke said, 'this Zakharov is not just "aligned" with GAMMA – he's taken over and tried to assassinate both leaders of the group.'

'It would appear so.'

'And now he's back in the United States,' the President observed. 'Any idea where he could have gone or what he might be up to?'

'No, Mr President,' Wentworth said, 'but it's imperative that we do everything we can to hunt this guy down. At one time this guy commanded a force of hundreds of battlefield nuclear weapons ranging in size from ten to two hundred kilotons. Stripped of their safety devices, fusing mechanisms, and reinforcements, making them suitable for mobile ballistic missile use, the warheads he commanded would make ideal portable nuclear weapons.

He's apparently not only got his hands on some, but he's managed to bring them into the United States – and it's obvious he's continuing to exact his revenge on TransGlobal Energy.'

'I would agree, Mr President,' Chamberlain agreed. 'We need to find this guy right away. It should be our top priority.'

'What do you suggest, George?' the President asked.

'The biggest worldwide manhunt since the hunt for Osama bin Laden, centered right here in the U.S.,' the Attorney General said. 'A joint coordination effort of all Cabinet-level agencies and Homeland Security military forces, headed by Director Kallis, reporting directly to you. All operations coordinated by Director Lemke from Washington for the U.S.'

Chamberlain shifted in his chair and nodded slightly but said nothing. 'I delegated operational control of antiterrorist activities to the National Security Adviser,' the President said. 'Director Kallis can continue to co-ordinate his activities with me through Mr Chamberlain.'

Both Wentworth and Lemke looked decidedly uncomfortable at that point. Wentworth finally took a deep breath and said, 'Mr President, we feel that Mr Chamberlain's efforts at organizing and directing our nation's antiterror activities have been completely ineffectual, and we request that you take control away from him and give it to Directors Kallis and Lemke.'

Chamberlain's face remained impassive. The President glanced at him, trying to gauge his reaction but was unable. 'Robert?'

'The Attorney General is referring to Task Force TALON, I'm sure,' Chamberlain said. 'I admit that the team hasn't lived up to expectations . . .'

' "Lived up to . . ." Chamberlain, are you serious?' Lemke exploded. 'The task force never came together – there's been infighting and a lack of coordination right from the beginning. Then several members of the task force – including the commander *you* picked, Jefferson – head off to Brazil . . .'

'I authorized that mission and got White House approval . . .'

'Chamberlain, those people nearly started a *war* in Brazil – not just in one city, but *two*,' Lemke went on.

'They were hot on the trail of this Zakharov character and nearly got him . . .'

'But only succeeded in almost getting everyone killed,' Wentworth said. 'SATCOM One News has agreed to keep the story quiet for now, but they won't do so for long. I'm afraid the government's liability in this incident is extreme . . .'

'Bull, George,' Chamberlain said. 'Skyy would've gone anyway, you know that – she's got a reputation to uphold. If Richter and Jefferson didn't go with her she would've gone alone and possibly gotten herself killed right away in São Paulo.'

'The unfortunate truth is that Jefferson and Richter *did* go, which could lead many to believe that it was a secret government-sanctioned action,' Wentworth said. 'We'd be forced to defend the decision, defend the task force, *reveal* the task force . . .'

'So what, George?' Chamberlain interjected. 'Americans *want* to see the United States government act, Americans are being greatly inconvenienced and challenged on their own soil every day because of restrictions, government intrusions, a loss of freedom and rights; some are suffering. I think they would feel better knowing their government is out there with our best technology hunting down the terrorists.'

Wentworth fell silent and looked at the President. They all knew that the President hated long arguments in the Oval Office – he wanted each side to present their arguments and then shut the hell up and wait for a decision. The President turned to Chamberlain. 'What's the status of Task Force TALON, Robert?' he asked.

'I confined them to their training base in New Mexico indefinitely until my office completed its investigation . . .'

'An investigation which so far does not include the FBI, CIA, or any other agency except for the office of the National Security Adviser,' Wentworth said. 'The execs at SATCOM One News are screaming bloody murder – they are completely incommunicado with their people. At best we're going to make some enemies in New York. At worst . . . well, we'd start with false imprisonment, habeas corpus, violations of the First, Third, Fifth, Sixth, and Eighth Amendments . . .'

The President looked suspiciously at Chamberlain, but apparently decided his actions, although extreme, were warranted. 'I think the quicker we hush this thing up, the better,' the President said. 'Robert, I'm disbanding the task force.'

'But, sir . . .'

'You can continue your investigation if necessary, but I'm going to turn the military guys back over to their units,' the President said. To Secretary of Defense Collier, he said, 'Russ, you're in charge of the task force personnel. If any indictments come down, refer them for punishment under the UCMJ; for the rest, issue them constant warnings to keep their mouths shut or else they'll be cleaning up polar bear shit in Greenland.'

'Yes, Mr President,' Collier said.

'George, assist Robert on investigating what happened with the task force in Brazil,' the President ordered. 'But I have a feeling these guys were just trying to do their jobs and they got a little overzealous. The FBI and civilians involved will still be included in the Justice Department and military investigations, of course, but they can be released immediately pending the outcome.'

'I agree, Mr President. I'll cooperate in any way I can.'

He paused for a moment; then he shook his head resignedly. 'I think, given what's happened with the task force lately and Mr Chamberlain's investigation into this Russian terrorist connection, it makes sense to hand off running the antiterror operation to other agencies. George, give your proposal to Victoria, let us staff it for a few days, and we'll give you a decision. Robert will, of course, be able to add his input to it, as usual.'

'Yes, Mr President,' the Attorney General said.

'Robert, you know I hate to go only halfway and turn around on anything,' the President went on, 'but your task force's actions leave me no choice. Complete your investigation, send any recommendations for criminal or punitive action to Justice and the Pentagon, then dissolve the task force.'

'Yes, Mr President,' he said simply.

'Anything else for me?' the President asked. When no one replied, he asked, 'What's the status of my proposal for a declaration of war on terrorism, George?'

'Mr President, I'm afraid it's a nonstarter,' Wentworth said. 'We simply cannot find any legal, legislative, or historical precedents for such a thing. For a congressional declaration to have the force of law, it must meet the basic legal structure: a victim, a crime, a loss, but more important a perpetrator. We simply can't indict a . . . a state of *mind*.'

'The word I'm getting from the congressional leadership says the same thing, Mr President,' White House chief of staff Victoria Collins said. 'Your supporters say the American people won't stand for any more hardships in their lives that declaring war on terrorism would certainly bring. Plus, if your request for a declaration of war is defeated in Congress, it would be a crushing defeat for you and your party, and they're not willing to risk their political futures on it. Your detractors say it would be perceived as nothing but grandstanding on the worst possible level, and win or lose they would be sure to present it as inflaming the nation's emotions for nothing but political gain. It's a loser either way.'

The President turned to Robert Chamberlain. 'Robert?'

'You know my thoughts already on this, Mr President,' Chamberlain said. 'I don't care about historical precedents or the political fallout – we need to *act* to defeat terrorism, plain and simple. Sure, the American people are getting tired of the restrictions, hassles, surveillance, and intrusions – but I don't think they would get so tired of it if the President *and his Cabinet* made an all-out commitment to defeating the forces that threaten their lives. If we don't at least go before Congress and the American people and make the case for all-out war against terrorism, people will forget why we're doing this . . . and soon, it'll just be our fault for making their lives miserable, not the terrorists.'

The President nodded his thanks, fell silent for a moment, then said, 'George, I'd like you to stay on it.'

'Mr President . . .'

'Mr Attorney General, instead of looking for precedents, how about let's come up with reasons why we should *set* a precedent,' Chamberlain interjected. 'Instead of finding out that no one's ever done it before, how about some good reasons why we *should* do it?'

'When I need *your* advice, Mr Chamberlain, I'll ask for it, thank you,' Wentworth said acidly.

'That'll be all, everybody, thank you,' the President said quickly, rising to his feet. Wentworth, Kallis, and Lemke departed the Oval Office silently, firing angry glares at Chamberlain.

'Well, I think you've succeeded in alienating just about everyone in the Cabinet now, Robert,' Victoria Collins remarked.

'What's the use in even *having* a Cabinet if they won't do what you tell them to do, Mr President?' Chamberlain asked. 'I understand this is no small task, but all I've heard so far is why it can't be done. Why don't you just *do it* and let the American people decide if they'll accept it or not?'

'I want the entire Cabinet squarely behind me before I proceed, Robert,' the President said. 'It's getting harder to get there when you browbeat and insult them like that.'

'I apologize, Mr President,' Chamberlain said. 'I'll stop antagonizing them. But I wish they'd show some backbone, that's all.'

The President looked at his National Security Adviser for a few moments, then nodded noncommittally and went back to the papers on his desk. 'Thanks, Robert.'

'Thank you, Mr President,' Chamberlain said, and departed the Oval Office.

The President waited a few minutes, then buzzed his inner office secretary. 'Bring him into my private office, please.' He went into the private room adjacent to the Oval Office and stood behind his desk. A few moments later the door opened, and the President straightened his suit jacket and smiled. 'Welcome, Harold,' he said, moving around to the front of his desk and extending a hand in greeting. 'Sorry to keep you waiting so long.'

'No problem at all, Sam,' Harold Chester Kingman, president of TransGlobal Energy, said. 'Your staff made me very comfortable.'

The President motioned to a leather chair in the small office as a tray of coffee was brought in and beverages were served. 'You've been briefed on the situation with these Russian terrorist suspects?'

'Yes, I have,' Kingman said. 'I appreciate being kept informed very much.'

'We definitely believe the terrorists are targeting your company around the world, Harold,' the President said, 'and we want to do as much as possible to protect your company. You and your company are very valuable to our nation's energy future. You heard our conversation in the Oval Office?'

'Yes,' Kingman said, taking a sip of coffee. 'Zakharov is in the United States? That's very worrisome. How could Chamberlain and your Homeland Security people miss that guy?'

'Apparently he had an airtight alias, developed many years ago – completely legitimate. Basically he used his money and connections in the Russian government – and his position in TransGlobal Energy, I'm afraid – to get passports and visas into Mexico. He got himself a legitimate business, got his American visas and entry documents. Then he turned himself into a sleeper agent, going about his normal activities right under our noses, just waiting to activate himself.'

'My lack of faith in this country's immigration system has been fully justified.'

'You remember this guy?'

'Of course,' Kingman said casually. 'Think of Joseph Stalin on a good day. The guy's a heartless, ruthless psychopathic killer. I cannot overemphasize the incredible danger we're in to have him loose in America, especially if he has valid identification and financial resources. And I remember Pavel Khalimov too, his "enforcer" in the KirovPyerviy oil company – he's even worse. At least Zakharov would consider your value to himself and his schemes first before putting a bullet in your head: Khalimov wouldn't waste the brainpower.'

'Why didn't you have Zakharov eliminated yourself, Harold?' the President asked. He knew that Harold Chester Kingman certainly chose murder as one of his tools for corporate success – and he also knew that he was probably the only man in the world that Kingman would allow to ask him such a question.

'He got away and disappeared before I could tag him – to South America, it now appears,' Kingman replied. 'I should have searched for him harder, but he had tons of money from his Russian oil company and he paid better than I did in Brazil.'

'What's Zakharov after, Harold?'

'Me,' Kingman replied matter-of-factly. He lit up a cigar without asking the President's permission – payback for him asking such uncomfortable questions. 'He's a twisted egomaniacal son of a bitch, Sam. He's engineered dozens of killings and attacks against TransGlobal facilities all over the world for months, and now he's after me here in the

U.S. Only a wacko could ever believe he'd get away with it. If he can't get me, he's content to kill thousands of innocent persons.'

'What's his next likely target?'

'Since he was based in the Bay area and returned there, I'd say he's lining up something out there,' Kingman said. 'Our corporate headquarters is in San Francisco, but it's a relatively useless target – we've dispersed corporate functions out to dozens of different and more secure locations long ago. An attack there would be mostly symbolic – and Zakharov doesn't really do "symbolic" stuff. He likes to go for the jugular. He's already gotten TransGlobal's number-one petroleum and natural gas facility in the U.S. at Kingman City, Texas. Our number-two facility is in Atlantic City, New Jersey, but our number three is in Long Beach, California, and our number-four is in Richmond, California. My best guess: Richmond. He'll kill several birds with one stone there: disrupt our Bay area oil terminal, along with five other companies' facilities; take a swipe at my corporate headquarters; and attack right in my hometown.'

'We'll deploy investigators and protective forces to all of your facilities in the U.S. and as many overseas as they'll allow, Harold,' the President said, 'but we'll concentrate on Richmond. If he's there, we'll get him.'

'Thanks, Sam. I appreciate that.'

'You and TransGlobal are important to America, Harold – it's in the government's best interest to protect you the best we can.'

Kingman nodded, letting the obvious buttering-up routine slide off his back unnoticed. 'So, how's Chamberlain working out for you?' he asked after a few more puffs.

'He's a great asset to me, Harold.'

'He seems to have matured a bit working for you in the White House, Sam,' Kingman observed. 'When he worked for me he was an insufferable scheming weasel who liked to prove to everyone how important he was, although he was competent enough. You mentioned to me several months ago about that task force you were going to place him in charge of – I take it it's not working out?'

'It was a great concept, but Robert seems to have picked some . . . unusual characters to be part of it,' the President responded. 'I left it up to him, thinking he had thought about it extensively and picked the absolute cream of the special-operations crop to spearhead it, but it turns out he just picked a bunch of untested paper shufflers and lab-bound mavericks that couldn't work well together.'

'Chamberlain can be an egotistic putz sometimes,' Kingman said, 'but I always found him to be a pretty good judge of character – picking the wrong guys for the job doesn't sound like him. Maybe he just got sloppy when he went into government service. I imagine being in Washington and having to deal with the brainless bureaucrats around here will do that to a man.' The President closed his eyes and chuckled, letting that comment slide off his back. 'That's why I stay away from this place as much as possible.'

'A couple of the task force members broke ranks and went down to Brazil to track down that environmentalist group, GAMMA,' the President went on, ignoring Kingman's remarks, 'and they stumbled across Zakharov and Khalimov. Got themselves shot up pretty good.'

'But they *did* track down this GAMMA and caught up

with Zakharov? Sounds like they might have something on the ball after all.'

'Half the Cabinet wants their heads on a platter.'

'As I said, Sam, my complete and utter lack of faith in most of the government and its leadership has been more than justified lately,' Kingman said, filling the air over his head with pungent smoke. 'Myself, I'd put my money on those guys that went down to Brazil, and fire everyone else.' The President nodded but said nothing, prompting Kingman to move on so he could get the hell out of there. 'Anyway, Sam, I wanted to talk to you about this energy summit that's coming up in Washington. You know I'm a big supporter of your alternative energy proposals, especially your nuclear power initiatives, which you're putting before Congress this fall, but I'm not so sure that it'll be safe enough here in Washington for this confab.'

'It'll be secure, Harold, I guarantee it,' the President said. 'It's important this be held in Washington – I want this to be a U.S. government–sponsored initiative, not a corporate one or something sponsored by another country or OPEC.'

'So why do I need to be involved?'

'There's no more powerful alliance we can think of than TransGlobal Energy and the U.S. government,' the President said. 'I want to show the world we two are standing together: the world's most powerful nation and the world's most powerful energy company, working together to give our nation and the world the energy it needs. You *are* TransGlobal Energy, Harold. You *have* to be there.'

'I don't go for these political dog-and-pony shows, Sam.'

'The world needs to know who the players are, Harold. If you just send some junior vice president of corporate communications or something, they'll lose interest.'

'What about the environmental and antimultinational corporate lobbies? Aren't you afraid of pissing them off? They represent a pretty substantial bloc of voters.'

'Yes they do, which makes it even more imperative that we stand together on this,' the President emphasized. 'The American people react emotionally to the environment and to abuses of big corporations – but what they *want* are cheap and plentiful gasoline, heating oil, and electricity. We'll convince them that with our domestic energy initiative we'll give them what they need and be conscious of the other stuff too. We'll *talk* about preserving and safeguarding the environment, but what we'll *do* is start building nuclear power plants and natural gas-fired power plants and storage terminals again.'

'You're the talker here, Sam – you always have been. Let me be the doer.'

'Do this summit for me, Harold, and you'll have your pick of the best contracts before they go out for bid,' the President said. 'I can also get you a heads-up on any congressional or regulatory agency probes coming out of the chutes.'

'I've already got all the spies I need on Capitol Hill, Sam.'

'Harold, do this for me, please,' the President said. 'You and me together on stage – it'll confuse the hell out of all your detractors. They'll think you're going to run for public office.'

'Hell, Sam, I'd shoot myself in the head first, and they know it,' Kingman said. He took another deep drag on his cigar, then shot a last cloud of smoke at the President of the United States. 'Tell me more about this task force that Chamberlain was heading. Who's in charge?'

'An Army Special Forces sergeant major by the name of Jefferson.'

'Chamberlain put a noncom in charge of a task force? That's odd. Who else?'

'That army major who rescued those people in Kingman City.'

'The guy inside the robot? That was pretty darn cool, Sam,' Kingman gushed. 'The robot too?'

'Of course. That's what got Robert interested.'

'He always did like the high-tech toys.'

'There's an FBI special agent too by the name of DeLaine cocommanding the unit. Runs an intelligence office out of FBI headquarters.'

'Military and FBI in the same unit? Chamberlain's showing extraordinary imagination,' Kingman admitted. 'It's a weird combination – I'm not surprised it didn't work out – but Chamberlain at least showed he still has an original thought in his head.' Kingman fell silent for a moment. Then: 'And you're shutting down this task force, even though they almost got Zakharov?'

'It was pretty obvious that Robert lost tactical control of them,' the President said. 'They got a little too . . . rambunctious, I'd say. Loose cannons. We thought for a second they *stole* a bunch of equipment and hightailed it to Brazil.'

Kingman nodded thoughtfully again. 'I'll do your circus in Washington, Sam, on one condition – you lend me this task force.'

' "Lend" it to you?'

'Call it a plant and port security assessment visit,' Kingman said. 'Let me have them for . . . oh, a year.

They'll be ordinary citizens, no federal powers; I'll pay their salaries and provide a secure location for them to train. Who knows – I might even snare Zakharov for you.'

It was the President's turn to lean forward in his seat this time, and he did so, just as Kingman expected him to do. 'It'll cost you more than a couple days in Washington, Harold,' the President said.

Kingman nodded – he enjoyed playing these quid pro quo games. 'Collins happened to mention to me that she's forming your reelection committee soon. I think TransGlobal would like to see to it that your committee is properly set up and running . . . shall we say, three million?'

'Let's say ten million, Hal,' the President said.

Kingman made a sigh as if he had just been out-maneuvered, but inwardly he was thinking that he was getting off cheap: he would've paid twenty million to get his hands on that super-strong bulletproof robot technology. 'You got it, Mr President,' Kingman said. 'How quickly can you load them up and send them on their way?'

'Where and when do you want them?' The President held up a hand. 'Wait, let me guess: San Francisco Bay area – today.'

'Great minds think alike, Mr President,' Kingman said. He leaned forward a bit and added, 'And maybe Chamberlain doesn't need to know about our deal?'

'I've already ordered him to wrap up his investigation and let them go,' the President said. 'I think he's pretty much washed his hands of them. He'll find out. But I don't want to see robots marching down the middle of Fisherman's Wharf or the Embarcadero, Harold. Don't make me look bad on the Left Coast.'

'They'll be out of sight, Mr President, I promise.' He got to his feet, approached the President's desk, and extended a hand. 'Thank you for a very productive meeting, sir.'

The President rose and shook his hand. 'Have fun with your new toys, Harold,' he said. 'If you happen to find this Zakharov guy, squash him for me, will you?'

'Gladly, Mr President. Gladly.'

Cannon Air Force Base, New Mexico
A short time later

She waited until Bolton was taking his turn in the shower, then got up and left to see where the other members of the task force were. She didn't sleep one bit, and the information she got from her colleague in Washington was like a leech sucking her blood – but at the same time, she didn't want to confront Bolton about it again.

There was a fair amount of activity happening for a disbanded military unit who were under criminal investigation, Kelsey DeLaine thought as she went out to the aircraft parking apron. Jefferson, Richter, Moore, the staff officers, and the TALON strike platoon looked like they were just getting ready to begin an early-morning run complete with rifles, Kevlar helmets, combat boots, and body armor with ammo pouches and CamelBak water bottles clipped to them; Ariadna Vega, her face still bruised and bandaged but already looking better, was handing out gear from the back of a Humvee. Kelsey hurried back to her barracks, put on a pair of fatigue pants, an athletic bra, black T-shirt, and boots, and ran out to go with them.

'Nice of you to join us, Agent DeLaine,' Sergeant Major Jefferson said.

Kelsey went over to him, very aware of all the angry, accusing eyes around her. 'Mind if I tag along, Sergeant Major?' she asked.

'Rumor has it the FBI Director and the Attorney General are going to get you pulled out of here today,' Jason Richter said. 'Sure you wouldn't rather be packing to go?'

'I want to go with you guys,' Kelsey said.

'How touching,' Ari said. 'Or do you just want to take another shot at Jason?'

'Dr Vega, put a cork in it, draw her some gear, and let's get going,' Jefferson said gruffly. Ari hesitated, glaring coldly at her, then picked out some gear and threw it on the ground behind the Humvee. The helmet and body armor were too big and the CamelBak was empty, but Kelsey didn't complain as she went over to fill up her bottle, then donned her gear and got in line. They did some stretching and a walk around the big hangar to warm up, then started an 'Airborne Shuffle' – a sort of a slow jog designed to cover long distances while wearing a heavy backpack or parachutes – out among the sage-brush and sand dunes of the Pecos East training range.

They took a break after about a kilometer's jog. 'How are you guys holding up?' Kelsey asked Jason after she sipped water from her CamelBak.

'Fine.'

'Are they letting you work on the CID unit?'

'Yes.'

'Are you going to talk to me just in one-word phrases from now on, Jason?'

'What do you want from me, Kelsey?' he asked. 'I've

taken full responsibility for everything I've done and I'll take my lumps. If it hurts anyone else . . . well, I'm sorry. But I still feel we're getting screwed, and I don't think we've heard the last of Zakharov or Khalimov. I don't know when or how, but they're going to strike again, and soon.' Kelsey's mouth turned dry when Jason said that, but she held her tongue, took a deep drink of water, and got ready for the next leg of their run.

The next two kilometers was a fast jog instead of the 'Airborne Shuffle,' and now there was a lot more huffing and puffing at the rest stop. Kelsey drifted around near Jason, hesitating, then finally made up her mind and went over to him. 'I wanted to let you know, Jason: we think Zakharov is in the United States,' she said.

Jason nearly spit out a mouthful of water. '*What*?' he exclaimed. 'Zakharov is *here*?' Now everyone's attention was fixed on them. 'How? When did you find out?'

'Early this morning,' Kelsey replied. 'He has a resident alien alias that he's been using for years. He's had full entry and exit privileges.'

'Where?'

'San Jose International.'

'What in hell is he doing in the U.S.?' Air Force Captain Frank Falcone asked.

'We don't know.'

'What's his alias?' Jason asked.

'He's a Mexican national with resident alien status,' Kelsey replied. 'Brokers and flies helicopters between the U.S. and Central America. Lives in San Mateo, California – has for years.'

'Jee-sus . . . !'

'Haven't the Fee-Bees picked him up yet?'

'We had his apartment under surveillance but missed

him,' Kelsey said. 'He either didn't return there or spotted the surveillance team and took off.'

'So now he's *loose* in the United States!' Jason exclaimed. 'My God . . .' He turned to Jefferson and said, 'Sergeant Major, we need to get the task force loaded up and sent out to the West Coast as soon as possible. He's going to strike somewhere out there, and we've got to be ready.'

'We're not authorized to do *anything* except cooperate with the investigators, Jason,' Jefferson said.

'We've been sitting around here for two days, and all they've been doing is asking us the same questions over and over again,' Jason said. 'Something's going on, Ray. We're being chopped out for some reason.' Jefferson fell silent, and Jason saw something that he'd rarely ever seen in the sergeant major before: doubt and confusion. 'Kelsey, we need to talk.'

'What about?'

'Zakharov. Who is he? We know he's an ex-Russian colonel and has apparently taken over this radical environmental group, but what else is he? We need some clues before we can take this guy down.'

'The FBI is tracking him down . . .'

'Kelsey, the guy used a nuclear weapon in the United States and is more than likely going to do some other attack – and if he's got access to more nuclear weapons . . .'

'He might,' Kelsey said hesitantly. 'He commanded a Soviet tactical nuclear rocket battalion back in the eighties.'

'Oh, my God . . . !' Lieutenant Jennifer McCracken breathed.

'After that, he was the head of a large private oil

company in Russia and a powerful right-wing political operative.' She paused before adding, 'He joined GAMMA when his oil company was bought out by . . .'

'Don't tell me, let me guess: TransGlobal Energy,' Jason said. 'That's why he's attacking all of those TransGlobal facilities in Brazil and the U.S. – he's on some sort of revenge kick. And now he's back in the U.S., on the West Coast . . .'

'TransGlobal Energy is headquartered in San Francisco,' Kelsey said, 'and they have a major terminal and storage facility in the Bay area . . .'

'That's his target – it's *got* to be,' Jason said. 'We've got to deploy the task force out there and hunt this guy down.'

'We've got the FBI, customs, Coast Guard, the National Guard, and every state and local law-enforcement agency within a hundred miles of San Francisco on the alert and after him,' Kelsey said. 'We're setting up surveillance on every possible target. What is the task force supposed to do that they can't?'

'Kelsey, you're acting as if this guy is just some sort of common criminal,' Jason said. 'He's a psycho with knowledge and probably access to military weapons, including nuclear weapons. You don't fight him with guys with a pistol and a badge – you fight him with superior firepower. You can't go out there expecting to apprehend him – you've got to go in expecting to hunt him down, battle it out, and kill the sonofabitch.'

'And what makes you such an expert, Major – the outstanding job you did down in Brazil?' Kelsey asked irritably. 'Listen, Jason, we've got folks on the case who figured this stuff out a long time ago and they've been on the move and setting up ever since . . .'

'Oh, really? How long have *you* known about this, Special Agent DeLaine?'

'. . . and Task Force TALON is alive in name only,' she went on. 'Let the professionals handle it.'

'Zakharov brought six squads of paramilitary troops, antitank weapons, and a helicopter gunship, all led by a former Russian commando, just to nab *one guy* – if he's going to attack a heavily armed target in the heart of a major city in America, he's going to bring a lot more fire-power than that,' Jason said. 'He'll be no match for the police department.' He turned to Jefferson. 'Ray, we've got to find a way to get out of here,' he said. 'Who else can you talk to besides Chamberlain? How about Secretary of Defense Collier?'

'I can try to contact him through friends of mine in the Pentagon,' Jefferson said. This time, there was no argument about trusting Chamberlain – he knew some-thing was wrong. 'I'm friends with the command sergeant major working in the office of the director of the Joint Staffs. He might be able to get a word to the SECDEF.' He pulled out his secure cellular phone and dialed. After a few moments, he closed the phone, and for the second time Jason saw a very uncommon sight – a confused look on his face. 'You're not going to believe this, sir,' he said. 'We've just been ordered to prepare to deploy – the *entire* task force. A C-17's on the way to pick us up.'

'Where are we going?' Jason asked – but when he saw Jefferson's face, he knew instantly: 'You're shitting me: San Francisco?'

'I shit you not, sir. San Francisco. They're calling it a "security assessment" for . . .'

'For TransGlobal Energy,' Jason said. 'Did they plant

listening devices on us, or what? Let's get back to the training area, Sergeant Major. Let's go, folks.'

'What if they're wrong about San Francisco?' Kelsey asked as they started jogging back to base. 'Zakharov could be anywhere.'

'I don't think he'd fly into San Jose and then risk flying somewhere else to do whatever he means to do,' Jason said. 'Whatever he's doing back in the States, he's going to do in the San Francisco Bay area.'

'It'll be like finding a needle in a haystack.'

'C'mon, Special Agent DeLaine, you're in the FBI, remember?' Jason said. 'Use your incredible powers of deductive reasoning, logic, and investigation. All you have to do is put this guy within smelling range of Task Force TALON, and we'll take him down – *hard*.'

San Francisco, California
Early the next day

Anyone who commuted regularly to the city of San Francisco knew that if you needed to be in the office by 8 A.M. you had better be actually on the Golden Gate Bridge from the north or on the San Francisco–Oakland Bay Bridge from the east, and actually pointed at the city itself, by 7 A.M., or you weren't going to make it on time. But folks who hadn't heard about the even more intense security setup on all three approaches to the City by the Bay would still never make it on time even if they allowed the full hour to cross the bridges.

Army National Guard Specialist Nick Howard walked between two lanes of traffic, not really fearing being struck by oncoming traffic because he was walking far faster than the traffic itself was moving. He was in full combat gear with body armor over his battle dress uniform, Kevlar gloves, and helmet. Clipped onto his body armor was his usual light-patrol field equipment, including radio, flashlight, ammo pouches for his M-16 rifle and Beretta M9 pistol, CamelBak water bottle, and first-aid kit. He also carried some specialized law-enforcement-style equipment such as plastic handcuffs, a can of pepper spray, cellular phone (his own, not government issued), and notepad and pencils.

The one thing he wished he had was a gas mask to help protect him against the carbon monoxide automobile exhaust fumes he had been sucking on for the past two hours while out here on patrol.

Howard looked at the faces behind all those windshields and saw nothing but anger and resentment. He couldn't blame them too much, but this was a national emergency. In civilian life Specialist Howard was a warehouse foreman in Berkeley, formerly a truck driver himself, and he knew that time spent idling was completely wasted. On the other hand, the San Francisco–Oakland Bay Bridge was certainly a major target for any terrorist. It would not only cripple San Francisco, but jam up most of the cities and freeways in all of Northern California. Certainly that was worth a little patience here.

'*Senegal One to Senegal,*' his command radio squawked. '*Be advised, CHP advises the wait lines to cross the tollbooths are exceeding ninety minutes, and they're recommending we speed up inspections. Go to one every twelve trucks. Advise on any other suspicious vehicles. Senegal One out.*'

Howard sent a short 'Echo Eight' in response. He knew that had to happen. Their initial instructions that morning were to inspect every fifth multiaxle vehicle or any vehicle that looked suspicious – i.e., ridden in by anyone looking as if they were wearing military gear, who looked nervous, or any vehicle that showed any sign of unusual activity, such as grossly overweight, rocking unsteadily as if lots of persons were moving around inside, or any vehicle suddenly changing lanes to avoid scrutiny. The inspections nabbed several suspicious vehicles, such as a small U-Haul moving truck with at least twenty Hispanic men and women inside the cargo compartment, probably undocumented workers heading off to work. But mostly it only nabbed rolling eyeballs, shaking heads, and a few epithets muttered behind Howard's back.

It took a very, very long time to search those vehicles, and the parameters had to change quickly or else they were going to be there all day. It went from one every five vehicles to one every seven and currently one every twelve; now they had to just 'report' suspicious vehicles, not search them. And the commute had been going on only for two hours, with at least two more hours to go – it would only get worse. Howard believed they'd have to go to at least one inspection every twenty trucks to get through this mess quickly enough.

Of course, he thought, these folks could help themselves by carpooling. At least 90 percent of the private vehicles in this huge traffic jam were driver-only. Commuters too stupid to use BART or carpool deserved to sit in line like this.

The traffic inched forward less than a car-length. The ninety minutes his ops officer mentioned was ninety minutes to go *two stinking kilometers* – God, getting caught in this mess would drive him absolutely bonkers, as he was sure it was doing to most of the drivers trapped here.

The cars he was walking near had already cleared the tollbooths, which made most drivers think that the congestion was over and it was clear sailing from here on out. No such luck.

Time to do another inspection. Although he had lost count of how many trucks it had been since he last did an inspection, the National Guard specialist eyed his next target: a five-ton plain white local delivery truck, with two guys in the cab, that had just pulled out of the toll plaza and was in the section of the bridge on-ramp where it started to narrow from twelve lanes to four. He liked to pick the trucks without logos or advertisements on them, because that meant the drivers were usually nonunion, and Howard was a die-hard third-generation Teamster. As he approached the truck it seemed to him that the men inside were looking a little nervous – and then he saw one of them, the passenger, reaching down under his seat for something. He was desperately trying to remain upright, not bending over but staying upright, but he was definitely trying to get his hands on . . .

'Hey, bub,' he heard a gruff voice beside him yell. The sudden sound startled him, and he jumped. The driver of the red Ford compact car, about three cars ahead of the white truck, seemed to take some delight in seeing the soldier jump like that. 'Hey, what's the problem here?' he asked. 'I haven't moved one freakin' foot in ten minutes!'

'Security inspections, sir,' Howard said, keeping his eyes on the men in the white panel truck. Keeping his right hand on the hand grip of his M-16 rifle, he reached up to key the mike button on his headset transceiver. 'Senegal, Echo Eight . . .'

'Hey, soldier, I'm askin' you a question,' the driver of the red Ford shouted. 'I'm gonna be fuckin' late for work if we don't get movin' here, and I've been sittin' here for thirty minutes already!'

'*Senegal Echo Eight, Senegal, go*,' came the reply.

'Excuse me, sir,' Howard said to the irate driver. 'Senegal One, be advised, I've got sierra-alpha, two white males in a white GMC five-ton panel truck, license number . . .'

'Hey, I'm talkin' to you!' the driver of the Ford shouted. 'I paid my damned ten bucks, and I need to get goin'! Why are you on this side of the tollbooths anyway? This is a pretty stupid place to be!'

'Sir, please lower your voice,' Howard said. 'I'll get to you in a minute. Thank you.' Howard took a few more steps toward the truck. The passenger was scrunched way down in his seat, with only his head and shoulders visible now; the driver was making nervous glances down at the floor between their seats. He keyed the mike again: 'Senegal One, Echo Eight, request backup on my pos.' The code phrase 'sierra-alpha' meant 'suspicious activity' in their parlance, and the phrase certainly fit in this case. He could practically see the sweat pouring out of the guy in that truck.

'Echo Eight, Senegal, say license plate number for that vehicle.'

'Senegal One, Echo Eight, target vehicle has California plates, one-six-delta . . .'

Suddenly he heard, 'Fuck you, asshole!' and he felt a sudden burning sensation on the back of his neck. Howard reached up with his left hand as the burning intensified and started creeping down his back. He looked at his gloved hand and found some sort of dark liquid . . . *coffee*! The driver of that red Ford *just threw coffee on him*!

Something exploded in Howard's brain. Without

thinking, he whirled and raised his rifle, pointing it at the driver. '*You! Let me see your hands*!' he shouted.

'Don't point that thing at me, asshole!' the driver shouted. 'Back off!'

'I said *let me see your hands, now*!'

'Fuck you! You can't do anything to me!'

A fuse blew in Howard's head. He raised the muzzle of his rifle above the roof of the red Ford, flicked the selector switch on his M-16 from Safe to Single with his thumb, and fired one round. The driver – and every other driver within twenty meters – jerked in surprise. 'One last warning: *let me see your hands*!'

'*Echo Eight, Echo Eight, this is Senegal One! What's going on? Report*!'

'*Jee-sus*!' the driver said. He immediately stuck both hands out the driver's window of his car, a stainless steel Porsche coffee mug still in his left hand.

'Senegal One, Echo Eight, request immediate assistance!' Howard radioed.

But the driver of the red Ford had stopped paying attention to what he was doing when the gunshot rang out, and his car crept forward as he unconsciously took his foot off the brake and hit the car ahead of him. Startled again, Howard lowered the smoking muzzle of his weapon back down to the driver. 'Don't you move!' he shouted, his eyes bugging in surprise. '*Stop*!' But the red Ford rolled about two meters forward and hit the car in front of him.

The sudden impact made the stunned driver drop his coffee mug, and it made a loud clattering sound when it hit the pavement. The driver unconsciously leaned out of the car window as if he was going to try to catch the mug in mid-air, arms flailing. Already hot-wired for

extreme danger, Howard reacted . . . by pulling the
trigger of his M-16 three times. The driver's head
exploded into a cloud of bloody gore, and the corpse was
tossed into the empty passenger side of the car. Howard
immediately raised the muzzle and flicked the selector
switch to Safe, but of course there was no way to recall
the bullets. Pandemonium immediately erupted. Car
alarms and horns blared; men and women screamed and
started leaving their cars in droves, running in all directions; more cars hit each other as panicked drivers fled,
creating even more confusion.

In the white panel truck not far away, the two men
in the cab nearly jumped right out of their seats, watching
in horror as the soldier opened fire on the civilian. '*Nu
ni mudi!*' the passenger swore in Russian. 'He just shot
that guy!' He looked around at the almost instantaneous
confusion. 'Shit, everybody's panicking! People are
getting out and running across the damned freeway!'

The driver of the white panel truck looked over and
saw something even more horrible – several more soldiers
running toward them, rifles at the ready. He made an
instant decision. He picked up his walkie-talkie and keyed
the mike button: 'All units, this is Charlie, *baleet zheeyot*,
repeat, "stomachache," "stomachache." Out.' He put the
truck in Park, pulled a pistol from under his jacket, hid
it in his front pocket, and got out of the truck. The
passenger's face was blank with surprise when he heard
the order, but after a moment's hesitation he too got out,
his hands inside his coat pocket.

Hundreds of frightened people were running hysterically off the Bay Bridge toward the tollbooths – some so
scared that they were throwing themselves over the side
and plummeting several stories to the pavement below.

The police were reacting quickly. *'Stay in your vehicles!'* they shouted from public-address loudspeakers. *'Do not panic! There is no danger! Stay in your vehicles!'* But after 9/11, when the rumor that loudspeakers in the World Trade Center towers were telling workers not to panic and to go back to work just before the towers collapsed, nobody listened – in fact, it only seemed to intensify the panic.

The two Russians walked quickly amid the crowds, walking quickly enough to not get trampled but not too quickly so as to draw attention to themselves. CalTrans officers were emerging from the toll plaza, arms upraised, urging folks to go back to their vehicles so they could be moved. As hard as they tried to avoid them, one CalTrans worker appeared in front of the lead Russian. 'Sir, where the hell do you think you're goin'?' the hefty woman shouted. 'Go back to your vehicle, right now! You can't leave your . . .'

'Yop tvayu mat!' the Russian said. He pulled his pistol from his pocket, keeping it low and as out of sight as possible, and put two bullets into the woman from less than a meter away. The new gunshots didn't just create a new wave of panic – they created a virtual human stampede. Terrified drivers ran in every direction, trampling anyone who was unlucky enough to be trying to head in the opposite direction.

The two Russians followed the surging human tidal wave past the toll plaza, steering themselves toward the north side of the on-ramp where a new east span of the Bay Bridge was under construction. Stunned construction workers scrambled onto machinery and trucks as the mass of humanity surged closer. The Russians climbed atop an immense dump truck at the base of a concrete support structure. Moments later, several construction workers joined them. 'What happened?' one of them asked.

'We heard gunshots,' one of the Russians replied in a pretty good American accent. 'When we saw everyone else running, we ran too.'

'Shit, man, this is the biggest panic I've seen since the eighty-nine earthquake,' another worker said. 'What did you see?'

'A huge explosion,' the Russian replied. 'A huge fireball, as big as those suspension towers.'

'What?' the worker asked. 'What are you talking about? I didn't see no explosion.'

'Oh. *Uyobyvat!* Are you kidding!' And at that, he pulled out a small cell phone, hit a speed-dial button, then pressed the green Send key – and the white panel truck, loaded with almost two thousand kilos of high explosives, detonated in a massive fireball. The entire easternmost section of the Bay Bridge blew apart, sending hundreds of vehicles flying through the air and crashing down to the edge of San Francisco Bay. The toll plaza and hundreds more cars were swallowed up by the fireball, with thousands of liters of gasoline adding their fury to the tremendous blast.

But that was not the last explosion to occur on the Bay area bridges that morning.

When the terrorists' emergency call went out, a second terrorist team already caught in heavy traffic on the westbound span of the bridge west of Yerba Buena Island in a large Chevy panel van also exited their vehicle, ran through traffic toward San Francisco, and detonated the explosives by remote control when they saw police officers up ahead in their path. The terrorists had a brief firefight with police before both terrorists were killed – but not before another section of the Bay Bridge, this time high above San Francisco Bay, collapsed. Another explosion farther east on the eastbound deck of the bridge also created havoc as several dozen vehicles plunged hundreds of feet into the Bay through the decimated bridge.

The Golden Gate Bridge to the northwest was not spared. Another truck filled with explosives detonated in the northbound lane several meters from the toll plaza, and a second truck bomb exploded almost exactly at midspan in the southbound lanes. The suspension bridge twisted wildly, several of the cables holding the span snapped, and huge chunks of the roadway fell into the straits, but the bridge somehow held.

Market Street in the heart of San Francisco came under attack moments later. Huge explosions ripped just two blocks from the U.S. Mint, collapsing part of an old hotel onto the busy street, and another explosion on Market Street east of the U.S. Mint ruptured a natural gas line, sending a column of fire into the early-morning sky. Pedestrians scattered, pushing and shoving others in a frenzied attempt to get off the street before another explosion occurred.

Through clouds of smoke wafting in all directions, six Humvees and two large sports-utility vehicles made their way through the debris and craters in the street. Each Humvee had a soldier in regular-looking green camouflage fatigues in the gunner's turret, manning a fifty-caliber machine gun. Two Humvees blocked the intersections of Drumm, California, and Market Streets, deploying two terrorists from each vehicle. The terrorists hid small remote-control explosive devices in trash containers or under parked vehicles, then took up defensive positions on opposite street corners. The four remaining Humvee and the SUVs continued down Drumm Street to a high-rise just west of Justin Herman Plaza, overlooking the San Francisco Ferry Building and World Trade Center on the waterfront.

'Inner security units, report,' Pavel Khalimov ordered on his secure FM transceiver. One by one, each Humvee and dismounted reconnaissance commando reported in. 'Very good. Keep your eyes open and report any movement. Remember you are U.S. soldiers – tell anyone who approaches, including police, that you are army soldiers and order them away from the area. That should dissuade most of them. Engage only if they're stupid enough to stay. Strike team one, proceed with insertion.'

One Humvee and two SUVs proceeded right up to the front of the high-rise building – the Harold Chester Kingman Building, world headquarters of TransGlobal Energy. Two soldiers got out of the vehicle, retrieved TOW antitank missiles, aimed, and opened fire on the front doors of the building. While one soldier provided cover, the second carried two backpack-like satchel charges inside. Gunshots rang out, but otherwise the high-rise was quiet for several moments; then, the two terrorists ran back outside. Moments later the ground shook and thick clouds of smoke blew out the front of the building as the two high-explosive charges detonated.

'Elevators and main stairways eliminated,' came the report. The terrorists returned to the Humvee to retrieve several remote-control explosive devices, and then planted them around the outside of the building. Meanwhile, the two SUVs drove through the shattered front entryway and into the immense lobby of the Kingman Building.

'Security two, patrol cars coming,' one terrorist

reported on the FM frequency. Seconds later a loud explosion erupted east of their position as the terrorist detonated one of his remote-control roadside bombs, completely obliterating one San Francisco Police Department patrol car and overturning a second.

'Security Eight, two patrol cars on Market near Beale,' another terrorist reported. 'Looks like they're setting up a perimeter.'

'Security Ten, another one going up on California near Davis,' another reported. They heard several gunshots, then a loud explosion. 'Responders down, *huyisos*,' the terrorist radioed moments later. 'Fucker tried to take a shot at me! More patrol cars setting up on California out to Frost Street now.'

'Strike team is out,' the terrorists reported after leaving the two SUVs in the lobby of the Kingman Building. 'Device is in place.'

Khalimov entered the lobby, opened the back cargo doors of the first SUV, worked for a few moments, then carefully closed the cargo doors. 'Stand by to evacuate,' Khalimov radioed.

'Security Twelve, I've got something out here, Drumm and Washington,' another terrorist team radioed. 'It's a dune buggy, but it looks military.'

Khalimov looked north up Drumm Street, couldn't see it, but he didn't need to – he had a feeling he knew who it was. *They* were here. 'Anyone else?'

'Yes. Another one, Market and . . . wait one . . . *gas, gas*, Market Street, heading east fast!' The little dune buggy raced down Market Street, firing gas canisters up the street ahead of it, obscuring it from view. 'I lost it!'

'Stand by to repel, boys,' Khalimov said. 'All teams, follow plan Alpha, repeat, plan Alpha. Go! Go!' He turned and started to race down Drumm Street toward Market. As he reached the corner of Drumm and Market he saw the two dismounts running toward their Humvee stationed on Market Street . . .

. . . just as a streak of fire appeared down along Main Street and hit the Humvee, blowing it into a red-orange fireball!

'Security Eight is under attack!' Khalimov radioed. 'Let's move, move, *mo* – !'

And then he saw it, running up to the intersection of Market and Main Streets – the robot. It wore an immense backpack, but it moved as quickly and with the same agility as he first saw it in Porto do Santos. He saw what appeared to be a cannon barrel over its right shoulder, swiveling from side to side but finally centering on *him*. 'It is here,' he radioed. 'The fucking *mashina cheloveka* is here. All units, plan Alpha and evacuate. Repeat, plan Alpha and evacuate!'

Khalimov ran up Drumm Street while the Humvee that had been stationed at Drumm and California drove beside him to pick him up. He heard a sound and turned, just in time to see one of the military-looking dune buggies stopped at the intersection. A soldier was standing on the back, aiming a wicked-looking large-caliber machine gun or grenade launcher at him. The Humvee gunner opened fire, and the dune buggy returned fire and sped away, firing what appeared to be gas canisters at the terrorists.

'Everyone, get your gas masks on,' Khalimov ordered, quickly donning his own mask.

The Humvee gunner let loose a long burst of machine gun fire, then shouted, 'Captain! *Pasmatryet*!' Khalimov turned . . . and saw a *second* robot standing at the intersection of Drumm and California Streets, also wearing a grenade launcher backpack! Behind him, several soldiers in pixilated desert camouflage fatigues moved from corner to corner, guns trained on the Humvee.

'Get that bastard!' Khalimov shouted. The machine gunner in the Humvee opened fire on the robot. 'Not with that! Bullets won't hurt it! Use the TOWs!' Khalimov's soldiers jumped out of the Humvee with shoulder-fired TOW missile launchers, took quick aim, and fired. The robot moved too fast and both missiles missed – but both missiles hit the facade of the building behind it, causing most of the front of the three-story building to come down on top of the robot.

'We got it! We nailed it!' one terrorist shouted. But just as the terrorists began to celebrate their apparent victory, the robot started to climb out from under the collapsed building.

'Time has run out, *tovarischniys*,' Khalimov said on his secure FM transceiver. 'When it gets up, it will be after us, and it is virtually unstoppable. Anyone who is not on his way to point Alpha will be on his own.' He climbed inside the Humvee and screamed at the driver, '*Pashlee*! Move out!'

'Are you all right, sir?' Doug Moore in CID Two radioed. He had run over to where Jason was just now pulling himself out from the the building debris.

'Yes . . . maybe,' Jason Richter in CID One replied. 'I've got a warning tone somewhere – probably that access panel again, damaged in the blasts behind me. My grenade launcher is damaged too. You got that Humvee in front of you?'

'I've got him, sir.' His electronic crosshairs were locked

on the retreating Humvee in front of the Kingman Building.

'Nail him, Sergeant,' Jason Richter responded.

'Roger,' Moore radioed, and rapid-fired two forty-millimeter grenades from his backpack grenade launcher. The M430 high-explosive dual-purpose grenades shot one per second from the cannon and hit the Humvee dead-on, disintegrating the right front tire and somersaulting the vehicle over completely before it came to rest on its left side.

Khalimov opened the smoldering right rear passenger side door, and he and one surviving crewman scrambled out. Stunned and shaken, Khalimov and the other terrorist slumped to the ground beside the overturned Humvee. Khalimov coughed thick, acidic smoke out of his lungs. His face felt as if it was burned, and every joint in both legs ached. He looked up and saw the first robot standing beside the second one, just now crawling out from under the bricks and steel of the collapsed facade.

Those things were unstoppable, Khalimov thought. There was only one way to stop them . . . and he had it right in his hand. He had no choice, he thought as he pulled the remote detonator from his pocket, pressed and held the button, then ran as fast as he could down Market Street toward the Embarcadero. His joints and muscles ached, his vision was blurred, but he clutched that detonator with all his willpower, praying that the colonel's range estimate was correct. All he knew was he had to get the hell away from there, before . . .

Doug Moore helped Jason climb the rest of the way out of the rubble. 'Thanks, Doug,' Jason said. He disconnected the damaged grenade launcher backpack and let it drop to the pavement.

Jason had opened a small window in the front of the CID unit at the top of the robot's 'chest,' covered in bulletproof glass, and Doug could see Jason's face behind the glass, partially obscured by the oxygen mask–like breathing apparatus they both wore. 'Can you breathe okay in there, sir?' he asked.

'Yes, I'm fine,' Jason replied. 'Looks like my electronic visor failed, and I'm still getting a warning about the hydraulic power pack losing pressure, but I'm still operational. I'm going after these guys on foot . . .'

'I'll go, sir,' Moore said. 'You're damaged . . .'

'These guys on foot won't be much of a threat to me,' Jason said. 'I need you to search around and find any other terrorists in the streets, and then disarm as many of these booby traps as you can locate. Have all TALON units stay in position in case the terrorists try to make a break for it. We need to get the first responders organized so we don't have any terrorists try to slip in and out if they're still in disguise.'

'I'll get on it, sir,' Doug said.

Jason ran down Drumm Street to Market, and then down Market toward the Embarcadero, just three blocks away. The CID system was still working, although his limb movements were starting to get a little spasmodic. Terrified civilians ran out of his way, although a few excited bystanders pointed down toward the waterfront. Jason kept going.

Khalimov and one of the terrorist soldiers were helping each other escape the carnage behind them. They had just crossed the wide boulevard at the Embarcadero when they heard two helicopters flying overhead. 'Right on time,' Khalimov said. One helicopter touched down between Pier One and the Ferry Building, while the other hovered nearby. Both helicopters had twenty-millimeter machine guns mounted on the skids, ready to engage any police or military responders. Khalimov headed toward the helicopter on the ground. He didn't know how far he was from the warhead test kit, but he doubted if it wasn't anywhere near two kilometers – he would have to get on the helicopter and fly directly east to be as safe as . . .

. . . and at that moment he saw the second helicopter gunship wheel in his direction, bearing down on a target behind him. 'Don't look, just *run*!' Khalimov shouted, just as the helicopter's machine guns opened fire. The shells felt as if they were whizzing directly over their heads, which made them run even faster.

Jason dodged right and the first fusillade of bullets missed him, but the damaged microhydraulic actuators in the CID system couldn't keep up with his demand for even faster lateral movements and momentarily failed. At the same instant the helicopter pilot wheeled left, and Jason was sprayed by machine gun bullets. More warning tones blared. He sprawled on the pavement, unable to move – his legs felt as if they were locked in place.

He hurriedly commanded the CID system to shut down and then restart the microhydraulic system, hoping that resetting the system would remove whatever gremlins were running around in there. The helicopter gunship pirouetted in mid-air, lining up again to strafe the CID unit again. The composite armor was holding, but he didn't know how many more strafing runs he could survive before the 'magic bullet' would find a chink in his armor.

* * *

Back near the Kingman Building, Doug Moore in CID Two heard the gunfire just a few blocks away and started moving in that direction. 'Major, are you okay?' he radioed.

'My hydraulic system is resetting,' Jason replied. 'Head over to the Embarcadero on the double. Khalimov and the other terrorists are getting away by helicopter!'

Moore started running in that direction – but as he passed in front of the Kingman Building, Lieutenant Jake Maxwell, the TALON platoon leader, waved him down. They went inside the demolished front lobby of the building. 'We checked out the vehicles that crashed inside here, Sergeant,' Maxwell said. 'The one on the right is filled with high explosives, over a thousand kilos of some really nasty shit. We've disarmed the detonators, so I think we're okay. But check this one out.' Maxwell carefully opened the back cargo doors, exposing a steel box . . . they found a large cylindrical device inside, with the test kit attached. A steady green light on the control panel read Power, and another steady red light read Armed; a blinking green light was labeled Active and a blinking red light read Fire.

'Is that what I think it is?' Moore asked.

'I think so,' Maxwell said. 'Any idea how to deactivate this damned thing?'

'No clue, sir,' Doug admitted. 'But I suggest you notify the police and evacuate this area as fast as you can.'

'What about you?'

'I'll radio for help,' Doug said. 'If someone can talk me through disarming it, I will. Get going, sir.'

'I'll stay,' he said. He ordered his men out to clear the entire Financial District of anyone who still might be in the area.

Moore put in a call to Ariadna to contact someone in the military who could help identify and disarm the device, then turned to Maxwell. 'You'd better leave, sir. I'll handle this.'

'As you were, Sergeant – I'm staying,' Maxwell said. 'I think my fingers can maneuver around on this thing better than yours anyway.'

The big robot looked at him and nodded. 'Thank you, sir,' Moore said.

'Just don't forget to pick me up when you run the hell away from here, Sergeant,' Maxwell reminded him.

Khalimov and his soldier had reached the helicopter on the ground and piled in. He looked to check whether anyone else was on the way, but quickly saw that the two of them were the only ones. '*Idi slanu yaytsa kachat*!' he shouted. 'Let's go before that bastard gets up!' The helicopter gunship took one last shot at Jason, missed, and zoomed overhead, chasing the first helicopter over Pier One and over San Francisco Bay north of the stricken San Francisco–Oakland Bay Bridge toward Berkeley.

After the microhydraulic system restarted, Jason found most of the warning tones gone, and he was able to get to his feet – although he was still getting spurious inputs from the microhydraulic system to his limbs, he was in control of them. The helicopter had just lifted off, and Jason sprinted after it. The helicopter was picking up speed, and so was he – but he was running out of dry land to run on. Just before reaching the edge of the wharf between Pier One and the Ferry Building, Jason made a last-ditch leap . . . and grasped the left skid bar on the helicopter.

Holding on with his left hand, he reared back and punched at the belly of the helicopter with his right. His blow easily pierced the thin outer aluminum skin and continued on through, rupturing the helicopter's fuel tank. The engine sputtered and sounded as if it was going to quit, so Jason let go of the skid bar, fell about twenty meters, and splashed into San Francisco Bay just a few hundred meters from the piers.

He was able to swim easily to the nearest pier, where a crowd of stunned onlookers watched as the robot climbed out of the bay. But when he looked to see the crash, he found the helicopter was still flying along.

'Doug, the Department of Energy at Lawrence Livermore Labs has dispatched an Accident Response Group to your location, ETE twenty minutes,' Ariadna radioed to Doug Moore. 'They'll be able to defuse the device. They've looked at the images from your cameras. They can't positively identify it but they say it appears to be a nuclear device, probably a nuclear missile or artillery shell warhead.'

'Oh, shit,' Moore breathed.

'They're also dispatching a NEST crew to search for any other devices the terrorists might have left there.' NEST, or Nuclear Emergency Search Team, was a squad of trained engineers and scientists who used sophisticated sensors and other devices to locate nuclear weapons or components.

'Anything we can do while we're waiting?' Maxwell asked.

'According to the readouts on that yellow box attached to the device,' Ari said, 'the DOE guys say the warhead appears to be armed but the fusing is either not set or disrupted somehow. There is a radar transmitter in front of the device that can set it off, and it can also be detonated by impact or shock, so don't touch anything.'

'You don't have to worry about that,' Maxwell said.

'They're familiar with the yellow box attached to the device: it's a maintenance test kit, used to check those things before deployment,' Ari said. 'The blinking Fire light has them a little confused, and it might be a modification that the terrorists made so they could set it and then have time to get out of the area.'

'What are you saying, Ari?' Doug asked.

'If it's blinking, it's a good thing.' Ari replied. 'If it comes on steady . . . well, you'll probably never *see* it come on steady, if you know what I mean.'

'Unfortunately, I do.'

'The ARG guys say most likely it's a gun-type fission weapon, which means there are two chunks of uranium-235 on either end of the thing,' Ari went on. 'There's a mechanical safety device that's supposed to keep the two halves apart if it's accidentally triggered. If you can find that safety device and engage it, it won't detonate even if it's triggered. The ARG guys are setting up a video feed as they head out to you, so keep your CID cameras on the weapon and let them study it.'

'Rog,' Doug replied. He examined the device carefully. 'I see a space where a safety device might have gone, but it's been removed. Why don't I just break the sucker in half?'

'Better wait for the word from the ARG team,' Ari said.

'I'm okay with that.' He turned to Jake Maxwell. 'Sir,

I think I've got it from here. Why don't you get your men together and help the major?'

'If he needs our help, we'll go,' Maxwell said. It was pretty weird talking to the big robot like this, but since they had all been stuck at Pecos East together he had started thinking of the men inside the robots rather than just the machines themselves. 'I'll stay here for now. Okay, Sergeant?'

'Yes, sir. Thanks.'

A few minutes later: 'Doug, the ARG guys are about ten minutes out,' Ari radioed. 'How are you doing?'

'Fine, Ari,' Doug replied.

'I miss shooting with you, Doug,' Ariadna said. 'You taught me a lot. You're a good teacher.'

'I had a *very* good student.'

'We're going to keep on training after this is over, aren't we?' she asked. 'You said you'd teach me assault weapons and heavier stuff next.'

'I can't wait, Ari,' Doug said. 'Not just the gun stuff, but . . .'

'But what, Sarge?'

'I can't wait to be with you again,' Doug said. 'I miss you.'

'Hey, I miss you too, Doug,' Ari said. 'It's not just the gun stuff at all. I like being with you.'

'Ari, I wanted to tell you something a while ago, before all the stuff in Brazil happened . . .'

'You can tell me now, big boy.'

'I wanted to tell you . . .' Instead, he stopped . . .

. . . because the Fire light on the test kit stopped blinking.

Moore didn't hesitate – he immediately karate-chopped the device right in the middle, his microhydraulically

powered hand crushing the steel-encased device as easily
as a beer can, blocking the slug of uranium in the front
of the gun before it could reach the second slug in the
rear, form a critical mass, and create a thermonuclear
reaction.

That was the last action he would ever remember –
but it saved the lives of millions of souls that morning.

The explosive charge in the warhead exploded
milliseconds after Moore crushed the cannon. The ten
kilos of high explosive blew into a tremendous fireball,
scattering debris from the two uranium-235 slugs into
the atmosphere. The explosion triggered a second
explosion – this time, in the backup blasting caps
embedded in the one thousand kilos of octanitrocubane
explosive in the second SUV. Both Moore and Maxwell
were vaporized in the second explosion.

Buildings in San Francisco and most of the Bay area
are designed to withstand tremendous side-to-side
motions to guard against earthquake collapse, but this
design makes them vulnerable to upward and outward
forces. The first satchel charges set off by the terrorists
weakened the main stairwell and elevator shafts, whose
structures were the principal interior support structures
for the entire building except for the earthquake-resistant
outer shell . . . the ONC explosion would take care of the
rest of the building's interior support.

The fireball created by the ONC explosion traveled
directly upward through the entire thirty-two-story
building like an immense cannonball racing through an
old iron cannon, incinerating everything in its path. Once
the fireball reached the roof, pressure built up within the
building, shattering every window and completely
gutting the interior of the building, leaving the reinforced

outer shell intact – but without any interior supports, the building would never stand. Seconds later, the Kingman Building started to collapse inside itself like a planned demolition implosion. Within seconds, there was a huge pile of steel and concrete at the place where the Harold Chester Kingman Building once stood.

Jason Richter had just started jogging as fast as his malfunctioning CID unit could go back toward the Kingman Building when the ONC explosion ripped it apart. He watched in horror as the Kingman Building went down in a huge cloud of dust and debris. The sound was deafening. People were screaming behind him, running in all directions in panic. The fogbank of debris rushed over him, but he was still too stunned to move.

'Jason!' Ariadna radioed. 'Can you hear me? *Jason*!'

'I hear you, Ari,' he replied solemnly. Jason took a deep breath inside the CID unit. Soon the dust and debris was so thick he couldn't see a thing.

'What happened? I lost the video feed from Doug. Can you see him out there?'

He was being pummeled by chunks of flying steel, glass, and concrete as well as by the windblast created by the collapsing building, but he still could not make himself move for several long moments.

'*Jason . . . !*'

'He's gone, Ari,' Jason finally said. 'The Kingman Building blew up . . . he's gone. Doug is gone.'

'Wha . . . what?' Ari asked. 'Say again, Jason? What happened?'

'Zakharov has *got* to be stopped,' Jason said. 'We have got to pick up his trail and track him down *fast*, before he kills any more innocent people. We have to think of a way to find this guy before he strikes again. We have to take the fight to *him* this time.' He paused, taking another deep breath, then turned and started walking out of the river of debris swirling all around him. 'Sergeant Major Jefferson.'

'Sir?' Jefferson radioed from his spot on one of the 'Rat Patrol' dune buggies, which had evacuated on Maxwell's orders uptown on California Street.

'Recall Task Force TALON to Pecos East immediately. We've got work to do.'

'I'm sure the feds and the state of California will want a debriefing on . . .'

'Sergeant Major, I gave you an order,' Jason said. 'Assemble the team at Pecos East immediately.'

'What about Lieutenant Maxwell's and Sergeant Moore's bodies, sir?'

'When they're recovered, we'll return and take them back to their families,' Jason said. 'Our job is to get that sonofabitch Zakharov. Move out.'

Ray Jefferson liked the sound of the voice on the other end of that radio conversation. 'Yes, *sir*,' he responded, smiling. 'All Task Force TALON squads, secure your locations and assemble at rally point Delta. *Move*!'

Washington, D.C.
A short time later

This time there was none of the usual pomp and ceremony when the President of the United States visits Congress: no ceremonial banging on the chamber door requesting admittance; no loud announcement of his arrival by the sergeant-at-arms; no welcoming applause; no handshakes. The assembled members of both houses of Congress simply rose to their feet and remained silent as the President, surrounded by Secret Service, walked quickly down the aisle to the podium.

The Vice President was not there, still in a secure location outside the capital due to security concerns; his spot was taken by the Senate majority leader. The Speaker of the House was in his usual position, behind and to the President's left; the bulk of the bulletproof vest he wore obvious beneath his suit, as was the case with most of the ranking members of Congress. Most of the Supreme Court justices, Armed Forces chiefs of staff, Cabinet members, and White House senior staff were in attendance, as were the members of Congress themselves. There were just a few observers allowed. Every door was guarded by a uniformed U.S. Marine Corps soldier with full battle gear and assault rifle.

'Mr Chairman, Mr Speaker, members of Congress, thank you for responding so quickly to my request to address a joint session,' the President began moments after reaching the podium. 'I know over the past several weeks you have been informally debating the idea of declaring war on terrorism. Today, that's exactly what I'm asking Congress for this afternoon: I wish Congress to issue a declaration of war against terrorism.

'I have already declared the entire San Francisco Bay area a federal disaster area and have activated the Joint Civil Response Force to help the state of California deal with the emergency. As commander in chief, I have federalized the California National Guard and Reserve Forces Command to help local and state authorities in rescue, recovery, medical, relief, and security efforts; I have directed the Secretary of Defense to assign active-duty units based in the U.S. to U.S. Northern Command and to be made available for defense and security assignments throughout North America; and I have ordered the highest possible level of security for all oil and gas, chemical, power production, water, and transportation facilities all across the United States.

'But all of this not enough – not nearly enough. Our resources, which were already stretched thin after the attack on Kingman City, are now at the complete exhaustion point. My only option is to request from Congress full war authority to muster resources to defend our nation and to deploy worldwide to hunt down and destroy these terrorists. I am asking Congress for a declaration of war on terrorism.

'Specifically, I am asking Congress to authorize all available resources of the United States of America to investigate, indict, pursue, capture, or destroy terrorists anywhere in the world. I specifically refer to the man known as Colonel Yegor Viktorvich Zakharov, whom we believe was the mastermind and weapons procurer of the nuclear attacks on Kingman City, Texas, as well as the attacks this morning in San Francisco. This resolution also pertains to his coconspirators around the world, and to any person, group, organization, or nation that harbors, protects, assists, or facilitates his movements or activities, past or present.

'I am also requesting one more thing from Congress: repeal of the Posse Comitatus Act of 1878,' the President went on. 'The act was designed to keep federal military troops from violating the people's constitutional rights by acting in a warlike manner to civilians on American soil without due process. What it has succeeded in doing, however, is to keep America incapable of defending itself against an attack on its own soil. The President needs the authority to deploy the full range of military forces anywhere, at any time, for any and all purposes in order to defeat this enemy. It cannot be restrained or hampered by the fear of crossing state or local jurisdictions.

'The war is no longer "over there"; the oceans no longer insulate us; and the enemy is using weapons and tactics that were once reserved only for the most extremely desperate battlefields. We are not fighting in the aftermath of a civil war – we are fighting a strong and determined enemy that can destroy this nation if we allow it. It is time for the U.S. military to be given the authority to use its power right here on our own soil to defend our great nation. As commander in chief, I promise I will not waver or shirk my responsibility to defend our nation; but I must be given the tools I need to combat terrorism wherever I find it, whether foreign or domestic.

'I therefore ask Congress . . . no, I *demand* that you pass a war resolution against terrorism, and that you repeal the Posse Comitatus Act of 1878 and allow U.S. military commanders and the forces under their command to take any and all measures necessary to defend and protect the United States of America right here at home. Time is of the essence; the very future of our nation is at stake. May God bless and protect the United States of America.'

As the stunned members of Congress got to their feet, the President stepped off the dais and walked out of the chamber without speaking or shaking hands with anyone. He was escorted under very tight security to his waiting armored limousine. His chief of staff and National Security Adviser were already in the limo waiting. The President took a deep breath and loosened his tie, slumping in his seat. 'I picked one hell of a day to quit drinking,' he said wearily. 'When do you think the vote will come in?'

'They have a quorum, but they still might send the draft resolution down to committee,' Victoria Collins said.

'They won't do that – not with almost continuous images of San Francisco being played on TV,' the President said. 'What's the latest straw poll?'

'The war resolution is evenly split,' Collins replied. 'Repealing Posse Comitatus . . . still three to one against.'

'But that was before San Francisco,' Robert Chamberlain reminded her. 'They might change their votes now. There was a *nuclear bomb* planted right in downtown San Francisco, for God's sake!'

'They see enough National Guard troops in their cities, airports, and bus terminals now – they might think that's plenty,' Collins said uneasily.

'I'm done waiting around here,' the President said resolutely. 'Where do we start, Robert?'

'Task Force TALON is back at their base in New Mexico, sir,' Chamberlain replied. 'They're investigating several possibilities. The FBI is interviewing tollbooth operators to see if anyone can identify Pavel Khalimov, but we're fairly certain that he was involved in the bombings in San Francisco.'

'Be sure TALON is fully reconstituted and ready to fight,' the President said.

'Does that mean I get control of the unit back, sir?'

'Damn right it does. I don't want them on the backside of the power curve any longer – I want them right up front, wherever the investigation takes them. Get them moving, Robert. Find Zakharov and destroy him. Wherever it leads them, whatever it takes – find him and destroy him. They get anything they want: aircraft carriers, bombers, tankers, transport planes, troops, the works. But they find this Zakharov guy and *destroy* him.'

'Yes, *sir*,' Chamberlain responded. 'It will be my pleasure – my *extreme* pleasure.'

Chapter Eight

Dumyat, Egypt
Two nights later

It had not taken as long as he thought it might, but it was still well after 9 P.M. when Yusuf Gemici closed the last accounts receivable file on his computer and secured it with a password. He took a last sip of thick, strong Turkish coffee, popular in Egypt and around the Middle East, and was ready to start shutting the computer down when a gentleman and a lady came through the outer office door. The secretary – his slutty but very cute sister-in-law – was long gone for the day, so he rose and went out to the reception area. This was an intrusion, sure, but he wasn't yet rich enough to turn away customers, especially those who looked well-off enough.

'*Ahlan wa sahlan,*' Gemici said in Egyptian Arabic. '*Misae el kher.*'

'*Ahlan bik,*' the man said in response, in stilted but passable Arabic with an American accent. '*Enta bititkallim inglizi?*'

'Yes, of course, I speak English,' Gemici replied. 'Welcome to my place of business. How may I be of service?'

'I apologize for the late hour,' the man said. The woman, who had been unobtrusively hanging behind the man, walked off and began looking at the pictures of cargo vessels on the walls in front of the secretary's desk.

'Not at all. Please come in and sit.' The man came into Gemici's office; the woman stayed outside. 'I am Yusuf Gemici, the owner of this business. I shall make coffee, unless you prefer water? Juice?'

'Water, *min fadlak*.'

'Of course. You Americans are not accustomed to *ahwa turki*.' He retrieved bottles of mineral water from a small refrigerator next to the secretary's desk, along with a bowl of half-melted chips of ice and a couple small glasses. The woman stayed outside, as a woman who knew her place should always do. 'I do not forget how much you Americans like your ice cubes.'

'*Shukran*,' the man said.

'*Afwan*.' Gemici kept the door to his office partially open. The woman was still looking at the pictures of various ships on the wall – she hadn't said a thing, unusual for a Western woman. 'We do not see many Americans here in our little city, except for the oil workers and tourists taking the *felucca* tours. Have you been on the Mouth of the Nile tour?'

'No, not yet.'

Gemici gave the man his business card after scribbling some Arabic on the back. 'My brother runs the Timsaeh tour company. The best boats on the Mediterranean. Show him this card and he will get you a bottle of Omar Khayyam wine for your sunset cruise.'

'Thank you, sir.'

Pleasantries over, Gemici leaned back in his chair expansively. 'How may I help you, sir?'

'My company is in the process of negotiating a sale of newly designed natural-gas metering equipment to the Egyptian General Petroleum Company,' the man said. Gemici's eyes widened. The Egyptian General Petroleum

Company was Egypt's second-largest petroleum consortium, with an immense presence in the area because of its development of several natural-gas fields near Port Said, on the other side of the Gulf of Dumyat. 'The Point Fouad project is ready to expand, and my company has a contract to provide new equipment to be shipped from Newark, New Jersey, to Dumyat.'

'Very excellent,' Gemici said. 'I am glad you chose us. We have a very fine vessel to move your equipment.' He stood and went over to a large photograph of a ship on his office wall. 'My pride and joy: the *King Zoser*, named after the man who united the two desert kingdoms into one nation which became Mişr, or modern-day Egypt,' he said. 'She is fast, reliable, efficient, fully inspected and certified by the U.S. Coast Guard, and specially designed to safely and securely handle outsized and delicate machinery such as computerized field equipment. We require very little handling equipment at the pier, so we routinely go into smaller ports which is often much more convenient for our clients. We can even offload outsized equipment directly onto offshore platforms if necessary without the use of helicopters.'

'The crew is especially important to this shipment, sir,' the man said. 'To cut costs, I would like to know if the crew has any experience handling equipment such as ours. We would like to avoid sending a number of engineers on the ship if at all possible.'

'But of course!' Gemici said. 'As I said, we specialize in serving the oil and gas exploration industry with safe, secure, and professional transportation support.'

'Excellent,' the man said. 'In fact, I believe it was one name in particular from your company that came very highly recommended: Gennadyi Boroshev.'

Gemici kept his smile in place, but he could feel sweat start to pop out around his collar and in the soles of his feet. 'I am sorry to inform you, sir, that I do not know of any such man. He does not work for my company.'

'Then maybe you can tell us where to find him, Mr Gemici.' The woman had come into the office, followed by two younger men with obvious gun bulges under their sportcoats. He noted the shades in the windows in the outer office were all closed and the lights turned out. The woman held up a wallet and showed a gold badge. 'Special Agent Kelsey DeLaine, FBI,' she said. The men with her closed the rest of the blinds in Gemici's office and started going through his file drawers. 'Gennadyi Boroshev. Where is he?'

Gemici closed his eyes as his heart sank through his chest into his bowels. Shit, he *knew* this was going to happen. But he still motioned to the agents rifling his file cabinets. 'Do you not need a search warrant to do that, Special Agent DeLaine?'

'Do you want me to get a warrant, Yusuf?' Kelsey asked. 'Would you like me to call the *Mubahath el-Dawla*? I'm sure they'd want to know what you're up to.' The *Mubahath el-Dawla*, or State Security Investigations, was the Egyptian internal intelligence force, the secret Gestapo-like unit that provided information to the President and the Ministries of the Interior and Justice – any way they could, in whichever way the ministries wanted it, or so their reputations suggested.

Gemici's eyes were darting around the room now in confusion, but he was still trying to bluff his way out of this, waiting to hear exactly how much information they had or if they were just on a fishing expedition. 'Boroshev . . . Boroshev . . .'

'He was on board your vessel for several weeks on your last North and South American cruise,' Kelsey said. 'As far as we can tell, he was on board all the way from Damascus to Richmond and all the way back to here. You don't remember him?'

Crap, Gemici thought, they had *everything* . . . 'Ah! You said *Boro*shev! Your accent is difficult for me,' he said, smiling and bobbing his head. 'Of course I recognize him. Russian. Ugly. Sickly. A drug fiend, if I remember correctly. I do not know where he is.'

'Got the crew files, Kelsey,' one of the agents searching his file drawers said.

'Boroshev was not a crew member,' Gemici said. 'He was a courier, a messenger boy. We paid very little attention to him.'

'Wall safe,' the other agent said, moving the large photograph of the *King Zoser* aside. He immediately started searching around the area of the picture, especially in dark, out-of-the-way places.

'That is the owner's safe,' Gemici said.

'I thought you were the owner, Yusuf.'

'I am just a lowly ship's captain,' he said. 'I am not allowed to touch it. I do not have the . . .'

'Got it,' the second agent said. He copied a combination from the very edge of a piece of trim around the photograph on his notepad and then entered it into the wall safe, and the door popped open.

'You men are all alike – you can't remember combinations so you write it on something nearby, thinking no one will ever find it,' Kelsey said. The second agent withdrew another batch of personnel files.

'I told you, Boroshev was a courier, a representative of a client,' Gemici said. The second agent flipped quickly through the personnel files, then went back to the open wall safe. 'I have no records on him whatso . . .

'False bottom,' the agent said. He removed a piece of carpet from the floor of the safe, then a piece of metal.

'I'm afraid I must insist that I call the harbormaster and local police,' Gemici said. 'This is getting quite . . .'

'More files,' the agent said, withdrawing another handful of folders from the bottom of the safe.

'This is outrageous!' Gemici said, his eyes bugging out in panic. 'This is illegal! I shall report you to the ministry of justice in Cairo! You have no right to—'

'Got it,' the agent said, handing Kelsey a folder.

'Right on top – must be an important person, eh, Yusuf?' Kelsey said, flipping through the file. 'Bottom note here says something about two million. Dollars? Egyptian pounds? Is this what Boroshev got paid to bring a nuclear weapon into the United States?'

'*Nuclear weapon*?' Gemici cried. 'I know nothing of this! Nothing!'

'Sure you do,' Kelsey said. She continued to flip through the file, then gave up and handed it to the second agent, who began studying it himself. 'You're going to be extradited to the United States to face over two thousand counts of murder and conspiracy, Yusuf. I can pretty much guarantee you the death penalty. In fact, I don't think we're going to bother with going through an extradition – we're going to hog-tie you like the murderous pig you are and just take you back with us. Your first stop will be Guantanamo Bay, Cuba. Have you heard of it? Let's go.' The second agent collected all the folders into a backpack while the first secured Gemici's hands behind his back with plastic handcuffs.

'Wait! I will tell you all you want to know!' Gemici

said. 'But the real records of what Boroshev was doing are on board my ship, not here.'

'Ahmed?'

'Nothing in the files like addresses or phone numbers,' the second agent, an Arabic translator, said. 'Looks like a payment sheet, maybe receipts. Hard to tell.'

'You better not be lying to me, Yusuf,' Kelsey said, 'or I hope you can swim with your head bashed in.' She had the plastic handcuffs cut off. 'Move out.'

They left the office and crossed over to the other side of the wharf to where the *King Zoser* was docked. There was one watch stander at the top of the gangway, who exchanged words with Gemici as they started up the ramp. The watch stander lit a cigarette and nodded, obviously not concerned that the captain was coming on board so late at night with four foreigners.

About halfway up the gangway, when the Arabic-speaking agent reached out to grasp the handrails with both hands as the ramp got slippery, Gemici saw his chance, slid under the handrail, and dropped about twelve meters into the harbor. '*Ilha'uni*!' Gemici shouted in Arabic when he surfaced. '*Utlub el bolis! Ilha'uni*!'

The watch stander reacted immediately, flicking his cigarette overboard, raising a small rifle, and shouting a warning to the rest of the crew. Several floodlights snapped on in the wheelhouse and somewhere on the bow. DeLaine, Ray Jefferson, and their agents were caught out in the open halfway up the gangway.

'Kelsey . . . ?' one of the agents asked. 'What do we fucking do now?'

'Let's jump for it,' the other agent said. But at that instant the watch stander opened up with a short burst of machine gun fire and shouted something in Arabic, and the four Americans could do nothing else but raise their hands and remain still. More crewmen started rushing up on deck, converging on them, weapons at the ready . . .

Suddenly the searchlight up on the pilot's arch near the wheelhouse went out in a shower of sparks, and they heard the sound of ripping metal, a scream, and then two splashes as something – or undoubtedly someone – dropped from the pilot's arch into the harbor. As the terrified crew members ran over to the section of the rail to try to see what had gone overboard, there was another loud *bang*, the sound of crunching metal, and the searchlight on the bow went out.

'Move, everybody!' Jefferson said. He led the way up the gangway, drawing his sidearm.

'*Wa'if! Haelan*!' the watch stander shouted, then opened fire. One of the first rounds hit an agent in the leg; he screamed and dropped to the gangway. The other shots missed, but the watch stander kept on firing. Jefferson and DeLaine went back to help the injured agent to his feet, drawing their weapons and preparing to return fire. The watch stander had them all in his sights and was ready to squeeze the trigger . . .

. . . until he heard a loud *thud*! right beside him. He looked up and saw a massive figure standing beside him, as if he'd appeared out of thin air! The figure, a cross between a man and a machine, snatched the rifle out of his hands like a parent taking a noisy rattle away from an infant, then crumpled it up in his right hand as if it was nothing but a stick of cinnamon. Then its left hand snapped out, grasped the man by the throat, picked him up with ease, and casually dropped him over the side.

'Bolton, what are you doing up there?' Jason Richter

radioed from inside CID One. He looked toward the bow and saw Carl Bolton in CID Three, the newest model, climbing down from the bow lookout. 'Get down here and let's secure this tub.'

'I can't get the hang of this thing,' Bolton complained. He finally got the nerve to just jump the ten meters down to the deck and found the landing much softer than he expected. 'I don't know how Moore did it.' He and Jason stood guard at various places around the vessel, staying out of sight but still prepared to fight off any response from police or port security. DeLaine, Jefferson, and the two agents were belowdecks for about fifteen minutes. Soon they were back on the wharf, folding and stowing the CID units and hurrying away in a rental truck. They could see the police starting to arrive in the rearview mirrors as they sped away.

'We didn't find anything in Gemici's cabin, and we couldn't find Boroshev's cabin,' Kelsey said. 'But we did find several folders of notes. Looks like we're going sight-seeing, guys.'

A Secret Location
Early the next day

'We were *raided*!' Yegor Viktorvich Zakharov screamed into the secure satellite phone. 'You sonofabitch, we were *raided*!'

'*Shto ty priyibalsa ka mn'e, Yegor?*' the voice on the other end of the connection known as the Director asked in passable Russian. 'Calm yourself.'

'They had a firefight with Gemici's men on his ship – *with two of those damned robots*!' Zakharov shouted.

'They're here, right now. You knew about it, and you said *nothing*!'

'Don't give me that bullshit, Zakharov!' the Director retorted. 'I told you to stay out of the United States. Instead you engineer *another* attack! Now look at what you've accomplished: the fucking President of the United States has gone before Congress and asked for a declaration of war on *you*! You brought this on yourself!'

'What do you intend to do about it?'

' "Do?" I'm not going to do a fucking thing!' the man insisted. 'You've got one more job to do out there, and then you're *out*. You've already been paid half the cost of the last job – you'd better finish it. After you're done, you should take your money and go back to Brazil or the Caribbean or whatever rock you intend to hide under, and disappear. Stay that way.'

'The mission was, Kingman *dies*,' Zakharov said. 'He's managed to escape every time.'

'The mission was: you do as *I* say, when I say it, and you get paid,' the Director snapped. 'I *never* wanted you to strike inside the United States. If I told you once, I told you a dozen times: attack Kingman everywhere *but* the United States. No one is going to care if you blow up a trillion dollars' worth of oil infrastructure in Nigeria or a power plant in Brazil, but blow up one oil head in the United States and they'd send the Marines out after you. Now you've got something even *worse* than the Marines – this lousy little task force. The attack in San Francisco was a waste of time and resources. I *told* you he wouldn't be there, and blowing up that building hasn't stopped his operation even for one day! The only thing you've succeeded in is enraging the Americans, turning most of the world against you, and driving Kingman even deeper belowground.'

'You're nothing but a fucking *coward*!' Zakharov shouted. 'I knew what you wanted: you wanted to see Kingman dead . . .'

'Wrong, you idiot. I want Kingman bent, broken, humiliated, bankrupt, and defeated – *then* dead,' the Director said. 'But you're not going to do it by blowing up his headquarters in San Francisco. You're turning him into the aggrieved party – people are even starting to feel *sorry* for the conniving bastard!'

'If you'd give me all the money I need, I could have his entire worldwide operation in *flames* in a year!'

'You're being paid very well,' the Director said. 'These added expenses caused by your escapade in San Francisco are coming out of *your* pocket. Finish this one last job, then go on your way. I never want to speak to you again.'

'What about this task force?' Zakharov asked. 'What about those robots? What am I supposed to do about them?'

'Sounds to me like you might need a lot more men,' the Director said. 'They're *your* problem. It would definitely be in your best interest to smash them, before they get any more support or funding. Use every weapon and every man you can scrape up, but take them down once and for all.'

'I need more information on them,' Zakharov said. 'You can get me the data on their technology I need to destroy them.'

'I'm not your messenger boy, Zakharov . . . !'

'You're involved in this as much as I am,' Zakharov said. 'You can get the data. I'm busy doing your dirty work – you can sit back in your comfortable office, push a few buttons on your computer, and get what I need, and we'll both be better off.'

There was a short pause on the line. Just as Zakharov thought he had hung up, the Director said, 'Check your secure e-mail box when you can. I'll see what I can find out. But *you* are the fighter. You're being paid a lot of money to fight smart and win. Do it right this time, Zakharov. Don't screw it up again.'

The White House, Washington, D.C.
A short time later

'She's here, sir,' the outer office secretary said, standing in her boss's doorway, 'and I'm afraid she's not going to leave until she gets some time with you.'

Robert Chamberlain made a show of running a hand through his ever-thinning hair and turned in his seat. From there, he could see the west entrance to the White House – and sure enough, there she was, surrounded by her ever-present camera crew and a small crowd of curious onlookers: Kristen Skyy of SATCOM One News. 'She's persistent, I'll give her that,' he muttered.

'What do you want to do, sir?'

He shook his head with extreme, exaggerated irritation. 'She wants to talk to me, not the President?'

'She said only to you.'

'What did Collins say?' All press interviews had to be approved by the President's chief of staff first, but he knew that Collins rarely said 'no' to anyone, especially to a female correspondent.

'She hasn't spoken to the chief of staff. She showed up outside without an appointment and asked to talk to you. Do you want me to contact Miss Collins's office?'

'No, don't bother. I'm not going to give her a statement of any kind anyway.' The last thing he wanted now was for that busybody Collins to find out so soon that Skyy was here. Chamberlain sighed, then nodded. 'All right, let's get it over with. But the camera crew stays in the Appointments Lobby until I find out what she wants.'

Minutes later, Kristen Skyy breezed into Chamberlain's office. A couple of days locked away in New Mexico only helped to make her look even more beautiful, he thought. Although her handshake was sincere enough and the smile looked genuine, he could definitely feel that aura of anger inside her at being cooped up at the Task Force TALON training area after returning from Brazil. 'Have a seat, Miss Skyy. I have a really busy day, so I hope you don't mind if this meeting is short.'

She didn't sit, but marched right up to his desk before he could rise or sit elsewhere; he was forced to lean back in his chair to increase the distance between them, something he didn't like. 'I just have one question, Mr Chamberlain: why hasn't my request to accompany Task Force TALON overseas been approved?' Kristen asked.

'The answer should be obvious, Miss Skyy – TALON is moving fast and operational security is absolutely critical,' Chamberlain replied. 'They can't afford to watch over you while taking on Zakharov and his gang of terrorists all over the world.'

'Dammit, Mr Chamberlain, I *earned* the right to go with them!' Kristen said.

'You *what*?' Chamberlain retorted, rising from his chair and leaning forward on his desk, going nose to nose with the gorgeous television journalist. 'You did no such thing! If it was up to me you'd *still* be under investigation for luring Richter and Vega to Brazil . . .'

'I didn't "lure" anyone . . .'

'. . . and just because you managed to survive your encounters with the terrorists doesn't mean you can tag along with TALON anytime you feel the need to grab another headline!'

Kristen looked as if she was ready to bore into Chamberlain, but instead she took a step back away from the desk and averted her eyes. Chamberlain took his seat. 'Mr Chamberlain, I'm sorry for barging into your office like this,' she said. 'But I feel as if I'm intimately tied into everything that goes on with Task Force TALON now. I know . . . I know I was wrong to go around you to get Jason and his team to Brazil, but I felt we had to take the opportunity we had, and I made a decision. I know how it must have hurt you and affected your authority, and I apologize, deeply apologize.'

Chamberlain nodded, crossing his fingers before him. 'Well, that's a start,' he said.

'I mean it,' Kristen said. 'I know I like to behave like a big shot, and I like being in control, but I now realize that my attitude and actions have an enormous effect on many around me. I don't want to be an enemy, Mr Chamberlain, but I know sometimes my mouth and my bad-ass attitude makes me look that way.'

If mentioning her mouth and her ass was meant as a distraction, it worked – his eyes were automatically drawn to both those luscious parts of her body before flicking back to her eyes. She didn't seem to notice, but he was sure her remarks were deliberately intended to elicit just that very reaction. He turned in his chair to look out the window; after a moment's thought, he nodded. 'All right, Miss Skyy,' he said. 'I'll approve it.'

'Thank you so much, sir.'

'You *and* your network will sign all the usual waivers of responsibility and liability.'

'Of course.'

'TALON has already deployed, and they're incommunicado right now,' he went on. 'To preserve operational security, I'm going to put you on the next scheduled military logistical flight to their general location, and I'll arrange for Major Richter to meet you somewhere so you can join the team. The final decision whether or not to allow you to accompany the team will be his. Understand?'

'Yes, sir. Thank you.'

'How soon can you leave?'

'We're packed and ready to go right now, sir.'

'I should have guessed,' Chamberlain said. 'Report to base ops at Andrews right away; I'll have a security pass and travel orders waiting for you at the front gate. Tell your boss that you'll be out of touch, period – no communications with anyone from here on out until cleared by Major Richter himself. Clear?'

'Yes, sir.'

'Good. I just hope you know what you're doing, Kristen.' Chamberlain stood. 'I'll never understand this obsession with "the story," Miss Skyy,' he said. 'The only way I can begin to understand is to equate it with my deep desire to defend my homeland. But the comparison still always comes up short.'

'I think you have it right, sir,' Kristen said, extending a hand. Chamberlain shook her hand and nodded. 'Thank you again.'

'Sure. Remember, from here on out, no communications until Richter says it's okay. Good luck to you, Miss Skyy.' He took a seat and started typing e-mail notifications to the chief of staff and orders to his secretary for the security passes and travel orders. As he typed, he could see Kristen Skyy fairly running out to the west entrance, with her crew members hustling to keep up.

Jason Richter, he thought, had no idea what was coming his way, he thought, and he wondered how he was going to be able to handle it . . .

She knew she said she wouldn't tell anyone, but she had Jason's secure short messaging service address already programmed into her phone, so she shot him a quick message: 'CLEARED 2 GO BY NSA. C U SOON. LUV KRISTEN.' That couldn't hurt anyone, she thought . . . right?

Near Giza, Egypt
Three nights later

The Giza necropolis is one of the starkest yet one of the most beautiful places on earth, awe-inspiring enough to give even ruthless warrior-princes like Alexander the Great, Julius Caesar, Emperor Caligula, and Napoleon Bonaparte – men who conquered much of the then-known world – pause. The region has been the location of countless battles throughout history, and yet the pyramids, tombs, monuments, and ancient structures of the necropolis remain very much as they have been for over four thousand years. They have been invaded, desecrated, stripped of their wealth and beauty, and some have even been razed over the centuries to make way for newer ones, but there they are still, chilling and majestic.

Of course, the necropolis is no longer isolated on the limestone plateau on the edge of the Sahara Desert overlooking Giza. The city of Giza now engulfs the necropolis, so close that diners in a Pizza Hut restaurant right across the street can look out the front window and get a full awe-inspiring view of the Sphinx and the three Great Pyramids while munching on pineapple pizza. In turn, the sprawling Cairo metroplex have begun engulfing Giza as the Egyptian economy slowly improves and workers flock to the city. Thousands of visitors from all over the world still tour the pyramids and monuments every day, but it is no longer the mystical, mysterious, and magical place it once was.

Case in point: just five kilometers east of the Sphinx, near the town of Tirsa, was another sprawling complex of buildings, tunnels, and soaring structures rising out of the desert that, many thought, easily eclipsed even the majesty of the Pyramids: Kingman Tirsa, Africa's largest petroleum refinery complex. The refinery was so close, and the complex so large, that at night the flames from the refinery's numerous cracking towers were bright enough to fully illuminate the Great Pyramids when the floodlights were turned off.

While all of Egypt's existing refineries and petroleum handling facilities were meant to handle product coming out of the Gulf of Suez and the Nile Delta in the Mediterranean Sea, and had already begun to see a decline in both volume and efficiency, Kingman Tirsa's entire reason for being was to handle product coming out of Egypt's newly explored Western Desert, five hundred kilometers to the west. The Western Desert explorations had already resulted in proven oil and natural gas reserves that exceeded all of Egypt's previously known reserves *combined*.

Over four square kilometers in size, with thousands of kilometers of pipe controlled by a vast network of computers, the Kingman Tirsa refinery, twice as large as the Mostorod refinery northeast of Cairo, was designed to someday process three hundred thousand barrels of crude oil *per day*, over half of Egypt's total production, and produce a diverse range of petroleum products with modern efficiency. Vast underground pipelines under construction tied Kingman Tirsa to transshipment ports in the Red Sea and Mediterranean Sea, and pipeline routes were being tied in to oil fields in Sudan, Libya, and Chad.

As Egypt's largest refinery, Kingman Tirsa was vitally important to the Egyptian government, so much so that an entire brigade of the Egyptian Ministry of the Interior's Central Security Force, fully 20 percent of Egypt's entire paramilitary homeland defense force, was assigned to guard the facility. The Kingman Brigade, as it was called, headquartered in Tirsa, had responsibility to patrol not only the refinery complex itself but its network of pipelines and pumping stations stretching all the way to the Western Desert and its ports along the Nile River and along the Gulf of Suez, as well as provide security for the dozens of residential subdivisions built for the refinery that housed the workers.

As with all of TransGlobal Energy's facilities around the world, Harold Kingman employed his own hand-picked administrative, security, and engineering staff within the main part of the complex, which left the rest of the security forces far outside, around the periphery. While the Kingman Brigade paramilitary forces were only just a bit above standard Central Security Force quality in training and weapons, the security forces in the main headquarters and control building had the best of everything . . .

. . . which is why Boroshev and his Egyptian counterparts decided to recruit an additional one hundred and ninety men from four companies within the Kingman Brigade to turn on their comrades, leave their barracks and desert their posts, eliminate any opposition and any officers that dared try to get in their way, and take the headquarters building. Boroshev led a platoon of snipers and commandos and eliminated the outer Central Security Force guards that chose not to surrender or join the infiltrators, then cut the communications and power lines tied into the city's power grid. The security headquarters was quickly overwhelmed after a brief firefight with TransGlobal security forces, but the small cadre of loyal guards were no match for the sheer numbers of infiltrators, most of whom were wearing friendly forces uniforms. Within an hour, the headquarters building was safely in their hands.

Under cover of darkness, Boroshev brought several large delivery trucks filled with explosives into the Kingman Tirsa refinery complex. Squads of riggers began wiring explosives throughout the complex, starting with the entrances and roads responders might use. Most of the explosives were set right in the headquarters building itself. They didn't even bother to unload the explosives from the trucks – they simply drove the heavily laden trucks right up to vulnerable spots in the building and set the detonators. Crates of explosives were hand-trucked into the building to be set in the complex's massive computer facility, which controlled all of the valves, pumps, switches, and flow meters controlling 3 million liters of crude oil flowing through TransGlobal's pipelines daily. Captured refinery workers were sent to the entrances all around the sprawling facility and made to kneel facing outward as a deterrent to any military forces that might try to storm the refinery.

The terrorists didn't have to wire the entire complex, so within another hour the headquarters building was completely mined and set to blow. Squads of demolition experts fanned out through the complex to set more mines and explosives in key refinery locations to maximize the destruction and reconstruction costs: the pipelines, valves, and manifolds from the sixteen main lines from the Western Desert oil fields were mined, as were the massive oil, refined products, and natural-gas storage containers.

Two hours from start to finish, with very little opposition inside the facility and *no* response from outside, and the job was finished. 'All platoons reporting in, sir,' Boroshev's second in command reported. 'All demolitions set, the firing panel is in the green, full connectivity and continuity verified. Backups ready as well.'

'Looks to me like Kingman wasn't ready to defend his largest refinery after all,' Boroshev commented. He had the fleeting thought that this job was *too* easy, but the fact was that it was done – all they had to do was leave. 'Order all platoons to evacuate,' he ordered. 'Report to briefed rally points, and make sure the head count is accurate.'

'What about the hostages, sir?'

'Last man out, turn out their lights,' Boroshev said.

'We don't want any clever engineers trying to undo all our hard work.' Boroshev took one last look around the main facility control center – this room had almost two hundred kilos of high explosives set in it alone, with another one hundred kilos down below in the computer spaces. 'My young guest comes with me.' Boroshev strode quickly out of the headquarters building and headed over to his vehicle . . .

. . . when suddenly he saw a bright flash of light just ahead toward the main plant entrance, followed moments later by a loud explosion. 'What the hell was that?' Boroshev shouted.

'Patrols can't see anything yet,' his lieutenant reported. 'Apparently one of the platoons heading out the front got hit.'

Boroshev nodded and unslung his Kalashnikov assault rifle. Fun and games were over, he thought. Whoever was out there – undoubtedly the American antiterrorist task force called TALON, according to the data received from the Director – their plan was simple and now obvious: wait until everyone was inside the plant and the explosives set, then trap them inside. That was probably why it was so easy to recruit the extra men from inside the plant, and why opposition was so light: they were all in on the trap.

'Contact, sir,' the lieutenant reported. 'Just one small vehicle outside each entrance to the plant. Not an armored vehicle. Looks like a single dismount and single gunner on board.'

Boroshev looked perplexed for a moment, but shook it off. 'Continue the evacuation,' he ordered. 'Have the outer perimeter units move in and take them from the rear.'

*   *   *

Boroshev or his men couldn't see them, but high over-head three small Grenade-Launched Unmanned Observation System (GUOS) aircraft orbited the Kingman Tirsa complex at one thousand meters, keeping a careful watch on everything happening below. Their imaging-infrared sensors captured the movement of any object larger than a dog and uplinked the images via satellite to controllers back in the United States and back down to users right at the scene itself.

'TALON Rats, be advised, you've got vehicles approaching,' Ariadna Vega reported from a control station flown into Cairo Almaza Airport about twenty-five kilometers away. 'TALON Three, there's four ve-hicles heading toward you, about three kilometers at your six o'clock.'

'Got 'em,' Sergeant Major Jefferson responded from the southernmost 'Rat Patrol' dune buggy. He wore a monoc-ular datalink display on his Kevlar helmet over his left eye that displayed electronic data and downlinked sensor images to him. The gunner swung his Bushmaster auto-matic grenade launcher south. Jefferson grabbed his M-16 rifle and got out. 'Be careful what you're shooting at, boys,' he said, and ran across the limestone plateau to the east.

'They look like Egyptian Central Security Force ve-hicles, but I see no transponder – definitely hostile,' Ari reported. Per Task Force TALON's engagement agreement with the Egyptian government, any friendly vehicles brought into the area would carry a small transmitter that could be remotely activated and instructed to send a coded, invisible radio signal. If it didn't have such a beacon, it would be considered a bad guy.

Jefferson ran about two hundred meters east, checked his position on his electronic map through his monocular display, then moved two hundred meters south. He found the deepest depression in the hard-baked earth he could, lay down, and rechecked the sensor data. Sure enough, one of the oncoming vehicles looked like it had veered east, not quite leaving the formation but definitely moving toward him. He immediately withdrew a gray-silver blanket from a hip pouch and threw it over himself.

'Ray?' Ariadna asked.

'I'm good,' Jefferson responded. That call made him feel very good – that meant that the Goose drone's infrared sensors had lost him. The blanket he draped over himself was a cover designed to absorb and trap heat from his body so enemy soldiers with infrared scopes couldn't detect him, and its dark color would screen him somewhat from anyone using night-vision optics as well.

'Second vehicle heading your way, Ray,' Ari warned him.

The first vehicle must've lost him and he called on a second to help locate him, Jefferson surmised – the first one was still the main threat. Jefferson loaded an M433 high-explosive dual-purpose grenade into his M203 grenade launcher mounted under his M-16 rifle. With his left eye displaying sensor data to the oncoming vehicle, he waited until the vehicle was about a hundred meters away, fired, and immediately rolled to his left several meters before leaping to his feet and running south. The grenade round armed after flying a few meters and landed squarely on the front armored windscreen of the armored personnel carrier. Although most of the grenade's energy was deflected up and away, the explosion was enough to blow in the bulletproof windows and blind the crew members inside.

As soon as Jefferson rolled he lost the cover of his

infrared-absorbing blanket, and the machine gunner on the second APC opened fire at the spot where he saw the grenade launcher's muzzle flash. Still on the run, Jefferson loaded the first grenade round he could grab from his bandolier. The machine gun bursts thudded the ground with heavy raps, but they hadn't caught up with him yet. He waited for the gunner to pause, threw himself down to the hard-baked earth, took quick aim, and fired. The grenade exploded several meters in front of the second APC – clean miss, but the distraction factor was enormous. Jefferson immediately dodged west, reloading again as he ran.

It took several seconds for the machine gunner on the APC to spot him, but once he did the carrier raced after him, less than one hundred meters behind. Jefferson realized he was running out of breath and time – one dismount had little chance against an armored personnel carrier, no matter how good a shot he was with an M203. The machine gunner opened fire, and the rounds were now whizzing all around him, close enough to feel the air pressure. Bits of limestone were kicking up in his face after hitting the ground right in front of him. No more running – this was it.

He dropped to the earth again, lined up on the approaching APC, aimed carefully, and fired. The APC dodged left when the driver saw the muzzle flash, and the round exploded just a few meters away from the right rear tire. The APC looked like it was going to flip over, but it didn't. It skidded to a stop, unable to move – but it wasn't out of the fight yet. The gunner straightened himself in his cupola, reloaded, drew a bead on Ray Jefferson, and fired from about sixty meters away. At this range, it would only be a matter of seconds before . . .

Suddenly there was a tremendous explosion right on the machine gunner himself. When the fire and smoke cleared, Jefferson saw that the entire cupola had been blown off the APC. An armored door opened up and a couple of soldiers stumbled out of the smoking interior, dropping to the ground and crawling away from the thick oily smoke billowing from inside. A few rounds cooked off inside as the heat intensified. That APC was definitely out of business.

'You okay, Ray?' Jefferson heard Jason Richter call on his radio. He looked at his datalink display and saw a green icon moving about forty kilometers an hour from the south toward the refinery.

'Roger that, sir,' Jefferson said, getting to his feet and checking his equipment. 'Thanks for the assist.'

'I'm going to cover Rat Six, Ray,' Jason said.

'I'll catch up, sir. Don't worry about me.' Jefferson found a cigar in a pouch on his body armor and lit up as he headed toward the refinery. He was in no hurry now – the CID units of Task Force TALON were on the job. They could fight for a while without him.

The other six 'Rat Patrol' dune buggies were doing the exact same thing to every one of the approaching hijacked Central Security Force vehicles: one buggy looked like easy pickings, so the APCs were just driving right up to them ready for the ambush, while a CID unit or dismounted TALON commando sneaked up behind it and attacked. With the Goose drones overhead, it was simple for the CID units – piloted by Jason Richter, Carl Bolton, and the third by none other than Captain Frank Falcone, who volunteered to take Doug Moore's place in a new CID unit just delivered to the task force – to sneak up on them from a blind side in the darkness and nail them.

Within minutes, the battle around the periphery of
the refinery was over. Gennadyi Boroshev didn't have to
wait for the sentry reports to come in – he could hear
the fear, confusion, and cries of surrender on the radio
as the hijacked General Security Force vehicles were
taken down one by one. He also didn't need a report
from his lieutenant that the turncoat GSF fighters still
inside the refinery complex were starting to get nervous:
their job was to simply desert their posts and let the
terrorists inside, not get trapped inside the place after
hundreds of kilos of high explosives were set right behind
them. But soon he got the report anyway: 'Sir, the lousy
bl'ats are running!' he said.

'Let them run – those *zalupas* are just as likely to turn
on *us* if we didn't let them go,' Boroshev said. 'The
Egyptians will certainly be waiting to arrest them – or
gun them down – as they run out. We need a distraction.' He pulled out an arming panel from a satchel on
his shoulder, turned a key to power up the panel, twisted
a selector knob, opened two red-covered switches, held
one switch up with his left hand, then flicked the other
one up with his right. Nothing happened. He twisted the
knob again and activated the switches – still nothing.

'I thought you said connectivity was good!' he
screamed at the lieutenant. 'Did you even bother to check
it?' The lieutenant's eyes filled with fear and he remained
silent. That wouldn't be too surprising – if you weren't
trained in demolitions, it would be damned tough for
anyone to turn that key knowing it was set to blow
several hundred kilos of high explosives just a few steps
away. But this was *not* the time to find out it didn't work.
'Damn you! The radio signal's not getting out. The
Americans might be jamming us.' To the lieutenant, he

said, 'Go to the detonators in the computer room and set them to go off in ten minutes.'

'*Ten minutes?*' the lieutenant exclaimed. 'That's not enough time for me to get out!'

'It's all the time you'll have,' Boroshev said. 'Order all the men to slip out with the hostages and CSF guards when the explosives go off. They'll never be able to capture all of us, and while they're trying, this place will start going up in flames. At least we'll take out the most important location in this place. I trust you'll run faster than you ever have before after setting those detonators. *Go*!' Reluctantly, the lieutenant dashed back into the headquarters building.

'More people coming out,' Ariadna reported, studying the GUOS images. 'The GSF officers and Egyptian military are picking them up.'

'Good,' Kelsey DeLaine said. She was seated beside Vega in the temporary command center they had set up at Almaza airport. She pointed to one of the screens. 'But this is interesting: one man running *into* the headquarters building, while everyone else is running *out*.' She hit the Transmit button on her control panel: 'Carl, I need you to check something out for me.'

'Wait, Kelsey – we'll get some TALON units to look in there,' Ari said. 'The CID units aren't really designed to operate indoors without a lot of training. He'll feel like a bull in a china shop in there.'

'There's not enough time, and all of the "Rat Patrol" guys are on the perimeter,' Kelsey replied. 'Carl is out there doing nothing right now. I'll send him in.' Ari was worried, but she fell silent.

A few minutes later, Carl Bolton piloting the third CID unit carefully made his way down a set of stairs from the main floor at the rear of the headquarters building to the second subfloor. That short trip down those stairs was one of the most frustrating he'd ever had inside a CID unit. Being inside the Cybernetic Infantry Device didn't feel one bit like being inside a three-meter-tall robot; the haptic interfaces kept arms, legs, fingers, and other body parts moving normally in relation to one another. But nothing prepared Bolton for taking the big robot through normal man-sized spaces. He was constantly bumping into furniture and walls, hitting his head on the ceiling when he wasn't crouched over enough, and even tripped down the last flight of stairs on his way down. Plus, all the training he had ever done in the CID unit – one day actually piloting the device, plus lengthy and usually boring lectures – had been outdoors. The smallest building he had ever been inside while piloting the CID was an aircraft hangar.

He finally made it downstairs and went down a long hallway, breaking open locked doors and using his scanners to locate any sign of danger, until he came to the computer room. Maneuvering inside there would be even more difficult than going down the stairs – the place was chock-full of workstations, server racks, printers, monitors, and bookshelves. The suspended floor, which was ventilated underneath to provide cooling air to the servers and workstations, felt spongy and fragile. Every time he moved he knocked something over, until in complete frustration he simply pushed objects out of his way – he figured he wasn't making any *more* noise than before doing it that way.

'Whoever is in this room, come out immediately,'

Bolton said through his electronically synthesized voice. *'Sdacha teper*!' he tried in Russian, using his on-board voice translator. No movement. He turned up the gain on his audio sensors . . .

. . . and immediately turned in the direction of a very slight *'Snip*!' sound he heard coming from behind a rack of modems and servers. *'Vy pozadi stojki*!' Bolton shouted. *'Vyhodivshij tam*!' He heard a man's muffled cry of panic. *'Vyhodivshij tam*! Come out of there!'

'Izbegite menja!' the man cried in Russian. 'Stay away from me, or I'll blow this whole place to hell!'

Bolton reacted without thinking and deployed his Bushmaster grenade launcher from his backpack . . . before realizing that the barrel and part of the feed mechanism had to extend upward out of his backpack. Since he had to stoop to enter the room anyway, the top of the backpack was almost always scraping the ceiling. When he deployed the cannon, the barrel immediately shot through the drop-ceiling in the computer room. It immediately got tangled in electrical wires and ducting so it wouldn't retract when ordered.

The lieutenant jumped up from behind the server rack, aiming an AK-74 assault rifle. Bolton tried to pull himself free, but the more he tried to twist free the tighter he got stuck. *'Umrite vy ubljudok*! Die, you bastard!' the Russian shouted, and he opened fire. The heavy-caliber bullets had no effect on the CID unit, but now Bolton was starting to panic as he was showered with sparks from the electrical wires at the same time he was being pelted with bullets. The Russian was crossing back around toward the door, firing as he moved. In a few more steps, he'd be out the door.

Enraged, Bolton thrashed around harder, kicking

workstations and racks around as easily as a Lincoln Logs set in his attempts to get free and to stop that Russian from escaping. Finally, he remembered to simply detach the backpack, and the second he did so he was free. Just as the Russian made it to the door of the computer room, Bolton lunged for him. The Russian stumbled out the doors, with the CID unit right behind him, blasting through the glass doors, giving chase. Blinded with confusion and frustration, Bolton didn't even attempt to avoid crashing into things – he crushed, scraped, smashed, or shoved anything and everything in his path.

The Russian headed straight for the stairs leading up to the main level, and Bolton knew he had to catch him before he reached those stairs because he wasn't sure if he could go up them without tripping or otherwise looking like an ass. '*Ostanovka*! Halt!' Bolton shouted. With a last effort he managed to grab the guy just as he started up the stairs. The Russian battered him with the butt of his rifle until the stock shattered, then tried pounding him with his fists. 'What were you doing down here?' he asked. '*Shto vy delali zdes'*?'

'Let me go! Let me go!'

'Not until you tell me what you were doing down here!' Bolton shouted.

'CID Three, what's your status?' Kelsey radioed.

'I captured the Russian who came down here,' Bolton replied. 'Whatever he was doing, I interrupted him.'

'Bring him upstairs and clear the building.'

'I'm going to find out what he was doing first,' Bolton said. 'I'll be up in two minutes.'

'This is Richter. Bolton, get your ass up here,' Jason interjected. 'Our objective is to get Zakharov and the terrorists. If he was setting explosives down there, you could be walking into a trap. We'll let TransGlobal security and the Egyptians worry about bomb disposal.'

'Or maybe he was going to warn Zakharov,' Bolton said. 'I'm going to investigate. I'll be up in two.' Ignoring Jason's repeated calls, Bolton headed back to the computer room. The Russian's terrified cries and futile attempts to escape only indicated to Bolton that he was on the right track.

He had almost destroyed the computer room in his mad dash to get out and chase down the Russian – it looked like every desk and rack was on the floor and half the roof was caved in. Still carrying the Russian, Bolton walked over to the rack the Russian had been working behind, kicking desks out of his way. 'Okay, Ivan,' he said, 'what in hell were you doing back . . . ?'

And then he saw it – a timer set to what appeared to be forty or fifty blocks of C-4 explosives, with wires leading to a half-dozen similar stacks on other racks and workstations. The Russian was screaming his brains out, but Bolton needed no translation now. He turned and ran, crashing through what was left of the doors and racing down the hallway toward the stairs until he—

He hardly felt the shock of the first explosion, although its force blew the Russian clean out of his arms and into a fiery oblivion. But the fury of the first explosive discharge quickly set off a chain reaction that eventually ignited over three hundred kilos of C-4 high explosives in the headquarters building. Carl Bolton was crushed between two nearly simultaneous explosions both below and above him and died almost instantly.

*   *   *

The feeling of dread Jason Richter felt when Carl Bolton said, 'I'll be up in two' was so strong that he didn't jump or feel surprised in the least when the headquarters building exploded. He felt sorry for Carl. He didn't deserve to die like this. He was here only because Kelsey DeLaine was here, not because he felt he had anything to contribute or because he cared at all for TALON.

'Jason . . . ?' The fear and pain in Kelsey's voice was obvious, and he felt very sorry for her. She had ordered Carl into the building, not knowing that the CID units were not meant for indoor operations.

'Kelsey, it was the headquarters building,' Jason said. 'We'll search for him, don't worry.' But the tone in his voice made it plain: the destruction was total. What he was praying for now was that the explosions would stop and not ripple throughout the entire facility . . . and thankfully, they did. Men were screaming and running wildly out of the plant. 'Let them go as long as they're not armed!' he ordered. 'Let the police pick them up. Keep an eye on the facility for any armed men.'

And at that exact moment, Falcone radioed, 'Armored car coming out.' Jason flipped his electronic visor over to Falcone's camera and saw what appeared to be a Humvee or similar wheeled infantry vehicle, racing away to the west. 'Want me to blast it?'

'You like riding in that thing, don't you, Falcone?' Jason asked.

'You got me hooked, boss,' Falcone said happily. Frank Falcone had always been a cheerful guy, but ever since volunteering to ride in the new CID unit, he was like a kid in a candy store. 'I got legs again. Let me tag this SOB, okay?'

'Take it, Falcon – just don't destroy it,' Jason said. 'We want them alive.'

'You got it, boss. Fire in the hole.' One ride in the CID unit and a few hours of training on the C-17 Globemaster flight from New Mexico to Egypt, and Falcone was an expert. He deployed his 7.62-millimeter machine gun from his backpack, turned, locked on to the front right wheels of the armored vehicle, and opened fire with a one-second burst. The rounds shredded the tire and wheel, and the vehicle collapsed and spun around. When the left front wheel exposed itself, a second one-second burst destroyed that wheel as well, completely immobilizing the vehicle.

'Two . . . no, three persons getting out,' Falcone reported. Jason had switched back to his own cameras so he could continue observing the main entrance to the refinery. 'Two of them are armed. I'll get 'em.'

'Rat Nine, can you assist?' Jason radioed.

'A-firm,' the driver on the westernmost dune buggy responded.

Jason switched back to the view from Falcone's cameras. He saw the first two persons getting out . . . and was stunned to see a man virtually dragging another person with him with his left arm, while holding what appeared to be an AK-74 assault rifle in his right. Just as he was thinking about asking Falcone to zoom in on the two, that's exactly what he did. 'Looks like this butthead's trying to take a hostage with him,' Falcone radioed. 'Looks like a woman. That's not nice. I'm moving in.'

Jason switched the images from Falcone's camera back and forth to his own cameras so he could maintain watch on both. The woman clearly didn't want to go with the guy, but she appeared to be stunned or woozy or something . . . no, he saw, she was handcuffed and manacled. 'Falcon . . .'

'I got him, Jason,' Falcone responded. 'Looks to me like she's a hostage. Fucker. I'll teach him to take a woman hostage.'

'Don't forget about the third guy,' Jason reminded him. 'Let's have a look at him.'

'Rog.' Falcone zoomed his camera out and turned toward the stricken vehicle . . .

. . . just as the third terrorist fired what appeared to be a rocket-propelled grenade or TOW missile at Falcone! The missile flared; Jason saw a streak of fire, and then the camera went blank. '*Falcon*!' Jason cried. 'Rat Nine, Rat Nine, what happened?'

'I . . . I'm okay, Jason,' Falcone murmured. 'I'm . . . oh, *crap*, that hurt . . .'

'We got 'em, TALON One,' the driver of the westernmost dune buggy radioed. They had opened fire on the assailant with their Bushmaster automatic grenade launcher, peppering the terrorist with half a dozen high-explosive projectiles from short range. The terrorist was bracketed with explosions and was last seen flying through the air and landing several meters away in a blackened, smoking lump. 'Splash one tango.'

'Don't kill the other ones!' Jason shouted. 'I'm after them! Check on CID Three.' Jason took off running to the west at full speed.

On the western flank of the refinery complex there was an access road, a stretch of sand and dirt used by the construction crews, a highway, and then the beginnings of temporary trailer housing for the refinery workers. By the time Jason ran over there, the two escapees had made it to the trailer area. 'Ari, I need a Goose overhead my location,' Jason said. 'They're in the housing area.'

'Roger, on the way,' Ariadna responded. 'It'll be about two to three minutes.'

That was going to be way too long. Jason started running through the closely packed trailers, dodging around knots of onlookers who had come out of their homes to watch the spectacular explosion at the refinery. '*Ana badawwer 'ala muktal aqliyyan.* I am looking for a terrorist and his captive,' Jason said in Arabic in a loud electronic voice. 'Did anyone run through here with a captive in handcuffs?' People started either running away or pointing in all directions. Jason gave up and ran down another street, asking the next group of people he saw.

'Jason, I'm picking up a vehicle, traveling west at high speed about fifty meters west of you,' Ariadna radioed.

'It's the only lead I've got. I'm on it.' Jason ran, following Ariadna's directions. After crossing another highway, he found himself in a mostly business district, with dozens of small shops and restaurants, then another wide boulevard, and finally at the edge of the Giza necropolis itself. The floodlights were still on the Sphinx and Great Pyramids, creating an otherworldly image against the pitch-black Egyptian night sky. Hundreds of tourists and residents pointed at Jason in wonderment; a few screamed, a few started clapping, thinking he was part of some street show; others threw fruit or rocks at him. Traffic started backing up as drivers stopped to stare.

'Got him!' Ari radioed. 'He's on foot, thirty meters northwest of you!'

Jason leaped across the boulevard over the stopped cars, narrowly missing tourists on the other side where he landed, and started running across the excavation sites and monuments in the necropolis. He heard gunshots and saw the terrorist right in front of the Temple of the Great Sphinx, still dragging his hostage, and two police officers writhing in pain on the ground. Jason leaped over an excavation, took three large steps, and leaped again – right in front of the fleeing terrorist. Gennadyi Boroshev's face was illuminated by the reflection of the spotlights shining on the face of the Sphinx.

'*Ja ub'ju ee, esli Vy budete dvigati'sja*!' the terrorist screamed in Russian. 'I'll kill her if you move!' He pointed the muzzle of his AK-74 at his hostage . . .

. . . who was, Jason saw with complete surprise, Kristen Skyy! '*Jason*!' she shouted. 'Thank God you're here!'

'I'm here, Kristen,' Jason said. 'Stay calm. I'll get you out of this.'

'I'll kill her!' Gennadyi Boroshev shouted, his eyes wide in fear, his chest heaving from the long run. 'Stay away from me or I'll blow her brains out!'

'Jason . . .'

'Put away your weapon,' Boroshev ordered. '*Now*!'

'Don't do it, Jason,' Kristen said. 'Kill this bastard!' But Jason let his Bushmaster grenade launcher backpack detach itself and clatter to the ground.

'*Vy ne mozhete ubezhat'*,' Jason said in Russian. 'You can't escape.'

'Oh yes, I will,' Boroshev said. 'This is the famous Kristen Skyy. The world loves her. She will die if you do not let me go, and the world will hate you. Now back away, and tell all those other police officers to back away too. I want a police car and driver to take me wherever I want to go. When I'm safe, I'll release her.'

'He can't release me, Jason,' Kristen said. 'I know too much.'

'You! Get out of that thing!' Boroshev ordered. '*Out*!'

'Don't do it, Jason,' Kristen said. 'He'll kill all of us if you do!'

'*Zakrytyj*!' he shouted. 'Shut up! Get out now or she dies!'

'*Kill him, Jason*!' Kristen screamed.

The next few seconds were a blur. Several Egyptian General Security Forces and Cairo police officers shouted warnings, shining flashlights at Boroshev and Jason, covering both with pistols and automatic rifles. Boroshev shouted something in Arabic and tried to turn Kristen around so he could use her body to shield his . . .

. . . but he half-stumbled on a piece of limestone. At that moment, Kristen twisted her body to the left, pushing Boroshev in the same direction he was already stumbling . . .

. . . and at the same time the GSF and Cairo police officers opened fire. Boroshev screamed as the bullets plowed into his body . . .

He pulled the trigger of his AK-74 as he fell. Kristen Skyy's hair flew as if blown by a sudden gust of wind, and the muzzle flash froze her face in a terrifying mask of surprise as if caught by a strobe light.

'*Kristen*!' Jason shouted. He was out of the CID unit within seconds and by her side. He pulled off his T-shirt and pressed it against the side of her head, but he knew there was nothing he could do.

Her lips were moving, and he stooped closer, putting his ear to her lips. He heard the words, heard *something* . . . and then felt her last breath on his face.

Jason held her close to him, oblivious to the growing

throng of police and civilian onlookers, oblivious to the majesty of the Sphinx right over his left shoulder. He didn't move – *couldn't* move – even after several Task Force TALON dune buggies arrived to help clear the crowds away. He didn't move until Ray Jefferson himself arrived and held Kristen so Jason could climb inside CID One. After he did, he lifted her up himself as carefully as he could and strode through the crowds, heading east again toward their rendezvous point.

Kristen's war was over, Jason thought grimly – his was not.

Chapter Nine

York, Pennsylvania
That same time

The place looked deserted; the doors were locked. The rather small red-brick colonial building half-hidden in a clump of oak trees out near York Airport, a small general aviation airport about ten kilometers from the city, looked as if it had been built a hundred years ago. There was a forty-acre fenced storage lot behind the building topped with razor wire, with a collection of green camouflage trucks, trailers, service vehicles, Humvees, helicopters, and even some larger armored vehicles such as Bradley Fighting Vehicles. There was even what appeared to be a multiple rocket launcher or two out there – a pretty impressive collection of weaponry for a little Pennsylvania National Guard unit.

At the rear of the storage lot was a six-bay service building and three aircraft hangars, and one of the hangar doors was open about a meter or so, so that's where Special Agent Ramiro 'Rudy' Cortez decided to look first. He and the agent accompanying him on this trip, Agent Jerome Taylor from the Federal Bureau of Investigation office in Philadelphia, went around the side, looking for a gate. The large taxiway gate leading to the runway was double-chained with fresh-looking chains and locks. 'Hello!' Cortez called out. 'Anyone in there?' No response.

'What do you want to do?' Taylor asked.

'I'd sure hate to come out all this way and not speak with someone at this unit,' Cortez said. 'It looks to me like someone's in there.'

'How about I call the state military bureau in Harrisburg?'

'That'll take all day – I've got to be back in D.C. by three o'clock,' Cortez said. He thought for a moment, then asked, 'We don't need permission to go onto a National Guard installation . . . do we?'

'You got me.'

Cortez shrugged. 'At the very least, this compound is not secure – it's our responsibility to secure it,' he said.

'If you say so,' Taylor said. He pulled out a cigarette and lit up. 'I'll watch from here.'

'You're not going in right behind me?' Cortez asked.

'I haven't climbed a fence since the academy, Cortez. I'll watch.'

Cortez pulled his car up to the gate, removed his jacket and tie, and retrieved a thick quilted packing blanket from the trunk. He climbed up on the hood of his car, threw the blanket over the razor wire, and started to climb. He was halfway over the fence and ready to throw a leg over the top, surprised at how well he was doing, when he heard, *'Hey, yo, what do you think you're doin' there*?' A guy in camouflage trousers, spit-shined combat boots, web belt, and olive drab T-shirt, carrying a very large Crescent wrench, came trotting out of the garage. His hair was a little on the long side, and his T-shirt had large drips of oil on the front – in short, he looked like a typical mechanic.

Cortez climbed down from the fence, thankful he didn't rip his suit trousers on the razor wire or dent the hood of his Bureau car. He retrieved his badge case from a trouser pocket and opened it. 'Cortez, FBI. We came here to talk to the CO.'

'FBI?' the soldier asked. 'What's the FBI want with us?'

'I'd rather talk it over with the CO.'

'Why were you climbin' the fence?'

'I saw the hangar door open and thought I'd better check it out.'

'Why didn't you just use the front door?'

'It's locked. No one up there.'

'What? No, the secretary's there.' He motioned with a couple fingers at the badge and stepped toward the fence. Cortez showed it to him again. 'Did you knock or what?'

'No, I didn't knock, but I didn't see anyone up there. It looked like you were closed.'

'Well, you got that right.'

'Say again?'

'Closed. I mean, we're *closin'*. The unit's moving, back to Fort Indiantown Gap. Annville.'

'When?'

'End of the fiscal year, I guess,' the soldier said. 'That's better than an hour from where I live. Right now it's easy for me to just get off from work and go to drills, but with the move, it's a real hassle to . . .'

'Can you let us in so we can talk to the CO?' Cortez interjected.

'Oh. Oh, sure. C'mon over. The CO, he ain't here, but the first shirt is around here somewhere and he can fill ya in. Right over here.' The soldier walked toward the rear of the red-brick building. Cortez jumped off his car and retrieved his jacket, and he and Taylor went to the front entrance. A few moments later, the soldier opened the front door and let them in.

The reception area looked neat and tidy, just deserted. The floor was polished to a high sheen, the computers were on, there was no dust built up anywhere; the live plants looked well cared for. Obviously it was geared heavily toward recruiting, with lots of posters and brochures around touting the educational and training opportunities in the Pennsylvania National Guard. 'What's your name?' Cortez asked.

'Conway. Eddie Conway. Sergeant First Class. Helicopter maintenance specialist, Troop F, First Battalion, One-Oh-Fourth Cavalry.' He turned to Taylor and motioned again with two fingers. 'Do you mind?'

'Troop F?' Taylor asked as he showed his badge and ID card again. 'You mean, "F Troop"?'

'The first shirt, he don't like the negative connotation,' Conway said. 'I just learned what the big gag was, and I still don't get it – *F Troop*, the TV show, that part I get – but he's a baby boomer so he's pretty sensitive about it.'

'You guys usually closed on the weekdays like this?'

'We usually open a couple days before a drill weekend,' Conway said. 'But with the unit relocating, the schedule's all dicked up. The CO hasn't been around since, oh hell, I don't know – I haven't seen him in a while. I just see the first shirt. I try to stay out of the old man's crosshairs, know what I mean? But the choppers still need the maintenance, know what I mean?'

'Sure,' Cortez said. 'We'll just check in with the first sergeant and get out of your hair, let you get back to work.'

'Heck, I like the break, know what I mean?' Conway said with a smile. 'I got credit for a training day whether I crawl under one bird or six, know what I mean?' Cortez thought that this was the kind of guy who needed lots of supervision, but he remained silent as they headed toward the offices in back.

'What do you guys do?' Taylor asked.

'We're a maintenance unit detached from the rest of the aviation battalion,' Conway said. 'We fix 'em all – Apaches, Kiowa Scouts, Black Hawks, Hueys, everything, even the vehicles like the Bradleys and Humvees. We're not really a combat unit but we can do field maintenance behind enemy lines if necessary.'

'What about the rocket launchers?'

'Oh, that's just here for chassis maintenance – the carrier vehicle has the same chassis and drive train as a Bradley,' Conway said. 'It's been unloaded, safed, and secured twelve ways to Sunday or we don't touch it. I don't know nothin' about those things, the business end of it at least, know what I mean?'

'Sure. Are all these helicopters and armored vehicles armed?'

'Nope,' Conway replied. 'We can do field maintenance on the weapon systems if necessary, but usually that's just R&R – "remove and replace." We expect all the choppers and vehicles that come here to be completely unloaded, disarmed, and safetied, but we find ordnance in them all the time. So what are you guys looking for?'

'We're investigating National Guard units who have reported losses in the past few months,' Cortez said. 'This unit's reported losses have spiked, and I was hoping to get some indication as to why that might happen.'

'Well, I'm not exactly sure why, but I'd bet it has to do with the move to Fort Indiantown Gap,' Conway said. 'Things get misaudited all the time – drive a Humvee to Annville and log it into their TO&E, then forget to fill out the transfer sheet back here. Part of the unit got back from the Middle East just two months ago too.'

'The move might explain a lot,' Cortez agreed.

They passed a few more offices, went through the unit meeting room, and then to a door with two flags on either side of it. Conway knocked on the door. 'Come!' they heard.

'Good. He's in there. Right this way, gents.' He led the way through the doors, and Cortez and Taylor followed. Inside were several metal shelves and a large set tub – it looked like a janitor's . . .

Cortez heard several loud *thummps*! behind him – and then his vision exploded into a field of swirling shooting stars. Crushing pain shot through his head and neck, and he hit the linoleum floor hard. Another blow to his rib cage took the breath out of him. He felt several more sharp blows to his head and neck . . . then nothing.

'*Hey*!' Conway shouted. 'You didn't say nothin' about *killin'* these guys!'

'What the hell did you expect us to do – sit 'em in the corner and tell them to be quiet and behave themselves while we rip this place off?' the assailant asked derisively. 'They're FBI, for chrissakes!'

'Our job was to just get the vehicles and choppers ready to roll . . . !'

'Then get your ass out there and finish up while I clean up this mess,' the assailant said. 'We don't get paid unless those vehicles are on the road by sundown.'

'They said they were investigating losses at National Guard units,' Conway said nervously as the other man started checking the bodies for weapons and ID. 'Think they're on to us?'

'If they were, this place would be swarming with cops

and troops,' the assailant said. 'I know of at least a dozen
other units involved in this scheme too, and they haven't
been investigated yet either. But after tonight, we'll be
done and on our way to Argentina with our money.' He
looked at Conway, who had frozen in place looking at
the dark blood and brain matter oozing out of the FBI
agents' heads. 'What's up with you? You never seen a
dead guy before?'

'Sure. Two tours in the Sandbox in five years, I seen
plenty. Just not one clubbed to death right before my
eyes. One second I was talkin' to the guy, the next . . .
whammo. I didn't sign up for this to kill our own, know
what I mean?'

'Get real, Conway,' the assailant said. 'You signed up
for this because they're paying us a shitload of money
and a free airline ticket out of the country. What do you
think they're going to do with all this equipment – have
a fuckin' Fourth of July parade? They're gonna blow
somethin' up with it. Banks, the IRS office in Philly, a
bunch of raghead mosques, who knows? I don't give a
shit as long as I get my money and I'm not around to
watch it.'

'But *we killed two guys . . .* !'

'First of all, Conway, *you* didn't kill nobody, hear me?'
the other man said. 'You don't know who did it, you
didn't see or hear nothin'. Second, we'll be out of here
by tonight. Third, you made a deal. You back out now,
and those crazy motherfuckin' Russians will be back for
your eyeballs. Now get finished and let's get the choppers and tracks ready to roll so we can get the hell out
of here.'

The White House Press Briefing Room, Washington, D.C.
Two days later

The President of the United States emerged from the back of the White House Press Briefing Room in the west colonnade of the executive mansion and took the dais, followed by Harold Kingman of TransGlobal Energy, National Security Adviser Robert Chamberlain, White House Chief of Staff Victoria Collins, and other members of the President's staff. The reporters in the packed briefing room got to their feet as the cameras clicked and whirred furiously.

'Thank you, ladies and gentlemen, good morning,' the President began, the indication for everyone to be seated. He waited a few moments while the White House press corps found their seats; then: 'It gives me great pleasure to announce today that Mr Harold C. Kingman, president and CEO of TransGlobal Energy Corporation, will be the keynote speaker, panelist, and honored guest at the first annual American Energy Conference, to be held next month here in Washington.

'As one of the world's, and certainly one of America's, largest, most diverse, and most technologically advanced energy providers, TransGlobal Energy's role in shaping, defining, and implementing strategies to providing the energy the world needs is pivotal,' the President continued. 'In today's highly competitive energy industry, however, few companies wish to share their vision for fear of giving away their company's blueprint for profitability. But there is one American not afraid to share his vision with us, and that is this gentleman right here beside me, my friend Harold Kingman. He's not afraid to tell us what the future holds in store for him and his company because he is a leader in the industry. As a leader, he's not afraid to take new directions, explore new possibilities, and challenge the conventional notions of service to humanity versus profitability, responsible stewardship of the environment, and natural resources versus innovation.

'I know there are still many concerns about security for this energy summit,' the President went on. 'Our hearts and prayers go out to the victims of the terrorist bombings in the San Francisco Bay area, and more recently over in Cairo, Egypt, near the Great Pyramids. However, thanks to Robert Chamberlain, my National Security Adviser, along with Attorney General Wentworth, Secretary of Homeland Security Calhoun, and National Intelligence Director Kallis, I believe America has never been more secure and more aware, and we are strengthening our security every day with the help of the American people. Our country is safer and more secure because of you. I thank you for your efforts, and I urge you to keep up the fight. I and my administration stand shoulder to shoulder with you.

'I'd like to invite Mr Kingman to say a few words and then we'll take a few questions. But we have a tee time here soon at an undisclosed location, where I assure all of you that I will try my best not to look like the duffer I am. Harold?'

Kingman took his place behind the microphone, looking decidedly uncomfortable. 'Thank you, Mr President,' he began. 'I am honored and privileged to be a part of the energy summit, and I hope I can contribute something to the discussions.' Off to the side a clerk handed Victoria Collins a note; she read it, stared blankly

ahead for a few seconds, then stepped up behind
Kingman as he was speaking and whispered into the
President's ear. The President adopted that same blank
stare for a few seconds, then nodded reassuringly to his
chief of staff.

'I'll have much more to say during the summit,'
Kingman was saying, 'but for now, my primary goal and
the goal of everyone at TransGlobal Energy is energy independence for America. It *can* and *will* be achieved.
Thank you.'

The press corps started tossing questions to the
podium, but at that moment Collins took Kingman by
the sleeve and escorted him off the dais. The President
stepped to the microphone and said, 'Unfortunately
there's a development that warrants our attention, so
we're going to cut the press conference short. I ask all
of you to follow the staff's directions in a calm and
orderly fashion. Thank you.' The President left the dais,
which was immediately occupied by a tall, burly Secret
Service plainclothes agent. The press corps immediately
erupted into bedlam as the reporters scrambled to get
more information and contact their bureaus.

'What in hell is going on, Robert?' the President said
between clenched teeth as they were escorted by the
Secret Service to the west wing of the White House. It
was not quite an evacuation, but the Secret Service agents
were making all of them walk very quickly indeed.

'Homeland Security issued a code red terror warning
for Washington, D.C., and the surrounding area, sir,'
Chamberlain said, reading the notes passed to him by an
aide. 'Two National Guard armories in Pennsylvania and
Maryland and the Marine Corps base at Quantico had
quantities of weapons and vehicles stolen recently, and

two FBI agents were found bludgeoned to death at one of the National Guard armories. The Pentagon is setting THREATCON Delta and the Secret Service is recommending the same for all government buildings, including the White House. The thefts fit the same pattern as just prior to the attack on San Francisco.'

'Oh, my God . . .'

'The problem is, there are so many Guard and Reserve units deployed around the city that it's hard to tell which ones are the real ones and which are bogus,' Chamberlain went on, 'so Secretary Calhoun decided to call a Code Red until everything can be straightened out. Unfortunately, that means evacuating the leadership, sir. I hope you concur.'

'I most certainly do *not* concur, Robert!' the President said. 'I am not going to evacuate the capital just on a *suspicion* of danger!'

'Sir, I don't think that's wise,' Chamberlain said. 'Victoria?'

'I agree with the President – there's no concrete reason he should evacuate right now,' Chief of Staff Collins said. 'We don't have troops stationed around the White House, for God's sake! If we did, it would be active-duty forces, and they'd be properly vetted. This is nonsense, Robert . . . !'

'It's not nonsense. It's prudent and wise. We should . . .'

'I'm sorry, Robert, but I'm not leaving the White House,' the President said firmly. 'I'm going to monitor the situation in the West Wing. If anything happens we'll go to the Situation Room and we'll put the contingency evacuation plan into effect. But I'm not leaving the White House unless there's an attack in progress.'

'This is insane!' Harold Kingman exclaimed. 'What in *hell* is going on?'

'Relax, Harold, this is just a precaution,' the President said. 'You're perfectly safe here in the White House.'

'Your confidence in your people is reassuring, Sam, but I'd prefer my own security forces, if you don't mind.'

The President looked at his primary Secret Service escort, who immediately shook his head. 'Let's wait until the situation stabilizes before you run off, Harold,' the President said. 'Watch my boys in action. You'll be impressed.' Kingman was obviously still not convinced, but he fell silent and allowed himself to be hustled down the corridors to the West Wing of the White House.

No one at all challenged the convoy of two Humvees and a military tractor-trailer as it made its way south on Interstate 95 through Maryland to the District of Columbia. The military convoy raced down Interstate 95 at speeds sometimes exceeding seventy miles an hour. Upon reaching Exit 27 in the southbound lane near Powder Mills, Maryland, just before reaching the Beltway, the convoy stopped – right in the middle of the freeway. Traffic immediately began backing up behind it, and soon traffic in the northbound lane slowed to a crawl as 'rubber-neckers' strained to see what was going on. One Humvee in the convoy went on ahead and blocked access to the southbound freeway from the Capital Beltway on-ramp, while a second Humvee unloaded three soldiers and then covered the mounting traffic behind them in the southbound lane. A few cars that were already too close to the convoy were allowed to pass, but all others were kept at least a kilometer away.

While the Humvees set up a perimeter, the crews on the tractor-trailer in the middle of the convoy removed the chains holding an M270 Multiple Rocket Launcher System to the trailer and drove the vehicle off. It maneuvered in front of the tractor and turned. Two soldiers got into the fire control cab, while two others stood guard outside. The crowds on the northbound side of the freeway started to leave their vehicles – they were stopped anyway in what had quickly become an immense parking lot – and stood by the guardrails to watch.

The rocket platform on the M270 soon swiveled until the launcher was facing south-southwest, and soon the onlookers saw the platform elevate. A few of those watching applauded, and one of the soldiers in the cab waved. Police sirens off in the distance sounded like they were getting closer, and a few onlookers got back in their cars although the traffic jam, now over a kilometer long in both directions, wasn't moving at all. This was a pretty unusual demonstration, all right, but this was the District of Columbia, some thought; they were pretty close to the Naval Surface Weapons Center, and maybe these guys had broken down. Maybe the military guys had to practice doing things like . . .

Suddenly there was a tremendous *fwoooosh*! and a huge cloud of smoke, and five rockets ripple-fired off the M270 and streaked toward the capital. The launcher platform turned and elevated once again and a few seconds later another four-round salvo flew off into the distance. Then, as casually as if they were street performers just finishing a juggling act, the soldiers got out of the cab of the M270, loaded up into the Humvees, and drove off at high speed onto the Capital Beltway, abandoning the empty M270 and its tractor-trailer on the freeway.

The first salvo of rockets landed just south of The Mall between Fourteenth and Fifteenth Streets south of the Washington Monument, right along Independence Avenue, hitting just outside the Department of Agriculture Building and the Auditor's Building. The second salvo landed along Seventeeth Street northwest of the White House near the New Executive Office Building, with one rocket making a direct hit. Fires erupted almost instantly from natural gas leaks and burning vehicles.

The attacks did very little actual damage and did not hit the White House or any strategic or tactically important sites, but the fear and confusion factors were enormous. First responders reported the gas leaks as a chemical weapon attack and stayed away from the impact areas; panicked citizens clogged the streets, adding to the confusion. Soon the entire western Mall area was closed off as government buildings were evacuated and the streets filled with terrified citizens, confused politicians and government workers, and helpless police and firefighters.

The attacks had one purpose: slow or stop any response from the two army bases in the Military District of Washington whose responsibility it was to respond to attacks in the capital region: Fort McNair in the District of Columbia, and Fort Myer adjacent to Arlington National Cemetery in Arlington, Virginia. Fort Myer was the headquarters of the Third U.S. Infantry Regiment, the Old Guard, the unit specifically tasked with defending and protecting the capital. Although the Old Guard's day-to-day duties were mostly ceremonial, including providing honor guards at Arlington National Cemetery, marching in parades, and wearing Revolutionary War–era

ACT OF WAR 469

costumes in welcoming ceremonies for foreign digni-
taries, the Old Guard's primary mission was as a light
infantry unit capable of defending the capital against
attack, insurrection, or riots. Fort McNair is the home of
First Battalion, Alpha Company, called the Commander
in Chief's Guard, an army rifle company specifically
trained to respond to threats to the White House and
Capitol; it also had several military police units capable
of deploying in support of the Metropolitan Police
Department's Special Tactics Branch.

The MRLS attacks would not stop the Old Guard or
the Metropolitan Police Department of the District of
Columbia for very long, but it didn't have to – the second
and third phases of the attack on the Capital were already
underway.

Two convoys of four Humvees left hiding places in
Anacostia and traveled across the Anacostia River, one
convoy taking the South Capitol Street Bridge and the
other taking the Interstate 295 bridges to the Frontage
Road off-ramp to Twelfth Street. Police and firefighters
did not stop either convoy – the Capitol Street convoy
even had a police escort for several blocks. Once on
surface streets, both convoys made it to The Mall, then
traveled westbound on Madison and Jefferson Drives,
going off the paved roads if necessary to circumnavigate
traffic and fleeing panicked pedestrians now clogging the
streets and parks. Once at the Washington Monument,
the two convoys headed north, one on Fifteenth Street
and the other on Seventeenth Street, again going around
traffic or obstructions by simply going onto the park itself
– the Humvees even cleared curbs and short one meter
walls with ease. They raced up through The Ellipse with
National Park Police looking on in amazement before

reaching for radios to report the military vehicles heading toward the White House.

Their first significant barricade was at E Street and Executive Avenue, outside the South Lawn of the White House, where massive concrete planters had been placed to prevent anyone from parking near the wrought-iron fence that surrounded the South Lawn. But the lead Humvee in each convoy was equipped with a TOW missile launcher on the roof, and when the convoys came upon the barricades on E Street, they simply blew them apart with one TOW missile shot each. The wrought-iron fence was child's play to breach with the Humvees.

Once on the South Lawn, the Humvees maneuvered west and north around the South Lawn Fountain toward the White House. Except for the lead TOW-missile-equipped Humvees, each of the other Humvees was armed with either a 50-caliber machine gun, 7.62-millimeter machine gun, or an Mk19 automatic grenade launcher mounted on the roof cupola. The units equipped with grenade launchers started peppering guard units on the roof of the White House from long range, while the units equipped with machine guns began raking the South Portico of the White House and West Wing with bullets. One of the TOW gunners got off a shot at the West Wing, blowing apart the gracefully curved windows of the Oval Office itself.

Shortly after the second salvo of MRLS rockets hit Seventeenth Street between the Old Executive Office Building and the Corcoran Art Gallery, four Secret Service Presidential Protection Detail agents burst into the Oval Office and escorted the President, Harold Kingman, and Chief of Staff Victoria Collins from the room. '*What in hell is going on here*?' Kingman thundered as he was half-pulled, half-dragged out of the office.

'Just follow along, Harold,' the President said, the tension in his voice obvious. 'Let the Secret Service do their jobs.'

They were taken quickly along the south hallway through the West Wing, past the National Security Adviser's office, and down a flight of stairs to the basement area of the West Wing. The Secret Service was busy clearing the area of nonessential personnel, so the group was escorted to the Situation Room to wait. The President immediately picked up a telephone and punched a button. 'Robert? Where are you?'

'Still in my office, sir. I'm getting the latest from the Secret Service right now on the other line.'

'We've been brought down to the basement. Find out what in hell's going on and then meet up with us in the Situation Room.'

'Yes, Mr President.'

The President hung up the phone . . . and at that moment they heard the first explosion of grenades hitting the roof of the White House. '*Holy shit*!' Wentworth exclaimed. '*We're under attack*!'

The President pushed another button, this one direct to the PPD. 'What's happening, Carl?' he asked.

'A few minutes ago the Old Executive Office Building and The Mall near the Washington Monument were hit with heavy rocket fire, sir,' the chief of the Presidential Protection Detail said. 'No reports of casualties or damage yet. Then the National Park Police reported military vehicles going across The Ellipse heading toward the White House. They – stand by, sir – ' There was a long pause, then: 'Mr President, there appear to be six Humvees on the South Lawn. They blew up the barricades on E Street and crashed through the fences. They . . . sir, they are *launching grenades at the White House.* Our security forces on the rooftop are under attack. They . . . *gunfire,* they are hitting the Oval Office *with machine gun fire . . .* !'

'My God,' the President breathed. 'My family . . . ?'

'The First Lady was in the Correspondence Room – she's being taken to the evacuation tunnel, sir.' A series of tunnels and emergency bunkers had been constructed under the White House during its expansion in the early years of the Cold War to protect the President from sneak attack. The tunnels were mostly used by the sixty-agent Secret Service Presidential Protection Detail to move in and out of the White House grounds but were also used by the staff on occasion, most notably on 9/11 to house the Vice President and National Security Adviser during the first confusing hours of the terrorist attacks. 'The children are on their way to school but are being diverted to a secure location – no indications at all that they are targets. We'll be ready to evac you all in just a few minutes, sir. We're checking to see which egress routes are best. Please stand by.'

The President hung up the phone, a worried expression on his face. 'Well?' Kingman demanded. 'What are they going to do?'

'We're evacuating the White House,' the President said.

Collins gasped aloud. 'My God . . .'

'There are military vehicles up there on the South Lawn shooting at the White House.'

'Don't you have any goddamned security in this place?' Kingman thundered.

'The army has sharpshooters and infantry units on the roof, but they're under attack,' the President responded.

'Well, how do we get out of here?'

'There are pedestrian tunnels connecting the White House to several other government buildings,' the President said. 'The Old Executive Office building was hit by a rocket, so that's not an option . . .'

'A *rocket*?'

'There are other tunnels connecting the White House to the Treasury Building and the New Executive Office Building,' the President went on. 'There's also an underground rail system that connects the White House to the U.S. Naval Observatory and the Capitol. If necessary, we can get out via the Metro subway system, which we can access from the New Executive Office Building or the Treasury Building. We can be out of Washington in ten minutes.'

'What if they have a nuke, like in San Francisco or Kingman City . . . ?'

'The Situation Room isn't protected, but the bunker under the Treasury Building is protected against anything but a direct one-megaton hit,' the President said. 'We're safe, Harold. Relax.'

A few minutes later, Robert Chamberlain came trotting into the Situation Room, wearing a dark gray trench coat and breathing heavily. 'We're ready to go, Mr President. Follow me, please.' He hurried out of the Situation Room, past the White House dining facilities, and through the door to the tunnel system, which had already been unlocked.

'Where are we headed, Robert?' Collins asked.

'The New Executive Office Building,' Chamberlain replied.

'I thought it was hit by a rocket!' Kingman exclaimed.

'It was only slightly damaged,' Chamberlain said. Every ten meters or so there was a soldier in full combat gear standing at port arms in the tunnel or a man in a bulletproof vest marked POLICE or U.S. SECRET SERVICE. 'There are a number of police and firefighters up there, and they'll screen us as we come out.'

'Why don't we just go to the Treasury Building?' Victoria Collins asked.

'That route's been compromised,' Chamberlain said. 'We need to hurry.'

After a jog of about two blocks, they reached an elevator and a staircase, guarded by another soldier in black fatigues. He had a hand up to an earpiece; when Chamberlain reached out to touch the Up button for the elevator, the soldier stopped him. 'Stand by, please, sir,' he said. 'It's not secure upstairs yet.' Into his sleeve microphone, he spoke, 'Four protectees have arrived, we're secure.'

'Catch your breath,' Chamberlain said. All of them were breathing heavily, as much from the terror as the job. He turned to the soldier. 'How long?'

'Status?' he spoke into his microphone. A moment later: 'Armored vehicle will be in place in sixty seconds, sir.'

'How in hell could this have happened?' Harold Kingman asked hotly. 'A rocket attack against Washington, D.C.? How could anyone get *rockets* into the capital?'

'They were apparently launched from well outside the city, outside the Beltway near Knollwood,' Chamberlain said. 'Mobile rocket launcher.'

'But how can they get close enough to the White House to shoot grenades and machine guns . . . ?'

'We don't know that yet, Harold,' Chamberlain said.

The soldier reached out and touched the Up button on the elevator. 'All right, follow me through the doors into the parking garage – the Suburban should be right there waiting for us.'

'Where are the PPD guys?' the President asked as the doors to the elevator slid open. 'Where's Carl? I thought he'd be escorting me.'

'He's up above, sir,' Chamberlain said. 'He'll be right beside you all the way. He's recommending we go to the Naval Observatory first, then fly out to Andrews and go airborne.'

The President nodded and removed his tie. 'This is a damned nightmare,' he said. 'I want some answers, dammit, and I want then *now*.' The doors to the elevator slid open . . .

. . . and they stepped into the center of an inferno. The entire parking garage was filled with smoke, and several vehicles were still on fire. Parts of the ceiling of the underground parking structure had collapsed, and bare wires and broken pipes were everywhere. 'What in hell . . . *Chamberlain, what did you do?*' the President shouted. 'The building *was* hit, and you led us right into it!'

'It was the only way I could be certain we'd be alone, Mr President,' a voice said through the crackle and roar of the fires all around them. They turned . . . and saw none other than Yegor Viktorvich Zakharov standing before them, his ever-present Dragunov sniper rifle cradled in his arms.

'Welcome, all, welcome,' he said with a broad grin on his face. They turned and saw Pavel Khalimov standing behind them with an M-16 rifle at the ready. 'Welcome to your worst nightmare.'

The White House South Lawn
That same time

It took only a few minutes for the uniformed Secret Service and the National Park Police to respond to the attack
on the White House, but they were far outgunned. After
initially responding only with small arms fire, the Secret
Service finally brought agents with assault rifles into the
fight, but they were still no match for the armed Humvees.
While the Humvees with the Mk19 grenade launchers
continued to pummel the White House, the other
Humvees turned their guns on the defenders, driving
them to cover.

But moments later heavier-caliber bullets started to
hit their location. 'From the roof of the Treasury
Building!' one of the terrorists shouted. 'Machine guns!'
The Secret Service had finally retrieved their heavier
weapons and were returning fire.

'How much longer do we have to sit here like this?'
another gunman shouted.

'Just shut up and keep firing!' the first terrorist shouted.
At that moment he received another radio call: 'Here they
come! Watch out!' They looked to the south from the
area of the Washington Monument and saw a pair of
Apache attack helicopters racing in from very low altitude. The gunners on the Humvees dropped down inside
their vehicles, but they knew that if the Apaches' thirty-
millimeter cannon shells hit them, they'd be toast – the
Humvees' thin armor would never protect them against
a devastating Chain Gun attack. The Apaches raced in
and the Chain Gun in the chin turret opened fire . . .

. . . but not on the Humvees, but on the Secret Service machine gun locations on the roof of the Treasury

Building! One pass by both helicopters was enough to destroy the hastily formed Secret Service machine gun nest. After they finished that pass, the Apaches hovered over the White House and fired the Chain Gun and 2.75-inch Hydra rockets at the army and Secret Service positions on the roof.

The terrorists in the Humvees were yelling and screaming in joy. '*Yibis ana v rot*!' one of them yelled in Russian. 'Nail those . . . !'

'Watch out!' someone yelled. 'Off to the right! *Get him*!' The terrorist swung his gun right . . . and centered his sights on a large robot figure standing in the tree line between the South Lawn and the Treasury Building, about twenty meters away. Just as he began to squeeze the trigger to his machine gun, the muzzle of the cannon on the robot's right shoulder flared . . . and the terrorist was blown completely apart by a forty-millimeter grenade fired at him from point-blank range.

'Another robot, off to the west!' But just as the warnings started coming, the Humvees one by one were pummeled by grenades. Two Humvees were destroyed within seconds.

'Splash two,' Captain Frank Falcone radioed. 'Two Hummers burning!'

'*Move, Falcon*!' Lieutenant Jennifer McCracken radioed. She was in CID Five near the Old Executive Office Building. 'Those Apaches are on you!'

'I got 'em, Jen,' Falcone said. He had been watching the Apaches approach with the help of the Goose drones orbiting over the White House. He ran several dozen meters south and fired a grenade at the first Apache, then dashed to the west. 'Ready, Jen?'

'Ready,' McCracken replied. She had fired grenades at

two more Humvees in front of her, then started tracking the Apaches. The lead Apache helicopter fired a volley of Hydra rockets at the spot where Falcone had been moments earlier, then wheeled hard right to line up again as he ran west. But when the Apache made its hard right turn it slowed considerably, making it a perfect target for McCracken. Two grenades hit precisely in the center of the Apache's rotor disk, blowing it out of the sky easily. It landed in a fiery heap at the very southern edge of the South Lawn.

The second Apache helicopter had enough. It kept on flying south, getting out of the kill zone as quickly as possible. It made it as far as the Tidal Basin . . . when it was shot down by an AIM-120 radar-guided missile fired from an F-22 Raptor jet fighter that had launched from Andrews Air Force Base just minutes earlier.

'We need some prisoners, guys,' Ariadna Vega radioed from her command position in the Treasury Building. She had been up there for days, coordinating the task force's defense against the expected attack on the capital.

'Roger,' Falcone responded. Instead of destroying the other two Humvees, he and McCracken in CID Five simply walked over to them before they could flee and overturned them. The survivors were quickly apprehended by the Secret Service.

'Thanks, guys,' Ari radioed. 'Rendezvous with Jason at the New Executive Office Building on the double.'

'Who in hell are you? Put that gun down!' Victoria Collins demanded.

'That's Colonel Yegor Zakharov,' the President said in a remarkably calm voice. He motioned over his shoulder.

'The man behind us is certainly Captain Pavel Khalimov. The whole attack on the White House was a setup.' The President nodded as he saw the confusion on Zakharov's face.

'I should have known,' Harold Kingman said. 'How could I be so damned blind?' He turned to National Security Adviser Chamberlain. 'Now let me guess: who among us would be clever yet twisted enough to engineer something like this, just to get to *me*?'

Robert Chamberlain smiled . . . and stepped over and stood beside Zakharov. 'That would be me, Harold,' he said.

'What?' Collins cried. 'Chamberlain . . . *you* set us up?'

'Vicki, I could be the biggest moron in D.C. and still be clever enough to put one over on *you*,' Chamberlain said, pulling a Secret Service MP5K submachine gun out from underneath his trench coat. 'Your immense ego kept you from seeing this plan, Harold.'

'So Richter was right,' the President said. 'There was only one person who knew where Task Force TALON was headed in Africa – *you*, Robert. Only you could have sent Kristen Skyy to the *exact* place where TALON was headed. But why? Why send her all the way into a battle zone?'

'The only thing I could think of that could stop Richter and his robots was not a bigger explosive, but Kristen Skyy,' Chamberlain said. 'I thought that sap Richter would try to sacrifice himself to save his lady love. It almost worked. I knew in the back of my head that it was strange that I hadn't heard from the task force after they finished with the Egypt job, but at that point I didn't really care. My mistake. So where are the major and his robots?'

'They've been stationed at the Treasury Building ever

since they returned from Egypt,' the President said. 'They figured out that Washington had to be your next target – it was just a matter of when. He thought the press conference with Kingman was the perfect moment.'

'He's a lot more clever than I gave him credit for,' Chamberlain said.

'Davajte vyhodit' zdes', Polkovnik,' Khalimov growled.

'Captain Khalimov is getting impatient,' Zakharov said. 'Harold, at first I was just going to shoot you through the head and get it over with, but now I think you'd be more valuable as a hostage. The President, his chief of staff, and Harold Chester Kingman as my hostages – if I have a chance of getting out of this city, this is it.' Chamberlain led the way out of the parking garage, with Khalimov following behind.

'There's no way you're getting out of Washington alive, Zakharov,' the President said.

'You forget, Mr President – the National Security Adviser, the man everyone calls your "copresident," arranged everything for us,' Zakharov said. 'Let's go.' Chamberlain removed his trench coat, threw it over the President's head, and held him tightly around the waist on one side while Khalimov held him from the other side, half-dragging him along.

They emerged from the parking garage surrounded by a phalanx of soldiers – more of Zakharov's men, dressed in army uniforms and Secret Service protective vests taken from the agents they executed – and were escorted past Blair House across Jackson Place to Lafayette Square. There, an Army UH-60 Black Hawk helicopter had just touched down right on Pennsylvania Avenue; a second Black Hawk was across Lafayette Square on H Street in front of the Hay Adams Hotel. Smoke was still rising from the roof of the White House. Metropolitan Police and National Park Police cruisers were arrayed along Pennsylvania and New York Avenues and H Street, but their confusion as to why regular army helicopters were on the ground in front of the White House was obvious. The starboard side door of the Black Hawk opened up, and more gunmen in battle dress uniforms with automatic weapons were visible inside. Zakharov and his captives were just a dozen meters from that door . . .

. . . when Khalimov shouted, '*Yop tvayu mat*!' and pulled the hostages even faster. There, standing just a few dozen meters in front of the Black Hawk, was one of the CID units. '*Otkrytyj ogon*!' Khalimov shouted. 'Open fire!' The Russian terrorists surrounding the Black Hawk opened fire with grenade launchers and automatic weapons. But the CID unit didn't move. It deployed a grenade launcher from its backpack and drew a finger across its throat, a clear signal to the helicopter's crewmen to shut down. '*Nyet*!' Khalimov shouted. 'Prepare to lift off, *now*!' The chopper pilot rolled up the throttle to liftoff power and held in a tiny bit of collective, just enough to make the Black Hawk dance on its wheels . . .

. . . but just before the hostages made it to the chopper, the CID unit fired a grenade directly into the Black Hawk's windscreen. The hostages were blown backward by the explosion, hugging the ground as shards of flaming metal and shattered rotor blades flew in every direction.

Jason Richter, piloting the CID unit, turned just as several uniformed Secret Service agents, Metropolitan Police Special Services, and U.S. Army soldiers ran up behind him. '*Freeze! Secret Service*!'

'This is Major Jason Richter, Task Force TALON! Don't shoot! I'm part of the President's protection detail . . . !'

Someone yelled, '*Drop the weapon*!' but they didn't wait for him to do so – they opened fire with automatic gunfire and what felt like a grenade launcher or LAWS rocket. The sustained gunfire on the backpack weapon unit did the trick – the second rocket hit made one of the grenades inside cook off, and the backpack exploded. Jason was thrown onto his face, the backpack burning, still attached to his back.

He immediately tried to eject the burning backpack, but it seemed to be fused tight. Warning tones and messages were flashing in his electronic visor, then everything went dark, and smoke began to fill the interior. Oh shit, he thought, I'm burning to death in here!

'*Jason*!' he heard someone shout. 'How do you open this damned thing?'

It was Ray Jefferson! Jason motioned behind him to his left belt area. Jefferson struggled through the smoke and heat coming from the backpack and felt around the waist area, finally locating the ridge and the two buttons underneath it. He pressed them both simultaneously and held them until he heard two loud *pops*! The burning backpack disengaged and the rear hatch flung itself open.

'*Richter*!' Ray climbed atop the stricken CID unit and pulled Jason out of the machine through a cloud of smoke. 'Are you all right?'

'What . . . what about . . . the President?' Jason croaked, gasping for breath.

Jefferson looked over to where the President, Kingman, and Victoria Collins were huddled on the street, surrounded by Secret Service agents. 'They're alive.'

'Where's Zakharov?' He looked around and saw Zakharov, Chamberlain, and Khalimov running across

Lafayette Square toward the other Black Hawk helicopter. 'I'm not letting that bastard get away,' he said. 'I'm going after Zakharov.'

'Khalimov is mine, Major!' Jefferson growled, and he picked up his M-16 rifle and ran off after them.

Pavel Khalimov pushed Zakharov ahead, ran away from the helicopter, took cover behind the statue of Andrew Jackson, and opened fire on Jefferson when he was less than twenty meters away. Jefferson's bulletproof vest protected his torso, but a bullet tore into his right shoulder, and he went down. Jason went over to him. 'Jesus, Ray, you're hit . . . !'

'Don't you let that chopper get away, Jason!' Jefferson said through teeth clenched in pain. He looked at Richter in surprise. 'You didn't bring a gun, Major? I knew you've spent too much time in those robots.' He pushed the M-16 rifle into Jason's hands. 'Don't let that traitorous bastard Chamberlain get away.'

Jason hesitated – he knew Khalimov was nearby, and the sergeant major was helpless – but the increased roar of the Black Hawk's rotors told him time was running out, and he hurried away.

When Richter ran off, Khalimov came out of cover, his weapon raised, and approached Jefferson. 'Why, it's the old sergeant,' he said. 'I owe you something, Sergeant.' Khalimov shouldered his rifle and started to trot as if he was a soccer player lining up for a game-winning penalty kick. 'I believe you said, "Hey, asshole," just before you kicked *me* in the head back in Brazil. Hey, asshole sergeant, this one is for you.' He aimed carefully at Jefferson's unprotected head . . .

. . . but at the last instant Jefferson caught Khalimov's boot centimeters before it landed and twisted it as hard as he could. The Russian cried out as his right foot was twisted at an unnatural angle and went down hard. He came up, roaring like a wild animal, with a huge knife in his right hand. Just as Jefferson was trying to get up to face this new threat, Khalimov lunged at him . . .

. . . but when the Russian tried to put weight on his right foot to make the final thrust, his broken ankle collapsed. Jefferson grabbed Khalimov's right hand and twisted the knife out of his fingers as he fell. Using the Russian's own momentum, he rolled on top of Khalimov, twirled the knife around in his left hand, and jammed it into Khalimov's unprotected throat.

'That's *Sergeant Major* to you, asshole,' Jefferson growled. He didn't let him go until he felt the last liter of blood pump out of his body.

It was the first time since Officer Candidate School that Richter had even held an M-16 rifle. The Black Hawk began to lift off, just a few dozen meters away now. He could see Chamberlain and Zakharov in the troop compartment – Chamberlain cowering in fear behind the sliding door, and Zakharov waving gaily and mugging Jason's awkward running with the rifle.

Jason dropped to one knee, raised the M-16, and squeezed the trigger. Nothing. He looked at both sides of the weapon before remembering the selector switch, found it, moved it from *safe* to *auto*, raised it again, and pulled and held the trigger. He saw the Black Hawk in his sights for just a split second before the muzzle suddenly took on a life of its own and jerked wildly into the air.

For Christ's sake, Jason admonished himself, he couldn't hit a huge helicopter just spitting distance in front of him! Jason fought to remain calm, and found when he did that he remembered sitting in on a couple of lessons Doug Moore gave Ariadna on the firing range. To his surprise, Doug's words came back to him, reinforcing his own shooting lessons from so many years back: relax; focus on the front sight; squeeze, don't pull the trigger; calm down and just *do it*.

Jason flipped the selector switch from *auto* to *semi*, lined up on the Black Hawk's open cabin door, took a deep breath, let some of it out, and started to gently squeeze the trigger. The weapon's sudden report startled him. To his surprise, he saw the Black Hawk starting to swerve in the air, and he also saw Robert Chamberlain lying on his side, his hands clenched on his stomach, his mouth and eyes wide open in obvious agony . . . and a dark stain spreading quickly on the front of his body.

Yegor Zakharov scrambled for his Dragunov sniper rifle – Jason could scarcely believe how fast he had it on his shoulder. He could practically feel Zakharov's eye on him through the Dragunov's telescopic sight, feel the crosshairs aligning on his forehead . . .

No! Jason screamed at himself. Remain calm! Remain focused! He lined up again on Zakharov, took a deep breath, and started to let it out . . .

He saw a wink of light from the helicopter door and knew it was the Dragunov's bullet heading for him . . . but he forced himself to relax, and squeezed the trigger, and again the M-16 barked before he expected it. Jason thought the sudden burst of air he felt across the right side of his forehead was the muzzle blast from his M-16 – it was probably a good thing he didn't know it was the Dragunov's 7.62-millimeter round whizzing just millimeters away from his head. He fired three more times before he forced himself to look, expecting a Russian bullet to obscure his sight as it zeroed in on his brain.

Instead, what he saw was Zakharov writhing in pain in the door of the Black Hawk helicopter, both hands over his left eye. He was kicking and thrashing in agony, yelling something hysterically at the pilot. The Black Hawk did a steep left turn over Lafayette Square, quickly picking up speed and altitude, and was soon lost to view.

'Good shooting, Jason.' Jason lowered his rifle and saw Ray Jefferson walking painfully over to him. He knelt down and motioned to a large patch of disturbed lawn where Zakharov's round had hit – well within the shadow of Jason's head cast on the ground. 'I'd say that one had your name on it, all right.'

'Doug Moore was talking to me, Sergeant Major,' Jason said. 'I could hear him coaching me.' He looked at the M-16 rifle in his hands, then slowly, deliberately, moved the selector switch back to *safe*. He turned it over a few times experimentally, then nodded in mock wonderment. 'So *this* is an M-16 assault rifle – a *real* infantryman's weapon, huh?' he remarked.

'That's right, sir,' Jefferson said. 'No batteries, no air data sensors, no targeting computers – but in the right hands, every bit as deadly as a CID unit.'

'Cool,' Richter said. 'Maybe you could teach me how to use it sometime, Sergeant Major?'

'Be glad to, Major,' Ray Jefferson said with a smile. 'Be glad to.'

Epilogue

Andrews Air Force Base, Maryland
Two days later

It was the very same hangar in which they had all first met, Jason realized, but so much had changed since that first demonstration. They had a nicer plane now, an Air Force C-37A, the military version of the Gulfstream Five, instead of the old C-130 Hercules; there were three Cybernetic Infantry Devices in the hangar instead of one, although one of them, the original CID, was pretty badly beaten up. But the most important thing was that they had a team, a *real* team . . .

. . . at least, he *hoped* they still did.

'I remember almost from the very beginning that you thought something was fishy about our task force, Jason,' Special Agent Kelsey DeLaine said. 'I never believed in what you were saying because I judged you by your looks.'

'No – you judged me because of my attitude, which I'll admit was nothing short of totally suck,' Jason said. 'I never believed we were meant to succeed, and it turns out that's exactly what Chamberlain had in mind right from the beginning: he picked two inexperienced, uncooperative rookies to lead a first of its kind unit; he picked an old hard-nosed noncommissioned officer to train us; he mixed experienced operators in with unproven technology just to make us butt heads; he encouraged us to make the wrong decisions.'

'All for revenge,' Kelsey said. 'Zakharov and

Chamberlain, both scorned employees, working together to kill thousands of innocent persons and attack two major U.S. cities – just to hurt their ex-boss.'

'Who are you calling "old," Major?' They turned and saw Sergeant Major Ray Jefferson walking toward them, wearing a suit and tie with the jacket draped over his shoulders, his right arm in a sling, supporting his injured shoulder.

'Is . . . is that *you*, Sergeant Major?' Jason remarked. 'You're . . . in a *tie*?'

'Button it, sir,' Ray said. 'I can still kick your butt up and down this hangar.' They clasped hands warmly.

'No doubt, Sergeant Major,' Jason said.

'Call me Ray, sir – you look a little constipated when you try to follow military protocol,' Jefferson said. He clasped hands with Kelsey, and she gave him a kiss on the cheek.

'I dunno – I was getting used to a buzz cut,' Jason said, running a hand over his newly close-cropped hair. 'I think I'll keep it.'

'At least I taught you *something*.'

A few moments later a dark Suburban was admitted to the hangar, and soon the President of the United States and Harold Kingman emerged from it, surrounded by Secret Service agents with submachine guns. The three snapped to attention. 'At ease,' the President said immediately. He shook hands with all three. 'I wanted to see you off personally. I would've had the meeting in the White House, but it's going to be closed for a while for renovations. Unfortunately it's going to be even more of a fortress than it had already become, but that's a sign of the times, I guess.' He turned to Ray Jefferson. 'Sergeant Jefferson, I'm going to ask you a favor . . .'

'Before you do, sir, one correction: it's *Sergeant Major*, not "Sergeant," ' Jason corrected him.

The President shot an exasperated glare at Richter. 'Of course, Major. Sergeant Major, it's going to be tough for me to trust anyone from the private sector anymore, and I've never trusted politicians because I know they'd be gunning for *my* job. I'm going to nominate *you* to be National Security Adviser. Will you accept the nomination and work with me in the White House?'

'Me, sir?' Jefferson asked. 'There's got to be hundreds of better-qualified candidates . . .'

'I can't think of any, Sergeant Major,' the President said. 'I just ask one thing from you: be straight with me. Talk to me, any time, day or night; tell me I'm full of shit; tell me I'm wrong; tell me I'm naïve – I don't care. Just be straight with me. That's all I ask.'

Jefferson glared at the President of the United States with that same evil-eyed stare that Jason always interpreted to mean 'Are you bullshitting me or what?' before apparently deciding he wasn't, snapping to attention, and nodding. 'It would be my honor, Mr President,' he replied.

'Good.' He turned to Jason and Kelsey. 'Special Agent DeLaine.'

'Yes, sir?'

'As effective as you've been in Task Force TALON, your talents are required elsewhere,' the President said. 'As you may know, Secretary Calhoun has resigned from her post as Secretary of Homeland Security, protesting the Oval Office's treatment of her during this whole debacle. Frankly, I don't blame her – I didn't back her up like a good chief executive should have. FBI Director Lemke privately told me he was going to resign as well, but I convinced him to stay . . . by offering him the position of Secretary of Homeland Security, which he's accepted. That leaves a vacancy at FBI Headquarters. I want you to fill it.'

'*Me*?' Kelsey blurted out. 'You want *me* to be director of the FBI?'

'You're a career investigator with an emphasis on antiterrorist operations – exactly what we need at the top of the FBI,' the President said. 'You're young, tough, dedicated, and have an outstanding record – the perfect choice. The Attorney General agrees. What do you say?'

She hesitated . . . but only for a second, then stuck out her hand. 'I'd be honored, Mr President.'

'Excellent.' He then turned to Jason. 'I have to apologize to you, Jason, on behalf of your team members who died, and especially to Kristen Skyy,' the President said. 'I was totally sucked in by Robert Chamberlain. I believed and trusted in him, and it got thousands of innocent persons around the world killed.'

'I'm sorry, Mr President.'

'Don't be – you saw right through him, or at the very least your gut was trying to tell you something, and you listened,' the President said. 'I have to tell you, Jason, that I didn't believe you. I was so blinded by my faith and loyalty to Robert Chamberlain that I didn't believe you . . . right up until he led us into Zakharov's trap, and even then I thought he might still be in charge of the take-down. I heard what you said about him authorizing Kristen Skyy to meet with you in Egypt, and I listened to all your other disconnects revolving around him, and I still didn't listen. I'm sorry. I'm truly sorry.'

He clasped Jason's shoulder, then straightened up and said, 'You two, Major Richter and Dr Vega, won't be getting a promotion or a new office in Washington. You are heading right back to Cannon Air Force Base. I want you to build CID units and whatever else you can come up with and put together the world's premier tactical strike force. You'll report directly to the President's Special Adviser on National Security Affairs, Sergeant Major Jefferson. Your mission will be to discover, locate, track, attack, and destroy the bad guys – clean, quick, simple, and deadly. You'll have all the resources of the United States of America at your disposal. But I'm not talking about a traditional army unit – I'm talking about the next generation, whatever it is. I think I saw a glimpse of it out there at the White House: I want to see *more* of it, soonest. Your first task will, of course, be to track down Yegor Zakharov and kill that murderous sonofabitch before he strikes again. Interested?'

'Yes, *sir*,' Jason said happily, without hesitation.

'Dr Vega? Interested in joining him as deputy commander?'

Ariadna looked at Jason, and Jason could see a slight shadow of doubt or fear in her face as she thought about returning to New Mexico to where she and Doug Moore became friends. But she smiled at Jason and nodded. 'Count me in, Mr President,' she said. 'Count me in.'

'Good. You start immediately. Good luck, all of you. Sergeant . . . er, *Sergeant Major* Jefferson, Special Agent DeLaine, you two are with me.' He nodded, turned, and headed back to his armored SUV limousine.

Kelsey DeLaine stopped, made like she was going to shake hands with Jason, then gave him a kiss on the cheek. 'I'm sure I'll be talking to you again very soon, Jason,' she said. 'Try to stay out of trouble, will you?'

'Sure . . . Miss *Director*,' Jason said, giving her a sly smile. 'You know me.'

'That's why I mentioned it, Major.' She smiled and headed off to the President's SUV.

Ray Jefferson stopped before him, smiled, then nodded. 'I'll be talking to you first thing in the morning, sir,' he said.

'It's not "sir" anymore, Sergeant Major – *you're* the boss now,' Jason reminded him.

Jefferson made a show of nodding in complete agreement. 'Why, I believe you're right . . . *Richter*,' he said, feigning his most deadly growl. 'Call me at oh-eight hundred hours tomorrow morning with a full report on regenerating your unit and with a plan to expand your operations capabilities. That'll be all.' He smiled. 'And one more thing, *sir*: thank you. Thank you for sticking with what you believe in. You're a good man. It'll be a pleasure working with you again.'

The last to shake hands with Jason was Harold Chester Kingman. When he clasped Jason's hand, he said in a low voice, 'We need to talk, Jason. Your technology and your talents will go to waste in the army. Come work for me.'

'I've got a job, Mr Kingman.'

'I'll put you in charge of a laboratory with a budget that'll make the Army Research Lab look like a preschool playground,' Kingman said. 'And you'll still be protecting America – just doing it without being tied down by government red tape and regulations. You'll be *the* power to be reckoned with in the world. You'll be in charge of an invincible force that will put all of the armies of the world to shame.'

Still clutching his hand so he couldn't squirm away, Jason pulled Kingman toward him and whispered directly in his face, 'Mr Kingman, I'm not interested in a job with you. And if I see any of your "ultimate army" gadgets on any of *my* battlefields, I'll take them apart and then come and stuff them down your *throat* piece by piece. Do I make myself clear?' Kingman blanched and retreated to the safety of the President's armored car as quickly as he could.

After the President and his party departed, Frank Falcone and Jennifer McCracken came up to Jason and Ari. 'Well, looks like we're still in business,' Falcon said. 'What's the word, boss?'

'The word is . . . I'm not going back to our damned base until they get some hot water, decent chow, and regular beds,' Jason said. 'We can write up an ops plan just as well on a beach in Florida. Daytona Beach is nice this time of year, isn't it? Jennifer, get us some nice Visiting Officers Quarters at Cape Canaveral or Patrick Air Force Base for a month or so, and get them working on fixing up Pecos East.'

'Yes, *sir*!' McCracken said happily.

Ariadna followed Jason to the cargo hold on the C-37A to supervise the loading of their folded CID units, then went inside to wait until Jennifer filed their flight plan and made preparations for departure. The interior of the C-37A was downright luxurious compared to the C-17 Hercules they had been flying around in. Jason found himself on a large L-shaped settee in a private compartment of the plane near the middle, with freshly made coffee, cold drinks, computer terminals, and large-screen plasma TVs waiting for them.

He stretched out on the settee, put his feet up, and patted the settee beside him. 'We got a few minutes to kill, Ari,' he said expansively. 'Why don't you and me relax a bit?'

Ariadna smiled warmly and seductively sauntered over to him. She stopped right in front of him, leaned forward, and let her dark hair cascade over his chest, letting him catch just a glimpse of her chest inside her partially unzipped warm-up suit top. 'Jason . . .' she breathed. Her lips moved closer to his . . . and then she dropped a glass of ice water into his lap. 'Like I said, *maybe* if we were stuck on a deserted island for like a *year*. Until then, keep dreaming.' She got up, tossed him a towel, and watched him wipe himself off with an amused gleam in her eye as she fired up a computer terminal and got ready to start writing up their report.

Well, she thought, maybe not a year . . . a *week*, maybe . . .

Acknowledgments

A personal Thank You to my friends Don Aldridge, Mike Alger, Kirk Caraway, Frankie Sue Del Papa, Darla Deville, Robert Gottlieb, Bruce James, Steve Martini, Jean and Sheamus McFadden, Jodi Rafkin, Don and Mary Savage, and of course my wonderful wife, Diane, for their support. It has been a rough year, but with your help and best wishes from you and many others, I think I'll be fine.

Thank you again to Dave and Cheryl Duffield for their extraordinary generosity and community service.